"I should never have let that happen."

Neither should he, Dallas thought. "You're not thinking straight."

"I'm not that tipsy," Paris said, her speech slurred. "I came here to convince you to hire me, not to make out with you."

"It was just a kiss, Paris. And I'm the one who should've stopped it."

Paris dropped down onto the mattress. "I'm not... normally... like this." She followed the comment with a hiccup and a giggle.

"You've got a good excuse. Now lie down and sleep it off."

"Thank you, Dallas Calloway. You're a nice man. I'm sorry I'm not acting like a nice girl."

"No need to apologize."

She sent him a sleepy smile. "Since I probably blew my chances at the job, I wouldn't mind a kiss goodnight."

He might have laughed if he hadn't been so damn tempted.

* * *

The Rancher's Marriage Pact

j

D0988235

THE RANCHER'S MARRIAGE PACT

BY
KRISTI GOLD

First Published in Great Britain 2016
By Mills & Boon, an imprint of HarperCollins*Publishers*
1 London Bridge Street, London, SE1 9GF

© 2016 Kristi Goldberg

ISBN: 978-0-263-91853-3

51-0316

Kristi Gold has a fondness for beaches, baseball and bridal reality shows. She firmly believes that love has remarkable healing powers, and she feels very fortunate to be able to weave stories of love and commitment. As a bestselling author, a National Readers' Choice Award winner and a Romance Writers of America three-time RITA® Award finalist, Kristi has learned that although accolades are wonderful, the most cherished rewards come from networking with readers. She can be reached through her website at www.kristigold.com, or through Facebook.

To my childhood companion,
very best friend and surrogate sister,
Charlotte L.

One

The Last Chance Ranch...

Her first thought, as she left her compact sedan and strode toward the single-story white stone structure set somewhere between San Antonio and the middle of nowhere. Her second thought—the South Texas weather was ridiculously hot for March. She should never have worn the tailored black blazer and skirt. Fortunately she'd twisted her hair up and off her neck that was now damp with perspiration. Of course in part, her current predicament could be attributed to nerves, not the afternoon sun. And a good dose of desperation.

Once she reached the threshold, Paris flipped her sunglasses up onto her head and noted the wooden plaque to the right of the entry.

"Welcome to the D Bar C, where cowboys and hospitality rule. Take off your boots, hang your hat and come in to sit a spell. And if we don't happen to be here, just reach out and ring the bell."

Cute. Very cute. Unfortunately she wasn't wearing a hat or boots, but what she wouldn't give to kick off her three-inch heels and barrel in barefoot. Not a banner idea when applying for a job, and boy did she need this job. Of course, the position hadn't exactly been announced, yet that hadn't stopped her from showing up, uninvited, which could result in rejection. Nothing new there.

After smoothing a palm down her jacket, Paris drew in a calming breath as she clutched the strap of the teal briefcase hanging from her shoulder. She exhaled slowly before opening the heavy mahogany door to find the place blessedly cool, otherwise she might have shed her blazer to reveal the sheer sleeveless white shell. The area happened to be completely deserted, not one soul in sight behind the lengthy mahogany counter, yet she did spot the aforementioned bell.

She could ring it to summon someone, or she could wait. She could leave, or she could convene some courage and see this through. But she had come too far to give up now.

In a fit of sheer procrastination, Paris took a few moments to study the area with a designer's eye. Aside from the usual office equipment behind the counter, she discovered typical Western decor—burnt-orange-and-white cowhide chairs set about the waiting area, massive stone fireplace with a heavy wood mantel, a set of horns hanging above said mantel. She moved closer to read the bronze plaque below the sad symbol of human cruelty to find it etched with "Prize twelve-point buck bagged by J. D. Calloway."

Lovely. Just lovely. She supposed she should be thankful dear J.D. had only saved the horns as a souvenir and not the poor deer's entire head.

More than ready to see this spontaneous plan through, Paris turned back to the counter and reached for the bell with a trembling hand. But before she could pick it up, a tall, dark-haired man emerged from an entry at the far end of the office, looking as if he had walked right out of an Old West time warp and into the future. He kept his attention trained on a document clasped in his rather large and masculine hands as he strode toward her, the jingle of spurs echoing against the beige walls, providing her the prime opportunity to do a comprehensive inspection. He was every bit a cowboy, from the top of his tan hat to the tip of his brown leather boots. He wore a faded blue shirt and equally faded blue jeans, yet the large silver belt buckle drew her immediate focus. She noticed the word *Champion* before her gaze traveled lower to a place no self-respecting, professional woman should go.

"Can I help you, ma'am?"

At the sound of the incredibly deep voice, Paris's attention returned to the cowboy's face, her cheeks flaming from mortification. "Uh, actually, I'm…" Heavens, the impact of his silver-blue eyes caused her to forget her name. She'd seen several photographs of him, yet none had done Dallas Calloway justice.

He reacted to her momentary mental lapse with a

half smile, revealing a deep dimple creasing the left of his whisker-shaded jaw. "Are you lost?"

"Not really," she managed to say although in a sense she did feel a bit lost. "I'm Paris Reynolds."

He leaned over the counter and offered a hand. "Dallas Calloway. What can I do for you?"

That question was as loaded as a shotgun. But since this man could hold the key to her future financial security, she had to regain her composure. "I'm here about your new venture."

Before he could respond, a petite woman dressed in a plain tailored floral blouse covering faded jeans, her silver-and-brown hair twisted into a braid, strode into the room and pulled up short when she caught sight of the pair. She eyed Paris with suspicion as she made her way to Dallas's side. "Whatever you're selling, we're not buying."

Paris had the feeling no one crossed this woman and lived to tell about it. "I'm not selling anything but my services."

She huffed. "For your information, my stepson doesn't have to pay for it."

When awareness dawned, another bout of embarrassment plagued Paris. "You've definitely misunderstood my motives. I'm here to discuss a *business* proposition." Not that the explanation sounded much better, evidenced by the woman's raised eyebrows.

"Stop jumping to conclusions, Mom," Dallas interjected. "I'm fairly sure that's not what she's selling."

The woman propped a hand on her hip and sneered.

"Dallas deals on a daily basis with females who come here under the guise of business."

"Oh, so true, Maria," came from behind Paris. "Our stepson is a regular chick magnet."

Paris turned to find a pretty middle-aged blonde dressed in a chic coral sundress, standing at the front door. Apparently the place was rife with the now-deceased J. D. Calloway's wives. Determined to get off on the right foot with this one, she held out her hand and smiled. "I'm Paris Reynolds."

The blonde returned her smile and shook her hand with much more gusto than Paris expected. "I'm Jenny Parks Calloway, J.D.'s third wife."

"Not officially," Maria added in a sour tone.

Paris assumed there must be a story behind that comment, but chose to remain silent and await the fallout between the feuding former spouses.

It came out in Jenny's intense frown. "Please forgive the second missus. Sometimes Maria forgets her manners. What shade on the color chart is your blond, if you don't mind me asking?"

Paris's hand immediately went to her hair. "I wouldn't know. I'm actually a natural blonde."

Jenny chuckled. "Oh, so am I."

"And I'm the queen of Texas," Maria said with a smirk.

Ignoring the other mother, Jenny turned her smile back on Paris. "By the way, I love, love, love your suit, sugar."

Paris grasped to find a return compliment. "Thank you, and I love your bracelet."

Jenny twisted the diamond and silver leaf bauble around her wrist. "And thank you. I picked this up at a silent auction at the art center in San Antonio last month."

Unbelievable. "Really? I was there, too." But she hadn't had the funds to bid. She'd been there to drum up business. An unsuccessful plan that had led her to this remote ranch.

Jenny laid a hand beneath the strand of pearls at her throat. "A small, small world it is."

"Way too small if you ask me," Maria grumbled.

Jenny sent her another scowl. "No one asked you, Maria, and no one appreciates your attitude or your sarcasm. You really should learn some Southern decorum."

"I think we all can work on that," Dallas chimed in as he opened the half door built into the counter. "Ms. Reynolds, if you'll follow me to my office, we can get away from all this verbal sparring and you can tell me what you need."

"But make it quick," Maria added. "He has work to do."

"Oh, hush," Jenny replied as Paris stepped through the opening. "He's not too busy to entertain a pretty girl. Also, their names go so well together—Paris and Dallas. Sounds like a match made in heaven."

"Sounds like an airport flight schedule," Maria muttered.

"It's high time he meets a nice girl, Maria," Jenny added. "Don't forget what's coming up at the end of the week and we both know what that means."

If only Paris knew what that meant. Regardless, she

could tell Dallas wasn't comfortable with the conversation when he rushed toward an opening to his left without responding.

With her mind riddled with confusion, Paris followed Dallas down a lengthy corridor, all the while unsuccessfully trying to keep her eyes off his derriere. She found the way he dangled his arms at his sides, his perfect lean build and the roll of his hips quite fascinating.

Good grief. Evidently the lengthy amount of time she'd been without male companionship had her falling head over common sense over some cowboy. Okay, not just any cowboy. An extremely gorgeous, rich cowboy who had succeeded at everything he'd tried, from rodeo to ranching, according to what she'd read on the internet. A far cry from her seedy ex-husband who'd managed to screw up everything he'd endeavored, including their marriage.

Dallas soon paused to lead Paris into a well-appointed office that served as a tribute to his success. The lush brown leather sofa and love seat set near the window complemented his masculine aura, and the massive mahogany desk spoke to his rugged persona. The hand-scraped dark wood floors topped off the decor that couldn't have been done any better if she'd done it herself, even if it wasn't exactly her cup of tea.

"Would you like something to drink?" he asked as he crossed the room to the elaborate granite-covered wet bar in the corner.

"Water would be fine," she said, *although wine would be better*, she thought.

"Water it is. Have a seat."

After settling in a beige club chair across from the desk, Paris set her case on the floor, crossed her legs, adjusted her skirt and prepared to make her pitch. She decided to begin with casual conversation and in the same instant, assuage her natural curiosity. "If you don't mind my asking, what's coming up at the end of the week?"

"I turn thirty-eight on Saturday," he said as he retrieved a crystal highball glass from the upper cabinet.

Six years her senior. Not too bad. Not that it mattered. "Big party planned?"

Once he filled the tumbler with ice from a bucket on the counter, then poured water into it from a pitcher he pulled from the built-in stainless refrigerator, he returned to the desk and set the glass on a coaster before her. "I hope like hell that's not going to happen. I'm not one for having people making a big deal over my birthday."

She sensed he would be that kind of man. "I have a feeling your stepmothers might be planning a big deal."

He dropped down into the chair behind the desk, leaned back and affected a relaxed posture, but his expression said he didn't exactly appreciate her conjecture. "They know better than to pull that on me."

Paris gathered he might be suffering from a severe case of the birthday blues. "Are you sure? It sounded as if at least one of them wants you to have a date for some soiree, hence the *nice girl* comment."

He sent her that sexy, crooked smile again. "If that's the case, are you volunteering to fill the role?"

If she were only that brave. Then again, if it helped

her secure the job… "I generally avoid mixing business with pleasure, although your family seemed to jump to the conclusion that my business is pleasure."

He narrowed his eyes and studied her straight on. "Speaking of that, what exactly do you do for a living?"

The suspicion in his tone ruffled her feminine feathers. "It doesn't involve a nine hundred number or a pimp, I promise you that."

Now he looked amused. "Glad you cleared the air."

So was she, and she planned to be perfectly clear. "In reality, I'm—"

"Wait. Let me guess." He inclined his head and pointed at her. "You're a stockbroker and you want to get your hands on my investments."

She might like to get her hands on something of his that happened to be a far cry from his portfolio. Since when had she become a purveyor of naughty thoughts? "Not even close."

He rubbed a palm over his chin. "I would bet the back forty you have an accounting degree."

If he only knew about her lack of accounting skills, he would never have assumed such a thing. That downfall had landed her in deep trouble and served as another reason for being there, about to beg for employment. "Believe me, math is not my forte."

"Marketing?"

In an effort to clear her parched throat, Paris took a quick sip of water. "Try again."

His gaze landed on her fingers still wrapped around the glass. "Considering your perfectly manicured nails, I'm guessing you're not a ranch hand."

"I haven't even seen a cow up close."

"Not even on your dinner plate in the form of filet mignon?"

"I'm primarily a vegetarian."

"I'm strictly a meat-and-potatoes kind of guy."

What a shocker. "I won't judge your food preferences if you won't judge mine."

"Agreed." He took off his hat to place it brim up on the desk, then forked a hand through his dark brown hair that worked well with those deadly blue eyes. "If you're a beautician, I don't need one. Just a quick round with the clippers and I'm good to go."

Yes, he was. Good enough to go anywhere he might want to take her. "No, I'm not a hairstylist. Do you give up now?"

"Yep. I'm all out of guesses."

The time had come to lay all her cards on the table, less a few secrets he didn't need to know. "I'm a commercial interior designer." Disgraced designer.

"No kidding?" he said, sounding somewhat awed over the admission.

"No kidding. And that's why I'm here. I wanted to speak to you about—"

"Hey, Dallas, I'm about to head out."

Paris shifted in her seat to see a young, buff blond guy filling the doorway. Aside from the tattered jeans and worn cowboy boots, he looked more surfer than rancher. Or body builder in light of the fit of the lime-green T-shirt hugging his muscled arms and torso.

"Where are you going now?" Dallas asked, looking and sounding none too pleased.

"To the beach for the weekend," the stranger replied as he strode to the wet bar.

Aha! Paris had pegged him right on his surfer status, though she still didn't know his relationship to the Calloways. He certainly didn't resemble Dallas.

"Did you talk to Fort yet, Worth?" Dallas asked.

"I called him," the man with the unusual name said as he pulled a soda from the fridge and popped it open. "But he's still pissed I left him high and dry and came here. He refuses to call me back."

"Figures," Dallas muttered. "By the way, does Houston know you're leaving?"

"Yeah, and Austin's agreed to hang around in case any of the heifers calve."

"That's good because Tyler's going to be gone until Monday."

Paris felt as though she'd just gone on a Cities of Texas tour. Without further hesitation, she stood to face Surfer Worth and smiled, bent on introducing herself since her potential boss evidently wasn't going to do the honors. "Hi, my name is Paris Reynolds."

Worth grinned and shook her extended hand, revealing the same dimple Dallas sported. "Pleasure to meet you, ma'am. Are you a friend of my big brother's?"

That confirmed her supposition that he was a Calloway sibling, although she couldn't recall any mention of him in any of the press releases she'd recently read. "Actually, we just met today."

Worth winked. "Well, if he doesn't treat you right, you're welcome to come to Padre Island with me. I'm a helluva lot more fun."

And way too young for her, Paris decided. Plus, she had always been attracted to brown-haired men, like the one seated not far away.

Dallas pointed at the door. "Get out, Worthless. Ms. Reynolds doesn't need you coming on to her."

Worth backed toward the exit with hands held up, palms forward. "All right. And when you find out where the hell you left your sense of humor, let me know."

With that, the younger Calloway son winked at Paris again before striding out of the room.

"I apologize for his behavior," Dallas said as he resumed holding cowboy court from his place behind the desk.

Paris dropped back down into her designated chair. "No need. He seems relatively harmless."

"He's a skirt chaser, according to his mother, and I've seen more than enough evidence of that fact."

The identity of Worth's mother didn't require a lot of guessing. "Is that Jenny?"

"Yeah, my father's third wife. Maria is the second."

"And your mother is?"

Dallas's gaze drifted away for a moment. "Gone. She died when I was pretty young."

"I'm sorry, Dallas." And she sincerely was. "I'm sure that's been really difficult for you."

"Not so much," he said. "I barely remember her. Now let's get back to the reason why you're here."

Being summarily dismissed wasn't all that surprising to Paris. Most men clammed up when it came to emotional issues, including her own father. "Well, as I was saying, I'm a commercial interior designer, and since it's apparent you'll need my services soon, I'm here to apply for the position."

He frowned. "Why do you believe I need an interior decorator?"

She wasn't certain if he was kidding, or he really didn't have a clue. "Look, I saw an article in the San Antonio paper about this Texas Extreme project and how you're going to cater to people who want to enjoy the whole high-risk rodeo experience." Though she couldn't imagine why anyone would want to do that. "I also read about your plans to build a lodge to house your guests, and that's where I come in. I would like the opportunity to oversee the design of that lodge."

"We haven't even broken ground yet," he said. "In fact, we haven't seen the final plans from the architect."

That could definitely work to her advantage. "All the better. If I'm involved in the beginning, then I can make suggestions that will only enhance the guests' experience. I have extensive knowledge in hotel design. I have a strong attention to detail and—"

"Ms. Reynolds—"

"Paris."

"Okay, Paris, first of all, these guests are wannabe cowboys. They don't need a fancy room. They only need a bunk and a bathroom. Hell, they might be satisfied with an outhouse and a creek."

The thought made her shudder. Yet he had made a good point, darn it. Still... "What if some of them want to bring their wives? Women have much higher standards. What if some of the wives or girlfriends want to participate, too?"

He mulled that over a moment before addressing her again. "I hadn't thought about that."

Now she was getting somewhere. "Have you given any consideration to the kitchen? You are having one installed, aren't you? Or will you be roasting marshmallows and wieners?"

He favored her with a sexy grin. "That's a thought."

"Seriously? A wiener roast for every meal?"

"Maybe that's not a great idea. But the kitchen doesn't have to be all that elaborate. Just the basics."

He truly didn't grasp the concept of hospitality. "How many people do you plan to house at one time?"

"Fifty if we're at capacity, but we want to be able to accommodate more in the future."

"Feeding fifty hungry men and/or women will require more than a four-burner stove, a side-by-side refrigerator and a single oven. You'll need commercial-grade appliances, plenty of prep space—"

"I understand what you're saying," he said, effectively cutting her off. "But we don't plan to open for business for a year, maybe longer if we can't get all the facilities set up by then. Not only do we have to build the lodge, we have to build a new arena and catch pens, plus a first-aid station and acquire rodeo stock. I wouldn't even need you for a good six months."

She would be destitute in two months. The unwelcome sense of extreme anxiety came home to roost, prompting Paris to make a final plea. "Again, you would be better off hiring me now than fixing something later. That will only cost you more money. I could meet with the architect before the plans are finalized. I could take care of all the details from the ground up. Besides, I live in San Antonio and since that's only an hour and a half away, that's convenient for us both. And I'm going to work cheaper than many firms you might decide to hire, but I don't do cheap work or cut corners. To be perfectly honest, you can't do better than me. And most important, I really, really need this job."

He tilted his head again and eyed her suspiciously. "If you're so good at it, why is that?"

She'd gone too far with the tirade, and probably blown any chance at the opportunity to oversee his project. Yet she was somewhat bolstered by the fact he hadn't kicked her out...yet. "Due to personal circumstances beyond my control, I've been forced to start over, but I won't bother you with the details. I would like to show you my work."

As she drew a breath, Paris fumbled for the briefcase resting on the floor and lifted it up. "I have my portfolio right here if you care to take a quick look."

Dallas sat in silence for a few moments while Paris's pulse raced out of control. "I'm sure you're more than qualified for the job," he finally said, "but like I told you, I don't see the need to hire a decorator—"

"Designer," Paris corrected without regard to helping her cause.

"Hiring a *designer* right now doesn't make much sense to me."

Plagued with the bitter taste of defeat, Paris stood. "Fine, but you should be aware, in six months, I might not be available." She might even be in jail. Or worse—

living with her folks on a potato farm in Idaho. "It's been a pleasure to meet you."

Dallas came to his feet and rounded the desk. "One question before you leave. What exactly did you mean by having to start over?"

She certainly wasn't prepared to get into that, but if it meant he might possibly reconsider, she would tell him everything. Almost everything. "Okay, as long as you understand I'm not looking for pity."

"Understood."

Oh, how she hated having to explain the sordid details. "Almost two years ago, my ex-husband left in the middle of the night, took every penny I owned and then took off to the Dominican Republic to get a quickie divorce."

The anger that flashed in his eyes took her aback. "Where is the bastard now?"

"Still there, with my hard-earned money and a new girlfriend. Shortly thereafter, the firm where I'd been working for eight years laid me off. I have very few funds to maintain my apartment for much longer, so I might be forced to move in with my family until I get back on my feet." That last part had wounded her pride beyond belief. The part she'd left out—the reasons why she'd lost her job—had caused her great shame.

He attempted a slight smile. "I can relate to living with family."

"Your stepmothers live with you?"

"No, they live in the main house. I built my own place a few years ago. But I see them every day, whether I want to or not."

They just stood there in uncomfortable silence until Paris decided to end the meeting and escape from her humiliating revelations. She retrieved a card from her bag's side pocket and offered it to him. "If you happen to change your mind, here's my contact information. If not, I wish you the best of luck with your new venture."

"Good luck to you, too," he said as he escorted her to the door. "And if I happen to need a date to a surprise birthday party, I just might give you a call."

Oh, sure he would. In some ways she wished he would. Who wouldn't want to spend an evening with a gorgeous macho guy? And since he obviously wasn't going to hire her…"You know, I just might take you up on the invitation."

Without gauging his response, Paris worked her way back to the front office and out the door, pausing only long enough to tell both mothers to have a good day. Once she slid into her car, she experienced overwhelming dejection over the epic failure. But she refused to cry. She'd already done enough of that to last a lifetime.

"Why in the hell did you let her leave, Dallas?"

At the moment, a lecture from Maria—his long time maternal influence—was the very last thing Dallas needed. He still hadn't gotten over the impact of the pretty green-eyed, golden-haired, determined woman named after a European city who had landed on his doorstep. He didn't quite understand his reaction to her, either. A strong reaction that had had him wanting to suggest things to her that any man with an ounce of honor wouldn't dare mention to a woman he'd just met. And if Maria Leone Calloway could read his mind, she would nix the speech and wash his mouth out with homemade soap even if he hadn't uttered a dirty word.

He cleared the uncomfortable hitch from his throat and shifted in his chair. "I don't know why her departure is bothering you, Mom. I figured you didn't like her all that much."

Without invitation, the current burr in his backside took the seat Paris Reynolds had vacated a few minutes before. "She's a little too uppity in my opinion, *mijo*. But as bad as I hate to admit it, Jenny was right about one thing. You need to find a woman, and maybe this Paris is that woman."

Dallas rocked back in his chair and sighed. "First of all, you both need to forget about that. It's too late. Secondly, I've come to terms with staying single and you just need to accept it."

Maria narrowed her dark eyes. "You're telling me you're going to let your no-account little brother gain control over this ranch?"

The thought left a bad taste in his mouth. "Blame your husband for putting that stupid marriage codicil in the will, although it still doesn't make any sense why Dad would leave this place to Fort. From what Jenny says, the kid was a rebel most of his life, plus he already owns the horse farm in Louisiana."

Maria tightened the band securing her braid, a nervous habit for as long as Dallas could remember. "You're right. It doesn't make a damn bit of sense what J.D. did, particularly since Fort wants nothing to do with you or any of his brothers. Then again, what your father did to me and Jenny didn't make any sense, either."

Dallas would never forget that day six years ago when during the reading of his father's will, he'd not only discovered he had twin half-brothers, he'd learned his father had been living as a bigamist. "I'm hoping Fort's disdain for the family will be enough for him to ignore the stipulation." Even if he wasn't banking on it.

"That's a big chance you'd be taking, Dallas," Maria said. "If you're wrong, he'll put a stop to your dream of turning this place into Texas Extreme. Hell, he could even toss you and your brothers off the property, take over the houses you all built and legally he could do it."

He knew that all too well. He also knew Fort would probably turn the place into a subdivision just to spite them. "I don't have a choice, Mom. I can't find a proper wife in four days, nor do I even want to attempt it."

The other mother—every bit the Southern belle—suddenly breezed into the room and stood behind Maria. "I think Paris is quite proper and sophisticated, and a man of your financial means and social status needs that in a life partner. If you make an effort to get to know her, who knows what could happen in a few days? You might find yourself falling hopelessly in love for the first time in your life, sugar. Why, I met your father on a Saturday night and we were married two weeks later."

"And look how that turned out, Jenny," Maria said. "Don't give him reason not to give this a shot."

Over the past few years, Dallas had learned one important thing about Jenny Parks Calloway—she was a flighty romantic who spent most of her days with stars in her eyes. "That's good in theory, Jen, but the chances of it happening are slim to none. And even if I wanted to pursue a relationship with Paris Reynolds, who's to say she would agree? And even if she did agree to go out with me, do you really think she'd jump at the chance to marry me two days later? Get real."

"She sounded pretty desperate to us," Jenny chimed in, then clamped her mouth closed after Maria shot her a nasty look over her shoulder.

Dallas wasn't all that shocked, but he was pretty pissed off over the intrusion. "You two were listening to our conversation?"

"Just a little bit," Jenny said sheepishly. "Your phone's intercom was on."

He looked at the key pad, noted the button was depressed and then muttered a few mild oaths. "Why didn't you tell me?"

"We didn't want to disturb you, *mijo*," Maria said.

Dallas didn't buy that for a minute. "You wanted to eavesdrop. Regardless of how desperate Paris might be, I don't see her as the kind of woman who'd agree to marry a stranger in exchange for a job. And I'm not the kind of man who would ask that of any woman."

Jenny put on her sweeter-than-honey expression. "Sugar, I love my son, but I also know Fort doesn't deserve this place given how much grief he's showered on me and Worth. Why don't you just invite Paris to dinner tonight and see what happens?"

He'd like to see what happened, but not in the way she was thinking. "I'm sure she's already halfway to

San Antonio by now and I've got a lot do before I fly
to Houston in two days."

"You can take one night off," Maria stated, a totally
out-of-character comment.

"Yes, you can, for the cause," Jenny added. "Now go
after her, sugar, and escort her back here. I can make
you both my famous chateaubriand."

He saw one big problem with that, and a prime excuse to halt all the nonsense. "She's a vegetarian."

Maria shook her head. "Yeah, we heard her say that,
but it's not normal. Not normal at all."

"We'll work around it," Jenny said. "I'll make a wonderful assortment of spring vegetables. That will allow
Dallas and Paris to get to know each other better in an
intimate setting, not a crowded restaurant."

Dallas barked out a laugh. "Sure, while the two of
you hang out in the next room, listening to every word
we say."

Jenny raised her hand like she was about to take an
oath. "I swear I will leave as soon as the food is served.
Maria will, too. Right?"

Maria stared up at Jenny. "Why do you need me
there anyway?"

"For moral support," Jenny answered. "And you can
make Dallas his usual T-bone, since that's not my forte."

Maria sighed. "It's easy. Remove the horns, slap it
on the stove, make sure it's not mooing and put it on
the plate."

Jenny ignored Maria and took his hand. "Sugar, we'll
work out the dinner details. In the meantime, you just
have to convince Paris to join you by telling her you

want to discuss the particulars of the job, sort of like an interview. Then you can see what comes up after that."

He had a sneaking suspicion he knew exactly what would come up if he didn't get a rein on his libido. Logical or not, he did like the plan, if for no other reason than to spend a little more time with Paris. As far as the mothers' harebrained matrimony scheme was concerned, no way would that happen.

After pushing away from the desk, he stood and propped his hat on his head. "All right, you two. Get to cooking and I'll go get the girl."

Two

Seated in her compact sedan, Paris stared at the private number displayed on her phone. Normally she would ignore the call, but some mysterious force propelled her to answer. "Hello?"

"Where are you right now?"

Overcome with sudden paranoia, she looked around the almost empty lot for some seedy no-account who'd magically come upon her cell number. "Who is this?"

"Sorry. It's Dallas Calloway. Are you back in San Antonio?"

"No," she said after she'd regained enough composure to speak. "I'm at a convenience store somewhere between Cotulla and Dilley. Or maybe I've already passed Dilley and missed it when I blinked."

"Right off the interstate?"

"Yes. It's a red-and-white building with some weird creature on the sign, but I can't see the name from here."

"I know the place. Stay put. I'll be there in a few."

Paris didn't have the opportunity to say another word before the line went dead, leaving her with a laundry list of questions bombarding her brain. Why would he want to come after her? Had she left something important at the office? She glanced at the passenger seat to verify the presence of her briefcase, although only a few moments ago she'd just carried it into the store to pay for gas and buy a snack. Speaking of snacks…she yanked down the visor and pulled up the vanity mirror to check for the presence of chocolate, which she found smeared in the corner of her mouth.

Paris scrambled around in the center console for a napkin, then swiped furiously over the offensive spot while cursing herself for being such a cliché. Have stress, grab candy. Preferably chocolate candy. Dark, light, didn't matter. As long as it contained cocoa and no nuts.

After reapplying her lipstick, and tightening the hair band securing the low twist at her nape, she waited for the enigmatic cowboy to arrive in a pickup, or possibly ride up on his trusty horse.

The first assumption had been correct, she realized, when a large dual-wheeled black monstrosity of a truck pulled in the space to her right and its dashing driver left the cab.

As Dallas approached the door, Paris powered down her window to find out what his surprise appearance was all about. "Did I forget something?" she asked as soon as he arrived.

"Nope," he said. "But I forgot to ask you something."

"What would that be, pray tell?"

"If you'd care to stay for dinner."

Only moments ago, she'd consumed a large bar of candy and washed it down with cola so dinner wasn't all that appealing. But maybe this was his way of saying he might be considering her for the position after all. "Dinner would be nice, but wouldn't it have been much easier for you to call me and ask me to come back rather than you drive all the way here?"

"Yep, that fifteen-minute drive was a real hardship, but here the West is still wild, and the men go after their women."

She'd give him a speech on the death of chauvinism if he didn't look so gorgeous displaying that grin and a delightful dimple. "Far be it from me to question archaic tradition."

He leaned over and folded his arms on the window's ledge. "Are you going to follow me home, or do you want to ride with me and I'll bring you back later to get your car?"

Although he seemed harmless enough, Paris wasn't stupid. If she didn't have her vehicle, she couldn't determine when it was time to go. "I know the way now. I'll drive."

He pushed away from the car and straightened. "Fine by me. See you in a bit."

In less time than it took Paris to fasten her seat belt, Dallas shot out of the lot on spinning tires, kicking up a flurry of dust in his wake as he turned onto the access road. She took a little more time following suit, still questioning the reason behind his surprise invitation.

Yet life wasn't without risk, and she'd taken plenty in her formative years. Some had turned out well, others, not so much. She hoped this risk proved to be a good one.

After traveling ten or so miles, she found Dallas had pulled over on the shoulder to wait for her. He seemed to slow down to accommodate her caution, and remained that way until they turned off the interstate and onto the rural road leading to the ranch.

Once they traveled through the elaborate stone entry containing the iron sign announcing their arrival at the D Bar C, Dallas drove past the office where the barren terrain took a dramatic turn. Paris glanced from the road long enough to ogle the massive white rock ranch house to her left as Dallas continued on. They passed by several other large houses set back off the road, each one appearing to include transplanted trees, lovely landscaping, first-rate barns and expensive vehicles, including one black Porsche that she would wager belonged to Worth. After Dallas took a left, pavement soon turned to gravel as they navigated through pastureland lined with barbwire fence and dotted with mesquite.

They soon passed a large pond lined with weeping willows where a two-story, expansive home came into view, dealing Paris another stunning mental blow. The structure was also stone trimmed with cedar accents, like the rest of the residences, only this one had a gleaming silver metal roof and seemed to be twice the size, as well as a tad more elaborate. If she didn't know better, she would have thought she'd happened upon a resort hotel.

Dallas pulled beneath the portico and Paris followed his lead, half expecting to be greeted by a parking attendant. When that didn't happen, she slid out of the car and joined her host for the evening at the entry. "Nice place you have here," she said as he opened one of the heavy pine double doors.

"It'll do," he replied with surprising nonchalance.

It would more than do, she realized after she stepped over the threshold. A grand staircase with a wrought iron banister centered in the soaring foyer, and dark slate floors could be deemed somewhat elegant. Yet that was where the elegance ended, right before the West began.

As Paris trailed behind Dallas into the great room, the cowboy culture came shining through in the floor-to-ceiling rock fireplace anchoring the room along with the macho leather furniture in shades of gray and black. And hanging from the towering ceiling, a chandelier, for lack of a better term, appeared to be made out of metallic animal horns, although she would swear they weren't authentic. At least she hoped not.

"Welcome to Dallas's little piece of heaven, Paris," Jenny said as she floated into the room wearing a frilly pink apron and a vibrant smile.

Odd that Dallas didn't have household staff and had to rely on his stepmother to play hostess. "Thanks for having me, and I have to agree. This place is paradise."

Jenny's grin deepened. "You should see the veranda overlooking the pool, which is where you two will dine so you can watch the sunset. The view is breathtaking."

Dallas frowned. "I'm thinking the dining room might be better since it's still fairly hot outside and the mosquitoes are big as airplanes."

Jenny waved her hand in a dismissive gesture. "Oh, posh, Dallas. You don't have a romantic bone in your body. Besides, the temperature will go down with the sun and it's too early in the year for a lot of bugs, including mosquitoes."

A sunset dinner was conducive to romance, but Paris was not in the market for wining and dining or mosquitoes. "The dining room will be fine." When Jenny looked absolutely disappointed, she added, "Or the veranda. I'm sure the sunset is very impressive."

"The veranda it is," Jenny said as she started to back away. "Dinner will be ready very soon and I assure you, Paris, I'm preparing a delectable vegetarian meal. In the meantime, Dallas can give you the VIP tour. His master suite is to die for."

She questioned the wisdom in viewing Dallas's bedroom. "I'm looking forward to it. The tour, I mean."

Jenny smiled before she hurried away, leaving Dallas and Paris standing in the middle of the great room cloaked in uncomfortable silence.

"Are you ready for the tour?" he asked.

As long as he didn't get too close to her in the boudoir; otherwise she might forget herself in the shadow of that smile. "I'm more than a little curious, so lead the way."

"Okay. Follow me."

And she did, up the stairs, trying desperately to avoid studying his butt before they took an immediate right at the top landing. They walked by several closed doors before reaching the end of the corridor where Dallas paused at a pair of double doors.

"Prepare yourself," he said. "You're about to see where all the action happens."

Holding her breath, Paris expected to discover a large bed, but she only saw what appeared to be a cowboy man cave with an at least seventy-inch television screen, a large old-fashioned bar straight out of a saloon and a series of round wooden tables and straight-backed chairs. She strolled toward a large glass display case to her right that housed trophies and belt buckles and trinkets from days past. "Is this the Dallas Calloway Hall of Fame?"

"Not exactly," he said from behind her. "If I had my way, those things would've stayed in the trunk in the tack room."

She glanced at him over one shoulder. "You should be proud of these. Not many men can lay claim to being a three-time world champion all-around cowboy."

"Funny, that's what Maria said." He came to her side, showing his handsome profile to full advantage. "She set this up after I built the house."

Time to get to know him a bit better. "You two are close, huh?"

He streaked a palm over his neck. "Yeah. She's the only mother I've ever really known. Then Jen came into the mix and now I have two mothers. Double trouble. They mean well but sometimes they're both a little too motherly."

"Right down to choosing your mate?"

He shot her a smile, throwing her for a mental loop.

"They try but I don't listen to them when it comes to my choice in female companionship."

That led Paris to a question she'd been dying to ask, perhaps at her own detriment if she dared. "You really don't have a girlfriend waiting somewhere in the wings?"

He turned those silver-blue eyes on her. "Nope. I've had a couple of steady girlfriends in the past, but rodeo and relationships didn't mix well."

"Apparently you no longer rodeo, so do you see yourself eventually settling down?"

He sent her an odd look before he brought his attention back to the mementos from his past. "Only if and when the time is right."

"I'm sure you're considered quite the catch in these parts. Probably throughout the state."

He turned and leaned a shoulder against the case. "I've had my share of propositions, but it's kind of hard to tell if they're more interested in my personality, or my personal finances."

Or his stellar physical attributes. "I'm sure more than a few are drawn to the cowboy fantasy and the notion you'll scoop them up and ride off into the sunset."

"Is that your fantasy?"

Not until that moment. Not until he favored her with that winning, dimpled grin again. "My exposure to cowboys has been nonexistent, so I'd have to say no."

He inched a little closer. "Now that you've been exposed, do you think you might change your mind?"

Heaven help her, he was flirting like a teenage jock. And she responded like an adolescent schoolgirl with a self-conscious smile. "The jury is still out. I'll let you know after dinner."

"And I'll do my best to show you there's something to be said for the cowboy way."

They stood there in silence, tension as thick as a morning haze hanging over them as Dallas's focus landed on her mouth. Paris sensed if she moved just a little closer, gave him just a little encouragement, he might actually kiss her. And she might actually hurl caution to the warm wind and let him.

The sound of staccato footsteps interrupted the moment and drew Paris back into reality and her attention to the doorway where Jenny now stood sporting a knowing look. "Dinner is served, y'all. Just come on out to the veranda when you're finished doing whatever it is you're doing."

As soon as Jenny disappeared, Paris turned back to Dallas. "Shall we go? I'm suddenly starving."

"So am I," he replied, keeping his gaze centered on hers. "Food sounds pretty good, too."

Paris released a nervous laugh. "I can tell you have a little bad boy in you."

"Yeah, darlin', I do. But don't ever doubt I'm every bit a man."

That wasn't up for debate. Paris had a sneaking suspicion if she hung around too long after dinner and let down her guard, she could very well see exactly how manly he could be.

She was getting under his skin, a dangerous prospect. He didn't need to lose all control around her, but he almost had. He didn't need a woman complicating his life, even if he couldn't deny he needed a woman. But not just any woman. *This* woman.

Dallas pushed his empty plate aside and watched as Paris sipped at the second mint julep Jenny had served her. He'd settled for a beer, but only one, in order to keep his wits about him. He didn't know enough about Paris to bring out the usual moves, even if those fantastic green eyes had reeled him in like a trout on a fly from the minute she'd walked into the office. He brought his attention to her hands, imagined those slender fingers raking across his chest, then traveling lower to the nagging place down south that craved some female attention.

Shaking off the images, Dallas thought it best to talk, not fantasize about her being naked beneath him. "How long have you been a vegetarian?"

She dabbed at her lips then set the napkin aside. "When I started college, I was determined not to gain the typical freshman fifteen. And honestly, when I was in my teens, I was somewhat...chunky."

He couldn't even imagine that. "Are you kidding?"

"It's true. I wasn't obese, but I was anything but thin. My family moved around a lot and I tended to use food to compensate for the fact I didn't have time to make friends. Before I knew it, I was a regular porker who lived on cheeseburgers and fries."

"The only way I'd believe that is to see some pictures."

She shook her head. "No way. Besides, I think I probably destroyed all evidence."

He downed the last of the beer and pushed the mug away. "You said you moved a lot. Why is that?"

"I was a navy brat. We were rarely in one place for any length of time."

"Do you have any siblings?"

"An older sister. She's living around the corner from my parents in Idaho with her husband and three kids. My folks are so proud."

"They're not proud of you?"

She rimmed a fingertip around the edge of the glass. "Let's just say they don't understand my creative nature. Or at least my father never did. He preferred I become a nurse or teacher."

"A traditionalist, huh?"

"More like a taskmaster. It was always his way or the highway."

He could relate to that. His father was still controlling his life from the grave. "My dad never liked me devoting all my time to the rodeo. That made him a damn hypocrite since he met my mother on the circuit."

"Really?"

"Yeah. She was a barrel racer and he was a bull-dogger."

"Bulldogger?"

"Steer wrestler."

She frowned. "Why would you want to wrestle a steer? That sounds rather dangerous."

He chuckled over her lack of comprehension. "Sorry. I'm just surrounded by women who lived with rodeo cowboys. Most of the time they think they know more about it than I do."

After downing the last of her drink, she took off her jacket and laid it in her lap, revealing a sleeveless silk top that sparked his imagination. And suddenly he started to sweat.

"Well, you'll never have to worry about that with me," she began, "because obviously I know nothing about the rodeo. Not that I'm averse to learning. I'm a quick study."

Just seeing her bare arms, and a hint of cleavage, brought to mind a few lessons involving his second favorite sport. "I'm a good teacher."

Smiling, she bent her elbow on the table and supported her cheek with her palm. "When is my first lesson?"

He wanted to suggest tonight, but the fact her voice sounded a little thick led him to believe she might be feeling the effects of the alcohol. "You name the place and the time, and I'll be there."

After a moment's hesitation, she straightened and stared out at the horizon. "This place really surprised me. I was expecting a lot more desertlike terrain, not all this green pastureland. The scenery is really beautiful."

So was she, and the fact she didn't seem to realize that only elevated Dallas's opinion of her. "Yeah, when the sky turns orange at sunset, it makes all the mesquite trees look good."

She sent him a smile. "Where are you going to put the lodge?"

"On the east side of the property. We've surveyed about five acres that will be dedicated to Texas Extreme."

"How many acres do you have?"

"Ten thousand."

Her eyes went wide. "Wow. That's a lot of land."

He resisted reaching across the table and pushing the strand of hair away from her cheek. "We have a large herd of cattle. In fact, Texas Extreme is going to offer the experience of a good old-fashioned cattle drive, including a camp-out under the stars, complete with a chuck wagon."

"That actually sounds fun. I'd like to join you."

"You'd have to learn to ride a horse first."

"I'm game, as long as it's a gentle horse."

"That can be arranged. I have a good gelding. He's so broke I'd put a five-year-old on him."

"That would be about my speed."

"Something tells me you'd be a natural."

Her cheeks turned a light shade of pink. "Thanks, but don't count on it. I'm not sure I've ever been a natural at anything except designing."

That put all sorts of questionable images in his mind. "I doubt that. In fact, I'm fairly sure you're a natural at several things."

She barked out a soft laugh. "I can't think of one."

"I can, but I'm guessing your ex never tapped into your innate abilities."

"My ex rarely tapped into anything after our first year of marriage."

Without giving it a thought, Dallas reached over and pushed that sliver of golden hair away from her face. "The man had to be an idiot. Is that why you divorced him?"

She suddenly looked more than a little uncomfortable. "He divorced me, remember? Not that I thought the marriage had any chance of surviving at that juncture. Anyway, I should probably be going before it gets any later."

He really didn't want her to leave but he had no one to blame but himself for bringing up past history. "It's barely eight."

"And I still have to drive back to San Antonio."

When Paris pushed back from the table, came to her feet and swayed, Dallas stood and caught her arm. "Are you okay?"

She pinched the bridge of her nose with her fingers. "I was fine until I got up. Guess I'm a little tired. That drink went straight to my head."

As he'd predicted, Jenny's mint juleps had claimed another unsuspecting victim. He should've warned Paris that she could be heavy-handed with the bourbon. "Come to think of it, you had two."

She sent him a shaky smile. "I did, didn't I?"

"Yeah, you did, which means you're in no shape to drive."

Her stern expression didn't take away from her fantastic face. "I can't very well stay here."

"You can, and you will. I have several guest rooms. Five, in fact. Take your pick." If he had his way, she'd pick his room. But he'd been taught never to take advantage of a woman under the influence.

"I didn't pack a bag," she protested. "I'm sure if I lie down for a little while, I'll be fine."

He didn't have much faith in that. "We'll see how

you feel later, but I'm not going to let you get behind
the wheel tonight if I think you're not fit to drive. End
of discussion."

Clasping her elbow, Dallas led Paris through the double sliding doors, into the sunroom and guided her to
the great room. He took one look at the towering staircase and decided showing her to his downstairs quarters would be the better part of valor.

He continued down the corridor and past the kitchen
where he noticed Jenny cleaning up the dishes. He didn't
dare stop although he knew he'd have to do some serious explaining if she caught sight of them heading to
the bedroom. He'd wager his inheritance she had. Not a
problem. He had a bone to pick with her over the booze.

Once they arrived at the back of the house, he let go
of Paris long enough to open the double doors before
grasping her arm to steady her.

She took him by surprise when she wrenched out of
his hold and headed to the bed. "This looks heavenly,"
she said as she fell back on the mattress and laughed.
"What a lovely guest room."

"It's my room," he muttered. "I wasn't sure you could
make it up the stairs."

She giggled again when she kicked off her shoes
and one landed on top of the dresser several feet away,
barely missing the mirror. "Are you trying to ruin my
reputation, sir?"

"I'm trying to keep you from breaking your neck."
He crossed the room and held out his hands. "Hop up
so I can turn down the covers."

She accepted the gesture but instead of stepping

aside, she stepped right into his arms. And then she did the one thing he'd been avoiding all night, yet wanted more than anything. She planted her mouth on his.

She looked like a saint and kissed like a sinner. Oh, yeah, she was a natural. She had mighty fine lips and met his tongue stroke for stroke. He roved his palms down her slender back and paused right before he reached her butt, which took a lot of effort.

He intended to stop it before they went too far. Stop short before it went too deep. But when she pressed that sweet body against his, he tossed all those well-intentioned plans to the plains. And the longer this went on, the more he wanted to take her back onto the bed… or ignore all formality and take her down to the floor.

Without warning, Paris pulled away and touched her fingertips to her mouth like she'd been burned. "I'm not normally that bold."

He liked her *that* bold. "You're not thinking straight."

"I'm a little bit tipsy," she said, her speech slurred. "I came here to convince you to hire me, not to drink and make out with you."

That made him feel like an oversexed teenager. "It was just a kiss, Paris." One knock-em-dead kiss. "And I'm the one who should've stopped it."

Paris dropped down on the edge of the mattress. "I'm really not…normally…like this." She followed the comment with a hiccup and a giggle.

"You've got a good excuse," he said as he pulled her up again and set her aside to turn down the comforter. "Now lie down and sleep it off."

"Okay," she said through a yawn. "But don't let me

sleep too long. I have to…" Her eyes drifted closed then opened again. "Hmmm. I have to do something tomorrow but I can't remember what."

Dallas suspected she'd be there all night, and he'd be spending the evening in another bed, wishing he was beside her. He hooked a thumb behind him. "The bathroom's there if you need it. Make yourself at home."

She pulled the band that secured her low ponytail and set it on the nightstand before she perched on the edge of the mattress. "Thank you, Dallas Calloway. You're a nice man, and I'm sorry I'm not acting like a nice girl."

He liked his girls a little naughty, he started to say, but began backing to the door when he noticed how sexy she looked with that blond hair curling around her shoulders. "No need to apologize. Just get some rest."

She stretched her arms over her head and sent him a sleepy smile. "Since I probably blew my chances at the job, I wouldn't mind another kiss good-night." She tapped her cheek and smiled. "Just a peck."

He might laugh at that if he hadn't been so damn uncomfortable, or tempted to do more than give her *just* a peck. "We'll talk later when you're sober. I'll check on you in a bit."

Before he traded in his honor and gave in to animal urges, Dallas rushed out of the room, closed the door behind him and then headed down the hall to confront the culprit who'd created the chaos. Once he reached the kitchen, he found Jenny loading the last of the dishes into the washer. "What in the hell did you put in those drinks?"

Jenny turned toward him and had the gall to look

surprised. "Why, honey, just the usual. A little mint, some sugar and water, bourbon. And maybe a touch of tequila."

That explained a lot. "You added tequila on top of the bourbon?"

She didn't bother to look contrite. "Yes. It gives the julep that special kick everyone raves about."

"It kicked my date right into drunk mode."

Jenny grinned. "Your date?"

"Guest," he corrected, although he didn't see much point in getting the details right.

"Maybe I put a little too much alcohol into the drink," she said, "but I thought it would help Paris relax."

"Hell, she's relaxed all right. She's passed out in my bed."

"Then why are you in here?"

He was asking himself that same question. "Because there is no way I'm going to seduce a woman who's intoxicated."

Jenny leaned back against the counter. "Of course you wouldn't, sugar. You're too good for that. However, she won't be drunk in the morning."

Of all the confounded suggestions. "I'm going to check on Paris and then I'm going upstairs."

"I'll have a nice breakfast waiting for the two of you in the morning."

"Great."

Without further comment, Dallas turned around and nearly ran into his other stepmother. "'Night," he muttered, looking for a quick escape.

Maria had other ideas, he realized, when she grabbed his arm. "Why is the woman still here?"

He didn't have the energy to explain. "Ask Jenny," he said as he brushed past her and headed toward his bedroom.

Once there, he opened the door to find Paris curled up on her side, the covers shoved to the end of the bed. She'd stripped down to a white strapless bra and damn if she hadn't taken off her skirt, giving him a prime view of a pair of lacy, black panties.

Damn, damn, damn...

He should probably turn tail and run, but he worried about leaving her all night in her current state. He could crawl in next to her, or he could be the man Maria had raised him to be. A gentleman.

With that in mind, he strode into the bathroom, dressed in his boxers and a T-shirt, then prepared to sleep in the lounger. But before he settled in for the duration, he paused a few moments to study the gorgeous woman in his bed.

With her arm crooked beneath her head, her hair a sexy, tangled mess, she looked somewhat innocent in sleep, and someone he wouldn't mind waking up to in the morning. He liked her wit, her brain and her body. Definitely her body. Too bad he hadn't met her a year ago, when he still had time to court a woman in an effort to meet his match, and circumvent the terms of the will.

But unfortunately that time had passed, and unless he wanted to propose to someone he'd met only a few hours ago, he could just let go of that pipe dream. Then something suddenly occurred to him. Something the mothers had suggested.

Nah. That would be too weird, not to mention she would never agree to it.

Following a quick shower, Dallas took one last look at the pretty lady, turned off the lights and kicked back in the lounge chair. He still had trouble shutting down his thoughts for several reasons, including the damned deadline on the will. He'd be better served if he accepted his fate—his youngest brother would have controlling interest over the ranch. Short of a miracle, that would come to pass. Unless…

Maybe the harebrained idea could work if he handled it right. If he made it worth Paris's while. Or she could laugh in his face and leave. Still, it couldn't hurt to ask, if he found the courage to do it. Hell, he'd ridden some of the rankest bulls in the world. He could propose a marriage pact to a woman.

Probably best to sleep on it for now and decide in the morning—if he actually got any sleep at all.

Three

Shaking off the fog of sleep, Paris came into conscious-
ness slowly in reaction to a ribbon of light landing on
her face. She opened her eyes and squinted at first,
until she spotted the man with an open chambray shirt
sitting in the chair in the corner, putting on his boots.
Her eyes went wide when she remembered her current
location—a stranger's bed.

Then it all came back to her, one frame at a time, like
a mortifying slide show. Dinner with Dallas Calloway.
Two drinks. Getting drunk. Getting into his bed. And
that kiss she'd instigated.

Paris resisted the urge to pull the covers over her
head and hide away until he left. Or she could choose
the mature path and apologize again for her stupid behavior.

After scooting up against the tufted leather head-board, Paris pushed her hair away from her face and cleared her throat to garner his attention. "What time is it?"

He glanced at her, rose to his feet and began buttoning his shirt, but not before she caught a good glimpse of his toned chest, ridged abdomen and the thin happy trail leading to his open fly. "It's after nine," he said. "I thought for a minute there you might sleep until lunchtime."

She thought for a minute there she might swallow her tongue due to his sheer male perfection. "You should have woken me sooner."

"I tried."

"Apparently not very hard."

"I nearly shook your shoulder off, but you didn't budge." He cracked a crooked smile. "How's your head?"

"Fuzzy." But not so fuzzy that she couldn't recall what a fool she'd made of herself.

"Need an aspirin?" he asked as he tucked his shirt into the jeans' waistband.

She needed an escape route when she noticed her skirt and top hanging on the end of the bedpost. "No, I'm fine," she said as she clutched the covers tighter. "I do need to get dressed and go home."

He barked out a laugh. "That's usually my morning line."

It suddenly occurred to her she might not remember everything about their evening, although she couldn't imagine forgetting *that*. "Uh, we didn't do anything... you know."

He buckled his belt and approached the side of the bed. "Unfortunately 'you know' wasn't involved. You did strip down to your underwear, but I didn't look."

"I've definitely heard that before." She determined an amendment would be best before he assumed she slept around. "From my ex-husband, and he was telling the truth. He rarely looked at me the last few years of our wedded non-bliss."

"Your husband sounds like an idiot. No offense."

"No offense taken. You've pegged him right, although my actions last evening would probably qualify as idiotic. I'm so sorry I subjected you to that."

He grabbed an off-white straw cowboy hat hanging from a hook near the door. "Look, you had a little too much to drink. It happens."

"Not to me," she muttered. "I can't recall ever drinking so much that I took off my clothes and climbed into a stranger's bed."

"Darlin', since all you did was climb into my bed, I think you can stop worrying about your actions."

"But I kissed you. Or at least I think I did."

His grin expanded. "Oh, yeah, you did. And you won't hear me complainin' about that at all."

At least that was reassuring. "I want to be clear I have never done anything like this before."

"Kissed someone?"

"Kissed someone I just met."

"I kind of like knowing I was your first."

"I like knowing you're not completely disgusted with me."

"Nothing about you disgusts me, sweetheart." He

settled the hat on his head and smiled. "Stay in bed as
long as you'd like, and I'll see you in a bit."

"In bed?" Now why had she said something so leading and ludicrous?

He didn't seem at all affected by the faux pas. "Is
that an invitation?"

She shook her aching head. "No. Just proof that I
sometimes speak before I think."

He winked. "That's too bad."

Paris fought the temptation to tell him she'd reconsidered. "Where are you going now?"

"I have to check on some of the livestock."

"Well, I guess I'll just say goodbye then. I'll probably be on my way home before you get back."

"You can't leave yet. Jenny went to town this morning and bought you a dress and some underclothes and
laundered them. She left them in the bathroom along
with some toiletries. She's also keeping breakfast warm
for you."

Jenny could be nominated for Southern sainthood,
in her opinion. But how embarrassing to have one of
the Calloway stepmothers learn she'd spent the night in
the stepson's bed. "Although I appreciate the gesture,
that's not really necessary. I'll just put on the clothes I
wore last night and get out of your hair."

"I want you to stay a while longer so we can talk."

"About what?"

"Business," he said as he clasped the knob and
opened the door. "So don't go anywhere."

Paris fought the urge to salute over his demanding
tone, but Dallas had already disappeared before she

could deliver the gesture. Assured he had left the premises, she slipped out of bed and wandered into the bathroom. Spa bathroom.

The beige marble tub seemed as large as her whole apartment, and so was the stone shower. She had a good mind to take a soak, but she didn't want to prolong her stay in Dallas's domain or delay the breakfast Jenny had prepared.

She retrieved shampoo and shower gel from the basket on the double vanity, gathered a towel from the heated rack on the wall, then took a quick spray until she finally felt somewhat refreshed and energized.

She dressed in the aforementioned underwear, and donned the yellow sundress hanging on a hook on the back of the door. Evidently Jenny had thought of everything, right down to the matching sandals and hair dryer.

After completing the morning ritual, Paris strode back into the bedroom where she thankfully found her case that held her makeup bag. She didn't have her complete beauty arsenal, but she did have mascara and lip gloss, which would have to do.

After pulling her hair back into a low ponytail, Paris carefully folded her suit, shoved it into the bag and then headed toward the luscious scents wafting through the hallway. Once there, she found Jenny standing at the massive six-burner stainless stove, flipping pancakes, surrounded by a chef's dream kitchen. She had finally uncovered the one place that shouted ultramodern, not macho rustic.

"Good morning, Jenny," she said as she sent her a somewhat self-conscious smile.

The friendly stepmom favored her with a bright grin. "Good morning to you, sugar. Did you sleep well?"

"Like a rock." Like a drunken sailor. "The mint juleps saw to that."

Jenny pushed the spatula under one cake and slid it onto a plate. "I am so sorry, sugar. I didn't know you were such a lightweight."

Paris leaned against the cabinet adjacent to the huge fridge and rested an elbow on the gray quartz countertop. "I really don't drink too often. Just the occasional glass of wine."

Jenny sent her a sideways glance. "Would you like a mimosa? Or perhaps a screwdriver. Nothing relieves a hangover better than that old hair of the hound dog."

The thought twisted her stomach into a knot. "Heavens no. I mean, no thank you. I wouldn't mind some orange juice, without the champagne or vodka."

Jenny retrieved a pitcher of juice from the refrigerator, poured Paris a glass and handed it to her. "You're not from the South, are you, sugar?"

"No. Why?"

"Because good Southern girls like their toddies now and again."

Now and again could possibly be an understatement when it came to Jenny. "I'm not really from anywhere. My family traveled all over the country during my youth."

That earned Paris a sympathetic look. "Everyone

should have a place to call home, honey. Mine was the New Orleans area, until I moved here."

Paris had fond memories of New Orleans, the place where she'd headed her first hotel design project. Little had she known that a few years later, she would suffer a major fall from grace. "Do you miss Louisiana?"

Jenny shrugged. "At times, but I can always go back whenever I choose."

She gestured toward a small bistro table set near a bank of windows at the end of the expansive kitchen. "Have a seat, sugar. How many slices of bacon with your pancakes?"

Apparently Jenny had forgotten the meal she'd prepared the night before. "None, please. And only one pancake."

The woman looked as if Paris had uttered the ultimate blasphemy. "Oh, that's right. You're a vegetarian."

After setting her glass on the round table, Paris pulled back a cute red chair and sat. The color definitely indicated a woman's touch, and most likely an unwelcome concession on Dallas's part. "I do eat eggs and some seafood. I just avoid pork, poultry and beef."

Jenny slid a plate piled high with the cakes onto the table in front of Paris. "You'd have a hard time living here, honey. Beef is a mainstay with almost every meal."

She wrinkled her nose. "Sounds like a cholesterol catastrophe to me."

After claiming the chair across from her, Jenny smiled. "You'd be surprised how good old hard work keeps that in check. I tell you, Dallas is in prime shape and in perfect health."

From what she'd seen, Paris wouldn't debate the *prime shape* part. She grabbed the pitcher of warm syrup and poured only a small amount, ignoring the pats of butter to her right. "Is Dallas not joining us for breakfast?"

Jenny laid a hand on her throat. "Oh, sugar, he gets up with the chickens. He ate at five a.m."

Paris couldn't imagine dragging out of bed at that hour, much less eating a full breakfast. "What exactly does he do at that time of the morning?"

"He tends to the ranch," came from behind Paris. "He's a rancher and that's what they do."

She didn't have to turn around to recognize the voice, but she did glance over her shoulder to see Maria Calloway pouring a cup of coffee from the carafe on the counter. "I guess that makes sense," Paris said. "I'm surprised it requires working sunup to sundown."

Maria took the chair next to Jenny and leveled her stare on Paris. "Have you ever lived on a large parcel of land?"

Paris swallowed the bite she'd just taken and rested her fork on the plate. "No, I've never lived on a farm or a ranch."

"She's never really had a home, Maria," Jenny said sympathetically. "Isn't that just so sad?"

Maria appeared unaffected by the revelation. "Then you're not accustomed to working with your hands?"

She didn't understand the reasons behind the obvious interrogation. After all, she'd be leaving in hopefully less than an hour. Then again, Dallas had mentioned a business talk, so she could be coming back to the ranch, if luck prevailed. "Any work I do with my hands involves sketching designs and using a computer keyboard."

Maria took a long drink of coffee before speaking again. "It's a hard life on a ranch. Not for the weak of spirit or faint of heart."

"It's not that bad, Maria," Jenny said. "I've adjusted just fine, but then I did spend several years on a horse farm."

Maria turned her frown on the other mother. "You spent those years throwing garden parties, so your opinion doesn't count. And since you've been here, I don't recall you even picking up a garden rake, much less muck a stall."

"Don't listen to her, Paris," Jenny said. "I planted the roses in the hedges."

"Bully for you," Maria muttered.

Feeling the need to play peacemaker, Paris decided to change the subject. "Where exactly is Dallas now?"

"In the barn, of course," Maria said. "He told me to send you there as soon as you're done eating."

Wearing a pair of sandals in a barn didn't seem wise, but anything beat dueling stepmoms. After consuming only half her food, Paris dabbed at her mouth, put the napkin aside, pushed away from the table and stood. "Ladies, it's been a pleasure meeting both of you, and thanks so much for your hospitality. Now if you'll direct me to the barn, I'll be on my way."

Maria pointed behind her. "It's that way. Big building with a big door. Can't miss it."

Jenny rose and took Paris's hand. "Sugar, I am so glad you showed up here. I know Dallas is, too."

Paris only wished she could be sure of that. "Thanks, Jenny, and if we don't see each other again, I'll always remember our meeting fondly."

"Oh, you'll be seeing her again," Maria said from her perch at the table. "Me, too. A lot."

She wanted to jump for joy. "Then he's decided to hire me?"

Jenny and Maria exchanged a strange look before Jenny regarded her again. "You could say that in a manner of speaking. Now run along, sugar. Dallas doesn't like to be kept waiting."

If a chance existed that Dallas Calloway would soon be her boss, she would run all the way to the barn.

When he noticed Paris picking her way carefully down the rock path, Dallas propped the shovel against the rough-hewn wall and smiled. His amusement was short-lived when he realized what he was about to do, and what was at stake—his future as the head of the D Bar C Ranch and his project, Texas Extreme.

If he went through with his plan, some might consider him pretty mercenary. Or insane. Or both. But at the moment, he only cared about the opinion of the good-looking woman entering the barn.

"Maria said you wanted to see me," Paris said as she balanced on one foot and shook the sawdust out of her sandal.

"Yeah," he told her, although he was seeing a little more than he should, namely a nice glimpse of the curve of her breast when she leaned over and removed the other shoe.

After she straightened and tugged at the hem on the sundress, her attention turned to some focal point behind him. "What a beautiful horse."

Dallas glanced over his shoulder to find the black gelding poking his head through the opening in the stall. "That's Raven. Even though he lost his stud status years ago, he still knows a beautiful woman when he sees one."

A slight blush colored her cheeks. "He must not get out much."

Dallas still couldn't get why she didn't realize her worth. He'd be happy to take a turn at trying to convince her. But not now. Not yet. He had something more pressing that required her consideration. "How was breakfast?"

She leaned back against the opposite wall. "Wonderful. Maria said you wanted to speak with me."

"Yeah. I thought I could show you around."

"Around where?"

"The barn." *Although the bedroom would be better*, a thought that luckily hadn't jumped out of his mouth.

She folded her arms beneath her breasts. "You're not going to ask me to be one of your ranch hands, are you?"

He couldn't stop a laugh. "Not hardly. Just trying to be hospitable."

"Oh. You said earlier you wanted to talk to me about business, so I assumed maybe that's why I'm here."

Obviously she wanted to get right down to it. Normally that would suit him fine, but this proposition would take some time easing into it. "We'll cover that in a minute. First, I want you to officially meet Raven."

She looked almost alarmed. "Is that necessary? I mean, he is rather big."

He crossed the aisle and took her hand. "He's big all right. A big baby. He won't hurt you."

"Are you sure?" she asked, a good dose of wariness in her voice.

"Positive."

He guided her to the gelding's stall, stood behind her and told her, "Just pet him on his muzzle."

"Huh?"

"His nose. Or rub him right between his eyes on that white part, which is known as a blaze. He'll follow you anywhere if you do that."

She glanced back at him and frowned. "I'm not sure I want him following me."

"Give it a try, darlin'. You'll see he's a gentle giant. Besides, if you're serious about going on that cattle drive, you better get used to being around a horse before you climb on his back."

After a moment's hesitation, Paris reached out and touched Raven carefully, then slowly began to stroke him. The gelding didn't move an inch, as predicted, and soon began to close his eyes like he'd been hypnotized. Dallas, on the other hand, began to twitch as he followed her movements and imagined her hands on him...

He had a dirty mind full of devilish thoughts that

could land him in trouble, or on his ass if he acted on them. To make matters worse, Paris suddenly turned and ended up way too close for his comfort.

He figured it would be best if he continued the tour, but when she wet her lips, he could only move toward her, not away. And this time, he took the reins. He lowered his head and kissed her like he hadn't kissed a woman in years.

The next thing he knew, he had her spun around and backed up against the wall. She had her hands wrapped around his neck and that sweet little body pressed against his. All thoughts of wedding pacts and proposing to a virtual stranger flew out of his brain in lieu of what was going on below his belt.

Without warning, Paris broke the kiss and ducked under his arm. "This should not be happening."

Dallas braced both palms on the wall and tipped his forehead against the wood. "Maybe not, but it did. Too late to take it back."

"I wish I could take it back," she said from behind him. "I don't understand what is wrong with me. I see no reason whatsoever why I keep acting this way."

That ticked him off a bit and turned him around to face her. "Are you going to try to ignore the chemistry between us? Because I'm sure as hell not going to even try. From the minute you marched into the office, I knew something was brewing."

She looked away for a few seconds. "It's immaterial whether we share chemistry or not. I've made it a point not to do anything rash, and I'm not inclined to sleep with someone outside a committed relationship."

Hell, not only was she sexy, she could read minds. "I don't remember asking you to sleep with me."

She sent a pointed look south of his buckle. "You might not have verbally asked, but the message was loud and clear."

That wasn't up for discussion. "Hey, I'm a man. We don't always have control over physical reactions."

She gave him a good eye-rolling. "That could be true, but I do have control over mine."

"Lady, you could've fooled me a few minutes ago. And don't forget that kiss last night."

"Evidently I forgot myself."

"Maybe you've just forgotten what it feels like to be with a man who really wants you."

Her indignant look told him he'd struck a nerve. "Look, I have a few rules. I don't believe in casual sex, and I don't become intimate with anyone I've known such a short time. Never have. Never will."

A good lead-in to his crazy scheme, *crazy* being the operative word. But for the first time in a long time, he saw a possible end to his dilemma. Not to mention being married to Paris Reynolds carried a couple of perks, the least of which would be some nice, hot lovemaking. First, he had to convince her to give his plan credence.

He paced down the aisle and back again before he paused in front of her. "No sex outside a committed relationship, huh?"

"That is correct."

He rubbed a palm over his neck and prepared to propose. "Then if that's the case, I can only see one answer to the problem."

"What would that be?"

"Marry me."

Four

"Have you lost your mind?"

"Nope."

Paris found it difficult to believe a man like Dallas Calloway—a reputed confirmed bachelor—would blurt out a proposal to a woman he'd known less than twenty-four hours. "Let me get this straight. You'd be willing to marry me in order to sleep with me?"

"Yep."

This simply had to be a joke with an impending punch line. "Shouldn't we go steady first?"

"I'm serious, Paris, and I'm not asking just so I can get you into my bed."

From the somber look on his face, she could tell he was dead serious. "If it's not only the sex, then why would you want to rush into a marriage?"

"Because I need a wife and I need one fairly fast."

Her head started spinning from confusion. "Could you be any more vague?"

"It's kind of complicated. But I believe getting married would benefit both of us."

In what universe? "This doesn't make any sense to me, Dallas. As I said before, you could probably have any woman you wanted and—"

"I don't want any other woman. And in all honesty, I'm running out of time to find a bride."

Paris entertained visions of gloom and doom. "Is there something physically wrong with you?"

"Do you mean a terminal illness?"

"Yes."

"No, but I am suffering from an incurable codicil."

"Now I'm really perplexed."

"Join the club." He gestured toward the end of the lengthy barn. "Let's go into the office. You're going to need to sit down while I explain."

That sounded like a good plan. Her knees were still weak from their mini make-out session and the bombshell proposal. "Lead the way."

Paris followed Dallas into the office that was surprisingly simple and blessedly cool. She took a black-and-chrome chair situated in the corner while he leaned back on the industrial metal desk opposite her.

Dallas released a rough sigh as he centered his gaze on her. "Before I launch into this mess, I need to know I can trust you with the information I'm about to disclose."

She braced for deep secrets, an all too familiar concept. "I promise I won't say anything. Besides, I really don't have anyone to tell, at least not around here. And I promise you I have no intention of mentioning any of this conversation to my mother and father."

"No best friend?"

"Not really. I basically lost touch with my friends from college." A sad commentary on the state of her life.

"Good, because some of my current predicament involves a scandal."

Her curiosity was considerably piqued. "Go ahead."

After looking away a few moments, Dallas finally regarded her again. "A few years ago, during the reading of my dad's will, we discovered he had another family we didn't know a damn thing about."

"You mean Jenny?"

"Yeah, and the twins."

Both shocking and scandalous. "I didn't realize your dad and Maria divorced."

"They didn't."

The cogs started spinning in her head as she added outrageous to the adjectives describing the situation. "You mean he was—"

"A bigamist."

"How did he get away with that?"

"By leaving the state to screw around on Maria. He bought a horse farm in Louisiana when Maria was pregnant with my half brother Houston. He met Jenny in New Orleans, married her and proceeded to get her pregnant not long after my other half brother Tyler was born. For over twenty years he lived the lie and no one was the wiser."

Paris felt as if she'd been thrust into a spaghetti Western soap opera. "I can't imagine keeping a secret of that magnitude for weeks, much less decades."

"J. D. Calloway was a conniving, cheating, lying son of a bitch," he said, venom in his voice. "Pardon my French."

She couldn't believe he would be concerned about cursing in light of what he'd just told her. "No worries. My father speaks the language fluently."

Her attempt at humor obviously fell flat when Dallas didn't even crack a smile. "But that part of the sorry story isn't even the worst of it."

Paris had a difficult time believing it could get much worse. Then again… "Please don't tell me he had another wife."

"Not that we're aware of, although I wouldn't put it past him. But he did have it out for me."

"Why is that?"

"Because he never could control me in life, so he decided to do it in death."

She definitely didn't think she'd care for the late Calloway patriarch. "How exactly did he manage that?"

"By using ownership of the ranch. He knew my grandfather insisted the controlling interest of the D Bar C be passed down to his first-born grandson, and my dad was forced to adhere to that request. But then he added a condition that would allow me to continue to run this place only if I did his bidding."

She was almost afraid to ask. "Such as?"

"I have to get married before my thirty-eighth birthday. If not, controlling interest reverts to my half brother Fort who doesn't give a tinker's damn about this place. He's so ate up with anger he'd like to see all of us fail."

So now she knew why that milestone held so much importance with the mothers. And she suspected she knew the reason behind the spontaneous proposal. "Am I correct in assuming you want me to prevent that from happening by entering into a bogus marriage?"

He scowled. "When you put it that way, it makes me sound like a jerk. But after I met you yesterday and learned about your current situation, I figured it would benefit us both."

"How am I going to benefit from a lie?"

"Financially."

She'd begun to feel a bit like the prostitute Maria had believed her to be. "Marriage for money. Interesting. And out of the question."

"Will you at least hear me out?"

"I wouldn't miss it for the world. But first, I have to know one thing."

"Go ahead."

"How could you put that much faith in this plan when you know so little about me?"

He paused for a brief moment. "Your parents are Howard and Sheila Reynolds. You were born in San Diego thirty-two years ago on November second. You graduated from a prestigious college, worked for an equally prestigious firm in Nevada and you married Peter L. Smith in Vegas eight years ago. I didn't find any record of your divorce though."

She was floored he'd gained so much information in such a short time. "I have the documents although they're in Spanish, and a photo of the book where the registrar recorded the divorce. And exactly when did you do this background check on me?"

"I couldn't sleep last night so I did an internet search. This morning I called a friend who's in security. He took it from there."

Security meant criminal history. Momentary panic set in. "Did he find anything interesting?"

"Nope. Not one felony or misdemeanor or even a speeding ticket."

She relaxed for a moment knowing he hadn't discovered her primary secret, but then no one knew about that. No one ever would, thanks to a nondisclosure order arranged by her attorney. "I'd expect you to thoroughly investigate someone you intend to hire, but not someone you intend to marry."

"I'm a businessman, Paris, and this is a business proposition. Maybe that sounds kind of crass, but before we go any further, I wouldn't want you to have expectations of it being anything else."

For some odd reason that stung like a hornet, as if she was stupid enough to think it might be more. "Really? Again I ask, what's in it for me? Aside from being wed to the object of many a woman's lust, of course."

He didn't seem affected at all by her sarcasm. "First of all, you have a fairly substantial debt you're dealing with."

Had he somehow discovered the money she owed

her former firm? Impossible. Or so she hoped. "Did you run a report on my finances?"

"No. I figured that out when you came begging for a job, and confirmed it when you mentioned your ex taking your money and cutting out of the country. I also recall some issue with staying in your apartment and possibly having to move to Idaho. Am I wrong?"

If he only knew the true magnitude of her problems. "No, you're not wrong."

"Exactly how much debt are you carrying?"

"That's really none of your—"

"Business? If you want me to help you, you'll have to be honest about the money aspects."

He had a lot of nerve making the request when she hadn't agreed to anything. "I believe I asked you for a job, not for your help."

"Yeah, but I'm asking for yours. We could help each other. How much debt?"

She momentarily swallowed her pride. "Over seventy thousand dollars." Most of which she owed to her former firm.

"Are you a chronic shopper?" he asked.

"No, but my ex is. He left me with all the bills." Including money he'd stolen that she was having to reimburse.

"Okay. If you agree to this, I'll make sure you're debt-free. I'll give you twenty thousand up front and you can live here rent-free. You can also design the lodge and I'll pay you monthly for that. If you see that through, I'll provide a reference and the seed money to start your own company."

Wow. She would finally be solvent, liberated from her former employer and on her way to a bright future. But at what cost? A nagging voice told her to go for it. Her mother's voice told her to proceed with caution. "If I did agree to this, and I'm not saying I am, how long would I be expected to remain in this marriage?"

"The will states a year," he said. "It's going to take at least that long to get Texas Extreme up and running and the lodge ready for guests. If you'll stay until then, I'll throw in another bonus. I'll buy you a new car so you can put that rusty sedan out to pasture."

She took offense to him insulting her car. "Bubba is not rusty."

He chuckled. "You gave that clunker a name?"

"Yes. He's been very reliable, unlike most men I've known."

"Bubba sounds like he's barely running."

"He does need a little work." Now for a very pertinent question. "There is the very important matter of dissolving the marriage. I'm personally not keen on being labeled a two-time loser with another divorce."

"We could look into an annulment."

"Under what grounds after we've hung in there for a year?"

He streaked a palm over his shaded jaw. "I'm not sure."

Neither was she, but she intended to find out. "Mind if I borrow your laptop to do a little research?"

He reached behind him and offered her the computer. "Knock yourself out."

After setting it on her lap, Paris began the search

for annulment criteria. She selected the most official-looking article and began to read. "Let's see here. The first condition states the parties are family members, but I highly doubt we're related to each other."

"Did you not pay attention to me telling you about my father's philandering ways? I wouldn't be surprised to discover you're the sister I've always wanted but never had."

"Very funny and kind of creepy."

"I'm kidding, Paris. I don't harbor any brotherly feelings for you whatsoever."

She looked up to see Dallas's smile before scanning the text again. "On to the next point. I guess one of us could get drunk during the ceremony and claim we weren't coherent enough to consent. We could then say we didn't sober up until after our first anniversary."

His low laugh gave her pleasant chills. "Sounds like you could handle that with a couple of Jen's mint juleps, pre-ceremony. I'm sure she'll keep you supplied for the next twelve months."

This time she didn't bother to look up. "Clever, but not anything either of us should consider. Coercion is out because I wouldn't agree to this unless we're both sure. Bigamy is also out. And fraud unless one of us is lying about our age."

"Nope," he said. "But back to that bigamy thing. Are you sure you're divorced?"

Realizing she'd inadvertently hit a nerve bringing up bigamy, Paris closed the computer and frowned. "Yes, I'm sure I'm divorced. Peter couldn't get out of the marriage quick enough. He's a CPA so he's fastidious and detail oriented." As well as a con artist, a fact she chose to withhold. "That leaves us with the final possibility. Do you have issues with impotence that would lead to the old standby, failure to consummate?"

He looked more amused than insulted. "You and I both know the answer to that after what happened a few minutes ago."

She'd realized very quickly he hadn't been poking fun. "That's too bad since it would make the whole failure to consummate much easier, which appears to be our only option. Get married, no whoopee."

He looked like he'd just bitten into a dill pickle. "You expect me to go without sex for a year?"

Paris thought that would be the greatest challenge of all, and a possible reason for him to rescind the offer. "Cowboy up, cowboy. You can handle it if you want to keep the ranch. Which leads me to another question."

"Shoot."

"Does maintaining control of this place mean so much to you that you would enter into a fake marriage that requires celibacy for a year?"

"I don't like the celibacy clause one damn bit, but I can only promise I'll try. And it would have to be a real marriage in order to meet the will's requirements."

She saw a possible alternative. "Who would know if we only pretended we married?"

"Fort will make a point to check it out."

The decision would be so much easier for Paris if that weren't the case. "You're obviously a rich guy, Dallas. I imagine you could buy a ranch just like this one anywhere in the world. Maybe even a bigger and better ranch. Then you wouldn't have to resort to this ruse."

"It wouldn't be the same," he said. "To risk sounding like Jenny, the D Bar C is equivalent to losing the plantation that's been in the family for generations."

"Wouldn't it still be in the family if Fort takes over? Have you even bothered to work out some agreement that wouldn't force you to go to such extremes?"

Anger flashed in his eyes. "Fort doesn't talk to anyone but Worth. He'd have the power to do anything he pleases, including selling it off piece by piece. I wouldn't put it past him to do that just for spite. He hates anything associated with the Calloways, including me. Especially me."

A family feud of grand proportions. "Because I grew up traveling the world, I've never experienced having a real home place. But I do understand why it would be difficult to give up a legacy."

"And even harder to give up the memories."

"Of your dad?"

"Of my mother. I have very few as it is."

That revelation yanked hard on her heartstrings. At times her own mother could drive her insane with her penchant for being overprotective, yet Paris couldn't imagine not having her mom in her life. "How old were you when she passed?"

"Not quite five years old, but I still recall the little things. If I'm forced to leave here, I'm afraid the memories might fade completely."

Hearing the pain in his voice almost pushed Paris over the marriage edge. But she couldn't let emotions rule common sense. She'd done that too often as it was. "You've given me a lot to consider," she said as she handed him the laptop.

"Then you're not completely ruling it out?"

"No, but I have to think about it long and hard. And you'd have to promise we'd find some way to go the annulment route."

"Believe me, my lawyer will find a loophole if that's how we want to end the marriage. And I'd be willing to put all the terms in writing if that would make you feel better."

She'd feel better if she had more time to weigh the verdict. "When do you want my answer?"

"I'm flying to Houston on Friday and I thought we could just do it there. It'll be easier to blend in at that courthouse rather than do it around here. Word travels fast in small towns."

"I don't know if I can make such a serious decision that soon."

"That's all the time I have since my birthday's Saturday," he said as he pushed off the desk. "When it comes right down to it, it makes sense to get it done the day before."

If only she could be so sure. "I'm going to go home and think it over," she told him as she stood. "But if I were you, I wouldn't get my hopes up. I'll call you as soon as I've made up my mind."

After leaving him behind in the barn, Paris managed to return to Dallas's house, gather her things and sneak out without being detected. She drove the ninety miles home in a haze, ticking off a mental list of pros and cons. She entered her barren apartment and thought about how she'd hoped to settle in a loft downtown, with a view of the River Walk. Yet her budget had only allowed her to rent a one-bedroom in a cookie-cutter complex outside the magic of the city.

Her life had turned into an absolute mess, devoid of security and absent of even a shred of a sincere social life. She had a closet full of expensive shoes and nowhere to wear them, a large stack of unpaid bills, including one that if ignored could take away her freedom, and a solid sense of defeat. But she still had an option—accept Dallas's proposal. What was the worst that could happen? Paris could think of one thing—she might lose her heart to a man who didn't return the sentiment. Again.

Not this time. Not if she approached the proposal as strictly business. She married for love the first time, why not marry for financial gain the second? A lot of people did it. Unfortunately she'd never imagined herself fitting into that mercenary mold. But she'd never dreamed she would be caught in this dire position.

Damn her bad luck. Damn Peter Smith for his criminal acts and betrayal and leaving her to take the fall. Damn Dallas Calloway for putting her on the verge of accepting his offer.

Knowing she needed advice had her reaching for the cell phone, although she would have to be very, very careful.

On that thought, Paris dropped down onto the sofa and pounded out her parents' number. After two rings,

"Reynolds residence" filtered through the line in Sheila's usual sing-song voice.

"Hey, Mom. It's Paris."

"Well I'll be, it's the prodigal daughter checking in and it's not even a holiday."

Her mom did have a tendency to make her kids feel guilty at times. "I know, Mother. It's been a while since I called, but I've been rather busy."

"Do you have a job?"

That depended on whether she took a husband. "Actually, I have a good prospect." Now for adding that other little tidbit of information. "I also have a new man in my life."

"Oh, Paris, are you sure that's a good idea? The ink has barely dried on your divorce decree."

"It's been twenty-two months, Mom." And four days.

"Oh. Time does fly, doesn't it?"

"Yes, it does. Anyway, I think you and Dad would like him."

"Does *he* have a job?"

"Yes, he does. He's a rancher. An honest to goodness cowboy."

"Interesting. Does he have a nice butt?"

Heavens, leave it to her matriarch to bring that up. "What difference does it make?"

"Believe me, it does. I married your father for his butt and we're approaching forty years of marital bliss."

Definitely too much information. "Yes, he has a nice butt and a nice house and a lucrative ranching operation. Are you happy now?"

"I'm happy if you're happy, dear."

Now for the moment of truth. A prelude to what possibly could be in the offing. "Good, because the *M* word has been mentioned."

"Meatloaf? Manners? *Mistake*?"

"Very funny, Mom. Marriage."

"Darn, I'd hoped that wasn't it."

"Nothing is set in stone yet, but I didn't want you to be blindsided if it does happen."

"I certainly hope we get to meet this one before you take that step."

Not likely that would occur in two days. "I'm sure you'll have the opportunity in the near future."

"Paris, if this man treats you well, then you'll have our blessing. Just make certain this time you're doing the right thing."

An obvious slam on her lack of judgment when it came to her former relationship. "Believe me, I'm going to be very certain before I end up at the altar. A part of me says I should go for it. Another part tells me maybe I'm not cut out for matrimony."

"I don't want to ever hear you say that again," her mother said in a no nonsense tone. "You have the capacity to make a marriage work, as long as you can trust and love your mate for life."

Therein lay the problem—love didn't figure into the deal. "How do you ever really know that, Mother? Marriage doesn't come with guarantees."

"True, but it does come with certain risks if it's not right. If you happen to be lucky enough to find your soul mate, then don't be afraid to take the chance. One bad apple named Peter shouldn't spoil the whole bunch. By the way, what is this man's name?"

"Dallas." And sadly he would never be her soul mate, though he could be her financial savior.

"How nice that he carries the moniker of your father's favorite football team. That should earn him a few points."

They shared in a laugh before Paris decided to end the conversation. "Thanks for listening, Mom. I'll take all your advice to heart."

"You're welcome, dear. And don't forget to follow that heart. If it feels right, do it. It's high time to leave the past behind and look forward to a brighter future."

"You know, Mom, you're right. Love you bunches and tell Dad I love him, too."

"We love you, dear. And don't wait so long to call, okay?"

"I won't." And that next call could be a bombshell that might blow up in her face.

After Paris hung up, she mulled over her mother's words and clung to one thing in particular—leaving the past behind and looking forward to a brighter future.

Maybe she should choose a different direction, journey down a new path, even an unorthodox one. Maybe marriage to Dallas Calloway could provide all of that, and more. Maybe his offer would be the best way to start over.

Too much to consider, and far too little time.

Right then, Dallas only wanted enough time to enjoy his lunch alone. But the two women hovering at the dinette where he now sat had no intention of giving him some peace. Maybe if he ignored them, they'd go away. And pigs would probably sprout wings first.

Jenny propped one hand on her hip and stared at him. "Well?"

He swallowed the last bite of the barbecue sandwich before he responded. "Well what?"

"Where is Paris?"

"She went home."

Maria flipped her braid over one shoulder and folded her arms. "Are you gonna ask her out again, *mijo*?"

"Nope."

Jenny sighed. "Sugar, you really should have given her another chance. A lot of women get drunk on a first date."

He saw an opportunity to rattle their chains and jumped on it. "I decided I didn't need to ask her for a second date."

Jen looked crestfallen. "Why not?"

"Because I asked her to marry me. I figured we'd pretty much moved past the dating game at that point."

That effectively shut them up for the time being, but he suspected not for long.

"You really did it?" Jenny asked, confirming his suspicions.

"Yeah, I did."

"Don't just sit there, *mijo*," Maria said. "Give us all the down and dirty details."

Jenny took on that same old wistful, romantic look. "Did you get down on one knee? Did you give her a ring?"

That beat all he'd ever heard. "No, I didn't get down on one knee. I approached it as a business proposition, which it is. And when would I have found time to buy a ring?"

"You have your mother's ring, Dallas. It's in the safe."

Maria didn't have to remind him of that. He'd thought about it often, even though he'd never really looked inside the blue velvet box. Giving it to Paris under the circumstances would be as false as the marriage. Ironically, that trinket had been reserved for true love, according to his dad. "A ring is the least of my concerns."

Jenny's face fell like it had weights attached to it. "She said no?"

He pushed back from the table and came to his feet. "She said she'd think about it."

"Then it's not a lost cause?" Maria asked.

"Okay, you two, don't get your hopes up." Exactly what Paris had said to him before she'd left. "My guess is she's going to think it over and then refuse the offer."

"You should have knelt before her," Jenny said. "Women like that."

"And given her the damn ring," Maria added. "I'm not sappy like Blondie here, but I do know most gals like to be treated with dignity when a man pops the question. Even your father knew that."

"That's true," Jenny began. "J.D. could be quite the romantic even if he was a jackass."

He didn't want to hear anything else about the aforementioned jackass since he was the reason Dallas found himself in this predicament. "It wasn't going to matter to Paris if I rode in on a white horse, considering what I'm asking of her."

"A white horse would have been nice," Jenny added. "That would be hard to resist."

He wanted to shake some sense into the woman and dislodge her visions of hearts and flowers. "Again, the ball is now in Paris's court. If she wants to agree to the marriage terms, then she'll let me know."

"Maybe you should go after her," Maria added. "Give her a little nudge in the right direction."

He had actually thought about doing that very thing before deciding he didn't want to pressure her more than he already had. "If she wants to go forward, she'll come to me. I'm not going to coerce her into a decision." Although that would be a reason for ending the marriage, provided it actually happened. Nah. His sense of honor wouldn't allow him to use that tactic.

"I hope she does say yes," Jenny said. "We could plan a grand wedding on the grounds of the main house. I could make canapés and my famous mint juleps."

That's all he needed—a drunk bride. Then again, that would be grounds for the annulment. He really had to get a grip. "If she decides to go through with it, and that's a big *if*, there won't be any wedding. Just a simple courthouse ceremony and no publicity."

Jenny pretended to pout. "That's no fun, Dallas. You should have your family present for the nuptials."

Before she called a caterer, Dallas had to get out of there. "You ladies have a good afternoon talking about me behind my back."

With that, he left the kitchen and headed to the barn,

all the while recalling how he'd watched Paris drive away. Probably for the last time.

In reality, the marriage pact was the craziest thing he'd ever conjured up. He sure as hell couldn't imagine keeping his hands to himself for a day in her presence, much less a year. If everything fell through, he'd be better off. He'd just turn the place over to Fort and find somewhere else to start up Texas Extreme, even if it wouldn't be the same.

Accepting the fact that Paris would turn him down flat would be best. He'd bet his last buck that's exactly what she'd do.

Five

"With the power vested in me by the state of Texas, I now pronounce you husband and wife."

The man should probably be pronouncing them certifiably insane. Four days ago she hadn't even known Dallas Calloway. Two days ago she'd packed up her limited belongings and moved in with him. Today she wore a diamond-encrusted wedding band and vowed to be his wife. Unbelievable.

Paris waited for Dallas to follow the justice of the peace's declaration, expecting a peck on the cheek. Perhaps a brush across her mouth. She got a full-on, well-deep kiss that curled her toes in the white satin pumps she'd purchased with the sleeveless matching dress before she'd left San Antonio.

After Dallas pulled away and winked, she automatically touched her tingling lips. "That certainly sealed the deal."

He leaned over and whispered, "There's more of that to come if you want more of it."

Yes, she wanted more. Much more than she should. "Now that we've made this official, what's the next step?"

"I have a driver waiting outside the north entrance. He'll take us back to the plane."

The private plane that had whisked her to Houston a few hours ago to meet up with the groom following his appearance at the grand opening of his newest saddle shop. An elaborate aircraft that could pass for a flying motel with a high-class bar and sleeping quarters, of all things.

Dallas clasped her hand to guide her through the courthouse vestibule and when they stepped outside, Paris was shocked to find hoards of reporters milling around the steps outside. "What is going on?"

"They're here for us," Dallas muttered, followed by a few strong oaths. "Just keep walking and stay close to me."

"Not a problem." She had no intention of crawling into the lion's den without a proper escort.

As soon as they started their descent, cameras immediately began to flash, film began to roll and some woman with red hair as big as Jenny's started hurling questions at Paris. "How does it feel to be married to one of the most eligible bachelors in the state?" she asked as she thrust a microphone in Paris's face.

Before she could respond, Dallas practically dragged

her toward the black limo waiting at the curb as he shoved his way through the crowd. She could swear someone tugged at the hem of her dress right before the chauffeur helped her into the car and away from the chaos.

Dallas slid in bedside her and immediately began to loosen his tie. "Dammit, I wanted to avoid all this nonsense. I'd like to know who the hell tipped them off."

"That's anyone's guess. Maybe someone in the courthouse when you obtained our marriage license. By the way, how did you manage to circumvent the normal waiting period?"

He shrugged out of his beige jacket and laid it on the seat beside him. "I know people. Obviously people that can't be trusted."

She imagined he did know a lot of people in high places. She also imagined him taking off the white tailored shirt, his best pair of jeans and cowboy boots, and laying her down on the leather seat. Maybe she'd request he leave the boots on. Maybe she should exit the car now before she found herself in a lot of trouble. As if she wasn't already. "You know, marriages are a matter of public record, Dallas. I'm sure that's how the media learned about us."

"We haven't even been married fifteen minutes. Someone at the courthouse must've leaked the info. Probably an employee who wanted to make a buck selling a story."

Curious over how far the news had traveled, Paris pulled her cell from her silk bag and did a quick internet search of their names. In less than five seconds, she had her answer from a renowned celebrity gossip site. "Oh, my gosh. I can't believe this headline. Sexy Former Rodeo Superstar Dallas Calloway Marries Longtime Girlfriend Paris Reynolds."

"Don't know why you're so shocked," he said with a grin. "Some women think I'm sexy. My truck, too."

He was just too darned cute not to tolerate his wry wit. "I'm referring to the *longtime* part. Talk about a misprint. It should read His Girlfriend of Three Days. Or more accurately, His Business Partner."

He scooted a little closer to her, providing another heady whiff of his clean-scent cologne. "I wouldn't be surprised if they didn't get hold of Jenny for an interview. She'd say something like that to make the situation more socially acceptable."

"I suppose she would do that since she's definitely all about decorum."

"She's also still mad she wasn't invited to witness the wedding. So is Maria." After his cell began to ring, he pulled it from his jeans' pocket and said, "Speak of the devil."

"Which one?"

"Jen."

When he simply stared at the phone, Paris wondered why he was hesitating. "What are you waiting for?"

"I'm tryin' to decide if I want to speak to her."

"Of course you do. It might be an emergency."

"Yeah, her pantyhose could be shot or her hairdresser canceled her appointment."

"Answer it, Dallas."

"Fine." He swiped the screen and grumbled, "What's

up, Jen?" followed by a few *yeahs* and couple of *yeps* and one *big deal*. Then he added, "I'll take that into consideration, and I don't give a horse's rear what he thinks. And yeah, I forgive you but only because he's your kid. Talk to you later."

"What was that all about?" Paris asked after he disconnected.

Dallas forked a hand through his hair and sighed. "It seems Jen decided to call Fort and tell him we were getting married and where. When she saw the story at five a couple of minutes ago—"

"Why does our marriage warrant coverage on the news channels?"

He looked at her as if she'd lost her mind. "She was watching some tabloid channel, not the national news. But be prepared for that to happen. Weddings, babies and divorces of the rich and infamous equal good ratings."

Apparently their surprising little wedding was worthy of major coverage, thanks to the notoriety of the man sitting beside her. The man who happened to legally be her husband. "I knew you were popular with the ladies, but I had no idea losing your bachelor status would have such an impact on the general public."

He shrugged. "No one thought it would ever happen. Anyway, Fort evidently called the press just to piss me off. Jen says a lot of reporters are camped out near the ranch. Maria's doing her best to run them off, hopefully not with a shotgun. Like I suspected, Jen also said it was her idea to claim we've been a couple for a long time."

"How long?"

"Three years, and she's real proud of the plan."

The *plan* could be a major problem. "Unfortunately that would make me an adulteress since I've been divorced less than two years. I hope that doesn't come back to haunt us."

He reached into the built-in cooler centered between the opposing rows of seats and withdrew a bottle of high-dollar champagne. "If it does create problems, we'll deal with it. In the meantime, let's celebrate our nuptials."

Celebrating wasn't foremost on her mind. Not when she continued to worry that somehow someone might dig up the dirt from the debacle at her former firm. But she couldn't concern herself with something that happened to be beyond her control. Besides, if Dallas found out, she'd simply explain she'd only been guilty of being too gullible. "Nice touch," she said after he poured them each a glass of the bubbly and offered one to her. "But I wouldn't peg you as a wine drinker."

"Normally, I'm not, but I think we deserve a toast." He held the glass aloft. "To an arrangement that will allow us to both win in the end."

As long as *the end* didn't include an emotional hijacking, she'd drink to that. "To winning," she said as she touched the flute to his.

After taking a few sips, Paris leaned back in the seat, looked out the window and noticed the slow-moving traffic. "It's going to take forever to get to the airport."

Dallas downed the rest of the champagne and grimaced before setting the glass aside. "That's what happens in Houston during rush hour. Guess we should have planned better."

The situation could work to their advantage. "Since we have the extra time, we should probably use it to get to know each other."

He scooted closer, draped his arm over the back of the seat and grinned. "I'm game."

"I don't mean that." Even though *that* would be tempting.

He slid a fingertip down her cheek. "Are you sure? I mean, we are newlyweds and we're in this big old limo with all this room. The driver can't see a thing with the window up."

More very vivid images filtered into her thoughts. Risqué images that caused her face to fire up. She didn't know whether to fan herself or faint. "I'm referring to discussing details about each other, in case anyone asks. After all, we've presumably been together for three years."

He released a rough sigh. "Talking wasn't what I had in mind."

"Of course not. You're a man. You're averse to conversation."

He traced a random pattern on her knee. "Not always. Just at the moment."

She slapped her palm on his hand and placed it on the seat between them, even though she considered sliding it up her thigh. "Now, now. Be a good groom. We both know the terms."

"I don't like the terms one damn bit."

In reality, neither did she. But she liked the thought

of another divorce even less. "First get-to-know-you question. What's your favorite color?"

"Brown. Yours?"

"Coral. Favorite pastime?"

"I thought I made that clear right before you threw the no-sex terms up in my face."

Definitely a bad boy. "Your second favorite then."

"Taking a long, hard ride on a—"

"Dallas," she said in a scolding tone.

"Bull." He tried on an innocent look that didn't quite erase the devilish gleam in his blue eyes. "What did you think I was going to say?"

The man knew exactly what she'd been thinking, and with good reason. "Moving on. Favorite food?"

"Steak."

She knew the answer to that before she'd asked the question. "I love hummus with red peppers."

He frowned. "I'd rather eat hay. Your favorite vacation spot?"

"I haven't been on a vacation in so long I couldn't really say. I do know it's not Vegas. I've seen enough of that place to last a lifetime."

"Never been a big fan," he said. "Except when I was at the National Finals Rodeo. Now that I've retired, give me a fishing trip any day."

"I've never been fishing," she said.

"Never?"

"No. My father spent his career on boats so he avoided taking us anywhere that involved water."

Dallas remained quiet for a while before he asked, "How would you feel about going fishing?"

"Today?"

"Sure. We've got to spend our honeymoon somewhere, not to mention the press is hanging out at the ranch, waiting for our return. We could just kick back a couple of days. I can teach you how to cast a line and we can just relax."

Had this been a traditional marriage, she might have preferred a tropical paradise in lieu of a fishing excursion. However, that fit Dallas's cowboy persona, not consuming fruity drinks with umbrellas during an island escape. Avoiding any more media coverage for the time being sounded like a good idea no matter where they went. She did see one problem. "I didn't pack a bag, Dallas."

"Just leave it all up to me. I promise you'll have everything you need."

She trusted he would make good on that promise. "Okay. Exactly where will we go?"

"Lady, this is your lucky day. I just happen to know this little cabin on a lake."

It had to be the biggest log cabin she'd ever seen.

When they'd arrived at the airport an hour ago, they'd been greeted by a fiftysomething-year-old man who'd delivered Dallas a tricked-out black truck, complete with leather seats, satellite radio and a high-tech computer. They'd immediately set off for Texas Hill Country, northwest of San Antonio, luggage on board as promised, for their impromptu honeymoon. And now they traveled up a steep drive lined by a myriad of trees toward another magnificent property.

"This place is really yours?" Paris asked as Dallas pulled into the circular drive and stopped before the front door.

He turned off the ignition and gave her a prideful smile. "Yep. I helped build it with my own two hands a couple of years ago. It's a nice place to escape, although I don't get to enjoy it often enough. Now wait right here."

After undoing her seat belt, Paris remained in her seat while Dallas rounded the hood and helped her out. He only let go of her hand to open the pine door, and then caught her completely off guard when he picked her up into his arms.

She had a little trouble catching her breath as he stepped inside. "What on earth are you doing, Dallas?"

"Carrying my bride over the threshold."

Even her *official* first husband hadn't done that. "Isn't this a bit of overkill considering our situation?"

"The caretaker doesn't know our situation," he said as he set her on her feet atop the wood plank floors. "And I don't know if he's left yet. I'm going to check the place over then I'll bring in the bags."

After Dallas left her alone to her devices, Paris readjusted her dress and tightened the band at her nape. The man had literally swept her off her feet. Imagine that. If not careful, she might actually start viewing him as a real husband. Not wise at all.

Pushing the concerns aside, she surveyed the great room with floor-to-towering-ceiling windows that afforded a view of the wooded terrain. Or what she could see of it now that the sun had disappeared. The place was rustic, like its owner, but charming all the same. Most of the accent pieces appeared to be antiques, with a lot of Western art and bronze statues. The heavy wood furniture with tufted cushions could have been hand-made, and the decor most likely had been strictly selected by Dallas. She could also tell it wasn't nearly as large as his ranch house, but just as masculine if not more so. In fact, she saw no evidence whatsoever of a woman's touch.

A few minutes later, Dallas came back through the front door, toting the suitcases, and startling her sense-less. "All clear."

"How did you manage to sneak by me?"

He set the suitcases down by the oversize sectional. "I went out the back door then walked around to the front."

Logical, though she couldn't lay claim to much logic of late. "Oh. Makes sense."

He pointed to his left. "Kitchen and dining room are in there, along with the back door." He then pointed to his right. "Bedrooms are that way. All have their own private bath. You can pick whichever one you want."

"Which one is yours?"

He cracked a crooked grin. "I was hoping you'd pick that one."

Apparently he didn't intend to give up on the sex thing very easily. "You and I both know that's not a good idea, sleeping in the same bed."

"I know no such thing. I think it's a great idea. That way if someone comes calling, we'll at least appear to be the happy couple."

Stubborn man. "Do you routinely have people randomly show up in your bedroom?"

He rubbed his chin and looked as if he had to think about that. "Maybe a time or two back when I was a teen and managed to sneak a girl into my bedroom. But I'm fairly sure Maria isn't going to make a trip down here for that. In fact, she would expect us to be sharing a bed. Jenny, too."

"Do they not know the terms of this marriage?"

"Not exactly, but they do know me."

She had begun to know him, too. She'd also begun to realize resisting him would prove to be a major challenge. "Humor me and show me to my own room, okay?"

He gave her that little boy shrug. "Okay. But this isn't like any honeymoon I've ever read about."

This wasn't like any marriage she'd ever heard of, either. "You'll survive."

"Maybe, but I will be walking funny."

"Ha, ha."

She shadowed Dallas's steps as he led her into a hallway, bags in hand, and stopped at the first open door. "This is probably the smaller of the three, but I think it suits you."

Paris stepped into the room to find the four-poster queen bed draped in an orange-and-white cowhide. "I refuse to sleep with a dead animal."

Dallas chuckled behind her. "It's not real, just made to look that way."

She turned around and scowled. "It's not very tasteful."

"It's my taste. Get used to it. Are you hungry?"

Not anymore. "The little vegetable sandwiches they served us on the plane will tide me over. Right now I'd like to get these shoes off and get into something more comfortable."

"Need any help with that?"

"No, but I do need my suitcase."

He laid her bag on a bench at the foot of the bed. "Lady, you seem to be lacking in the fun department."

"And you seem to have an overabundance of testosterone."

"That I do, and I won't apologize for it."

"I wouldn't dream of asking for an apology." She brushed past him and unzipped the case, only to find some skimpy barely-there bright red nightie. "Who packed this?"

He leaned over her shoulder, his warm breath filtering over her neck. "I'd guess Jenny. She wants to make sure the groom is happy."

"I'm never going to wear this, you know."

He slid his arms around her and whispered, "Stranger things have happened."

She couldn't argue with that. This whole marriage pact was incredibly strange. The butterflies in her tummy were stranger, still. She couldn't recall the last time she'd been so sexually charged she wanted to jump out of her own skin. Or jump into bed with a man she barely knew. Easy. Never.

For her own protection, Paris wrested away from Dallas and strode to the door. "Now run along like a good boy, and take your suitcase with you."

He headed toward her, a determined look on his face.

"They're both yours. I have everything I need in my bedroom. Almost everything."

She didn't have to ask what he meant by that. "Before you go, is it safe to take a walk before bed?"

"Sure. Go out the back door and you'll find a path to the lake."

"Is it well lit?"

"The moon is full tonight. That's enough light for you to see where you're going. Just don't fall into the water. And watch out for snakes."

She cringed. "Snakes?"

He had the gall to grin. "Just kidding. The cats keep them away."

"Cats?"

"Yeah. Big ones. Attack cats. But they've been trained not to bother pretty girls."

With that, he exited, closing the door behind him, leaving Paris alone to unpack, and ponder how she would find the strength of will to ignore his overtures, and her own needs.

She returned to the suitcases, thankful to find something other than naughty negligees in the mix. In the smaller one, Jenny had packed every toiletry known to womankind, and enough underwear to last two months, not two days. The woman had also packed jeans and a few T-shirts, and from those Paris picked her favorite coral knit top and pair of seen-better-days denim with a slash above the right knee, a small hole on the inside of her left thigh, and a pocket that was barely hanging on. That suited her current state of mind.

After exchanging her formal dress for comfort, she

kicked out of her heels and donned the slide-on sneakers that had been stashed in a side pocket. Now she felt more human, if not more calm. Too bad they'd left the champagne in the limo.

She didn't need alcohol, she needed some peace and quiet. Time alone to reflect. With that in mind, she headed into the hall and located the well-equipped kitchen—which was almost as nice as the one back at the ranch—then made her way out the back door.

Dallas had been right about the moon. It cast the manicured lawn in an amber glow and helped guide Paris down the dirt path toward a copse of trees. Fortunately someone had had the foresight to cut a wide clearing in the woods, otherwise she might have been hesitant to continue. A few yards away she could see the shimmering lake and headed in that direction, all the while aware of the sounds of nature, including what sounded like an owl. She managed to make it to the dock without stepping on a critter or coming upon the attack cats.

Once there, she strolled to the end of the pier and lowered herself onto the wooden slats, then hugged her knees to her chest. A slight breeze blew across her face, bringing with it the pleasant scent of cedar. She heard the sound of chirping and an occasional rustle of leaves, which might have unnerved her if she would have still been walking.

On afterthought, she rolled up her jeans, took off her shoes and dangled her feet in the water that was much colder than she'd predicted. But after a while she acclimated to the temperature change and rocked back on her elbows to study the host of stars in the night sky.

For the first time that day, she experienced true tranquility. A sense of well-being as she soaked her sore feet in silence.

"Mind if I join you?"

Paris gasped and nearly vaulted right into the water. She shifted around, palm against her pounding heart, to find Dallas standing above her. "Jeez, you scared me to death!"

He sat beside her without waiting for an invitation and draped his arms on bent knees. "Did you think I was a snake? Or maybe one of the tomcats. Just so you know, they don't talk."

"You startled me because I wasn't expecting you."

"Next time I'll whistle."

Like that would help her anxiety over being accosted by random wildlife. "I'm surprised I didn't hear you."

"No kidding. This dock creaks like box springs on an old iron bed."

No real shock he would bring up a bed analogy. "I was very deep in thought."

"About?"

"Today. This whole thing seems so surreal."

He shifted slightly, leading Paris to believe maybe he was suffering from bride remorse. "Yeah, I know. Never thought it would happen to me."

Her conjecture could very well be right. She wouldn't know what might be on his mind unless she asked. "So what brings you here, other than this bizarre situation?"

"I owe you an apology."

That she hadn't expected. "For what?"

"I'm sorry for coming on too strong. But I won't apologize for wanting you so badly I ache."

She'd never felt so flattered in her life. "Apology accepted, and I'd be telling one colossal lie if I said I wasn't extremely attracted to you. But—"

"But what?" He gave her a meaningful look. "If you're worried about the whole annulment thing, I won't tell if you won't."

"I won't lie under oath. And I have a feeling your integrity won't allow that either."

His sigh cut through the silence. "You're right about that. One thing I learned from my father, deception takes no prisoners. I do think we can find other ways to answer our needs."

Was he suggesting an open marriage? "If you're going to ask if you can see other women, that's your call, but rest assured I wouldn't feel right seeing other men."

"I'm not saying that at all," he said. "We can explore each other without going beyond the limits."

"You mean only foreplay?"

"You got it, darlin'. It's my favorite kind of play."

The thought of his hands on her made her shiver in a very nice way. "That would certainly be new and different for me."

He frowned. "Your husband wasn't into foreplay?"

The understatement of the millennium. "Let me sum up our sex life in a few words. Hi, Paris, just passing through, only have a minute, got to go, see you later. That happened about once a week unless he wasn't in the mood. He always said I was too uptight about my body, but what did he expect when all he did was criticize me?"

"Why in the hell were you with that ass?"

The sheer anger in his voice took her aback. "I was young and stupid. He was my first lover and the first man who really paid attention to me. At least in the beginning. When I got him hired on at the firm, everything changed. I'm fairly certain he cheated on me, although I didn't have any proof. Eventually I didn't even care."

Dallas let go a litany of curses. "You're damn special, Paris. You deserve to be treated that way. And if you want me to show you how good it can be between a man and a woman, all you have to do is ask."

When he rose to his feet, Paris realized she didn't want him to leave. "Where are you going?"

"To grab a snack, take a cold shower and then head to bed."

"Could you stay a little longer?"

"I could, but being so close to you and not being able to touch you is killing me."

She recognized the risk she'd be taking, but she truly craved his attention because she knew with all her heart he would treat her with respect. "I want you to touch me, Dallas. I *need* you to touch me."

He stood statue still and after a few moments asked, "Are you sure?"

She held her hand toward him. "If you'll help me up, I'll go back to the house with you."

"No need for that."

Paris had no idea what he planned to do next when he, too, rolled up his jeans, sat back down, pulled off his socks and boots, then positioned himself behind her, his legs on either side of her thighs. Right at that moment, Paris felt something at her feet beneath the water and gasped again.

"Just relax sweetheart," he told her as he pulled the band away, pushed her hair aside and kissed the back of her neck.

"It's not you. Something was nibbling on my toes."

His slow laugh sent pleasurable chills down her spine. "Darlin', I can do that, but you'll have to wait until it's warmer or until you have your feet out of the lake."

She smiled back at him. "You mean you wouldn't jump in the water if I asked you?"

"Not unless you're waiting for me, naked."

Interesting concept, albeit not logical. "We probably should put that on hold for a couple of months."

"It's a deal."

He kissed her then, thoroughly, stroking her tongue softly with his in a heady rhythm that made her want to climb all over him. If she reacted so strongly to this simple show of affection, she couldn't imagine what she would do if he did anything else.

She would soon find out, she realized, when he broke the kiss and rested his cheek against her cheek, reached beneath her shirt and unclasped her bra. For a moment she felt like a schoolgirl making out with her first real boyfriend in a backseat, an experience she'd never really had. But when Dallas tugged the tee up over her head, taking the bra with it, she knew she was in the hands of a real man. Naked from the waist up. In wide-open spaces.

She should be mortified over being so exposed, but she honestly didn't care. She should have been self-conscious when Dallas whispered, "Watch," but instead she waited with excited anticipation. And the minute he began to circle her nipples simultaneously with his fingertips, she grew hotter than blazes in places still unseen.

As much as she wanted to continue to see what Dallas was doing, Paris closed her eyes and leaned back against him to savor the sensations.

"Feel good?" he asked, his voice low and grainy.

"Yes."

When Dallas slid his palm down her belly, Paris held her breath. And when he began to toy with the button on her jeans, she automatically tensed.

"Just tell me to stop and I will."

She frankly hoped he kept right on going, but then he suddenly halted everything, much to her disappointment. She opened her eyes and stared at him blankly. "I didn't say anything."

He moved from behind her, rolled down his jeans, put on his boots then stood. "I think that's enough for tonight."

She snatched the discarded shirt and clutched it to her bare breasts. "I don't understand."

"Put your shirt on and I'll walk you to the house."

Somewhat miffed, Paris slid the tee over her head,

stood and shoved the bra in her back pocket. "I can find my way."

"Are you mad at me?"

"No. I'm mad at myself for falling into your trap. Nothing good could ever come of mixing business with pleasure and in reality, this is a business arrangement as you have reminded me several times."

"Between two consenting adults who have the hots for each other." He had the nerve to wink. "Darlin', a lot of good could come from it, as soon as you realize sometimes you can't control chemistry. Just let me know when you're ready to explore all our options."

"Don't count on that happening," she said to Dallas as he strode away, leaving her alone to wonder why she couldn't resist him. Why she had let him go so far. Why he could so completely splinter her coveted control, and she welcomed it.

He might have caught her in a moment of weakness, but from that point forward, she vowed to reclaim her power. Call all the shots in this sexual game he seemed determined to play. Turn the tables on him. The time had come to shed her insecurities and prove to him— and to herself—that she could be a strong woman capable of going after what she wanted, wisdom be damned. Business be damned. Fact was, she wanted him.

Perhaps she hadn't been born a natural seductress, or acquired any real skills in thirty-two years, but it was never too late to learn. When it came right down to it, celibacy wasn't the least bit fun.

Six

Celibacy sucked swamp water.

Dallas had discovered that recently but learned long ago the lack of merit in a cold shower. He'd taken one anyway at dawn, following one helluva restless night. Afterward, he'd headed to the kitchen, made a strong pot of coffee, a couple of scrambled eggs and ate them at the kitchen island like he did every morning at the cabin. But his normal news catch-up routine had been disrupted by visions of the woman sleeping down the hall. Just the thought of touching Paris again, going further, going all the way, kept him from focusing on the state of the global markets. But he had to remember the annulment terms—no sex in the real sense.

If he had any hope of maintaining his sanity for the next twelve months, he had two options—take care of the problem himself, or convince Paris they should take care of each other, even if it meant not fully consummating the marriage. He liked the second plan best. Taking it slow seemed to be the only way to accomplish that goal, even though it would damn sure prove to be real hard. Literally. Now if he'd been a dishonorable jerk, he would've crawled into bed with her last night to solve the problem, knowing he'd had her exactly where he'd wanted her before he left her on the dock.

The *problem* only grew more obvious when Paris padded into the room on bare feet, wearing some short flimsy peach-colored robe, her hair piled on top of her head in a messy ponytail. On one hand, she was about as cute as a newborn foal. On the other, she looked sexy as hell, even with her face free of makeup.

She sauntered over to the counter, poured herself a cup of coffee, then turned a sleepy smile on him. "Happy birthday and good morning, handsome husband."

She looked like a birthday gift he wanted to thoroughly investigate. "Mornin', pretty wife." He'd never dreamed those words would ever leave his mouth. But then he'd never imagined meeting anyone like her, either. He liked the way she moved. The way she talked. Her intelligence. Her body. And he knew he would seriously like the way she loved if she gave him the chance to partake of all the benefits that most married couples enjoyed.

Wait a minute. For all intents and purposes, they'd entered into a fabricated union. They weren't playing house, they were doing business. If it was up to her, that's all they'd ever be doing.

Maybe not, he decided, when she sauntered over to the island, sat on the barstool across from him and didn't bother to close the opening of the robe, allowing him a nice view of the curve of her breasts. "Sleep well?"

Not hardly. "Fairly well. And you?"

"You mean after you left me alone topless on the dock? I've had better nights."

"Sorry," he muttered, although he really wasn't all that sorry, except maybe about the leaving part.

She then leaned completely across the granite surface to study the newspaper in front him, causing the robe to gape more and giving him full view of her bare breasts, nipples and all. "*Wall Street Journal*, huh? I expected you to be reading some ranching magazine."

He expected to elevate the island at any moment. "I've been interested in financial news since I acquired my MBA."

Her green eyes went wide as she sat back down, taking his fun away but giving him some moderate relief. "I had no idea you have a graduate degree. Where did you go to school?"

He couldn't resist rattling her chain a little. "Got it online from the University of Dumb Cowpokes."

She laughed softly as she rimmed a fingertip around the coffee cup, drawing Dallas's undivided attention. "Be serious for a change."

He had a serious need to see what else she might be wearing underneath that robe. Or what she wasn't wearing. "I got the undergraduate degree at a small college in Stephenville, Texas, while on a rodeo scholarship. A few years later, when I decided to open the saddle shops, I decided to go for the masters at a bigger university in Fort Worth."

"Impressive. Why saddle shops?"

Recounting his history could calm his rowdy libido. "When I was growing up, a ranch hand named Gordy taught me how to tool roping saddles. I used his design, started my own line of saddles and began to market it."

"Gordy doesn't have a problem with that?"

"Nope. He's happily retired living off the royalties."

"You are a man of many talents, I must say. Do you have any sugar?"

Ignoring the urge to tell her he could give her something really sweet, Dallas nodded toward the cabinet behind her. "Right next to the coffee maker."

She glanced over one shoulder before sending him another smile. "Oh. I didn't see it," she said as she slid out of her chair.

She sure had great legs, he realized, when she walked to the counter to sweeten her coffee. The robe was so short that if she lifted her arms, he felt sure he could see her bottom. He should've told her the canister was in an upper cabinet. He'd give a month's worth of pay to find some excuse for her to bend over. He didn't have to let go of a dime when she dropped the spoon on the floor and reached down to pick it up.

Damn if she didn't have on a thing. Damn if she didn't have one fantastic butt. And damn if he didn't have the mother of all erections.

She turned around and leaned back against the counter. "What are your plans for the day?"

He could offer up a few that involved staying horizontal for the next twenty-four hours, but remembered his aim to take it easy. "I thought we'd go fishing."

She sipped her coffee then set the cup aside. "Sounds like fun. When do you want to do it?"

Right now on the kitchen island. "We need to get going before it gets much later, while the fish are still biting."

"Then I should hurry. What should I wear?"

Not a damn thing. "T-shirt and jeans, I guess. Or shorts. It's going to be close to eighty degrees today."

While Dallas sat there suffering from lack of sex, Paris rinsed her cup out in the sink and put it in the dishwasher, unaware of his predicament. "I'll take a quick shower and be back in a few. Where should I meet you once I'm finished?"

In my bed. Your bed. Any bed. "The dock."

"The dock it is. Maybe I'll just show up without my top to save time."

Taking Dallas totally by surprise, Paris untied the sash at her waist, turned around and let the robe fall from her shoulders onto the floor as she walked away.

The image of her slender back and shapely butt remained burned in his brain long after she disappeared.

Was she just trying to torture him, or give him a taste of his own medicine? He didn't know the answer, but he sure as hell intended to find out.

Paris wondered what effect, if any, her little attempt at seduction had had on Dallas. If he only knew how difficult it had been to completely let go of her inhibitions, then maybe he might have said *something*. When

she'd left him in the kitchen, she hadn't had the forti-
tude to wait around. He certainly hadn't sought her out
in the shower, or showed up at the bedroom door. Only
time would tell what he might have in store for her during their little excursion, and the closer she came to the
dock, the more the excitement escalated.

She discovered him waiting for her, dressed in khaki
cargo shorts and a sleeveless army-green tank, revealing
a pair of very masculine legs and muscled biceps that
sent her heart on a marathon. A few moments passed
before she noticed the sleek silver-and-red boat with the
covered hull tied to the side of the pier.

After sliding her sunglasses into place, Paris stepped
onto the creaky planks and made her way to her tour
guide for the day. "Is this yours?"

"Yep," he replied.

"How did it get here?"

"George."

Clearly he'd decided to be cryptic. "Who is George?"

"My neighbor. He looks after the place when I'm not
here, and in exchange I let him use the boat. I called
and had him deliver it a few minutes ago."

Evidently George wasn't going to join them, a very
good thing. "I see. I've never been on this kind of boat
before. It looks like it costs a pretty penny."

"About eighty grand."

Paris nearly swallowed the gum she'd been chewing. "Eighty thousand dollars? For that price, it should
clean the house, or at least do more than float around
the water looking pretty."

"It can fly," he said as he held out his hand. "If you're lucky, I might let you drive it."

As long as he had sufficient insurance since she'd never been behind the wheel of a boat before. "I might take you up on that, if you're lucky."

He cracked a crooked grin. "I have a feeling we could both be lucky today."

She returned his smile. "Could be." Or not, depending on how far she wanted the seduction scheme to go.

After Dallas helped Paris down into the space-age looking seat, he untied the boat then claimed the space next to her. One hand on the wheel, he backed away from the dock slowly, said, "Hang on," then turned the craft around and shot off into open water.

Yes, the thing could fly, and she couldn't hold a conversation with him due to all the wind noise. She basically clutched the sides of the seats, gritted her teeth and only breathed easier when he navigated the boat into a secluded cove fifteen minutes later.

She pulled away the band securing her high ponytail and finger-combed her hair. "You need to turn around and go back."

He frowned. "Why?"

"Because I think I left my stomach a few miles back."

He barked a laugh. "I take it you're not much of a thrill seeker."

Only partially true. She'd married him on a moment's notice, hadn't she? And she was definitely seeking some thrills today. "I've ridden a few roller coasters on several occasions, but I wasn't quite prepared for this."

Paris *had* prepared to turn on the charms and hopefully turn him on in the process. On that note, she crossed her arms, grabbed the T-shirt's hem and tugged it over her head, leaving her clad in a red bikini top.

Dallas cleared his throat and shut down the ignition. "Didn't know you had a swimsuit."

"Actually, I didn't either," she said as she stood. "Jenny thought of everything." Including massage oil and lubricants, a veritable sex shop in a bag.

"No surprise there," he replied, his voice sounding somewhat grainy.

Paris realized she didn't have a lot of room to maneuver, so she pointed to the enclosed hull. "What's under there?"

"A live well to keep fresh bait and fish and a place to store equipment." He climbed over the smoked glass minidash and stood on the decking to toss an anchor overboard into the murky green water. "You basically turn on the trolling motor and stand here to fish, but we're going to stay stationary until you learn how to cast."

"Or I could sunbathe," she said as she retraced his steps and stood before him. "I can do that while we fish, right?"

"Not a whole lot of sun with all the trees, but whatever floats your boat, pun intended."

She shimmied out of the shorts and tossed them back onto the seat, revealing the scant swimsuit bottoms. "I'm ready for a pole now."

That earned her a wily grin. "I can fix you right up."

"Fishing pole, Dallas."

"I've got one of those, too."

"You have an evil mind."

"You have an unbelievable body."

She felt a head-to-toe blush coming on, and the same old belief he'd simply been trying to be nice. "I bet you say that to all your first mates."

He tucked one side of her hair behind her ear. "You're technically my first mate."

If only she could say the same for herself. If only she could erase Peter from her past and if only this arrangement with Dallas was real. "Well, I suppose we should start fishing before they stop biting."

He stared at her a few moments before leaning over, opening a hatch and pulling out a rod. "I've got this rigged to catch a bass. I also have some blood bait for catfish if you'd prefer to try for one of those."

She wrinkled her nose. "Any bait that includes *blood* in the name is out."

"Good call, because it's also known as stink bait."

Ewww… "Definitely bass."

"Bass it is. Now move to the edge of the boat."

After she complied, Paris surveyed the wooded bank and noticed not a house, or soul, in sight. "How many people live on this lake?"

"Just me and George," he said. "It's a private lake."

Of course it was. "So there's no chance anyone will see me making a fool of myself?"

"Not likely." Dallas came up behind her and handed her the pole with the little yellow frog-looking thingy dangling from the end. "Hold this in your left hand, and grasp the reel in your right."

Simple enough. "Like this?"

"Yep. Now push that button with your thumb, pull the rod back to the side and let it go, but not over your head or you'll hook me."

She did exactly as he'd instructed, yet nothing happened. "I knew I wasn't cut out for this."

"I don't mind helping you out." He moved behind her, wrapped his hand around the rod below her hand and replaced her thumb on the release with his. "It's just one smooth action," he said as he cast the line in the water with ease.

He didn't make a move away from her. In fact, Paris would swear he moved closer. "Okay. What now?"

He rested a palm on her belly and pushed her hair to one side with the other. "It's a top-water jig, so the fish will hit it on top of the water."

"How long does that take?"

"Until the fish decides to bite."

When Dallas rimmed the shell of her ear with his tongue, Paris almost dropped the pole. "So it might take a while."

"Probably not."

After Dallas dropped his arms from around her, Paris glanced back to find he'd removed his shirt. And oh, what a sight to behold. He had a board-flat belly and a chest that wouldn't quit. "Hot already?"

"Lady, you have no idea how hot."

She had a sneaking suspicion she might soon find out when he came back to her and began kissing her neck again. "What are you up to, Dallas Calloway?"

He moved flush against her back. "Pay me no mind and watch your line, in case you get a bite."

"Aren't you going to fish?"

"Maybe later. I have something I'd rather do at the moment."

Paris held her breath when he tugged the string at her neck and unclasped the strap at back. Now the bikini top lay in a pool at her feet and she found herself exactly where she'd been last night—naked from the waist up.

"Dallas, are you sure no one will see us?" Her voice sounded tinny, thanks to the cowboy's hands roving over her breasts.

"George left for Kerrville this morning to visit his mother." He feathered more kisses along her neck. "Besides, the possibility of getting caught makes this a little more exciting."

Her legs began to shake like a leaf in the breeze. "Any more excitement and I might actually not be able to stand."

"I'll make sure you don't fall. Just relax."

Relaxing proved to be impossible when his palm came to rest on her midriff and began to drift lower… and lower. "What are you doing now?"

"Scratching your itch."

When he slipped his hand beneath her bathing suit bottoms, Paris was powerless to stop him. When he began to stroke her softly, she could no longer hold onto the fishing pole. After she dropped it on the deck, she reached back and wrapped her hand around his nape to ground herself. She briefly envisioned how this would look to a passerby—him with his hand down her pants and her in the throes of a sexual frenzy—and that only amplified her need for release.

In a matter of seconds, her pulse accelerated and her respiration picked up speed as the impending climax began to build. The orgasm slammed into her hard with a series of strong spasms that seemed as if they went on forever. She literally shook from the force of it and Dallas, as if he sensed she might not remain upright, turned her into his arms and kissed her.

She came back to reality slowly and broke the kiss to tip her forehead against his shoulder. "Wow."

"Been a while, has it?"

"Try never. At least not with Peter."

He set her back and stared at her. "He never got you off?"

She shook her head. "Sadly no, because he really didn't try, or care. And go ahead and say it. I'm a fool for staying with him as long as I did."

His expression turned somber. "Then why did you?"

"Because I'd convinced myself I couldn't do any better." An admission she'd not made to herself, much less to another soul.

He hugged her for a few moments then pulled away to study her eyes. "Sweetheart, you deserve better. You deserve to have a lover who takes care of you first and puts himself second. That's the way a man should treat his woman, especially a woman as special as you."

His woman? Once upon a time she would have made a snide comment about beating his chest, but oddly she liked the sound of it. "Thank you. That means more than you know. But I'm nothing special."

He looked mock serious. "Yes, you are, and don't argue with me."

"I wouldn't dare, Mr. Macho. Not after what you just did for me." That brought about an important question. "Speaking of that, what about you? You've clearly got an itch that needs scratching, too."

"True, but I'm fine for now." He grinned. "Later this evening is another story altogether. We still have a whole lot of exploring to do, if you're game."

Paris imagined giving him the pleasure he'd just given her and that made her tingle. "I'm definitely game." The sound of the reel suddenly drew her attention and prompted her to snatch the rod off the ground. "I think I have something. What do I do now?"

"Bring it in, darlin'."

"How?"

Without responding, Dallas stepped to her side, took the pole and turned the reel's handle until he brought up the line, a smallish silver fish dangling from the hook. "Not quite big enough for dinner."

"It's so cute, but hurry and take it off."

"It's a baby," he said as he unhooked the bass, crouched down and released it into the water. "Grow up, bud, and maybe I'll catch ya later."

That made Paris smile. "I'm glad you let him go."

"I don't like fishermen who hang on to undersized fish just because they can. It's a waste, and I don't like waste."

She liked him more and more with each passing moment. She predicted that beneath the tough-guy exterior resided a heart of gold. "It's nice to know you have respect for wildlife. And women."

He offered her the pole. "Want to try for something bigger?"

"Are you referring to a fish?" she teased.

"Well, sweetheart, what else do you have in mind?"

"Maybe I'll show you later this evening." She took the rod and this time managed to cast it all by herself. "How was that?"

"Looks like you're a fast learner."

She handed him back the pole. "But I'm not very patient. You fish, I'll just kick back on the deck, get some sun and watch you bring in dinner."

He nodded toward the hatch. "There's a towel in there, so have fun. But don't get too comfortable because we might not be here much longer. It's almost time for lunch."

Paris realized she hadn't eaten a thing since the whole grain bar she'd consumed in the bedroom following her novice strip tease. "I admit I'm getting a little hungry, too."

After casting toward the bank, Dallas shot her a grin. "From this point forward, you can always depend on me to take care of all your appetites. How am I doing so far?"

She returned his smile. "Best fishing trip ever."

And she couldn't wait to find out what else he had planned.

Seven

His plans for Paris had unfortunately been put on hold.

The woman had been so relaxed that immediately after she'd eaten lunch—if you wanted to call a tomato and lettuce sandwich *lunch*—she'd taken a nap. A long nap.

His mind whirled back to earlier in the day, when she'd been as hot as a branding iron and quick to fire. The bastard she'd married had done a number on her, and he really wanted to right the wrongs. Show her all the ways a man could please a woman. Convince her that she was as close to perfect as they come. No doubt he'd be up for the challenge, in every way possible.

Dallas had thought about joining her in bed, but he'd taken a trip to the nearest grocery store—fifteen miles away—then returned a few calls, including one from his attorney. As a result of that conversation, he had to break some serious news that wouldn't make Paris happy in the least. She might not want anything more to do with him.

And now, with the sun working its way down the horizon, Dallas grabbed a beer, fired up the grill and contemplated how he would tell her the sorry news. He didn't have a lot of time left, he realized, when Paris made an appearance on the back deck a few minutes later, looking like she'd walked right off the cover of a fashion magazine.

Her straight blond hair fell past her shoulders like homespun silk. She wore just enough makeup to show off her features to full advantage, and a short blue dress with thin straps that showed enough cleavage to make him want to growl. He couldn't believe his luck in finding such a good-looking fake wife.

She kicked off her flip-flops, curled up on the wicker sofa and pulled her legs beneath her on the blue cushions. "Whatcha doing, cowboy?"

Imagining what it would be like to make fast, hard love to you on that sofa. For the sake of distraction, Dallas turned the burgers before lowering the lid on the grill to regard her again. "I'm making us some dinner. You must've been really tired considering how long you slept."

"I only slept about an hour. I spent the rest of the time rehearsing what I would tell my parents about our marriage and then I called them."

He would have liked to have been a fly on the wall during that conversation. "How did it go?"

She shrugged. "As expected. My mom bemoaned the fact that once again she didn't have the opportunity to throw a lavish wedding for her youngest daughter due to a whirlwind courtship. The conversation with my dad wasn't much better."

"What did he say?"

"He said, and I quote, 'This guy better not treat you as poorly as that other SOB.' And then he went on to say to let him know where he can find Peter so he can beat the…well…some sense into him."

Although Dallas could understand her father's attitude toward the ex-husband, he didn't like the thought of winding up on the wrong side of a retired military man when that man learned his daughter's latest marriage wasn't permanent. "How big is your dad?"

"How tall are you?"

"Six-two."

"He's five inches shorter and stocky. My mom is five-seven, and so is my sister. I fell on the shorter side at five-five."

"I would've guessed you to be a little bit taller. Must be those long legs."

"Must be your imagination."

Yeah, his imagination was running amok when he thought about having those legs wrapped around his waist. Again he looked to his cooking duty to keep him from acting on his fantasies. At least until he could confess…after dinner.

"Speaking of family dynamics," Paris began, "I assume all your brothers know about the will, but do they know that our marriage isn't exactly the real thing?"

"They're all pretty busy right now so I'm not sure what Jen or Maria have told them. I plan to say as little as possible when we get back to the ranch."

"Do you think they would actually believe you would rush into a marriage on a whim because of a will?"

Probably not. "It doesn't matter what they believe. It's an unspoken rule that we don't get into each other's business."

After a span of silence, Paris leaned slightly and studied the grill. "Color me crazy, Dallas, but those look a lot like beef patties."

"Only two of them," he said as he flipped them again before turning back to Paris. "I found some kind of veggie burgers at the store. I figured they couldn't be too bad. Heck, you could serve up a boot as long as you've grilled it with mesquite wood chips."

"Heavens, I hope it doesn't taste like a boot."

Honestly, so did Dallas. He didn't want to let her down, although he suspected he eventually would before night's end. "The cashier who checked me out told me she loved them."

"I'll bet she checked you out thoroughly."

The jealously in her voice surprised him, and in some ways pleased him. "She had to be at least sixty-five."

She lifted her chin. "Just because a woman matures doesn't mean she can't recognize a sexy cowboy when she sees one."

"And just because I'm a man doesn't mean I'm gonna flirt with a grandmother."

"Men flirt with any woman who'll flirt back."

At least she'd said it with a smile. She wouldn't be

smiling when he lowered the legal boom. "Do you want something to drink?"

"I wouldn't turn down a glass of white wine, if you happen to have some. If not, water will work."

"I have wine." Thankfully he'd had the foresight to stock up a few months ago, the last time he'd had a female guest at the cabin. The last time he'd had a woman, period. Tina, or maybe it was Terry. What the hell did it matter? He'd only spent one weekend with her. Plus, she couldn't hold a candle to Paris in any way, shape or form.

When Paris came to her feet, Dallas caught a good glimpse of a thigh and one stubborn part of him stood, too. He needed to get the hell out of Dodge before she noticed. He'd begun to wonder if any man had ever expired due to a perpetual erection. "Sit. I'll bring it to you. In the meantime, you enjoy the sunset."

"If you leave, you'll miss it since it's almost gone."

So was his sanity. "I've seen it before." He'd also seen a feminine leg before, but for some reason, viewing even an inch of her bare skin kicked his libido into overdrive.

After one last look at the burgers, Dallas rushed into the house, braced both palms on the kitchen island and took a few deep breaths. If he didn't calm down and get with the program, all his plans for the evening would go up in smoke. He couldn't act on his need for her until she knew all the truth.

When he finally gained his composure, he took the plate full of lettuce, tomatoes and pickles from the fridge, along with the bottle of chardonnay. He thought about popping the top on another beer but figured that wouldn't help his predicament at all. He needed to keep his guard up and his sex drive down for the time being.

He brought the hamburger fixings and put them on the wooden picnic table, then handed Paris the wine. "Sorry about the plastic cup. I don't have any fancy barware here. Hell, I don't have any fancy dinnerware, either. That's why we're eating on disposable plates."

She took a drink of the chardonnay and rested the cup in her lap. "Not exactly environmentally friendly, but I suppose they'll do if we don't have a choice."

He didn't want her to believe he was a total Neanderthal. "They're plastic, too. I throw them in the recycle bin before I leave so George can properly dispose of them."

"That's good to know. How is dinner coming along?"

He checked the burgers, all the while considering giving her a kiss. Only one kiss. But like the potato chips resting on the red checkerboard tablecloth, he wouldn't be able to stop with just one. "Looks like they're about ready. Do you want cheese on yours?"

"Sure. I'm in the mood to splurge a little."

Dallas hadn't realized she was standing behind him until that moment. After laying the cheese slices on the burgers, he put the spatula down and turned around, only to run headlong into some fairly fantastic green eyes and a mouth that looked like it wanted to be kissed. Maybe that was just wishful thinking. "What else are you in the mood for?"

She slid her arms around his neck and pressed her great body against his, indicating she might be willing to make his wish come true. "Oh, I don't know. Maybe a little slap and tickle after we eat. Maybe a little of that before we eat."

Man, she was killing him. "Aren't you hungry?"

"Yes, but not only for food." She rubbed against him and it hadn't been an accident. "Just humor me, okay?"

With the last scrap of his control in shambles, Dallas gave her a full-throttle, no-holds-barred kiss. A tongue-dueling, fire-starting kiss that gave the barbecue grill behind him a run for its money.

But damn, he wanted more. He wanted to use his mouth somewhere else, and that meant disregarding his original plan of ignoring her. To hell with it.

He pushed the straps off her shoulders and then lowered the dress's bodice to do what he'd wanted to do earlier that day. He bent his head and took one breast into his mouth while Paris threaded her hands through his hair to hang on. When he circled her nipple with his tongue, she released a purely sexual sound that made him so hard he wanted to strip out of his jeans then and there. Instead, he slid his palms down her back, clasped her butt and pulled her against the erection that wouldn't die unless he did something about it. But if he acted in haste, he could make a mistake of monumental proportions. As bad as he wanted to be inside her, he thought of all the reasons why he couldn't.

Dallas let her go and took a step back. He had to look her straight in the eye when he made the revelation. "We need to have a serious talk before this goes any further."

Paris's lips looked swollen and her eyes hazy, but she

didn't seem to be too mad over the interruption. Yet. "Talk about what?"

"A change in the marriage terms."

"I'm sorry, Dallas, but I'm confused."

She wouldn't be confused much longer, but she sure as hell might be ready to slug him. He saw no choice but to blurt out the sorry truth.

"Darlin', we're going to have to get divorced."

Surely she hadn't heard him correctly. "Are you serious?"

"Yeah, I am."

Paris pulled the dress back into place as her mind reeled from Dallas's proclamation. "Now? We've barely been married a day."

"No, not now. When the year ends."

She could not believe he would go back on his word. So much for trusting another man. "We both agreed we would get an annulment. In fact, you promised your attorney would find some way to accomplish that goal."

Dallas took her by the hand and showed her to the table where they sat on opposing benches. "I spoke to him today," he began, "to ask him why it was taking so long to get the final agreement drawn up. He informed me that if we annul the marriage, that would be like it never existed in the first place, and that would go against the terms of the will."

Darn the family feud. She struggled to remain calm and sensible when she wanted to shout from frustration. "Then Worth could take control of the ranch and this charade would have been for naught."

"That about sums it up."

And she didn't like it one iota. "Great. We'll be forced to get a divorce and I'll be marked as a woman who just can't make any marriage work."

"Not if the divorce is my fault and I take the fall."

She supposed at this point they didn't have any choice. "How would you do that?"

"You could tell everyone I cheated on you."

Impossible. "That would be two cheating husbands. People could interpret that as I'm a total fool, or a cold fish in bed. What else do you have?"

"Maybe I drink too much."

She'd never seen him have more than one beer. "Anyone who knows you could disprove that. Any other brilliant ideas?"

"Yeah, I could tell the truth. I don't want any kids and that's a deal breaker for you."

Shock rendered her momentarily silent. Under the circumstances, that shouldn't matter to her, but it did. His disclosure did put the kibosh on any future with him, as if she'd really believed that would happen. "You don't want a child to continue your legacy?"

"Nope. I have five brothers who can take care of the procreating."

For a man who appeared to be all about family, he certainly seemed opposed to having one of his own. "Why exactly do you feel this way?"

He stared at some unknown focal point behind her. "When you have the misfortune of being born to a man like my dad, it makes you doubt yourself and your ability to be a good husband and father."

She reached over and touched his hand to garner his attention. "As far as I know, infidelity isn't genetic, and I sense you'd be a great father."

"You don't know me that well."

True, but she believed she was getting there. And she still had twelve months to learn even more, although she realized that was all she would ever have with him. "I know you love animals and you're willing to set a baby bass free. That speaks to your patience and compassion and some paternal instinct."

"I'm basically married to someone for the sake of a parcel of land. Some might say that speaks to my selfishness."

Obviously both of them put a lot of stock in other people's opinions. "I don't see you as selfish, just desperate. Besides, I'm basically in the same situation since I married for financial stability. Mr. and Mrs. Desperation. It has a nice ring to it."

He rubbed his chin then grinned. "Yeah, it does. So you're not too mad at me over the annulment issue?"

She wanted to be angry, but in essence she could only blame faulty research and jumping in feet first before they knew all the facts. "Let's just say I'm disappointed we rushed into this before I fully investigated our options"

"Would you have changed your mind if you'd known?"

She had to think about that a few seconds. "Possibly, but it doesn't matter since we can't do anything about it now. Besides, we still have twelve months to figure out how we're going to end it."

"Yeah, you're right, unless you can't tolerate me that long."

She gave him a mock stern look. "That's a strong possibility if you don't finish those burgers. I'm suddenly so hungry I could eat the tablecloth."

"No more slap and tickle?" he asked, clear disappointment in his tone.

She wanted to say definitely, but she hadn't quite digested the divorce issue. "Let's worry about dinner right now, okay?"

He stood and leaned over to kiss her forehead. "Sure thing, sweetheart."

Something suddenly occurred to her. "Since it is your birthday, I should have cooked for you."

He studied her a long moment before speaking again. "You know what I'd really like from you to make this day special?"

"Does it start with an 's' and rhyme with vex?"

He shook his head. "No. I want you to tell me you believe that I didn't know the annulment wasn't going to work."

"I'm going to give you the benefit of the doubt." And she hoped her faith wasn't misplaced again. "I only wish we'd had more time to think things through before we rushed into this arrangement."

"Unfortunately time wasn't on our side. But I'll try to make it up to you after dinner."

That could create more problems from an emotional standpoint if she succumbed to her strong desire for him. "How are you going to do that?"

"You'll have to wait and see."

* * *

The sound of a sultry country ballad drew Paris from the kitchen back onto the deck. As the music filtered through the outdoor speakers, the sun had disappeared from the horizon, washing the sky in an orange glow, providing the perfect backdrop to the man leaning back against the railing. A cowboy knight wearing a crisp light blue shirt rolled up at the sleeves, slightly faded jeans and the usual boots, one substantial hand wrapped around a beer.

"Did you shower?" she asked as she approached Dallas, immediately catching a whiff of his clean-scented cologne.

"I wanted to get rid of the barbecue smells."

"I really don't mind that at all." And she didn't, though she still worried she'd made a mistake with their fake marriage. She worried she might make another if she didn't keep her wits about her.

"Thanks for cleaning up the mess," he said.

"After those great veggie burgers, it was the least I could do."

A few moments of silence ticked off as they stood there steeped in palpable tension. Dallas shifted his weight from one leg to the other before setting the bottle atop the nearby table. "Let's dance," he said as he offered his hand to her.

Paris was plagued with a serious case of nerves. "I'm not very good. Not when it comes to country dancing."

He pulled her gently into his arms. "You just have to hold on to me."

And she did as they swayed in time to the tune, moving easily through the last of the song and onto the next, his palms roving softly over her back, her cheek resting against his shoulder.

She briefly wondered how many women had fallen under his spell. How many would have given anything to be in her shoes right now. That shouldn't matter. After all, they were married, at least for a year until it all came to an end.

Maybe they could take the time to learn more about each other. Perhaps she should spend the months finding herself, without getting lost in him. But she felt lost right then as they moved closer, held each other tighter.

When Dallas paused, Paris lifted her head and met his mesmerizing blue eyes. "Mind if I kiss you?" he asked.

She found that odd. "You've never needed my permission before."

"Yeah, but I do now since I didn't keep my promise to you about the annulment."

"It's done, Dallas. We can't go back and undo it. We can only move forward."

"True. You didn't answer my question."

She did, but not with words, despite the lack of wisdom. Instead, she wrapped her hands around his neck and kissed him. A soft, almost quiet kiss that seemed strangely emotional. The way newlyweds who had entered a real union would kiss. A kiss that took a drastic turn toward mutual need in a matter of moments.

Dallas broke the contact first and sighed. "I wish I didn't want you so damn bad."

In some ways she wished the same for herself. But

life was short, and their time limited. She could reject his advances, or take another risk that would most definitely come with rewards. Foolish as it might be, she wanted to experience all that he had to offer, and suffer the possible consequences later. "Maybe we shouldn't overthink this too much."

He frowned. "I'm not following you."

"Do you know what this divorce requirement means?"

"Yeah. I'm going to be padding my lawyer's pockets even more."

Evidently he was having a lapse in comprehension. "No. What it means for us."

He grinned. "We don't have to stop with only slappin' and ticklin'?"

She did a little smiling, too. "Correct."

His smile faded into a serious expression. "That's a big step, Paris."

A step she hadn't planned to take, but… "As you've said, we're both consenting adults and we'll be spending a lot of time together. Since the consummation issue no longer exists, we have no reason not to let nature take its course." And during the journey, she vowed to keep a good grip on her heart.

Taking her by the hand, he led her back to the table, claimed the bench across from her, folded his hands and gave her a somber look. "Are you sure you want to do this? I don't want you to feel like you're being pressured into something that makes you uncomfortable."

Evidently he didn't get it. "Let me put it to you this way. For the first thirty years of my life, I walked a straight line. I ignorantly thought if I followed all the rules, did what was expected, didn't make waves, everything would be rosy. I learned a painful lesson when I realized that wasn't always the case two years ago."

"After your divorce?"

She wanted so badly to tell him the whole truth, but only one person could verify that, and Peter wasn't talking. "The divorce turned out to be only the beginning. Once I lost my job, I recognized that no matter how well you walk the line, situations arise that steer you off your path. I determined then and there I would make my own decisions and guide my own future. As ridiculous as it seems, this agreement we made happened to be a step in the right direction. Otherwise, I would not have entered into it."

He frowned. "You still haven't answered my concerns."

"Actually, yes I have. If I want to be carefree and enjoy intimacy with my pseudohusband, then I'm going to do it. More importantly, I trust you, Dallas. I know you're going to treat me well and make me feel respected. So there."

He finally sent her that wonderful smile again. "Okay then. You've convinced me you're ready."

She wondered if maybe he was experiencing a little hesitation. "Are you ready?"

"Darlin' that is not a question you should have to ask."

Paris felt a disclaimer coming on. "We can do this as long as we go inside and turn off the lights since I assume I'm going to be completely naked."

He stood, rounded the table and held out his hand to help her up. "Inside is okay and we're both going to be naked. Besides, I've already seen a lot of your body, and I want to see it all, so I won't promise I'll turn off lights."

"Dallas—"

He cut off her protest with a quick kiss. "If you really trust me, then let me show you the benefits of seeing all the details."

Exactly what she wanted to avoid. But maybe the time had come to shed her self-consciousness in earnest. Maybe she could actually take charge of the situation and finally relax.

Mulling that over, Paris followed Dallas inside, expecting to be led into the bedroom. Instead, he went to the opposite end of the house and past the kitchen to an all-glass sun porch with rustic, wide, cushioned chaises and plush, rug-covered slate floors. Through the wall of windows, she glimpsed a small creek and two deer foraging in the grassy area in the last remnants of daylight. "Why have I never seen this place?"

"Because you haven't been here long enough to explore," he said. "During the day, you get sun. At night, you can see all the stars. If you notice, there aren't any light fixtures."

She looked around to confirm that fact. She also noted the room was illuminated enough to view all those details she preferred he not see. "Is this where you bring all your dates?"

He didn't appear too pleased over the question. "This is where I come to wind down."

"It's a good place to do it. Unwind, I mean."

He cupped her cheek with his palm. "It's a good place for us to get to know each other in every way."

They stood there face-to-face, as if neither knew what to do next. Dallas broke the standoff by taking her back into his arms and holding her for a long moment. He pulled away and searched her eyes. "If you change your mind at any point, let me know. I want you to be totally comfortable."

She very much appreciated his consideration. She also felt confident he would show her great care, and probably a very good time. "I'm not going to change my mind."

He sent her a soft smile. "Good. I've been waiting all night to see you undress for me."

Oh, mercy. "Are you going to watch?"

He flashed a grin and a dimple. "Do politicians lie?"

"All right. I suppose I can do that. As you pointed out, you've seen almost all of me anyway." And now he would see it all—from head to toe and too-wide hips in between.

You're too uptight, Paris.

The ghost of that chunky, awkward girl came back to haunt her, along with the voice of her ex criticizing her butt and in his opinion, inadequate breasts. She lowered her eyes to avoid Dallas's scrutiny. "I'm not sure I can do this while you're staring at me."

He came to her then, tipped up her chin with his fingertips and kissed her softly. "Yeah, you can. Don't forget the boat."

"That was different. I had on a bikini until you took the top off me. And that was only the top."

She could tell by his expression that his patience was waning. "You're a beautiful woman, Paris. All of you. Now we can talk about this all night, or we can act on this all-fire need between us."

"Okay, I admit there is a tad bit of chemistry."

"You know we've both been hot for each other since we met. You can keep denying it, but you know I'm right. I figured that out in the kitchen this morning when you dropped the robe. If that wasn't a hint, then I don't know what is."

She couldn't be shocked when she'd intentionally been transparent. She'd also allowed him a peek of her backside, and he hadn't run away yet. "Okay, I'll make a deal with you. Since you've already seen more of me than I care to admit, it's only fair you go first."

Without hesitating, he stepped back and lowered his fly. "Just so you know, something's come up. It's been up for days."

She managed a smile. "Nothing I haven't seen before."

After stripping out of his clothes and underwear, he looked no less proud. Every inch of him. And frankly, her very limited sexual experience had not included such an absolutely impressive…man.

"It's your turn, sweetheart."

Okay, she could do this. She'd been pretty gutsy this morning. Why not carry that over to this moment?

Following a deep breath, Paris shimmied out of the dress and let it fall to her feet, then shoved her panties down and kicked them aside. And there she stood, totally nude in the middle of a dimly-lit, glass-walled room with a fantasy man raking his gaze over her, clear approval in his eyes.

He inclined his head and pointed at her. "Lady, if I had my choice, you'd never wear a thing again when you're with me."

She released an anxious laugh. "Something tells me that could be awkward with both the mothers darting in and out all the time."

"True. Now come here and let me give you the time of your life."

Paris felt much less ill at ease and very ready to be in his arms. "Gladly."

Dallas grabbed a pillow from one chaise, set it down on the largest rug, then signaled her to join him on the floor. He laid her back and hovered above her a few moments as he stroked her cheek. They kissed for a long while as if they didn't have a worry in the world. She did find it strange that he hadn't exactly ravished her, and very curious when he said, "I need to get something."

When Dallas left her embrace, Paris felt bereft. "Hope you hurry back."

"Darlin', you won't even know I'm gone."

Perhaps he wasn't quite that quick, but he did return in less than two minutes, carrying that "something" in his hand. She sat up and braced on bent arms. "Just so you know, I am on the pill."

"Doesn't matter," he said as he stretched out next to her on his side. "No birth control is fail proof so having both is better. Nothing wrong with a double bucket, as we say in the horse world."

The seriousness in his tone told Paris he truly didn't want a child, and she found that sad. However, getting pregnant in this situation would be completely inadvisable and cause for great concern. "I totally agree with using both. Besides, in this day and time, safety should also come into play."

"I'm safe, just don't want to be sorry."

After Dallas tossed the condom aside, he kissed his way down her throat, pausing to pay special attention to her breasts, barring all thoughts or concerns from her brain. But he didn't linger very long before sending his talented mouth down her torso, lower and lower, causing Paris to shift with anticipation.

He lifted his head and rested his chin on her belly. "Are you okay?"

Apparently he'd misinterpreted her movement. "Never better."

"Just wanted to be sure this is something you want."

"It's something I've never had before." Only one more admission that pointed to the sad state of her sex life and the severe lack of intimacy with her former husband.

Her current husband, on the other hand, looked as if she'd awarded him the grand prize for being such a gracious lover. "I will almost guarantee you're going to like it. But if not, let me know."

When Dallas's mouth hit home between her trembling legs, Paris couldn't speak if her life depended it. She could barely even breathe. She couldn't manage to keep her eyes open, though. Every featherlight stroke of his tongue brought her closer to the brink of madness. Every pull of his lips drove her further into oblivion, but not enough to tune out the steady build of the climax as he lifted her hips with his palms, bringing her closer to his expert mouth. And then came the strongest, mind-blowing climax she'd ever experienced.

She almost screamed but somehow quelled it. She couldn't stop the slight moan that drifted from her mouth or the inadvertent movement of her hips. She did miss the moment Dallas rose up, she realized, when her eyes fluttered open to discover him tearing at the silver package with his teeth.

He seemed to be quite in a hurry and that might have made her smile except she wanted him to hurry, too. He also seemed to be a pro when he had the condom in place in a matter of seconds.

Paris refused to think about his past conquests. She wanted only to concentrate on all the sensations as Dallas shifted over and eased inside. She rubbed her palms over his muscled back as he moved in a slow, delicious rhythm. She circled her legs around his waist, allowing him to go deeper with each thrust. He demonstrated his stamina, his control, as they continued this dance she'd been determined to avoid. And when that control slipped, his body tensed and he collapsed against her with a low groan.

Paris truly cherished the feel of his weight, the feel of this man who'd entered her life and turned her world upside down. She honestly mourned the loss of him when he rolled onto his back and draped one arm over his eyes.

"That happened way too fast," he said.

She shifted to her side and studied him a few minutes. "Out of ten, I'd give that a twelve."

"A twenty," he muttered. "You're definitely a natural."

"And you're definitely an expert."

He turned to face her. "Don't ever doubt that you're special, sweetheart."

Funny, he made her feel that way. "I must admit I did surprise myself."

He could move mountains with that grin. "I'm ready for another round. How about you?"

"Maybe we could do it under the table outside since we have yet to explore that scenario. Heck, maybe we could do it *on* the table."

He narrowed his eyes and tried to look disapproving. "Have I turned my good girl bad?"

My good girl... If only that were true. "You know, I think you have."

"I'm glad. I wouldn't want you any other way."

She wished he wanted her for all time.

The sudden thought took Paris by storm. She had to emotionally stand firm and avoid any fuzzy feelings if she wanted to protect herself. Yet when Dallas held her again, she worried she might travel straight into the land of heartache.

Eight

During the past week, his good girl turned bad had pretty much worn him out. Not at all a complaint, just an accurate observation. But as soon as they returned to the ranch today, Dallas had to resume his usual routine.

He'd let a lot of things slide, including joining Tyler to search for prime rodeo stock for Texas Extreme. But as he felt his wife's hand beneath the sheet, he didn't give a damn about duty. He had to have her. Now.

They came together in a rush of kisses, a hot, quick roll. A morning drive-by, as Paris had put it. He knew exactly how to touch her to give her what she needed. She knew exactly how to move to send him over the edge. By the time they were done, they were both pretty much exhausted.

Dallas rolled onto his back and studied the ceiling,

waiting for his breathing to calm and his heart to slow down. "You're incredible, darlin'."

"You're not so bad yourself, cowboy." She draped her arm across his belly. "I wish we could stay here a little longer."

He stacked his hands behind his head and sighed. "I didn't intend to be here this long, but a pretty little lady decided to hold me hostage."

She playfully slapped at his arm. "I didn't hold you hostage, Dallas. You were free to go at any point in time."

"Let me rephrase that. You made me a prisoner with your good loving."

She remained quiet for a moment before asking, "What's going to happen after we're back at the ranch?"

"Business as usual."

"I meant with us. Do I sleep in the guest room or in your room?"

He hadn't given that much thought, but he didn't like not having her in his bed. "We should probably give the appearance of the happily married newlyweds."

She laid her head on his shoulder and sighed. "Honestly, I can't remember the last time I've been this happy. It's been a wonderful week."

Uh-oh. If she got stars in her eyes, that could spell trouble. "It's been great, but it's not reality. You and I both know this arrangement comes to an end in a year."

She rose up and stared at him. "You don't have to remind me of that. But if I'm going to be stuck in this pretense, I don't see any reason why we can't enjoy each other's company, unless you decide that once we leave here, the party's over."

He saw a major reason why they shouldn't enjoy it too much. "I still want to be with you, just as long as you know I'm not looking for anything permanent."

The comment sent her out of the bed to grab her robe and slide it on before she faced him. "Of course it's not permanent, Dallas. If I learned anything about you at all since we met, it's that for some reason you run from emotional commitment."

That made him sound like a coward. "Look, I'm not running from anything. I just know who I am, darlin', and if you expect too much, I'll break your heart."

She tightened the sash and pushed her hair away from her face. "Don't flatter yourself. I'm much tougher than you think."

Spinning around, Paris headed into the bathroom and shut the door a little harder than necessary. Dallas remained in the same spot, pondering her words. Maybe in some ways she'd been right. Maybe he had been running away. But one thing he'd learned in life—aside from most of his immediate family, people never stayed around for very long, if not physically, then emotionally. He recalled the loneliness following his mother's death. He'd witnessed both Maria's and Jen's devastation when they'd learned of his dad's betrayal. He wasn't going to put himself out there to be hung up to dry.

He'd been a loner much of his life, and he liked it that way. Even a special woman like Paris couldn't change his mind.

* * *

Little by little, everything had begun to change over the past few days. Even though Paris had opted to stay in his suite, he hadn't touched her. She'd gone to bed before him, and he'd started getting up before her. No more predawn lovemaking. No more joking around. In fact, he'd barely spoken to her aside from general conversation over meals. When she'd asked Dallas if something was wrong, he'd only said he'd been busy playing catch-up. It seemed as if everything they'd shared at the cabin had all been a dream. Today she planned to get to the bottom of his sudden turnaround.

After a futile search for him in the barn, Paris hopped into her new black luxury sedan—a wedding gift from her new husband—then drove to the main office and marched in, bent on seeking him out. "Is Dallas here?"

Jenny patted her big hair and smiled. "No, sugar, he's not here. He left for the house about a half hour ago. I believe he's in the media room."

Oh, for heavens sake. She should have checked there first. "Are you sure?"

"That's what he told me when I put your dinner in the oven. I made a nice vegetarian lasagna. It should be ready in ten minutes or so and you'll find a salad in the fridge."

Eating alone didn't exactly appeal to her. "Thanks, but I need to talk to Dallas before I even think about dinner."

Jenny took on a concerned look. "Is something wrong, sugar?"

"No." She reconsidered when she realized the stepmom could be a solid sounding board. "Actually, yes. Since we returned from the cabin, he's been rather aloof."

"Oh, that. I'm not surprised."

Clearly everyone else in the Calloway family held the key to Dallas's mood. "Could you let me in on the secret?"

"I will gladly fill you in, since my stepson isn't one to talk about his feelings."

Paris knew that all too well. "Go ahead. I'm all ears."

"First of all, his mother died on April second, which happens to be tomorrow. Coincidentally, J.D. died April third. According to Maria, and I've seen it myself since I've been here, Dallas goes into this funk. Give him a week or so and he'll come back around."

Most of that made sense, but she believed there could be more. She also found it hard to believe he would do a one-eighty when it came to their floundering personal relationship. "Maybe it's time someone encourages him to get in touch with his feelings."

"Be careful, Paris," Jenny cautioned. "If you push too hard, he'll only withdraw more."

Not if she could help it. "I'll approach the issue slowly. Thanks for telling me."

"You're welcome, sugar, and good luck. By the way, you never said if you enjoyed your honeymoon."

She had been intentionally guarded in what she'd revealed for fear Jenny would read too much into it. Regardless, the honeymoon phase was basically over before it had really begun. "We had a very nice time. I'll see you later."

Paris rushed out of the office before Jenny began requesting details. After she made it back to the house, she hurried up the stairs and headed to the cowboy cave, only to find the door closed. She considered knocking but since he might not answer, she decided to walk right in.

Dallas looked surprised to see her, but she happened to be more surprised to see him seated at a round table, a slew of photographs spread out before him.

"I thought I might find you here," she said as she pulled out a chair. "What are those, if you don't mind me asking?"

He slid a picture of a brown-haired, blue-eyed young woman holding a toddler, a black horse grazing beside them. "That's my mom, Carol."

The first time she'd heard him mention his mother's name. "And you?"

"Yeah and her mare, Kenya."

"She's beautiful. Your mom, not the horse, although the horse is pretty, too. You definitely have her eyes. Your mom's eyes, not the horse."

Finally she'd unearthed his smile but it faded fast. "That's the horse that killed her."

Paris swallowed around her shock. "How did that happen?"

He leaned back in the chair and streaked a hand over his jaw. "She was training her for speed events. Kenya spooked one day and threw her into a barrel. She sustained a serious head injury and died two days later."

The pain in his voice was palpable. "Do you remember any of that?"

"No. I just recall she was there one day and not the next. I didn't find out what happened until I asked my dad when I turned thirteen. Of course, he didn't want to talk about it so Maria told me."

Thank heavens he'd been spared the details when he'd been too young to understand. She leaned over and picked up a photo of a twentysomething, tall, handsome man with a single prominent dimple. The resemblance to Dallas was almost uncanny. "I assume this is your father."

"The one and only. That was taken right after he married Maria."

She'd always wanted to know how that had come about, and now she had her chance. "When and how did they meet?"

"He hired her as our nanny after my mom died. Next thing I knew, they married a few months later. Then came Houston and Tyler."

"No doubt about it, your dad didn't waste any time."

"No. He just wasted the truth."

Paris wished he could find a way to heal, and she could find a way to help. "Don't waste your life being bitter, Dallas. I had to tell myself if I let my anger toward Peter continue to rule my life, I would lose and he would win."

He nailed her with a stern look. "Maybe I'm not the eternal optimist, like you."

"Then it seems to me you're very much like Fort."

He mulled that over for a moment, as if he'd never considered that notion, before the ire returned. "I'm nothing like him. I didn't abandon the entire family due to the sins of the father."

She might as well beat her forehead against the table. "No, but you might be abandoning your happiness by keeping yourself closed off to it. And shutting me out isn't going to make me go away, if that's what you're thinking."

He failed to look at her. "I'm not shutting you out."

"Oh, really? I don't remember the last time you kissed me, much less touched me. I wake up in the middle of the night and you're on the edge of the bed as if you can't stand to be near me. If you find it so appalling to sleep with me, just let me know. I'll be glad to move to a guest room."

"I don't find you appalling, dammit. It's just that—"

"What?"

"I never wanted to hurt you, Paris, but it sure looks like I'm doing that now. I'm worried maybe you have expectations I can't meet."

Feeling a bit more benevolent, she laid a palm on his arm. "You can't hurt me unless I allow it, and I'm not going to do that. And I don't expect anything from you that you can't give. I'm a big girl and I know what I agreed to when I married you. But I would like better communication between us."

"I'm not real good at that and I'm not sure I can change."

With a retort on the tip of her tongue, Paris suddenly remembered she hadn't removed the food from the oven. "Dinner should be ready by now. We can continue this conversation while we eat."

"I'm not hungry," he said. "You go ahead. I'll grab something later."

Paris's frustration began to mount. "I don't deserve this, Dallas."

He shuffled through the pictures to avoid her gaze. "Deserve what?"

"Your disregard. I'm trying to be your friend but you're making it pretty darned difficult."

"Don't need a friend," he said. "I need to be left alone."

She shoved back from the table and stood. "Sure you do. That's the way you operate, isn't it? Always the tough guy. But let me tell you something, Dallas Calloway. A future with the prospect of happiness is a terrible thing to squander, and you're the one who's afraid of getting hurt, not me."

Without awaiting his response, she rushed out the door and slammed it behind her. She despised the overwhelming disappointment. Hated that she couldn't reach him and probably never would. Most important, she detested the emotions welling inside her. She couldn't save him from himself and for some reason that made her so sad.

Somehow, someway, she had come perilously close to falling in love with the wounded cowboy, or at least the one she'd known while they were away. If she let the cycle complete, she would most surely collide head-on with devastation.

To prevent that from happening, and for self-protection, she would let Dallas continue to brood, and in the meantime, she would get out of his bed. But as far as their arrangement went, she vowed to see it through. No matter how hard he might try to drive her away, she wasn't going to budge until she saw the arrangement through.

When he retired at midnight, Dallas found nothing but a deserted room and an empty bed. He also discovered all her clothes were gone, and the toiletries, too. Not one sign that Paris had ever been in his life.

Unexpected panic set in and sent him to the garage first, where he found the Mercedes parked next to the truck. That didn't mean she hadn't abandoned the car and found another way to leave him.

He wouldn't blame her if she'd left. He'd been a moody bastard and he'd pushed her away. He couldn't stand the thought of her taking off without telling him goodbye. Taking off at all.

He took the stairs two at a time, flipped on the hallway lights and started opening doors to the additional rooms. By the time he reached the final one at the end of the corridor, he'd all but given up…until he found her in the black sleigh bed wearing a pink nightshirt, a pillow propped behind her back, her legs crossed before her and a computer in her lap.

"Mind if I come in?"

"Depends on why you're here," she said without taking her attention from the laptop.

"I'm here to talk."

Finally she looked up. "Wow. That's new and different. Are you ill?"

Sick over hurting her feelings. He perched on the edge of the mattress near the footboard and sighed.

"First, I want to say I'm sorry. You're right, I haven't been treating you well and it's not fair. My problems aren't your fault."

"Apology accepted. Go on."

"Secondly, I suck at being a boyfriend."

That made her laugh. "In case you've forgotten, we kind of skipped the boyfriend-girlfriend stage and went right to the marriage. Besides, I wasn't looking for a boyfriend when I entered into this mess."

The "mess" thing didn't bode well for him. "Okay, I suck at relationships. And I didn't come looking for you, either. But here you are, and honestly, it does scare me."

She closed the computer and set it aside. "Why?"

Now for the admission he didn't count on making. "Because I do care about you, Paris. I don't think I realized how much until I thought you'd left."

"I promised you I'd stay until the bitter end."

"And I promised you an annulment."

"As I've previously stated, that was due to faulty research and an unreasonable timeline."

"Do you regret marrying me?"

She paused for a few seconds. "I regret that more couldn't exist between us aside from you keeping the ranch and me alleviating my debt. But hey, I'm a realist. This is a unique situation. I don't regret our time at the cabin, even if it was only temporary and apparently over."

"It doesn't have to be."

She frowned. "All signs point to the contrary, Dallas. I refuse to make love to a man who won't give me the time of day."

"What if I try to do better?" He drew in a breath and released it slowly. "What if I told you I want to see where this thing goes between us in the next year?"

He green eyes widened. "Do you mean exploring the possibility of making it permanent?"

"Yeah. There's no guarantee it will work, but I'd like to try. It would require starting over, since we put the cart before the horse."

"You mean like dating?"

"I guess you could call it that. I want to take you out to dinner and maybe go see a movie or two. I definitely want to teach you how to ride if you're going to be a rancher's wife."

She held up her hands, palms forward. "Wait a minute. I'm still trying to digest the whole dating thing."

So was he. "Okay. I'll slow down. But just so you know, I've never had a relationship that lasted longer than six months. Maybe that's because I don't know what it takes."

Paris unfolded her legs, draped them over the bed and scooted next to him. "My mother always said that when you evaluate who you're going to have as a life partner, you have to ask yourself, *Will they make me a better person?*"

Solid advice. "I believe that could be true when it comes to you making me a better man. You'd probably be getting the short end of the stick with me."

She hooked her arm through his and kissed his cheek. "I think we could make each other better."

For the first time in two weeks, he felt optimistic

and not quite as afraid of making her life miserable. "As long as we both can trust each other."

"We can do that."

"Can we still have sex while we're dating?"

That earned him a mild punch in the biceps and her smile. "Is that all you men think about?"

"Pretty much."

She released an exaggerated sigh. "Oh, all right. I suppose we can tango between the sheets now and then."

He came to his feet, ready for the dance to begin. "Let's get back to our bedroom, wife."

She stood, grabbed the nightshirt's hem and pulled it over her head. "We have a perfectly good bed here, husband, so let's mix it up."

Up would be the operative word when she slid her panties down and tossed them onto the nearby chair. "You won't catch me arguing with a naked woman."

Dallas undressed in a rush, took her down on the bed, kissed her thoroughly and then sent his lips and hands on a mission over her body. She responded strongly to his touch and climaxed quickly beneath his mouth. He realized he didn't have a condom, but this time he didn't care. He trusted Paris completely, not to mention he'd seen her birth control pills.

When he started to move over her, Paris said, "Not this time," before nudging him onto his back. "I want to play cowgirl."

Damned if she wasn't full of surprises. "Lady, ride away. I just hope this lasts longer than eight seconds."

It took all his strength to hold back the orgasm when

she climbed on top and guided him inside her. Having no barriers between them only increased the sensations, and he realized he'd never had sex without protection, a lesson that had been drilled into his brain by his dad. The wait had been worth it. But it also happened to be playing hell with his control, and no matter how hard he tried to hold back the tide, the dam broke all too soon.

After Paris collapsed against him, Dallas rubbed her back and felt a strong sense of peace, like this is where they belonged. Like the way love might feel.

Whoa. He sure as hell wasn't going to go there yet.

"Did you enjoy that?" Paris whispered in his ear.

"Hell yeah. I always like new adventures."

She lifted her head and smiled. "So do I."

He brushed her hair away from her cheek. "Darlin', get ready for all the adventure you can handle."

For the past three weeks, the adventures had kept coming like hits on a radio. She'd learned to ride a horse—kind of—spent three days holed up in a cabin in Wyoming with Dallas and attended a country music award ceremony on his arm in Nashville.

Paris couldn't remember when she'd had so much fun, or so much fantastic sex. No place had been off-limits, from hot tubs to home-theater chairs to pickup trucks. And yesterday, when she'd walked in the office to show Dallas the latest plans for the lodge, she ended up with her dress hiked up to her waist and her panties down at her ankles while her husband ravished her on his desk without taking off his boots.

Memories of those moments brought about a blush

when she returned to the office today and came face-to-face with both the mothers. "It sure is getting hotter outside," she said as she entered the opening at the counter.

"Hotter inside, too," Maria muttered while Jenny giggled. "Real hot yesterday."

Mortified, Paris rushed toward Dallas's study, hurried inside, closed the door behind her and leaned back against it. "They know."

Dallas glanced up from a document and frowned. "Know what?"

She walked to his desk and collapsed into the chair. "They know what we did in here yesterday."

"Why do you say that?"

"Because Maria just made a comment about it being hot inside when I said it was hot outside." She snapped a finger and pointed. "You pressed the intercom and told Jenny to hold all your calls and I bet the button got stuck. You need to get that fixed before we do it in here again."

He grinned. "Darlin', are you ready for another round?"

Yes. "No. I came here to tell you to schedule the groundbreaking for the lodge next week. I've been working with the architect and we've almost finalized the design. If you have a few minutes, I want to fill you in on the details."

He stood and rounded the desk. "We might not be ready to build yet, but that's still cause for celebration."

When he bent down and nibbled her ear, Paris shivered. "Stop it, you bad, bad cowboy, and let your fake wife tell you about the lodge."

He pulled her out of her chair and brought her into his arms. "You like me when I'm bad, Mrs. Calloway."

"And you like me bad, too, Mr. Calloway."

"That I do."

Just as Dallas planted his mouth on hers for a hair-curling kiss, the pesky intercom sounded. When the buzz repeated twice, Paris pulled back. "Aren't you going to answer that?"

"Do I have to?"

"It could be important."

He looked thoroughly put out. "You're right. I have an appointment in about fifteen minutes with a supplier. He's probably early, dammit."

She stood on tiptoe and kissed his chin. "I suppose I'll see you at the house for dinner."

"Yep, and when I get there, be naked."

"I can do that."

He let her go to depress the pesky button. "Yeah, Jen."

"There's someone here to see your wife."

Dallas sent her a confused look, prompting Paris to say, "I'm not expecting anyone."

"Who is it, Jen?" he asked.

"Maybe she should just come out here, sugar."

"A name, Jen," Dallas said. "Stop beatin' around the bush."

"He says he's her husband."

Nine

From the panic on Paris's face, Dallas figured she hadn't expected this blast from her past. "What the hell does he want?"

"I have no idea," she said as she started toward the door. "But I'm going to find out."

"Don't go out there," he said as he pushed the button. "Send him in, Jen."

When she spun, fear flashed in her eyes. "I need to handle this myself."

"Fine, but I want to be there when you do." In case he needed to take matters into his own hands with the bastard.

The loud rap obviously startled Paris, sending her around to open the door to a lanky, blond-haired guy wearing a prissy pink polo shirt, chinos and a smirk. "Hello, Paris."

"Hello, jerk."

Dallas wanted to applaud when the idiot reached for her and she sidestepped him. He also wanted to punch the guy and wasn't ruling that out.

Paris held on to the doorframe but didn't invite him into the room. "Why are you here?"

He leaned over and eyed Dallas. "I have information that would interest you and your new *husband*." He had the nerve to push past Paris, stride to the desk and stick out a bony hand. "It's a pleasure to meet the other husband."

Dallas ignored the gesture. "Pleasure's all mine, Dick."

"It's Peter."

"Whatever. Now state your business and get the hell out of here."

The bastard dropped his arm and sneered. "You might not be so quick to dismiss me once I say what I have to say."

He fought the urge to wrap a hand around that skinny neck and toss him out. "Hurry up."

"Dallas, could I have a few moments alone with him?" Paris asked.

No way. No how. "Not on your life, sweetheart. But I am going to step out and tell Jen to reschedule my appointment." He intended to tell her more than that. "In the meantime, don't say anything to him until I get back."

He hated to leave Paris alone, but he didn't trust the

son of a bitch or his motives. For that reason, he strode to the reception area and gestured Jen aside. "Do you still have that digital recorder?"

She looked a little clueless. "Yes. Why?"

"Because as soon as I get back in there, I want you to turn it on and press the intercom. Can you handle that?"

"Of course."

"Good. I also want you to go outside, call the sheriff on your cell phone and have him send a deputy over to be on standby."

Now she looked alarmed. "Are you afraid he's going to harm you, sugar?"

"No. I'm afraid I might hurt him. And I'm also thinking he might be up to no good."

He turned around to head back to the office and hoped like hell Jen followed his instructions to a tee. If the bastard tried to pull anything at all, at least they'd have proof and the law on their side.

When he entered the room, he found Paris seated in the chair under the window while the ex roosted in the one across from the desk. They both sat silent like they'd been engaged in a standoff.

Dallas decided to stand next to his wife. "Okay, the floor's yours, Pete," he said. "Have at it."

The guy crossed one leg over the other, looking every bit the wimp he was. "How much do you know about Paris, Mr. Calloway?"

"All that I need to know," he answered before Paris could open her mouth.

"Then she told you about her criminal history."

"I don't have a criminal history," Paris shot back. "I covered for yours."

Dallas didn't care for where this was heading. "What is he talking about, Paris?"

"He embezzled funds from our former employer," she said. "He led them to believe it was all my idea, which it was not. I'm only guilty of being gullible and stupid."

The SOB let go a grating laugh. "Don't play innocent, Paris. You had no problem spending the funds that I borrowed from the company."

"You mean stole, don't you?" Paris scooted up to the edge of the chair. "I didn't have time to spend a dime other than what we needed for bills. I was too busy working. You, on the other hand, were hitting on every woman in Vegas. They reaped the benefits of your ill-begotten gains and now I'm charged with paying off your debt or risk going to jail."

Dallas wasn't at all pleased that Paris had withheld this level of information. "Looks like I'm a walking example of 'the husband is the last to know.'"

"About that husband thing," Peter chimed in. "There's a bit of a problem with that."

Dallas leveled his gaze on the bastard. "What kind of problem?"

"Paris and I are still married."

A strong wave of nausea hit Paris, driving her to take a few calming breaths before she could respond. "I don't understand."

"It's simple," Peter said. "I didn't complete the divorce process in the Dominican Republic for leverage."

Dallas released a few unflattering oaths aimed at the once-believed-to-be-ex-husband. He then turned his obvious anger on her. "You told me you had the documents, Paris."

She'd never felt so hopeless, or foolish, in her life. "I did. I do."

Peter's laugh sounded maniacal. "Since I knew you know very little Spanish, I sent you a record of a civil lawsuit that I obtained from the internet and I altered a photo of the official record from the Dominican Republic to include our names. You should have hired an attorney to protect your interests, dear. You did have that option."

She had the strongest urge to dump him out of the chair. How could she have been so blind to believe he was a decent guy when she'd married him? Easy. He'd been a chameleon and a con, and she'd been a naive girl. "I spent all the money I had left on attorney fees to stay out of jail, all because of you."

"Someday perhaps you will learn not to be so trusting, Paris."

She had another urge to slap that condescending grin off his face but settled for a verbal slug. "You should get help for your short man's syndrome, although it does apply in every sense of the word, you miscreant con artist."

Dallas took a step toward Peter. "You could've told her this in a phone call, which leads me to believe you're up to something."

"I considered calling," he replied. "But I couldn't be certain she would tell you everything."

Paris shot out of the chair. "You're the liar, not me."

"What do you want?" Dallas asked, his fists balled at his sides.

"Well, for starters," Peter began, "I'm sure you wouldn't want this scandalous secret to taint your good name. If you give me fifty thousand dollars, I won't go to the media and tell them you married another man's wife. A hundred thousand buys Paris a proper and legal divorce so you two can resume your life together."

Before Paris could react, Dallas had Peter by the collar and backed up to the wall. "Listen, you son of a bitch, I strongly suggest you take your blackmail attempts and get the hell out of here before I forget there's a lady present and I throw you out the window."

For the first time she saw fear in Peter's eyes. "It's your choice. If I don't have the money by tomorrow, in cash, I will notify the press. As far as the divorce is concerned, it's immaterial to me what you do. It's no skin off my nose to stay married to the most gullible woman I've ever known."

Dallas balled his fist but before he could throw a punch, someone said, "Don't do it, Calloway, or I'll have to arrest you, too."

Paris looked straight ahead to see a deputy filling the doorframe, Jenny cowering behind him.

Dallas shoved Peter toward the officer. "Did you get it all recorded?" he asked Jenny.

"Every bit, sugar."

He addressed the deputy then. "Did you hear it, Rowdy?"

The man patted his rounded belly. "Every word, Dallas."

The deputy stepped toward Peter and withdrew a pair of handcuffs. "Turn around and put your hands behind your back."

Peter stood in stunned silence for a few seconds. "Why are you arresting me? He should be cuffed for assault."

"I don't see any signs of assault," Rowdy said as he turned him around and snapped the cuffs into place. "You, my man, are in a heap of hot water."

Peter shot a menacing look in Paris's direction. "What are the charges?"

"Extortion. Embezzlement," Rowdy answered. "Take your pick. You want me to lock him up, Dallas?"

"Not yet." He stared at Peter for a long moment. "I'll make you a deal, Pete. If you never show your face here again, I'll let you slide for now. But if I ever lay eyes on your sorry self, and if I learn you uttered one word about this to even the clerk at the convenience store, I'll have you thrown in jail so fast your head will spin. I'll also play your confession to your former boss."

Peter practically cowered. "All right."

"And as far as that divorce goes," Dallas continued, "I want you back on a plane to finish the procedure and I plan to hire that lawyer to make sure you follow through this time. Understand?"

"Yes, I understand."

"Good. Rowdy, get him out of my sight before I forget why I didn't coldcock him the minute he opened his mouth."

As the deputy led Peter away, Paris waited for the shock to subside before facing Dallas again. "I am so, so sorry."

His somber expression spoke volumes. "Sorry about which part? That we're not legally married or that you lied to me about your past?"

She should have seen this coming. "I didn't exactly lie about the theft at the firm since I legally couldn't tell you. When Peter left the country before he could answer to the allegations, both parties signed a nondisclosure in exchange for my agreement to pay off the debt. My former employer was convinced I played some role, but I swear I didn't."

"You mean to tell me that you lived and worked with the man and you didn't know a damn thing about it?"

His distrust burned like a hot poker to the heart, though she couldn't exactly blame him under the circumstances. "I didn't have a clue because we had separate checking accounts. He was double billing vendors and depositing the excess in various places. Of course, he did give me funds to pay his half of the bills, so in essence I did benefit from his illegal activities, but I didn't know that's what I was doing."

Skeptical would be the best way to describe the look Dallas gave her. "Well, darlin', at least you won't have to worry about getting our divorce now. You're free to go do what you please."

She expected him to be angry. Livid even. But not to be totally written off. "You're being unreasonable."

"I'm being practical."

His attitude absolutely floored her. "Look, I understand why you're upset. I even understand why you might question my role in the embezzlement. But I can't quite comprehend after all we've been through why you can't give me the benefit of the doubt when I afforded you that courtesy over the annulment issue. I've never given you any reason not to trust me."

"You just did, by deceiving me. Lying by omission is as bad as a bald-face lie."

She truly wanted to scream. "So that's it? All the time we've spent together means nothing?"

"If you're worried about losing the money I fronted you, keep it. Keep the car, too, since I sold the old one for scrap. I'll even give you a good reference for what you've already accomplished on the lodge design."

"I don't want your money or the car or the job. I also don't want any more of your excuses."

"Excuses?"

"You've been looking for an out and I handed it to you on a silver platter. In fact, you lied to me when you said you wanted to see where our relationship might go. You never had any intention of making this marriage work. You only told me that to keep me in your bed."

"That's not true, Paris."

"Oh, really? Well, listen up, cowboy. You were right when you said you don't know how to commit because committed couples weather the storms and forgive all the flaws. But then you don't know the first thing about forgiveness because you certainly haven't forgiven your father. Since he's a blood relative, and I'm little more than your playmate, I don't stand a chance."

Before she started to cry, she had to leave. But she still had one more thing to tell him. "Even after knowing what I know about you now, I still believe in you, because Dallas, I've fallen in love with you although that's the last thing I wanted to do. I only wish you believed in me, too. I'll be out of here tonight." She removed the wedding band from her finger and laid it on the desk. "Have a nice life."

As she walked away, tears began to flow, yet she managed to get outside before the dam completely burst. She left the Mercedes parked in front of the office and started to the house on foot, hoping that maybe Dallas would come to his senses and come after her. But by the time she reached the front door, she realized that wasn't going to happen.

Now all she had left were the memories, a few mementos, some money and a severely shattered heart.

"What in the hell are you doing, *mijo*?"

An hour after the sorry scene, Dallas turned from the office window to see the mothers filing into the room, led by Maria, along with a band of merry brothers. All his brothers—Austin, Tyler, Houston, Worth—except one. Judges and jury members all wrapped into one family unit, thanks to his matriarchs' role as family criers.

"Why are you all here?"

"We're here to talk to you about Paris," Maria answered.

Figured. "Nothing to talk about, so you can leave and take the boys with you."

"We've filled them all in on the details, sugar," Jen said. "We're worried about you."

He had a good mind to walk out before the show started, but they'd probably follow him. "If you're going to take turns taking potshots and me, that's the last thing I need at the moment."

Austin stepped forward first. "I'd personally like to knock some sense into you. Do you have any idea what you've done to that little gal?"

"He's stomped on her heart," Tyler replied for Dallas. "I saw her walking up the road, crying like a baby."

"And now he's lost the ranch in the process," Worth added.

Houston took a step forward. "Hell, Dallas, Fort is going to have a field day with this once he knows you're no longer married."

Dallas had about had enough. "We weren't married in the first place, dammit, and that's not my fault."

"It's not Paris's fault either, sugar," Jenny chimed in. "She was victimized by a man and the fact that you dismissed her so easily means you've done the same thing to her."

He hadn't done that. Or had he? "You all know how much I hate deception. She could've told me what happened with her former employer because I wouldn't have told a soul. I didn't have to hear it from that SOB ex-husband. Oh, yeah. Her current husband."

"And you're so damned perfect, Dallas," Austin added. "You tossed her out before you gave her a chance."

His temper was close to reaching the boiling point. "And you're a damned hypocrite, Austin. You were married to Lilly, what, less than a year?"

Austin looked like he wanted to throw a left hook. "At least I made it to a year. Plus we both decided the marriage wasn't working."

"That's what happens when you get drunk and get hitched."

"Kiss my—"

Maria clapped her hands and pointed toward the door. "Everyone out. This kangaroo court is dismissed."

"Yes, boys, you should all go because we need to talk to Dallas alone," Jenny said.

Maria scowled. "When I said everyone, that means you, too, Jenny. I'm going to handle this."

Jenny looked dejected. "But—"

"No buts. Go."

After the crowd disappeared, Maria gestured toward the desk chair. "Sit down, *mijo*, and I'm going to tell you how the cow ate the cabbage."

Great. Just great. "I'd rather go work off some steam in the barn."

"I don't care what you want, Dallas Calloway. You're going to hear me out. *Comprendes?*"

He understood all too well. He was about to get a butt chewing. "Fine. But make it fast."

Maria took a seat in front of the desk. "I will make it very fast because you're running out of time. If you don't get your head on straight, Paris is going to leave and she won't be coming back."

The thought left a bitter taste in his mouth even though it's what he wanted. Or what he thought he wanted. "The damage is done and it can't be repaired, Mom."

"Love fixes anything."

That nearly shocked him out of his boots. "I've never said I love her."

"I'm sure you haven't, but that doesn't mean you don't. I've seen the way you look at her, *mijo*."

"You're seeing lust."

"Like hell I am. I've lived long enough to know the difference. She walks in the room and you hang on her every word. You open doors for her and you put your hand on her back when you're walking out together. You always let her speak without interrupting and you're always asking if she needs anything, and I don't mean sex. I've even heard you say hurry back if you're watching TV and she goes into the kitchen."

"And your point?"

Maria muttered a few choice words in her native tongue. Words he'd learned from some of the hands. "Let me ask you something. Do you wake up every morning thinking about her and go to bed every night glad she's going to be by your side?"

As bad as he hated to admit it, all that was true. "Yeah."

"Do you imagine growing old with her?"

Damn. "Maybe."

"Do you wonder what it would be like if she had your babies?"

"I've always made it clear I don't want kids."

"Answer me."

He released a rough sigh. "Not at first, but lately, yeah."

"Have you ever felt this way about any other woman?"

The answer was easy, and pretty damn telling. "Nope."

Maria slapped her palms on the desk and stood. "You're in love, although you're too damn hardheaded to admit it to yourself. If you don't get to the house, get on your knees and beg Paris for forgiveness for being a *cobarde*, you're going to live the rest of your life with a belly full of regrets. She'll forever be known to you as the one who got away when she should be the one who saved you from one helluva lonely life."

Deep down he recognized everything Maria had said made sense. He also realized he had one major problem. "What if she doesn't accept my apology?"

"She will if you offer her the ring."

He didn't have to ask which ring. The one meant for his true love. And damned if he hadn't found her. But... "You think it's a good idea I propose?"

"Do you still want to marry her?"

Did horses like hay? "Yeah."

"Then I'll go get the ring, and you go get the girl."

Ten

"Sugar, are you sure you can't wait until the morning before you go?"

Paris kept right on packing. And sniffling. And occasionally sobbing. "He doesn't want me here, Jenny, so the faster I leave, the better it will be for all concerned, myself included."

"Not as far as we're all concerned," Jenny said. "You should have seen the boys take him on for his cruelty. I thought Austin and Dallas were going to actually fight."

Wherever she went, clearly trouble followed. "I'm sorry this has caused a divide in the family. I never meant for that to happen."

Jenny handed her a tissue. "Honey, none of this is your fault. If Dallas wasn't so darned pigheaded, he'd realize you had no choice but to lie. He would also realize what the two of you have together is worth fighting for."

"You can't fight for something you don't care to win. Dallas has already decided what he wants, and it's not me. I need to be with someone who's willing to accept me for who I am, an imperfect woman."

"Sugar, he believes in you. He just doesn't believe in himself."

After dabbing at her eyes, Paris zipped the last suitcase and set it next to the other two at the foot of the bed. "Dallas hates deception, justified or not. And he doesn't feel he's capable of a long-term commitment. He has his father to thank for that. No offense."

"Oh, sugar, we all know J.D. was a lying philanderer, but we loved him all the same."

"That's because you know how to forgive. Dallas hasn't learned that lesson yet."

"Dallas hasn't figured out everyone lies now and then. Why, my mother passed herself off for years as the consummate Southern lady when in fact she grew up in the Bronx. She got away with it because she mastered the accent perfectly. And she learned how to make those luscious mint juleps. Would you like me to make you one before you go?"

It would only delay her departure if she passed out. "No, thank you, but if you could call a cab I would definitely appreciate it."

"Dallas bought you a perfectly good car."

"I don't want it." She didn't want anything more from him aside from some good memories to override the bad.

"Honey, there aren't any cabs that come out here. But

I would be glad to drive you anywhere you want to go, although I don't see why you won't take the Mercedes since it was a gift from Dallas."

A gift that came with conditions—marry me, make love with me but don't get too close. "He can give it to the next faux bride. I'm sure he'll get to work on that first thing in the morning, before Fort finds out we aren't married."

Jenny drew her into a hug. "I promise you, he won't go looking for someone else. Besides, the birthday deadline has passed, not to mention he doesn't want anyone but you."

If only that were true. "He doesn't want me, Jenny. I'm no longer of any use to him."

"I guess we'll see, won't we?" She sounded as if she knew a secret.

Paris pulled the handles from the rolling bags and slid the duffel's strap over her shoulder. "I won't see anything since I'm ready to go. If you could just drop me off in the nearest town, I'll find a room and rent a car tomorrow." At least she had enough money to get her to Idaho to stay with her parents and explain once again how she'd been duped by another man. Oh, joy.

Jenny gave her a pretend pout. "Are you sure you won't change your mind about that drink? Or how about some dinner? I could make you a nice vegetable frittata."

Her stomach roiled over the thought of choking down any food. "You've done enough already. And by the way, Dallas has enough money to hire a private chef, so why doesn't he?"

"Because he knows I like to make sure all the boys are fed. It makes me feel useful."

Unbelievable. "You make dinner for the other four?"

"Almost every night unless they're out of town or engaged in activities with women that no mother should be exposed to. Which is sometimes quite often with Worth. That little apple didn't fall far from the family tree."

They shared a laugh and another hug before heading out of the bedroom…and running right into none other than her erstwhile pretend husband. Her heart sank a little over the sight of him, and the regrets tugged at her soul.

When Paris muttered an apology and tried to push past him, he clasped her arm, halting her progress. "We need to talk."

"I think we've said all we have to say. No need to belabor the point and my shortcomings."

Jenny took the duffel from Paris. "Hear him out, sugar."

Maria appeared in the hall to give her two cents worth. "It's important, *mija*. Let's go to the kitchen, Jenny."

"No, stay," Dallas said. "I don't care if the whole damn county hears this, as long as the two of you don't interrupt. Besides, you're going to eavesdrop anyway."

Paris wasn't at all certain how to take any of this. "Then make it quick so I can get out of here."

"I don't want you to go. It's going to kill me if you go."

A stunning development. "I can't stay with a man who can't trust me, Dallas."

"I trust you, darlin'. I don't always trust me. But I'm going to learn if it's the last thing I do. And you were right, I got cold feet and blamed you for it."

Oh, how she wanted to believe him. "If that's the case, why the sudden change of heart?"

He looked somewhat sheepish. "I had a little help with that."

"From me," Maria stated without regard for the non-interruption directive. "I verbally beat him over the head."

"She just said things that made sense," he countered. "She made me take inventory of my feelings for you, and it led to a fairly obvious conclusion."

"Which is?"

"I love you, sweetheart."

She lost her grip on the bags' handles, sending the upright suitcases onto the floor. "Could you repeat that, please?"

He circled his arms around her. "I love you more than this ranch. More than I ever thought I could love anyone. We'll find our own place and build a house, along with a future together."

"And we'll all go with you if we have to," Jenny said.

"Don't give her any reason not to stay with him," Maria scolded.

She let that proposition soak in for a moment. "I love you, too, but is that enough?"

"It's a start. And we won't know unless you stay."

"You do realize we're not married anymore and it's bound to get out."

"We can fix that real quick." He pulled a blue velvet

box from his shirt pocket, opened it to reveal a gorgeous marquise diamond that had to be at least two carats and lowered to one knee. "Paris, this belonged to my mom and it was given to me to give to the woman I want to spend my life with. That woman is you. So will you marry me again and have our babies and make this miserable cowboy a better man?"

Paris stood there, mouth agape, basking in the emotion in his eyes, the sincerity in his words, until reality jumped into the euphoria. "I'm not divorced yet."

"We don't have to be in a hurry. We're going to need time to plan a proper wedding anyway."

"I can't wait," Jenny practically shouted.

A proper wedding would be wonderful. However, another issue still remained. "But you'll lose the D Bar C if Fort finds out we're not married anymore. Maybe we should hurry up and do it."

"I don't care about Fort or the will. I only want to be with you. This isn't about keeping the ranch—it's about keeping you close, always."

As much as she wanted to accept his heartfelt proposal, she still had one more question. "You're serious about wanting babies?"

"Yep. I actually like them. I help with the rodeo club at the local high school and I plan to have a summer riding camp for the younger ones. If I can ride a bull, I can take on a baby. Or babies."

Paris managed a smile around the mist forming in her eyes. "As long as you don't expect us to keep them in the barn."

"I promise. And by the way, I have a bum knee,

thanks to a rank horse that bucked me off two years ago, so if you could give me an answer, my joints would appreciate it."

She laughed through the tears. "Yes, I will marry you, bad knees and all, so you can get up now."

After sliding the ring on her finger, Dallas rose and drew her into a soft kiss. "We're going to have a lot of adventures. And when we find our own place, you can design the house to your liking."

"Actually, you probably won't have to move after all, sugar."

Dallas let her go long enough to stare at Jenny. "Fort will probably say otherwise."

She shook her head. "No, he won't. I told him if he wouldn't pursue the terms of the will, I'd give him my half of the horse farm in Louisiana."

"I thought you'd already done that," Dallas said.

Jenny grinned. "I conveniently forgot to do it, just in case I need some leverage, even though he didn't know that. Sometimes you just have to tell a little white lie."

"When did this happen?" Paris asked.

Jenny stared at her pink peep-toe pumps. "The day you arrived here after the wedding. I had a feeling you two would be a good fit if given the chance. Also, around these parts, available women are few and far between."

"And you just let the marriage plans go on without telling me?" Both his tone and expression revealed Dallas's displeasure.

Jenny propped her hands on her hips. "Yes, sugar, and you should thank your lucky stars I didn't tell you.

Otherwise, you wouldn't be engaged to the woman of your dreams."

Dallas turned his attention to Maria. "Did you know, too?"

"Yep. I figured it was the only way to get you hitched so you can have me some grandbabies."

He pointed to the hall behind him. "Both of you can leave now."

Ignoring the order, Maria gave Paris a hug. "Welcome to the family, *mija*. Get ready for one wild ride."

After Jenny and Maria departed, Dallas pulled Paris back into his arms. "Looks like everything is going to work out after all. I keep the ranch and the girl. Who would've guessed that would happen?"

Not Paris. Not in a million years. "Did you know I almost decided to settle in New York? If I had, we would never have met."

"What changed your mind?"

"Actually, I'd picked out an apartment to rent and the landlord decided to sell it right before I left Vegas. Then I turned on my computer to search for another one, and I saw an ad for San Antonio. Something told me I needed to be in Texas, and here I am with my very own cowboy whom I love with all my heart."

He kissed her again, a little longer and deeper this time. "Care to take that cowboy and show him how much you love him?"

"I'll race you to the bedroom."

"Who said anything about the bedroom?"

"We're not going to do it here in the hall, Dallas. Not

with the probability that Jenny and Maria are some-where nearby."

"True, and we're going to set some ground rules about that. But I'm actually thinking I want to make love to you in a place we haven't tried yet."

Paris tapped her chin with a fingertip and pretended to think. "I can't recall a place where we haven't done it."

"It's the place where we won't be keeping the kids."

They exchanged a smile and simultaneously said, "The barn."

Most women wouldn't agree to get hitched in front of a barn. But Paris Reynolds Calloway wasn't most women, Dallas decided. She'd turned out to be one in a million, and now she belonged to him. And he defi-nitely belonged to her.

He stood next to Maria, choking down one of Jenny's gut-burning brews so he wouldn't hurt her feelings, even if he preferred beer. As he watched Paris visiting with her parents beneath the tent's canopy, he noticed she'd only been drinking punch.

"She looks beautiful, *mijo*. And very happy."

"Yeah, she does." When he'd seen Paris coming down the makeshift aisle an hour ago, wearing that form-fitting, long, sleeveless silk gown, sparkling tiny flowers sprinkled through her hair, he couldn't believe he'd gotten so lucky. "Her folks seem fairly nice, too."

"Her dad's a piece of work," she said. "He told me he brought a shotgun in case you bowed out. I told him I had one handy, too."

Dallas couldn't help but laugh over the image of his stepmom wielding a weapon while wearing a dress. "In-laws and outlaws. Works for me."

At that moment, Paris caught his eye, smiled and started toward him. Once she arrived, he leaned over and kissed her. "Do you think we can have a few minutes alone before dinner is served?"

"I'm going now," Maria said. "I've got to make sure Jen isn't putting too much tequila in those drinks."

After his mom disappeared into the tent, Dallas wrapped his arms around his wife. "How are you holding up?"

"Pretty well for a woman who planned a wedding in less than two months."

"Any regrets so far?"

"No, other than we have to wait another four hours or so before we can start the honeymoon. Actually, second honeymoon. And speaking of that, are you going to tell me where you're taking me?"

"I'll give you a hint. It involves a boat."

"The cabin?"

"No. It involves a big boat. Worth offered his yacht with a full crew and captain. I figure we can mosey on down to the Mexican Caribbean for two weeks where I've rented a private villa."

She hugged him hard and kissed him soundly. "That sounds wonderful, honey."

"And since I'm not getting any younger, I also figure we can get on with the baby-making."

She glanced at the ground before raising her gaze

to his. "Now that you mention it, I probably should tell you it's too late for that."

For a second he couldn't speak. "How? When?"

"Well, *how* is pretty obvious, although exactly where is up for grabs. I estimate it happened around six weeks ago. And in case you're wondering why, it's been crazy with the wedding plans and I might have missed a pill or two. But I swear on my mother's favorite blue flats, which she's wearing now, I did not plan this."

He waited for the urge to head for the hills, but it didn't come. He might be a bit nervous, but he wasn't spooked. "I believe you, darlin'. And I'm looking forward to being a dad."

She immediately relaxed. "I am so glad. I wasn't sure how I was going to tell you after I confirmed it this morning."

"This morning?"

"Yes. I looked at the calendar on my phone and thought something's missing, and it ain't only my mind."

"Ain't? Looks like you're picking up the cowboy vernacular. I'm impressed."

"Vernacular? Now I'm impressed."

"Hey, I might be a hayseed, but I have a little class in me, too. I also have a hankering to kiss my bride and the mother of my baby."

She draped her arms around his neck. "Kiss away, cowboy."

Before he could, he felt a tap on his shoulder and turned to find his brother standing there. "What do you want, Austin?"

"We want you both in the tent for a toast."

"Are you going to make it?"

"Nope. Worth drew the shortest straw."

Paris laughed. "This should be interesting."

"Or a train wreck," Dallas said.

When they walked beneath the canopy, Dallas spotted his youngest brother standing on the stage reserved for the band, Jenny standing at his side. A roving waiter offered them champagne, which Paris nixed for a glass of water, while Dallas picked up a flute.

Worth held his glass up and cleared his throat. "To my brother Dallas, who had the good sense to wed a woman like Paris. And to my new sister-in-law, I hope you own a pair of boots because he'll probably have you muck the stalls before you know it. Best of luck to you both and may your trail ride together be a long one."

After the applause died down, Dallas put down the wine and grabbed his wife's hand to lead her to the stage.

"Dallas, what are we doing?" she asked once they reached their destination.

"You'll see." He circled his arm around her waist and prepared to say a few words. "We'd like to thank all you folks for sharing in this day with us. I'd also like to thank Jen for pulling together one heck of a party in a short amount of time, and my mom, Maria, for being there for me through thick or thin after I lost my own mother. If my dad were here, he'd pat me on the back and tell me *You did good, son*, and I did." He looked into Paris's eyes and saw honest-to-goodness love there. "And Paris, I never expected to find someone as special as you, and I sure as hell never really thought I'd settle down, but I'm damn glad I did. Thank you for honoring me with your vows, and for carrying our baby."

That caused a spattering of gasps among the onlookers and another toast from Houston. "To the Calloway sperm, known for being good swimmers."

"And I hope it's not catching," Tyler said, spurring a lot of laughter in the crowd.

Dallas guided Paris through the maze of guests offering their congratulations and managed to get her alone again, this time in the barn. "I hope you don't mind me telling everyone," he told her after they arrived. "I just couldn't wait to let everyone know."

"It's okay," she said. "I would have liked to have waited a little while since it's so early."

He held her again. "Darlin', I will do everything in my power to protect you. I promise you won't have to muck any stalls and I'll make sure you stay off your feet and get plenty of rest—"

She pressed a fingertip to his lips. "I'm having a baby, honey, not suffering from an incurable illness. Women do it every day. And I just know everything will turn out well with our little girl."

"Or boy."

She sighed. "You're probably right if you inherited the Calloway sperm that not only swims fast, it produces male children."

"Stranger things have happened. After all, the woman of my dreams said yes."

"Twice," she said. "And I am so glad I did. I love you, Mr. Calloway."

"I love you, too, Mrs. Calloway."

Maybe he had too much pride and too many trust issues. Maybe he still had a lot of learning to do about love, women, and most of all, himself. But with Paris by his side, Dallas felt confident he would master those lessons in time. One thing he did know for sure, when this beautiful blonde breezed through his door three months ago, that turned out to be the best day of his life. He expected to have many, many more.

* * * * *

Her entire body relaxed.

Of course he'd give her a sisterly kiss on the cheek. She closed her eyes.

His lips came down softly.

On her mouth.

Oh, she'd died and gone to heaven. His lips were warm and giving and soothing. She wrapped her arms around his neck and brazenly returned the kiss. Wow. It was all so new. And exciting. Dylan McKay was kissing her on Moonlight Beach at sunset, and she was fully in the moment this time. There were no gaps of memory from a fuzzy brain. There wasn't anything but right now, this speck of time, and she relished the taste of him.

But something still seemed slightly off with his kiss. She couldn't quite put her finger on it. Was it just that she was fully aware, fully attuned to him right now?

Dylan broke off the kiss first. "Thank you. I needed your company tonight, Emma."

What could she say? Was she foolish enough to think he remembered their night of passion and wanted more? No, that wasn't it. Dylan needed comforting. At least she could give him that.

Her secret was safe.

"You're welcome, Dylan."

* * *

One Secret Night, One Secret Baby
is part of the series Moonlight Beach Bachelors:
Three men living in paradise…
and longing for more.

ONE SECRET NIGHT, ONE SECRET BABY

BY
CHARLENE SANDS

First Published in Great Britain 2016
By Mills & Boon, an imprint of HarperCollins*Publishers*
1 London Bridge Street, London, SE1 9GF

© 2016 Charlene Swink

ISBN: 978-0-263-91853-3

51-0316

Our policy is to use papers that are natural, renewable and recyclable products and made from wood grown in sustainable forests.The logging and manufacturing processes conform to the legal environmental regulations of the country of origin.

Printed and bound in Spain
by CPI, Barcelona

Charlene Sands is a *USA TODAY* bestselling author of more than thirty-five romance novels. Her books have been honored with a National Readers' Choice Award, a CataRomance Reviewers' Choice Award, and she's a double recipient of the Booksellers' Best Award.

Charlene writes "hunky heroes with heart." She knows a little something about true romance—she married her high school sweetheart! When not writing, Charlene enjoys sunny Pacific beaches, great coffee, reading books from her favorite authors and spending time with her family. You can find her on Facebook and Twitter. Charlene loves to hear from her readers! You can write her at PO Box 4883, West Hills, CA 91308, USA, or sign up for her newsletter for fun blogs and ongoing contests at www.charlenesands.com.

Special thanks to my wonderful son-in-law, Zac Prange, who helped me with the on-set moviemaking details of this story. Your support and expertise really meant a great deal, keeping the story honest and authentic. With love to you, Nikki my fabulous daughter, and of course your two sweet princesses who brighten our lives every day, Everley and Lila.

One

She wasn't a one-night stand sort of girl.

Emma Rae Bloom was predictable, hardworking, ambitious and least of all, adventurous. *Boring.* She never did anything out of the ordinary. She was measured and sure and patient. *Double boring.* The one time she'd crushed that mold, breaking it to bits, was at her neighbor Eddie's blowout bash at Havens on Sunset Boulevard in celebration of his thirtieth birthday last month. She'd partied hard, lost her inhibitions as well as her mind during the now infamous Los Angeles blackout and wound up in bed with her best friend's brother, Hollywood heartthrob in the flesh, Dylan McKay.

She'd had secret dibs on Brooke's brother since the age of twelve. He was the older boy with sea-blue eyes and stubble on his face who'd treated her kindly and given her a measuring stick to compare all men against.

There was no going back to reclaim their night together, although her memory of her time with Dylan was almost nonexistent. Just her luck, she had her first ever one-night stand with the hottest guy on earth and her mind had gone as foggy as a London winter day. Too many mango mojitos could do that, she'd been told.

She stood at the port-side railing of Dylan's yacht now. As he approached her, his head wrapped with gauze bandages, a haunted look on his face spoke of sadness and grief. It was a somber day, but beaming rays of sunshine and stunning marshmallow fluff clouds didn't seem to know that. She pushed her sunglasses farther up her nose, grateful to hide her true emotions.

Roy Benjamin was gone, killed in the freakish stunt accident on the set of Dylan's Navy SEAL movie. The tragedy had rocked Hollywood insiders and made a big splash on the news, even eclipsing the story of how the lights went out in the city just the day before. It wasn't just Roy's death that had rocked the entertainment world and hit the headlines with a bang, but Dylan's amnesia resulting from the same blast that had killed his friend.

"Here, have a soda." Brooke walked up beside her brother and offered Emma a glass. "You look like you could use one."

"Thanks." She accepted the benign drink. No more alcohol for her, thank you very much. "It's a hard day for everyone." She sipped her cola.

Standing between her and Brooke, Dylan wrapped his arms around them. "I'm glad you both are here with me today."

Emma's nerves squeezed tight. She hadn't seen Dylan since the night of the blackout. The supportive arm around her shoulders shouldn't elicit any of the sensations she was having. It shouldn't. She sighed. His hand caressed her upper arm lightly, sending shock waves through her system. As the yacht backed out of its slip, his body lurched, two hundred pounds of solid granite shoulder to shoulder with her. She stopped breathing for a second and gripped the railing.

"Of course we'd be here," Brooke said. "Roy was a friend of ours, too. Right, Emma?"

She gave Dylan a quick smile. It was such a tragedy that a man so vital and strong as Roy had died at such a young age. He was a Dylan look-alike, his stunt double and a close friend to the McKays. Emma only knew Roy through them and he'd always been nice to her.

Dylan's lips curled up a little, the subdued smile of a man in mourning. "I miss him already."

He tightened his hold, bringing their bodies close. He was the consummate movie star, sunglasses shading his face, blond hair blowing in the breeze and a body carved from hard gym workouts and daily runs. He was Holly-wood royalty, a man who'd managed to steer clear of last-ing relationships his entire adult life. Darkly tanned, as talented and smart as he was good-looking, he had it all.

Emma should be concentrating on Roy's death instead of her dilemma. Yet as she'd dressed this morning ready-ing for Roy's memorial, she'd rehearsed what she would say if Dylan remembered anything that happened between them during the blackout.

I wasn't myself that night. The blackout freaked me out. I've been afraid of the dark since I was a kid and I begged you to stay with me. Can we just go on being friends?

Now it looked as if she could dodge that confession. Soul-melting blue eyes, dimmed now from grief, settled upon her as they always had. He saw her as his sister Brooke's friend, nothing more. He had no memory of their night together. The doctors termed it dissociative amne-sia. He was blocked and might never remember the hours or days leading up to the blast that took his friend's life and sent a hunk of shrapnel tunneling into his head. He'd been knocked unconscious and had woken up hours later, in the hospital.

He let her go to sip his soda and she began breathing normally again. Cautiously she took a step away from him. Having his hand on her played too much havoc with her brain. She had escaped telling him the truth today, and the devil on her shoulder whispered in her ear, *Why rock the boat?* Clever little fiend. *This can be your little secret.*

Could she really get away with not having to tell him?

She battled with the notion as the yacht made its way out of Marina del Rey, traveling past the docks at a snail's pace. Pungent sea scents filled her nostrils, seagulls squawked overhead and one white-winged bird landed on a buoy and quietly watched the yacht head into open seas.

"I guess it's time," Dylan said, minutes later, once they were far enough out to sea. Dylan wanted to do this alone, with just his family. Later today, a memorial would be held at his Moonlight Beach home open to Roy's friends and fellow crew and cast members, the only family he'd ever known. That's when Emma and Brooke would go to work, hosting an informal buffet dinner in Roy's honor. It definitely wasn't a Parties-To-Go kind of event, but Dylan had turned to them for help. "Roy always joked, if he missed the net from a ten-story fall, to make sure I tossed his ashes from the *Classy Lady*. He loved this boat, but I never thought I'd ever have to do this."

Brooke's doe eyes softened on her brother and Emma hurt inside for both of them. Brooke and Dylan were miles apart in most things, but when push came to shove, they were always there for each other. Emma envied that. She had no siblings. She had no real family, except for foster parents, two people who'd taken her in and then neglected her as a child. She hadn't hit the jackpot in the parent department, that was for sure. Not like Brooke. Brooke was Dylan's younger foster sister whom his parents had eventually adopted. They were totally amazing. They'd been better parents to Emma than the two who'd collected monthly checks on her behalf.

Dylan made swift work of saying heartfelt words about his friend, his voice tightening up to get it all out, right before he opened the urn, lifted it up and let the wind carry Roy's ashes out to sea. When he turned around, tears filled his eyes and his mouth quivered in heartbreak. She'd never seen this vulnerable side of Dylan and she gripped the railing tight to keep from going to him. It wasn't her place.

Brooke went to him and cradled him in her arms the way a mother would a child, whispering soft words of sympathy in his ear. Dylan nodded his head as he listened to his baby sister. After a few minutes he wiped the tears from his eyes and the solemn expression from his face. He gave Brooke a sweet smile.

Dylan McKay was back.

It was the first time Emma had ever seen him let his guard down.

It touched her soul.

Secret dibs.

Dylan's kitchen could swallow up her little apartment in one large gulp. Every kind of new age appliance ever conceived was set on the shiny onyx granite counter and in the textured white cabinets. It was a culinary dream kitchen and his housekeeper, Maisey, made great use of it. She'd cooked up a storm for the fifty-plus people who'd come to pay their respects to Roy Benjamin. Aside from Maisey's home cooking, the caterers Emma had commissioned delivered trays of finger foods, specialty breads and appetizers. Everyone from grips to the president of Stage One Studios was here. Emma and Brooke, dressed in appropriate black dresses with little ornamentation, set out the food and offered drinks to the guests. They weren't acting as Parties-To-Go planners today as much as they were Dylan's hostesses for this sad event.

"Did you see what Callista is wearing?" Brooke muttered under her breath.

Emma set out a plate of sweet-cream-and-berry tarts on the dessert table, shooting a quick glance to the living room, where many of the guests were gathered. Callista Lee Allen, daughter to the Stage One Studio mogul, was on Dylan's arm, hanging on his every word. She wore Versace, and the only reason Emma knew that was because she'd overheard the blonde gloating about it. It was a silver glimmer dress with detailed layering and jewels dripping off her throat and arms. "I see."

"It's not as if the Fashion Police are trolling. Roy deserves better. This day isn't about her."

Emma grinned. "Tell me how you really feel, Brooke. At least she talks to you. I'm invisible to her." Being a friend of Dylan's sister didn't rank high enough on Callista's status scale to award Emma an iota of her attention.

"Be grateful. Be very grateful."

Emma stood back from the arrangement, giving the presentation scrutiny. They'd draped the dessert table with tablecloths in varying colors and edged each platter with flowering vines. This is what they did. And they did it well.

"It's none of my business, but Dylan's on-again, off-again relationship with her isn't good for him," Brooke said.

Emma shot them another glance. Callista's eyes flashed on Dylan's bandage, one hand possessively on his arm as she reached up with the other to touch the injury. Emma watched the scene play out. Dylan was deep in conversation with Callista's father and didn't seem to notice her unabashed attention.

Sucking oxygen in, Emma glanced away and tamped down pangs of jealousy swimming through her body. She'd be ten times a fool to think she'd ever have a chance with Dylan. He was her friend. Period. "He's a big boy, Brooke."

"I never thought I'd say this, but thank God my brother doesn't commit. She's all wrong in so many ways." Brooke lifted her hands in a stopping motion that was her signature move. "But like I said, none of my beeswax."

Emma smiled at her friend and put the finishing touches on the dessert table. Maisey had made coffee and there was hot water and a sampler box of teas available.

Dylan approached, gorgeous in a tailored dark suit and tie. He'd changed his clothes from the jeans and black silk shirt he'd worn this morning on the yacht. "Do you two have a minute?" he asked quietly. His brows were gathered in question. Brooke and Emma nodded and he guided them to the far side of the kitchen, out of earshot of anyone. It was all so curious.

"You girls have done wonderful today. Thank you," he began and then shook his head. "I'm figuring you'd give it to me straight. Callista and I…are we a thing again?"

Emma held her breath. She wouldn't comment on her thoughts about the bottle blonde. Dylan didn't exactly confide in her about his love life, but his earnest question made her stomach ripple in guilt. She had a truth to tell him, too, and maybe it would help spark his memory, but it could also make things weird between them, which was the last thing she wanted.

Brooke seemed eager to answer, but shook her head as if formulating her thoughts. "You don't remember?"

"No. But she's acting like we're ready for the altar. From what I remember, that wasn't the case. Am I wrong?"

"No, you're certainly not wrong," Brooke shot back. "Not even close. Before…before your accident, you told me you were going to break it off with her for good."

"I did? I don't remember." Poor Dylan was struggling. His gaze lifted to the wide windows that opened out onto the sea, as if he were searching for answers there. He seemed lost right now, not his usual self-confident, always-one-step-ahead-of-everyone, charming self.

"If she says it's more, Dylan, I'd be careful," Brooke offered. "She's banking on your amnesia to worm her way back into your…"

Dylan turned to his sister, his brows lifting and a crooked smile emerging. "My what?"

"Your good graces," Emma finished for her.

Dylan slid her a knowing look. "Always the diplomat, Em. But somehow, I don't think that's what Brooke was going to say." He began nodding. "Okay, I get the picture." He glanced at Callista, who was now surrounded by a few other actors in the film. She was deep in conversation yet constantly casting him furtive glances at every opportunity, sizing him up and staking her claim.

Brooke was right—Callista was all wrong for Dylan. How difficult it must be for him not to remember some things, not to have a grasp on his feelings. "You're the only ones I can trust," he said. He rubbed his brow, just under his bandage. "I can't tell you how bizarre this feels. I see some things clearly. Other things are fuzzy at best. And then there's a whole chunk that I don't remember."

Emma plunked three ice cubes into a glass and poured him a root beer, his favorite from childhood. "Here, drink up."

"Thanks," he said, "though I could use something stronger."

"The doctor says not yet. You're still on pain meds." Brooke's internal mother came out. It really was sweet seeing how close the two had become since the move from Ohio to Los Angeles years ago.

"One drink won't kill me."

"Let's not find out, okay? I was worried enough when you were sent to the hospital. And Mom just went home two days ago. If I have to call her again to tell her you're back in Saint Joseph's, she'll have a heart attack."

Dylan rolled his eyes. "You see how good she is, Emma? She knows exactly how to lay on the guilt."

A chuckle rumbled from Emma's throat. "I know all about Brooke's tactics. I work with her."

"Hey!" Brooke said. "You're supposed to be on my side."

"Like I said, Emma's a diplomat. Thanks for the drink." He lifted his glass in mock toast and then pivoted around and walked away.

"He'll be okay," Brooke said, watching him head back to his guests. "We just have to do whatever it takes to help him along."

Dread formed a tight knot in Emma's stomach. She hated keeping secrets from Brooke. They usually shared everything. But how exactly could she come out and say, *I begged your brother to sleep with me the night of the blackout and all I remember is his body on mine, heated breaths and sexy words whispered in my ear.* She didn't remember how she got in bed or when he left her that night. She couldn't recall how they'd ended things. Were there parting words recognizing the big mistake? Or had he promised to call her? He had no knowledge of what they'd done, but geesh, she didn't recall much of that night, either.

"Oh, brother," she mumbled.

"What?" Brooke asked.

"Nothing. Nothing at all."

"Brooke, you did a wonderful job today," Callista said, leaning her arms over the granite island, spilling her cleavage and smiling her billion-dollar smile. The sun was setting and all but one guest had left the memorial service. "You helped make the day easier for your brother."

"It wasn't just me, Callie," Brooke said. "Emma did her

fair share of the work and we'd both do anything to help Dylan get through this day."

Callista's gaze darted Emma's way as if she'd just noticed her standing there. *Hello, I'm not invisible.* "Of course, you, too, Emma." She spoke to her as if she were a child. What was it with rich powerful women that made them feel superior, just by right of wealth? Emma could probably run circles around her SAT scores. "You did a marvelous job."

"Dylan's a special guy and I'm happy to help."

Callista gave her a cursory nod, eyeing her for just a second as if measuring the competition, and then turned away, writing her off.

"Brooke, do you know where Dylan is? I want to say goodbye to him and tell him his eulogy was touching."

"Yeah, I do. He said to say goodbye to you for him. The day tired him out. He went to sleep."

"He's in bed already?" Callista straightened and her gaze moved toward the hallway staircase. She knew exactly where Dylan's bedroom was. "Maybe I should go up and wish him good-night."

"He, uh, needs uninterrupted rest. Doctor's orders." Brooke's accomplished smile brought Emma a stream of silent chuckles. Leave it to Brooke. She was in defense mode now.

"Yes, of course, you're right." She nibbled on her lip, shooting another longing glance at the staircase. Then her expression changed. "He does need to rest up so he can be back on set as soon as possible."

The SEAL movie had been shut down for a month already and it was costing the studio big bucks, so Dylan's return to the set was essential. Even Callista recognized that fact. "Tell him I'll call him."

"Will do, Callie. I'll walk you out."

"Oh, that's not necessary," Callista said.

"I don't mind."

After the two left, Emma couldn't contain her laughter. She knew for certain Callista Lee Allen hated to be called Callie, yet she let Brooke get away with it because she was Dylan's sister.

What a day it had been. Selfishly, Emma was glad it was over. She didn't like walking around with a cloud of guilt over her head. She hoped "out of sight, out of mind" would work on her. As soon as she left Dylan's house, maybe her head would clear and she'd be free of this grating bug gnawing at her to tell Dylan what happened between them.

Finished with her duties, the house clean and back to normal, thanks to Maisey and her efforts, Emma took a seat on one of the many white leather sofas in the living room. A pastel pop of color fading on the horizon grabbed her attention as she looked out the window. The sunset was beautiful on Moonlight Beach. She leaned back, closed her eyes and listened to the sound of the waves breaking on the shore.

"Mission accomplished," Brooke said, clapping her hands. "She's gone."

Emma snapped to attention as Brooke sat down beside her. "You're a regular Mama Bear. Who knew?"

"Normally, Dylan can take care of himself, but right now, he needs a little help. What else are meddling little sisters for anyway?"

"To keep conniving women away from him?"

"I try my best." Brooke propped her feet on a cocktail table and sighed. "I'm getting excited about the celebrity golf tournament coming up. This is one of the biggest events we've ever booked. And we got it all on our own. No intervention from Dylan. They don't even know he's my brother. Dylan doesn't play golf."

"I don't?" Dylan walked into the room looking adorably rumpled. It was the five-o'clock shadow, the mussedto-perfection hair and those deep blue bedroom eyes that did Emma in. He wore a pair of black sweats and a white T-shirt.

"No, you don't," Brooke said, eyeing him carefully.

He grinned. "Just joking. I know I don't play golf. At least I have memories of tanking every shot. Never did get the hang of it."

"Brat. What are you doing up?"

On a long sigh, he ran a hand down his face. "I can't sleep. I'm going for a walk. I'll see you guys later. Thanks again for everything."

Brooke's mouth opened, but he was out the back door before she could stop him. "Darn it. He's still having dizzy spells. Will you go with him, Emma? Tell him you're in the mood for a walk, too. He already thinks I baby him enough."

Emma balked. She was three minutes away from escaping to go home. "I, uh…"

"Please?" Brooke begged. "If you're with him, he won't get it into his head to start jogging. I know he misses it. He's been complaining about not doing his daily runs. It's almost dark on the beach. He could collapse and no one would know."

It was true. The doctor said he shouldn't overdo any physical activity. How could she deny Brooke the peace of mind? She'd been worried sick about her brother lately. "Okay, I'll go."

"That's why I love you." Brooke sounded relieved.

Emma bent to remove her heels and rose from the sofa. "You better," she said. "I don't chase handsome A-list movie stars for just anyone." With that, she walked out the back entrance of Dylan's mansion, climbed down the stairs, searched for signs of him and took off at a jog when she'd seen how far he'd already traveled.

"Dylan," she called, her toes squishing into wet sand as she trudged rapidly after him. "Wait up."

He turned around and slowed his pace.

"Would you like company?" Her breathing ragged, she fibbed, "I feel like a walk, too."

"Let me guess. Brooke sent you."

She shrugged. "Maybe I just felt like taking a walk?"

His mouth lifted in a dubious smile. "And maybe the moon is green."

"Everyone knows the moon is made of cheese, therefore it's yellow."

He shook his head, seeming to relinquish his skepticism. "Okay, let's walk. Actually, I would like your company."

He took her hand, his fingers lacing with hers.

How…unexpected. Her breath froze in her chest.

"It was a nice memorial, wasn't it?" he asked as he resumed walking.

There was a slight tug on her hand that woke her from her stupor and she fell in step with him. "It was heartwarming. You honored Roy with a wonderful tribute to his life."

"I'm the only family he had, aside from his crew. He was a great guy and it's just a ridiculous shame. Roy was obsessed with his stunts. He spent his whole life perfecting them. He was the most cautious man I've ever known. It just doesn't make sense."

"They're saying it was a freakish accident."

Dylan took a sharp breath. "That's what they say when they don't know what happened. It's the standard answer."

They walked on in silence for a while, the heat from where he held her hand warming her entire body. It was actually a perfect evening for a stroll on the beach. Breezes blew at the twist of hair at the back of her head. She reached up and pulled it out of its band, freeing the long waves that touched the middle of her back.

"So tell me what's going on in your life, Emma."

Her brows gathered at the oddity of the request. Dylan knew just about everything about her. She was Brooke's friend and business partner. She lived in a tiny apartment twenty minutes away from Moonlight Beach. She loved her work and didn't go out much.

Oh, no! Did he remember something? Blood drained from her face as her mind worked overtime for signs that he'd remembered that blackout night. But as she dared to gaze at his profile, his eyes didn't probe her but stayed straight ahead, his neutral expression unchanged. She let out a relieved sigh. Maybe he needed to break the silence. Maybe he was just making conversation. And maybe her guilty conscience was wringing her dry.

"The same old, same old," she answered. "Work, work, work."

"Still hoping to make your first million before thirty?"

Her laugh came out a little too high-pitched. Brooke must've told him of her long-term goal. How embarrassing. Ever since she was a child, money had been scarce. Her foster parents didn't have much and were stingy in sharing. She didn't know that until she'd grown into a teen, of course, and witnessed how they'd splurge what they did have on each other. Never her. She grew up mostly wearing thrift store clothes. From the age of thirteen, Emma knew she'd have to find her own way in the world. She'd worked her ass off, achieving a full scholarship to college, and vowed she'd become financially independent one day. The promise she made herself was that by the age of thirty, she would make her first million. She had several years to go, but her hopes were high of expanding Parties-To-Go into a million-dollar franchise.

"Your sister, my best friend, needs to button her mouth."

"Don't blame Brooke," he said softly. "I think it's commendable to have goals."

"Lofty goals."

"Attainable goals and you work hard, Emma."

"Without your investment, we wouldn't even have a business."

"I just helped you get started, and in the two years since you've been working at it, you've come a long way."

"We owe you, Dylan. You've been amazing. We want to make you proud."

Dylan stopped, his Nikes digging into the sand, and when she turned to him, a genuine smile graced his handsome face. Gone was the sadness from before. A glint of appreciation twinkled in his eyes. "You don't owe me anything. And I am proud. You're a hard worker, and you're paying me back faster than I expected or wanted. But, Em, I have to tell you, as much as you believe Brooke has helped you through the growing-up years, you've helped her, too. She came to California hoping to become an actress. God, it's a tough business. I've been lucky…more fortunate than I could've hoped, but it's not the same for Brooke. She's much happier now, being in business with her best friend and earning a legitimate living doing what she loves. I owe that to you. So thank you for being…*you*."

Dylan leaned in, his face coming within inches of hers. Her heart rate escalated as she stared at his mouth. She understood now why his female fans swooned. He was breathtaking and yummy. There was no other way to describe it. "You're the amazing one, Emma," he whispered.

Her mind going fuzzy, she whispered back, "I am?"

As he inched closer, taking her into his arms, angling for her cheek, her entire body relaxed. Of course, he'd give her a sisterly kiss on the cheek. She closed her eyes.

His warm lips came down softly.

On her mouth.

Oh, she'd died and gone to heaven. His lips were warm and giving and soothing. She wrapped her arms around his neck and brazenly returned the kiss. Wow. It was all so new. And exciting. Dylan McKay was kissing her on Moonlight Beach at sunset and she was fully in the moment this time. There were no gaps of memory from a fuzzy brain. There wasn't anything but right now, this speck of time, and she relished the taste of him, the amazing texture of his firm lips caressing hers, the strength and power of his body close to hers.

But something still seemed slightly off with his kiss. She couldn't quite put her finger on it. Was it just that she was fully aware, fully attuned to him right now?

Dylan broke off the kiss first, and instead of backing away, he grasped Emma to his chest tightly like a little boy needing the comfort of his favorite stuffed toy. Elmo or Teddy or Winnie the Pooh.

She stood in his embrace for long moments. He sighed and continued to hold her. Then his mouth touched her right earlobe and he whispered, "Thank you. I needed your company tonight, Emma."

What could she say? Was she foolish enough to think he remembered their night of passion and wanted more? No, that wasn't it. Dylan needed comforting. Maybe what she considered to be a heart-melting kiss, only counted as a friendly measure of comfort for a man whose life was full of adoration. At least, she could give him that.

Her secret was safe.

"You're welcome, Dylan."

Glad to be of service.

Two

Dylan wasn't himself. That had to explain why he'd kissed Emma as though he meant it. Actually, he *had* meant it in that instant. She was familiar to him. He knew the score with her, his sister Brooke's best friend. Someone he could trust. Someone he could rely on. The meds he was taking lessened his headaches and he was recovering, feeling better every day. But having a chunk of his memory gone affected his decision making and confidence, made him vulnerable and uncertain.

But one thing he was certain about: kissing Emma had made him feel better. It was the best kiss he'd had in a long time. It packed a wallop. He knew that without question. Those big green eyes that sparkled like emeralds wouldn't steer him wrong. He'd needed the connection to feel whole again. To feel like himself.

Had he gotten all that from one mildly passionate kiss? Yeah. Because it was with Emma and he knew his limitations with her. She was untouchable and sweet with a side of sassy. So he'd kissed her and let the sugar in her fill him up and take away the pain in his heart.

"You're quiet," he said to her as they walked back toward his house. "Was the kiss out of line?"

"No. Not at all. You needed someone."

He covered her hand with his again and squeezed gently. "Not just anyone, Emma. I needed someone I could trust. You. Sorry if I came on too strong."

"You…didn't."

But she didn't sound so sure.

"It was just a kiss, Dylan. It's not as if you haven't kissed me before."

"Birthday kisses don't count."

She was quiet for a second. "I didn't have a lot of affection when I was younger. Those birthday kisses meant a lot to me."

He gave her another quick squeeze of the hand. "I know. Hey, remember the face-plant kiss?"

"Oh, God. Don't bring that up, Dylan. I'm still mortified. Your parents went to a lot of trouble to make that cake for me."

He chuckled at the image popping into his head. "Damn, that was funny."

"It was your fault!"

Dylan's smirk stayed plastered on his face. He couldn't wipe it clean. At least his long-term memory was intact. "How was it my fault?"

"Rusty was your dog, wasn't he? He tangled under my feet and in that moment I figured it was better to fall into the cake than snuff out your dog. I would've crushed that little Chihuahua if my full weight landed on him."

"What were you, twelve at the time?"

"Yes! It said so on the birthday cake I demolished."

Dylan snorted a laugh. "At least you got to taste it. It

was all over your face. The rest of us just got to watch. But it was worth it."

"You should've given me my birthday kiss before your mom kindly wiped my face clean. Then maybe you wouldn't have felt so deprived. The cake was good, you know. Chocolate marble."

"Oh, don't worry, Em. I wasn't deprived."

She stopped abruptly, taking a stand in the sand, pulling her hand free of his and folding her arms across her middle. "What's that supposed to mean? You enjoyed seeing me fall?"

The phony pout on her face brought him a lightness that he hadn't felt in more than a week, since before the accident.

"Oh, come on, Miss Drama Queen. It was many moons ago." And yes, he knew stuntmen, Roy included, who couldn't have done a better pratfall. It had been hilarious.

"Me? Drama queen? I don't think so. I'm standing here, looking at a true-life drama king. Mr. Winner of two Academy Awards and God only knows how many Golden Globes."

"Three." He grinned.

She rolled her eyes. "Three," she repeated.

He walked back to where she'd made her stand and grabbed up her hand again, tugging her along. He liked Emma Rae Bloom. She'd had a tough life, raised by neglectful foster parents. Just by the grace of all good things, she'd become his sister's best friend, and thus, a member of the McKay clan.

They were almost back to his house. It was sundown, a time when the beach was quiet but for the waves washing upon the shore. Moonlight illuminated the water and reflected off the sand where he stopped to face Emma. "Well, you've succeeded where many have failed this week, Em. You've put a smile on my face."

Her pert little chin lifted to him, and he balked at the urge to take her into his arms again. To kiss that mouth and feel the lushness of her long hair against his palms. She was petite in size and stature, especially without shoes on, and so different than the tall lean models and actresses he'd dated.

He wouldn't kiss her again. But it surprised him how badly he wanted to.

He pursed his lips and went with his gut. "Hey, you know, I've got this charity gig coming up. If the doctors say I'm good to go, I'd love for you to join me for the meet and greet at Children's West Hospital."

Emma turned away from him now, to gaze out to sea. "You want me to go with you?"

"Yep."

"Don't you have agents and personal assistants to do that sort of thing?"

"Em?"

"What?"

Tucking his hands in his pockets, he shrugged. "It's okay if you don't want to go."

She whipped her head around, her eyes a spark of brightness against the dim skies. "Why do you want *me* to go?"

"The truth? I'm a little mixed-up right now. Having a friend come along will make me feel a little safer. I haven't been out in public since the accident. Besides, I know the kids will love you. I was going to ask Brooke, too."

"Oh." She ducked her head, looking sheepish. "These kids, are they all ill?"

"Mostly, yes. But many are in recovery, thank goodness. I'm slated to do a promo spot in a few days with some of the kids to raise funds and awareness about the good the hospital does. I've donated a little to the new wing of the hospital and I guess that's why they've asked me."

"You donated 1.3 million dollars to the new wing, Dylan. I read that online. It's going to be amazing. The new wing will have a screening room with interactive games for the kids."

He smiled. "So what do you say?"

"Yes, of course I'll go."

"Thanks, Em. Now, let's get back inside before Brooke sends out a search party for us."

Emma's laughter filled his ears and made him smile again.

Late Wednesday afternoon, Emma hung up the phone with Mrs. Alma Montalvo, rested her arms on her office desk and hung her head. The client was delirious about details and had sapped Emma's energy for two long hours. Yes, they'd found a local band to play fifties tunes. Yes, they'd rented a '57 Chevy and it would be parked strategically at the top of their multitiered lawn for added effect. Yes, they'd have a photo booth decked out with leather jackets, poodle skirts and car club insignia for the guests to wear as they had their photos snapped. Yes, yes, yes.

Thank goodness the party was this Saturday night. After it was over, she and Brooke could take their big fat check from Mrs. Montalvo and say, *Hasta la vista, baby. Parties-To-Go has come and gone.*

The chime above the door rang out Leslie Gore's classic song "It's My Party" and Emma glanced up.

"Hey, I thought you were going home early today," Brooke said, entering their Santa Monica office.

"I thought I was, too, but Mrs. Montalvo had other ideas."

Brooke rolled her eyes. "We'll impress the hell out of her, Emma. The party is going to be top-notch."

"It better be. I've put in extra hours on this one."

Brooke grinned and set down shopping bags on the

desk adjacent to Emma's. The office furnishings were an eclectic mix, all colorful and light to convey a party atmosphere for clients. The desks were clear Plexiglas, the walls were painted bright pastels and the chairs were relics that had been upholstered in floral materials. Photos of their parties and events adorned the walls from hoedowns on local ranch properties to rich, elaborate weddings with a few celebrity endorsements mixed in, thanks to Dylan.

They had two part-time employees who came in after school and on weekends to answer phones, do online research and work the parties whenever needed.

"Take a look at this," Brooke said, pulling a mocha cocktail dress from a box in one of the bags. "Isn't it… perfect? I got it at the little shop on Broadway."

"Wow, it's gorgeous. And not black. I bet it's for the San Diego golf dinner, right?"

Brooke was shaking her head. "Nope, not at all. You'll never guess."

Emma's thoughts ran through a list of upcoming events and couldn't come up with anything. "Don't make me, then. Tell me!"

Brooke put the dress up to her chin, hugged it to her waist and twirled around, just like when they used to play dress-up and pretend to be princesses ready to meet their special prince.

"I have a date." Brooke sang out the words and stomped her feet.

It shouldn't be that monumental, but Brooke seldom dated. After graduating from college, they'd both been focused on the business. And Brooke was picky when it came to men. So this was a big deal, judging by the megawatt, light-up-Sunset-Boulevard smile on her face. "The best part is, he doesn't know who I am."

Or rather, who her brother was. Most people, men and women alike, showed interest in Brooke once they found out that Dylan was her big brother. It sucked big-time and made Brooke wary of any friendliness coming her way. She was never sure if there was an ulterior motive.

"I mean, of course he knows my name is Brooke. We met at Adele's Café. We were both waiting for our take-out lunch orders and it took forever. But once we got to talking, neither of us minded the long wait."

"When was this?"

"Yesterday."

"And you didn't tell me!" Wasn't that like breaking the BFF rule?

"I didn't know if he'd call." She hugged the dress one last time, before carefully stowing it back in the box. "But he did this morning and asked me out for the following weekend. And get this, he wanted to see me sooner but I told him about the event this weekend and he seemed really disappointed. We don't have anything next weekend. Tell me we don't. The golf tournament is in three weeks, right?"

Emma punched it up on her computer and glanced at their calendar. "Right, but you're so excited, even if we had an event, I'd relieve you of your duties. I've never seen you so gaga. What's his name?"

"Royce Brisbane. He's in financial planning."

Emma dug her teeth into her bottom lip to keep from chuckling. "You, with a suit?"

"Yes, but he looks dreamy in it."

"Wow, Brooke. You really like this guy. You shopped." Brooke was not a shopper. She had one color in her wardrobe arsenal, basic black, and she wore it like armor every day.

"I think I do like him. A lot. It was so easy talking to him. We have a lot in common."

"Tell me more."

After getting the full details on Royce Brisbane, Emma's thoughts went to Brooke's upcoming date on the drive home.

Emma had to admit, the guy sounded good on paper. If he made Brooke happy, then she was all for it. She hadn't seen Brooke smile so much in months. That could be a good thing, or a bad thing. A very bad thing. The more you care about someone, the more they could potentially hurt you. But Emma wouldn't poke a hole in Brooke's happy balloon; her friend deserved to have a good time.

Emma parked in her apartment structure and climbed out of her car. Her legs were two strands of thin spaghetti tonight. It was an effort to walk across the courtyard to her front door. She shoved the sticky door open with her body and glimpsed her comfy sofa with cushy pillows and a quilt she could curl up in. She dropped her purse unceremoniously onto the coffee table, sank down onto the sofa and let out a relieved sigh.

A hundred details ran through her head. The upcoming golf event was first and foremost in her mind. It wasn't for a few weeks yet, but it was a big opportunity for the business. She did yet another mental check, making sure all bases were covered, before she could really relax. Somewhat confident she hadn't forgotten anything, she lay her head down and stretched her legs out, allowing the cushions to envelop her weary body.

If only she could go mindless for a while. Sometimes she envied people who could close everything off and go blank. Just…be. She tended to overthink everything, which made her excellent at her job, but a sad prospect for a carefree lifestyle.

The night of the memorial for Roy Benjamin played in her head and she immediately zoomed in on Dylan McKay. The way he had held her on the beach, the way she had felt when his hand covered hers possessively, the way his mouth had moved over hers and claimed her in a kiss. It wasn't a birthday kiss. It wasn't a friend's kiss, either, though Dylan seemed to think so. It was much more for her. And the memory floated through her body and filled in all the lonely gaps.

Secret dibs.

She smiled. It was never going to happen, yet part of her fantasy had come true. Dylan had made glorious love to her. Okay, so she wasn't sure about the glorious part. She'd been too out of it to know if he was a good lover or not. But in her fantasy world, Dylan was the best. *Appeal* magazine had said so, too. He'd been voted Most Sexy Single this year. And there had been endorsements by his former girlfriends. So it had to be true.

Her eyes grew heavy. It was a battle to keep them open with the cushions supporting her fatigued body and the quilt covering her. All tucked in, she gave up the fight and surrendered to slumber.

Ruff, ruff...ruff, ruff.

Emma bolted upright, her eyes snapping to attention. She found herself on the sofa, half covered with her favorite quilt. How long had she been out? Squinting, she glanced at the wall clock. It was eight thirty. Wow, she'd been asleep for ninety minutes. She'd never taken a nighttime nap before.

Ruff, ruff...ruff, ruff.

Her phone rang again. She grappled for it inside her purse and put it to her ear. "Hello."

"Hello."

It was Dylan. There was no mistaking that deep baritone voice that had half the female movie-viewing population panting to hear more. "Oh, hi."

She hinged her body up, planted her feet on the ground and shook her head to clear away the grogginess.

"I didn't wake you, did I?"

Did she sound as if she'd been sleeping? She tried her best to pretend she was wide-awake. "Not at all. I'm up."

"Busy?"

"No. Just sitting here…going over a few details in my head." A yawn crept out and she cupped her hand over her mouth to hide the sound. "What are you doing?"

"Nothing much. I spoke with Darren on the phone and my manager stopped by to check on me tonight. To be honest, I'm going a little stir-crazy."

"You're used to being busy."

"I can't wait to get back to work. But then, I'm dreading it at the same time."

"I get it. It's because of Roy. It'll be strange for you to go about your daily routine knowing that he's gone and you're going on with your life."

"How come you're so smart, Em?"

"I got lucky in the brains department I guess." She chewed on her lip. She still wasn't comfortable speaking to Dylan with this big black cloud hanging over her head. It made her feel guilty and disingenuous. And why was he suddenly her best friend? Did that knock to his head change his perspective? They'd always been cordial, but since his rise to celebrity status, she hadn't exactly been on his radar. All of a sudden, he was behaving as if they were best buds.

He was disoriented. Fuzzy in the brain. And in need of someone he could trust. But as soon as he was comfortable in his own skin again, things would change. She had no doubt. Dylan was a busy, busy man, sought after by the masses and the media, with who knew how many opportunities for work.

She scrunched up her face. *Don't get used to his attention, Emma.*

"Well, I won't keep you," he said. "I'm calling to confirm our date."

Date? A bad choice of words. "You mean the hospital thing?"

"Yes, it's this Friday morning. How about I swing by your place around nine to pick you up?"

"That's fine. I'm still not sure of my part in all this, but I'm happy to help out."

"You are helping out. You're helping *me*."

The way he said it, with such deep sincerity, tugged her heart in ten different ways. And it dawned on her that it wasn't just returning to work he was partially dreading, but going out in public for the first time with everyone expecting to see Dylan McKay back in true form. That was clearly worrying him. He didn't know if he was ready for that. He needed the support of his sister and friend.

"And you're going to make a difference in a lot of children's lives."

"I hope to. See you around nine, Em. Sleep tight."

"You, too."

Emma ended the call and sat there for a few minutes taking it all in again. She had to stop dwelling on Dylan McKay. Food usually kept her mind occupied. But oddly, she wasn't hungry. In fact, the thought of eating right now turned her stomach, so she nixed that plan and picked up the TV remote. She hit the on button and her small flat-screen lit up the dark room. The channel, tuned to the local network, was airing a movie. She settled back, propping up her feet, and stared ahead.

Dylan McKay's handsome face popped up, filling most of the screen, his bone-melting blue eyes gazing into the pretty face of Hollywood's latest darling, Sophie Adams. The cowboy and his girl were about to ride into the sunset. The camera zoomed in for the movie-ending kiss, and just like that, something cold and painful snared Emma's heart as Dylan's mouth locked onto Sophie's.

Hitting the off button did little to calm her. Why couldn't she get away from Dylan?

Falling for the unattainable was romantic suicide. She wasn't that stupid.

She'd just have to get over her secret dibs.

End of story.

She was ready at precisely nine o'clock. When the doorbell rang, she took a quick glance in the mirror, checking her upswept hairstyle, snowy-white pants and the sherbet-pink blazer she wore over a dotted swiss top. A tiny locket nestled at the base of her throat; that, silver stud earrings and a fashionable chunky watch were all the jewelry she'd opted for. She was going for a professional look without appearing unapproachable to the children. A little thrill ran through her body. Seeing Dylan aside, she was looking forward to meeting the kids, knowing firsthand how hard it was for a youngster to be outside the mainstream. She'd been one of those kids. Lucky for her, she had been healthy, but she'd been different, unloved and unwanted, and she'd never really felt as if she belonged.

Today was all about the kids.

She opened the door and was immediately yanked out of her noble thoughts as she took one look at Dylan standing on her doorstep. She'd expected his driver. But there Dylan was, in the flesh, his bandage gone now, the scar on the side of his head that would eventually heal only making him appear more manly, more dangerous, more gorgeous. Dressed in new jeans and a tan jacket over a white shirt, he smiled at her. "Morning. You look great."

She didn't feel great. She had woken up pale as a ghost and feeling boneless from tossing and turning all night. But his compliments could get to her, if she put stock in them. He was smooth. He was the consummate lady-killer. He knew which buttons to push to make females fall at his feet. And with her, she was sure, he wasn't even trying.

"Thank you. Is Brooke with you?"

He shook his head. "Brooke cracked a tooth this morning. She called me in a panic and said she had to get it fixed right away. I guess it's because of your event tomorrow, but she bailed. She's got a hot date with the dentist in twenty minutes."

Or rather a hot date with Royce next week and she couldn't go toothless. "Oh. Poor Brooke."

"She didn't call you?"

Emma lifted her phone out of her purse and glanced at the screen. "Oh, yeah, she did," she said. "Looks like a voice mail this morning. I was probably in the shower."

Dylan's eyes flickered and roamed over her body. Gosh, he was Flirt Central without even knowing it.

"I'm ready. Or would you like to come in?" Oh, boy, had she really invited him in? The last time he'd been here, they'd…

He glanced behind her and scanned her apartment as if seeing it for the first time. It was clear he didn't remember coming here.

She put those thoughts out of her mind and wondered what he would think of her two-bedroom apartment tucked into an older residential area of Santa Monica. There were no views of the ocean, no trendy, glamorous furnishings or updated kitchen. But it was all hers. And she loved having…stuff of her own.

"Maybe some other time," he said politely. "We should probably hit the road."

After she locked up her apartment, Dylan took her arm and guided her through the courtyard to the limousine parked by the sidewalk. "Here you go," he said as the driver opened the door. She slid in and Dylan followed. "I haven't gotten clearance to drive yet," he explained as he settled into the seat across from her by the window.

But it wasn't as if being carted around in a limo was foreign to him.

"Thanks again for coming with me today."

Again, she was struck by his sincerity. "You're welcome. Actually, I'm looking forward to it."

He stared at her, waiting for more.

She shrugged. "It's just that my own childhood wasn't ideal. If I can do something for these kids, even just as a bystander, I'm all for it. But how are you doing? This is your first venture out in public since the…"

"Accident?" His lips tightened and he sighed. "Let's just say, I'm glad you're here."

"Even though you'll have your team waiting for you there?"

"My agent and PA are great, don't get me wrong. But they see me one way. I don't think they get how hard this has been for me. Losing those days of my life, and losing Roy, has put me at a disadvantage I'm not used to. There are missing pages in my life."

And she could fill in some of those blanks if she had the courage.

He reached for her hand and laid their entwined fingers on the middle seat between them. "Brooke had good reason to jump ship today. I'm just glad you didn't bail."

"I wouldn't."

"I know. That's why I asked you to join me. I can count on you."

They reached Children's West Hospital, a beautiful building with white marble walls and modern lines. The limo slowed to a stop right in the circular drive that led to the entrance.

"Ready for the show?"

Several news crews were waiting like vultures, snapping pictures even before the driver got out of the limo. Dylan made headlines everywhere he went, and his first time out in public since the accident was big news. She recognized Darren, his agent, and Rochelle, his prim assistant, also waiting along the lineup. "Ready." Emma gave off much more confidence than she was feeling.

Dylan waited two beats, sighed as if grasping for strength and then nodded to his driver, who had one hand on the door handle. The door opened and photos were snapped immediately. Dylan got out, waved to the crowd and then reached inside to take her hand. She exited the limo and was dragged into the fray by Dylan, who seemed to tighten his hold on her. A hospital official came forward to greet them and introductions were made as security guards ensured that none of the news media followed them into the hospital lobby. His agent and PA also followed behind, eyeing everyone. Still, Emma saw cameras pressed up against the windows, the paparazzi snapping photos of Dylan and his entourage as they moved along the corridors with Richard Jacoby, the hospital administrator, and a few other ranking hospital officials.

Mr. Jacoby stopped at a double-wide door and turned to their small group. "The children are excited to meet you, Dylan. We've gathered our recovering patients here, in the doctor's lounge. And later, we'll go up to see the other children who are still in treatment."

Emma assumed that he was talking about the kids who couldn't make it out of bed. Her heart lurched and she braced herself for what was to come.

"Afterward, we'll shoot your promo spot with Beth and Pauly."

"Sounds good to me," Dylan said.

"We had a little movie premiere of *His Rookie Year* last night for everyone to get acquainted with who you are. Most of them already knew of you. Eddie Renquist was quite a character."

The rated-G movie hadn't won Dylan any awards, but he'd garnered a whole new audience of youngsters with that role. It was on Emma's Top Ten Favorite list.

"After you," Mr. Jacoby said, and they entered a large room filled with kids of all ages, sitting on grown-up chairs, their eyes as big as the smiles on their faces. They began waving at Dylan. With Emma at his side, he made his way over and spoke to each child. The younger boys called him Eddie and asked him all about baseball, as if he really was a star athlete like his character in the film. Dylan was quite knowledgeable actually and always reminded them he was only acting out a role. Some of them got it, others weren't quite sure. The girls were all over the map, the teens telling him he was hot and they loved him, while the younger ones wanted to shake his hand or give him a hug.

Dylan wasn't stingy with his hugs. He gave them freely and laughed with the kids, shook hands and recited lines from his movies when asked. Some of the kids with shaved heads had peach fuzz growing. They were the lucky ones, the ones who would eventually go home to live normal lives. Some wore back braces or leg casts; others were in wheelchairs. But all in all, every one of them reacted positively to Dylan. He was good with them and managed to bring Emma into the conversation often.

"This is my friend Emma. She plans parties and knows a lot about everything," he said.

"Have you ever planned a Cinderella party?" one of the younger girls asked.

"Well, of course. Cinderella and Belle and Ariel are friends of mine," she said.

A cluster of little girls surrounded her and asked her dozens of questions.

Dylan caught her eye and nodded as he continued to make his way around the room. Once Dylan had greeted every single child, he came to stand at the front of the room and asked if they would like to sing a few songs. "Emma has a great voice and knows lots of songs."

It wasn't exactly out of her wheelhouse to entertain children, but this had come out of the blue. "Oh, of course. We can do that." She jumped right in.

She led them in Taylor Swift and Katy Perry songs as well as a song from *Frozen*, for the little ones, and then Mr. Jacoby signaled to her that their time was up. Dylan walked over to his personal assistant and she handed him a packet of cards.

"Thanks for giving me a chance to meet you all," he said to the kids. "I'm going to come around the room again one more time and hand out movie passes for you and your families."

And afterward, they were whisked away, riding up in the elevator to the third floor where the really ill children lay in beds. What really struck Emma was how happy all the children seemed to be, despite the bald heads, wires and tubes going through them, limbs in casts and machines humming. Experiencing their unqualified acceptance and genuine gladness to see them was as heartwarming as it was heartbreaking. Emma sent up silent prayers for all of them, wishing that affliction wouldn't strike ones so young. But their spirit was amazing and many adults, including her, could learn from their sense of joy and gratefulness.

Dylan treated these kids in the same way he had the others. No pity shone in his eyes; instead, there was a sense of camaraderie and friendship. He was one with them, talking movies and baseball and family with these wonderfully unaffected children.

"It's a lot to take in," Dylan said once they were alone in the hallway.

"They're sweet kids."

"They shouldn't have to deal with this crap. They should be allowed to be kids."

This wasn't just a photo op for Dylan. "You're a softy. Who knew?"

She knew. She'd seen it firsthand and she'd learned something about Dylan today. His compassion for the less fortunate was astounding.

"Shh. You don't want to wreck my image, do you?" He grinned.

"Heavens, not me."

His agent and PA called him away, and he excused himself. When he returned, he was frowning. "The little boy Pauly who was to do the shoot with us had a setback. He's not healthy enough to do the promo spot right now. They're giving me the option to do it with only Beth or to pick another child, or I can wait for Pauly. The camera crew is all here, everything's set up, but here's the thing. Pauly was really looking forward to this. They tell me it's all he's talked about all week." Dylan ran a hand down his face. "What do you think?"

He was asking her advice? She didn't know about the technical nature of this business or the cost involved, but she had only one answer for Dylan. "I'd wait for Pauly. It might make the difference in his recovery, if he has this to look forward to."

Dylan smiled wide, his eyes locking to hers in relief. "That's what I was thinking, too." He leaned over and kissed her cheek. "Thanks."

He turned away before he could take in her shocked expression. He'd kissed her again.

It had to be the surroundings, the children, the good that he'd done today to brighten lives here at Children's West Hospital, and that's all Emma would read into it.

When they walked out of the hospital a short time later, the press vultures were waiting, snapping pictures and shooting questions at him from behind a roped-off line. She stood in the background with Darren and Rochelle, noting how perfectly Dylan handled the situation, stopping them with a hand up. "I'll make a brief statement. As you can see, I'm doing well and recovering. I'll be back to work very soon, but today is not about me. It's about the wonderful work this hospital is doing for the children. The doctors and staff here are dedicated and so willing to give of themselves. We're hoping to shine a light on Children's West Hospital today. Visit their website to see how you can help these brave children. Thank you."

With that, Dylan ushered Emma into the limo and it sped off before she could get her seat belt on.

"Whoa," he said, and for the first time today, she glimpsed beads of sweat on his brow.

"Dylan, are you okay?"

He sank down, shrugged into his seat belt and tossed his head against the headrest. "I've been better."

"Dizzy spell?" She clamped her own seat belt on.

"Nope, it's just a little bit...crazy, isn't it? I'm not feeling myself just yet."

"That's understandable, Dylan. You've been through a lot. But you handled them like a pro."

He turned to her, shaking his head. "Maybe I should've kept you out of it. Your picture might just make the front page of some of those rags."

"I did hear several questions shouted about the redhead." A giggle sounding more like a hiccup escaped her mouth. She'd lived in Los Angeles long enough to know how desperate the paparazzi could be. "I noticed you ignored those."

"Think they'd believe me if I said you were a friend of the family? Not on your life. Let 'em guess."

"Yeah, let them guess." Bet they'd never guess she'd been the one-night stand Dylan McKay had no memory of. Now, that was a story for the tabloids.

"Thank you for coming with me today. It made a difference having you here."

She was his surrogate sister. She didn't mind. Not today.

"You know, I'm glad I came, too, and if I helped you in the process, that's a bonus."

"You did." Dylan leaned over, gave her a sweet kiss that seemed to linger on her lips, then retreated to his seat and closed his eyes. "Thanks."

She was pretty sure surrogate sisters didn't get kisses like that.

In fact, she didn't remember much about his kisses at all.

And that stumped her. A man like Dylan…well, a girl shouldn't forget something like that, drunk on mojitos and in a blackout or not.

The Montalvo party went off without a hitch, except for one boisterous guest who'd gotten smashed on martinis and fallen off the top tier of the multilevel grounds. Luckily for him, it was only a five-foot drop and he'd fallen on a shelf of border boxwoods that pinched like the dickens but broke his fall and prevented major damage. After causing a momentary ruckus, the man sobered up real fast, skulked off like a pup with his tail between his legs, and the party picked up again from there.

Emma was proud of the display they'd put on for the fifties party and their company was hired on the spot by a theatre producer in attendance to host a similar event. It had been a win-win night.

She'd worked her butt off these past few weeks. Brooke had her head in the clouds after her date with Royce and they'd seen each other three times since. Emma didn't mind picking up the slack, except that she'd been extremely tired and with her resistance down she managed to catch Brooke's cold. Now both of them weren't feeling well. But while Brooke had only sniffles and sneezes, Emma had an upset stomach, as well. She couldn't look at food for days and even now the thought of eating anything but a piece of fruit made her tummy grumble. And the big golf tournament event was in just four days.

"Emma, get your ducks in a row," she muttered. She lay on her bed praying for strength. A commercial for a big sloppy hamburger came on the television screen and she didn't turn her head away in time. "Oh, God." Her stomach soured instantly and her legs tangled in the sheets as she fumbled from bed and raced to the bathroom. She landed on her knees and made it to the toilet just as her stomach contracted.

Wonderful…just wonderful. After she flushed the toilet she sat back on her knees. The little energy she'd had this morning had seeped out of her. But the flu bug would not get her down. She wouldn't miss their big charity event coming up. She grasped the bathroom counter for support and lifted herself up. Her head spun for a second, until finally her eyes focused and she mustered every ounce of strength to stay upright.

"Okay, Emma," she whispered. "You can do this."

Carefully, she stepped away from the sink. The merry-go-round in her head was gone. *Thank you, Flu Gods.* But just a second later gripping pain attacked her stomach. "Oh." She held her belly and flew toward the toilet again. Sinking down onto the floor, she emptied everything into the porcelain bowl, until there was nothing left.

An hour later, after managing to climb her way back into bed, her body shaking, her bones weak, she clutched her cell and pushed Brooke's number. "Hi," she whispered.

"What's wrong?"

Brooke knew her so well.

"I'm down, Brooke. Can't make it out of bed right now. The flu."

"Oh, Em. I'm so sorry. I got you sick and now you're getting the brunt of it. You sound terrible."

"My stomach's finally eased off, but it wasn't pretty an

hour ago. I'm so…tired. I'm gonna try to make it into the office later today."

"No, you're not. You need to stay in bed all day and rest. I've got things handled here. You know we've been right on schedule with this charity event. I just have a few last-minute things to take care of. You rest up and get better so you can make it on Friday."

"Okay, I think you're right."

"Sleep. It's the best thing for you."

"Thanks, and, Brooke, no way am I missing this weekend."

"I'll come over later and bring you some soup."

"Ugh, no. Just the thought of food right now turns my stomach."

"All right. I'll call you later."

When the call ended, Emma turned her head into her pillow, closed her eyes and slept the entire day. She woke up bathed in a stream of dim light coming from the night-light on the opposite wall. She blinked herself awake. Outside, darkness had descended, but she was safe, protected. Since the night of the blackout, she kept night-lights on day and night in her apartment to keep from ever being alone in total darkness. She also now had an entire bedroom shelf devoted to pillar candles, scented and unscented. It didn't matter, as long as they did the trick. She took them with her when she traveled, too, just in case, and had also started carrying a mini flashlight in her purse. Not that she couldn't use her cell phone—someone had turned her onto a flashlight app, which came in handy—but cell phone batteries died on occasion and she couldn't chance it.

A look at her cell phone now revealed that it was seven twenty-five. Wow, she'd slept for nine hours. Funny, but she didn't feel rested at all. Or hungry. Just the thought of food made her queasy all over again.

Brooke called and they spoke for half an hour, going

over the final details of the golf event, the dinner, dancing, silent auction and raffle. At two thousand dollars a head and with an expected one hundred fifty guests in attendance, there were lots of fine points to check on.

"I'll see you tomorrow, Brooke," Emma said, feeling optimistic as she hung up the phone. Her stomach had eased back to normal and she figured she'd been through the worst of it.

By the morning of the next day, she knew that she'd figured wrong. She emptied her stomach twice before it settled down. She managed to go into the office, but once Brooke took a look at her pasty face, she ordered her back to bed. Emma didn't have the strength to argue.

By Thursday morning, nothing had changed. She spent the morning in the bathroom next to her new best friend. Suspicions were running rampant in her head. What if she didn't have the flu? What if there was something else wrong with her? Something permanent? Something rest and hot soup wouldn't cure?

Eyes wide-open now, she fought the invading rumblings in her belly, quickly dressed and dashed to the local drugstore. Once she got back home, she peed on a stick at three different intervals of the day, only to get the same result each time. Opening her laptop, she keyed it up and researched a subject she thought would be years down the road for her.

She was as sure now as she would ever be; she had all the symptoms.

She was pregnant.

And Dylan McKay was her blackout baby's father.

Three

"You're trying to hide a smile, Brooke. You don't fool me."

"I'm not trying to fool you, Emma. I think it's kinda cool that you and my brother…"

"No, it wasn't like that, really." Oh, boy.

Having Brooke stop everything at the office and come over right away might have been a mistake. But this was big and she couldn't hide her pregnancy from her best friend. Especially not when Brooke had a stake in this, too; she was Dylan's sister after all. Emma needed her right now. She had no one else to turn to and time was running out. She had morning sickness, big-time. Immediate decisions had to be made and she'd have to deal with Dylan at some point.

"We're not romantically involved," she said to Brooke.

Her friend sat on the sofa next to her, her mouth twitching, the smile she couldn't conceal spreading wider across her face. This was no laughing matter. Obviously, Brooke thought differently.

She'd given Brooke the bare facts about what had happened that night between her and Dylan, explaining how she'd panicked when all the lights had gone out in that nightclub. The entire city had gone dark from what she could tell and she hadn't been in any shape to drive home. At least she got that part right. No drunk driving for her.

But instead of Brooke coming to pick her up as she'd hoped, Dylan had come to her rescue, as any good guy would. Emma tried to make clear to Brooke that she'd been the one to initiate the lovemaking. Emma remembered that much; she'd begged him to stay with her. She had no recollection of exactly how it all went down, those hours fuzzy in her head, but it was all on her. She'd been scared out of her wits and inebriated. And Dylan was there. She'd lived out her fantasy with him that night, but she didn't tell Brooke that. Some things were better left unsaid.

"Brooke, I'll say it again, and this is hard to admit, but I probably climbed all over him that night. I swear, he didn't take advantage of me." The worst would be that Brooke would hold anything about that night against Dylan.

Brooke covered her ears. "Emma, pleeeze! No details. I can't think of Dylan that way." And then she lowered her hands. "But it's sweet that you're trying to protect him. You don't want me to think badly of my brother. I get that, Em. And I don't. No one's to blame."

"Okay, no details." Not that she could remember any. "Dylan doesn't know any of this happened."

"Are you sure of that?"

"I'm sure. I'd know it, if he remembered. I'd see something in his eyes. And he's never mentioned my phone call that night, or the fact that he came to pick me up from the nightclub. When he came to my apartment the day we went to the children's hospital, he didn't seem to recognize anything as familiar. I'm certain that night was erased from his memory."

"I think so, too. Just making sure there were no signs."

"Nope, not a one."

Brooke nodded and then gazed warmly into Emma's eyes for several ticks of a minute. "You're going to be the mother of my niece or nephew," she said as softly as Emma had ever heard her speak. The tone was rich and thick as honey. "And my brother is going to be a father."

The way Brooke put it was sort of beautiful. Emma could get lost in all the wonder of motherhood, of nurturing a new life and having a man like Dylan father her child. But the wonder didn't come close to erasing the plain facts. That she and Dylan didn't plan this child. That he didn't even have a clue what was happening, yet his life was about to change forever.

"Oh, Brooke. I'm just wrapping my head around it. The baby part has me feeling...I don't know, protective already and scared." Emma shivered. "Very scared."

"You'll be fine. You have me. And Dylan. He'd never turn his back on you."

"Gosh, it's all so new. Part of me feels guilty not telling him about that night. It might've triggered some of his memories."

"You'll have to tell him now, Em. He has a right to know."

It was inevitable that she tell Dylan. But she wasn't looking forward to that conversation. Gosh, he'd been like a big brother to her and now nothing between them would ever be the same.

"I know. I will."

"Good. You're in no shape to do the golf event, Em. You're exhausted and still having morning sickness."

Emma chewed on her bottom lip. She didn't want to miss this weekend. All those hours, all that planning. Brooke needed her, but how could she function when she was running to the bathroom all morning long? "Yes, but it's getting better. Maybe I could come along and help out in the afternoon and evening."

Brooke was shaking her head. When had she turned into a mama bear? "I've got it covered, Emma. You can't come. You'd be miserable. I've got Rocky and Wendy on standby."

The part-timers?

"I've been briefing them and they're up for the task. I don't want you to worry about a thing. You should concentrate on the baby and feeling better. We'll do fine."

"Are you saying you don't need me?"

"I'm saying, we'll make do without you, but of course, we'll miss you. Thanks to your unending efficiency, we've got all the bases covered. You should take this weekend to adjust to all of this. That's what I want for you. It's what you need."

Emma sighed and gave her friend a reluctant nod. Brooke was right. She couldn't very well carry out her duties in San Diego with her stomach on the blink every hour and her body feeling as though it had been hit by an eighteen-wheeler. "Okay, I'll be a good girl."

"It's too late for that," Brooke replied with a grin.

"Don't I know it."

Brooke's eyes melted in apology. "You're not letting anyone down, Emma. Just the opposite. I know the situation isn't ideal right now, but you're having a baby with Dylan. My best friend and my brother...how can I not think it's just a little bit wonderful?"

Brooke's arms came around her and the hug warmed all the frigid ice flowing through her veins. She was wrapped up in comfort and support and friendship. "How come you always know the right thing to say?"

"Since when?"

"Since...now."

"Oh, Emma. Do you want me to be there when you tell Dylan?"

"No!" Emma pulled away from her friend. The thought of having that conversation gave her hives, but having Dylan's baby sister there? There was no number on the Awkward Scale high enough to describe such a scene. "It'd be too weird. I can't even picture any of this in my head right now, but I suspect this is one time I need to be alone with Dylan."

The tight lines on Brooke's face crumbled and her expression resumed some semblance of normalcy. "Whew, thanks. I have to agree. I love my bro and I love you, but…"

"But I made my bed, now I have to toss off the tangled sheets and come clean."

"Yeah," Brooke said, giving her that same melting look. "Something like that, sweetie."

"Promise you won't worry about me this weekend?"

"If you promise me the same. Don't give a thought to the golf event."

They stared at each other, knowing unequivocally that would be impossible.

"Sure," Emma said.

"Gotcha," Brooke added, her smile falsely quick. Then Brooke kissed her goodbye on the cheek and brought her mouth near her ear to whisper, "The sooner you tell Dylan, the better."

"I know," she said, nodding. "I will."

Problem number one: she didn't have a clue *how* or *when* she could bring herself to do that.

"A little bit of fresh air will do wonders for you, Emma," Dylan said as he strolled into her apartment wearing jeans and a vintage T-shirt, the Stones logo stretching wide across his chest. The shirt hugged him tight and hinted at a ripped torso underneath. Before she got caught ogling, she shifted her attention to his face and was struck by the scruffy, tousled look that appealed to her on so many levels, it was ridiculous. "Brooke is worried sick about you."

Emma had had about half an hour advance warning from Dylan that he was coming to visit her, his text announcing he was on the way, leaving her no option. He was on a mission, commandeered by Brooke, no doubt, and Emma had raced around her apartment destroying evidence of just how sick she'd been. She'd picked up blankets tossed across the sofa and folded them, sprayed the room with cinnamon spice air freshener—the place now smelled like Christmas—slipped off her smelly sweats, taken a shower and put on a sleeveless denim dress and a pair of tan boots.

Evenings were her best time of day lately, so she was pretty sure that she could pull off seeing him without doing a sprint to the bathroom. "I'm feeling much better, Dylan. There's no need for you to be here. Gosh, you must have better things to do on a Friday night."

He smiled her way, that megawatt lady-killer smile that either slowed breathing or caused it to race. Right now, her breath caught in her throat and she reminded herself to breathe. He was just a man.

And the father of your baby.

"Nope, no plans. And since I'm already here, I was hoping not to eat alone tonight. Come back to the house with me. Maisey's made an amazing meal. We can eat on the patio. It's a gorgeous night."

God, getting some fresh Moonlight Beach air did sound appealing. She'd been stuck in her house for eons, it seemed.

Her hesitation wasn't lost on him. He eyed her carefully, taking a quick toll of her state of health. She didn't want to seem ungrateful for the gesture although she knew he was here solely at Brooke's bidding.

"Brooke says you haven't been eating. You need a good meal, Em."

She did, and her traitorous stomach growled quietly, but he didn't appear to notice, thank goodness. "I don't know."

"You want to. Come for an hour or two."

It was hard to refuse, with the look in those beautifully clear sky-blue eyes. When aimed at her, she usually succumbed. It had always been that way. What could she say? She, like a zillion other adoring fans, had it bad for Dylan McKay. And she knew darn well, he wouldn't be here if it weren't for Brooke's nagging. She wouldn't get off his case if he didn't succeed in making sure Emma was well cared for tonight.

Why had Brooke put her in this position? As sweet as it was, she wasn't anyone's charity case. She hadn't been for a long time, and she wasn't ever going back there. She'd learned to fend for herself since her foster care days and didn't want to be thought of as an obligation in order to ease anyone's conscience. She had a mind to refuse him flat, but those bone-melting eyes kept a vigil on her and a look of hope spread across his face.

"Well, maybe just for a little while, but only to get you off the hook with Brooke."

Gesturing in his own defense, he turned his palms up. "I don't know what you mean. This was my idea."

She snorted. "And the sun doesn't shine in LA."

Glancing out the window at the dimming skies, he grinned. "It isn't at the moment."

Okay, she could share a meal with him. She didn't have to tell him the truth. Not yet. She wasn't ready for that, and this way, he'd report back to Brooke that all was well and she'd have the rest of the weekend in peace. "I'll get my jacket, then."

He nodded, looking ridiculously satisfied.

A few minutes later, they were barreling down Pacific

Coast Highway in his licorice-black SUV, the windows down and warm spring breezes lifting her hair. Dylan, recently cleared to drive again, was concentrating on the road, and she took a second to gaze at his profile. He had classic good looks: a solid jawline, a strong chin, a nose that was just sharp enough to suit his face and eyes the color of Hawaiian waters, deep blue with a hint of turquoise. His hair was streaked by the sun, a little long right now so that it swept over his ears. Most times he wore it combed back away from his face, but there were these locks that always loosened from the pack to dip onto his forehead that drove her crazy.

Would their child have his hair? His eyes?

Or would the baby look more like her? Green-eyed with dark cranberry tresses?

Her stomach squeezed tight thinking of the secret life inside her, growing and thriving despite her frequent bouts of nausea. She really did need a nourishing meal and Maisey's cooking was too good to turn down.

"Here we are." Dylan pulled into the gated circular driveway of his beach home. There were times she couldn't believe this was all his. He'd grown up in a normal American household, the son of a high school principal and a civil engineer. Dylan's dad had died one year before he was due to retire, but Markus McKay had lived a full and happy life. The love he'd had for his wife and family, the life they'd led filled with generosity and kindness, had restored Emma's faith in mankind.

Once he parked in the multicar garage on the property, Dylan made an attempt to wind around the car to open the door for her, but she was too quick. She stepped out on her own, ignoring how his smile faded as she strode past him toward the service door that led into his house. "Hey, Sparky, wait up," he said, coming to stand beside her.

He unlocked the door and opened it for her. She took

a step to enter, just as his arm shot out, blocking her way in. Suddenly, surprisingly, she was trapped between his body and the door. Trapped by the compelling scent of him. Several beats ticked away and then she lifted her lids and locked onto his gaze.

"Do me a favor," he said softly, the fingers of his free hand coming to rest under her chin. His innocent touch kicked her senses into high gear. He didn't wait for her answer, but continued, "Don't pretend you're completely recovered just to prove a point. I see how tired you are. Your face is pale, and you've obviously lost weight."

He'd hit the nail on the head. The shudder that erupted inside probably wasn't visible on the outside, but boy, oh boy, how it rattled her all the way down to her toes. His noticing her body was shock enough, but noticing how bad she looked brought new meaning to her humiliation. What next? Would he point out her warts and moles, too?

"I've been around the theatre long enough to know an act when I see one. All I'm asking is for you to relax tonight, eat a delicious dinner and have a good time. You don't have to pretend with me. Just be yourself."

As he lowered his arm allowing her to pass, Emma blurted, "Yes, Dr. Dylan. Will do." All she needed now to accompany the nod she gave him was a military salute.

His eyebrows lifted at her sarcasm. "Your mouth… sometimes I want to—" And then he leaned in before she could grasp his intention and brushed a soft kiss to her lips.

She gasped, raking in air, but quickly recovered. "Shut me up?"

He shook his head, chuckling. "That's one way to put it. But I was thinking of it more as a way to sweeten the sass blistering your tongue."

Well, he'd shut her up *and* sweetened her mouth with one tiny kiss. Dylan could get away with things like that. He'd been gifted with an accommodating good nature that charmed any woman in his path. She'd seen it over and over again. His reputation with the ladies had been mulled over, talked about and dissected by the media. Magazine covers, television interviews and social media platforms had him figured out. He wasn't one to be tied down, but he'd gotten away with it with the press, because he never infringed. He'd been crowned a one-woman kind of man, and the woman he was currently dating received all of his attention. A smart move on his behalf, it kept him out of trouble.

And all it had taken was a power outage burdening most of the city one night to shake his very well-protected reputation. Only, he didn't know that yet.

Oh, boy, when Emma did things, she did them all the way.

The minute they entered his luxurious home, Dylan went about opening the massive beveled glass French doors in the living room. Balmy breezes immediately rushed in bringing scents of salty sea air and powdery sands. Emma followed him into the kitchen, where he opened the doors leading to the Italian-stone-and-marble patio deck. Succulents and vines grew vertically up one wall in a landscaping masterpiece Dylan had recently commissioned, adding just the right touch of greenery to the outdoor landing. Patio tables and a cozy set of lounge furniture were strategically placed around a stone fire pit to allow the best views of the Pacific.

"Want to have a seat out here?" he asked. "I'll heat up the food Maisey left for us and you can soak up some fresh air."

She'd rather do something with her hands than sit outside. Alone. In the dark. "No, thanks, I'll help you."

"Suit yourself. But I can handle it. I give Maisey the weekends off usually."

"You mean you cook for yourself?"

He smiled as he walked over to the double-door cabinet refrigerator and grabbed a covered dish. "Unless Maisey takes pity on me and leaves me something wonderful like this chicken piccata, I've been known to throw a meal together." He set the dish down and opened the oven door.

"Impressive," she said.

"I can also wash a dish and toss dirty clothes in the washing machine, too."

He gestured and she grabbed a casserole dish of rice pilaf from the fridge and handed it to him. Into the oven it went, right next to the chicken. A basket of bread, something garlicky with bits of sun-dried tomatoes, was nestled on the onyx counter next to a tray of homemade chocolate chip cookies. All the combined scents should make her queasy, but she found them actually whetting her appetite. She was hungrier than she'd been in a week. "Such skills. I'm impressed."

Once the meal was set to reheating, Dylan leaned against the granite island, folding his arms across his torso, and pinned her down with those baby blues. "You're forgetting how I grew up. Mom and Dad expected us to do everyday chores, just as they did. I washed cars, cooked meals, did laundry, made beds, and good God, I even scrubbed toilets."

"I bet you don't anymore."

He shrugged and slid her a crooked grin. "Not if I can help it."

Thinking about her recent toilet incidents, she didn't blame him. "Your mom and dad were wonderful people. They taught you well."

"Yeah, but at the time I didn't think so. I did more work than any of my friends. Before I could go out and play ball, I had a list of chores to get through. Weekends were especially gruesome."

"They were building character."

"Yeah, now I play characters on the screen."

"And you still wash dishes and make your own meals. The last conversation I had with your mom, she told me how proud she was of you."

"She is now, but when I left college in my sophomore year to pursue an acting career, my folks were both pretty bummed. Especially my dad. He had high hopes of me going to medical school. He lost his chance at being a doctor and tossed all of his hopes and guilt onto me. He wanted to be a pediatrician." He made a noisy sigh and scrubbed at the dark blond stubble on his chin. "I guess I really disappointed him when I ran away with Renee."

Renee had been no good for Dylan. Emma had heard that a zillion times from Brooke and Dylan's folks. Emma hadn't been too happy with her, either. At the tender age of fourteen, Emma's heart had been crushed when Dylan had fallen in love with a cheerleading beauty who'd convinced him he could make it big in the movies. She had connections. She could get him in to see all the right people.

"Maybe it wasn't in the cards for you to be a doctor. Your dad lived long enough to see your success. He had to know you made the right decision for yourself."

"Dad didn't think I knew what I was doing. And maybe I didn't. Renee was my first girlfriend and I was crazy about her." He pumped his shoulders a couple of times, hopelessly, and something faint and hidden entered his eyes. "But enough about ancient history. How about a soda?" He opened the fridge again. "Lemonade? Wine or beer? Anything else? Maisey keeps the fridge pretty stocked."

"Water sounds good." It was safe. She couldn't trust her stomach right now, and even before she'd found out about the baby, she'd given up alcohol.

He handed her one of those cobalt blue water bottles

that cost more than a glass of fine wine and then plucked out an Indian Brown Ale for himself. His throat moved as he tipped the bottle to his lips and took a swig. She looked away instantly. She was never one to hide her emotions and the last thing she needed was to have Dylan catch her eyeing him.

They'd had their one night. Unfortunately neither of them remembered it.

Dylan's cell phone rang out the theme song to his latest action flick. How many people actually had their very own ringtone? He grabbed it off the counter and frowned at the screen. "Sorry, Emma. I have to get this. I'll make it quick. It's the head of the studio."

"Go right ahead. I'm fine right here." She gestured for him to take the call.

He nodded, his eyes sparkling with gratitude as he walked out of the room, the cell to his ear. Emma grabbed the salad from the refrigerator, set it on the granite island and then scrounged through drawers to find tongs. Coming up with a pair, she leaned against the counter as Dylan's voice drifted to her ears.

"It's Callista's thirtieth birthday? Yeah, I think she'd love a party. Up at your house?"

And then after a long pause, "I'll do my best to be there, Maury. Yes, yes, I'm recovering nicely, thank you. I'm back at work on Monday. Thanks for the call. See you soon."

He walked back into the kitchen, frowning and running a hand down his face. "Sorry," he said. "Business crap."

"Sounds like Callista's having a party." She tilted her head. "Sorry, I overheard."

"Yeah, she's turning thirty. Maury likes to remind me he's not getting any younger. He expects me to be there." Dylan sighed.

Maury Allen had power and influence. That much, Emma knew. According to Brooke, he'd been pushing for

Dylan to make a commitment to his daughter, but so far, Dylan had resisted. Their relationship had been on and off for three years. "And you don't want to go?"

Dylan leaned back against the counter, picking up his beer. "Maury's been good to me. Gave me my first break. I sort of owe him my loyalty. If he wants me at his daughter's birthday celebration, I'll go."

Dylan McKay and Callista Lee Allen made a gorgeous couple. Whenever they were together, there were headlines. To all the world they probably seemed like a perfect match.

Which made Emma's predicament suddenly jump to the forefront of her thoughts and curdle her stomach. She was feeling a little weak-kneed anyway and needed to sit down.

Dylan's hand came to her elbow and his eyes locked onto hers. "Emma, are you okay? You're looking pale. I need to get food into you. Come, sit down."

Why was he always touching her? She had enough to deal with right now, without getting all fan crazy over Dylan's slightest brotherly touch. "Okay, maybe I should sit."

He guided her to the outside patio table closest to the kitchen. "Wait here. I'll get some plates and bring out the food."

She sat, dumbfounded by her fatigue, and stared straight out to sea. The waves gently rolled onto the shore, and stars above lit the sky as low-lying fixtures surrounding the deck gave off soothing light. Fresh scents from the vertical garden on her right drifted to her nose and the whole effect made her feel somewhat better.

Emma wasn't a wilting flower. Nothing much rattled her, well, except being alone in complete darkness. Overall, considering her lousy childhood, she'd fended well in the world, but this whole Dylan thing—secretly carrying his child, losing her cookies every morning and not holding up her end with Parties-To-Go—overwhelmed her. The walls were closing in from all directions and right now her body wasn't up for the fight.

Dylan came back loaded down with food and went about serving her as if she was the Queen of England. Then he offered her the tan suede jacket she'd brought from home. "It's getting a little cool out here," he said.

She nodded and he helped her put her arms through the sleeves. "There you go. Better?"

She nodded. The jacket fit her snugly. She wondered how much longer she could wear it and then, just like that, tears welled in her eyes. Her mouth began to quiver.

It had to be hormones.

Dylan didn't seem to notice. He was too busy making sure she had everything she needed at the table. "Eat up, Emma."

He finally sat and they both picked up their forks. The food was delicious and she managed to eat half of everything on her plate. An accomplishment, considering she hadn't eaten this much in days.

"You're not worried about your girlish figure, are you?" he asked, eyeing her plate. His grin and the twinkle in his eyes were right on par for Dylan.

"Should I be?"

His lids lowered as he slowly raked his gaze over her body. "Not from where I'm sitting."

She had no comeback. He'd once touched every inch of her and seemed to have no complaints that she could remember.

She managed a smile, though suddenly her energy waned. "The food was amazing. I feel full and satisfied," she fibbed. Actually, she wasn't feeling so great. "Please be sure to thank Maisey for me."

"I will."

"Dylan?"

"Hmm?"

"I'm really exhausted. Would you mind taking me home?"

He hesitated and something that resembled regret flickered in his eyes. "Sure…if that's what you want."

"It is." She rose and pushed back her chair. Before she could take a step, heat washed up and over her, spinning circles inside her head. Her legs buckled and soon she was falling, falling.

And then Dylan's arms were around her, easing her to the ground. "Emma!"

A sharp pat to the face snapped her eyes open. She'd been slapped.

"Emma, thank God. You fainted."

Her head felt light and she saw two Dylans leaning over her on bent knee. "I did?"

"Yeah, you were out for a few seconds. I'm going to get you inside and call 911."

"No, no!" His words were enough to rouse her and refocus her eyes. "I don't need the paramedics."

"You do, honey. You've been sick for days now. You should see a doctor." The resolve in his voice frightened her. This was going sideways fast.

"No, no. I'm not sick."

"Something's wrong with you, Emma. I have to get you help."

"Dylan, no." She gazed into his worried face. "I know what's wrong. I'm not sick."

"You're not?"

She shook her head. "No, I'm not. I'm…pregnant."

Four

"Pregnant?" Had he heard Emma right? He didn't know she'd been seeing anyone. He softened his voice, attempting to keep his surprise concealed. "You're pregnant, Em?"

She nodded, chewing on her lower lip, her eyes down.

Where was the guy? Did he bail on her? And why did he feel sharp pangs in his gut consisting of an emotion he refused to name? "Are you sure?"

"Yes," she whispered, still averting her eyes.

It seemed that she hadn't come to grips with it yet. Softly, he brushed fallen locks off her forehead, the tendrils flowing through his fingers like silk, which brought her pretty green eyes up to his. "Well, damn."

She swallowed.

"Is it okay for me to lift you up now?"

He was holding the top half of her body off the ground. Another few inches and she would've landed hard on stone.

"I think so. I'm not dizzy anymore."

He knew something about getting dizzy. Luckily, that

hadn't happened to him for days now. "Okay, slowly," he said.

He brought his face close to hers, breathing in a sweet scent that reminded him of lavender. God, he liked her. There was something sweet and real about Emma Bloom. She'd spent a lot of time in the McKay household while growing up and he'd always looked upon her as a second little sister. But now he wasn't altogether sure why he felt so close to her. Or why, whenever given a chance, he chose to kiss her. It was almost second nature with him lately, holding Emma and kissing her.

Gathering her in his arms, he guided her up, keeping her body pressed close to his. Her breasts crushed his chest and he tried not to think about how soft and supple they felt. Once they were upright, he kept his hold on her. "Do you think you can stand on your own?"

"Yes, I think so."

"I won't let go of you completely. I'll hold on to your waist, okay?"

She nodded. Color had come back to her face. It wasn't rosy, but she didn't look like a sheet, either, so that was a good thing.

She was unusually quiet and there was a stark look on her face. Stronger breezes had kicked up on the patio and it was getting chilly. "Let's go inside."

He stood beside her now, wrapping an arm around her slender waist. "I've got you." Shoulder to shoulder, they took small steps. They bypassed the kitchen and moved into the larger living room. Dylan stopped at his buttery leather couch, the most comfortable seat in the house, and helped her sit down. Her silence unnerved him. Was she embarrassed, scared, regretful? Hell, he didn't know what to say to her when she was like this.

"Thank you," she mumbled.

"You're sure you're okay?"

"I'm feeling better, Dylan.

"You really should see a doctor."

She looked down at the hands she'd folded in her lap. So unlike Emma. "I plan to."

"Does Brooke know?"

She nodded. "I told her just recently."

"I don't mean to pry, but what about the baby's father? Does he know?"

She shook her head. "Not yet."

Dylan didn't want to stick his nose into her business, but Emma hadn't led a charmed life. The kid didn't deserve to go through this alone. Dylan wasn't good with stuff like this, but she was here and had fainted in front of him. With Brooke gone for a few more days, Dylan had to step in. "I'm not taking you home until I'm sure you're feeling better."

"Dr. Dylan," she said, her lips quirking up. Signs of the real Emma Rae Bloom were emerging.

"Your friend Dylan."

She looked away.

"Let me get you some water. Hang on."

He left the room, and when he returned with a glass, Emma's eyes were closed, but there was no peace on her face. He sat down beside her quietly and put the glass in her hand.

She turned to him then and whispered, "Dylan...I need to talk to you."

"Sure. Okay. I'm listening."

Her chest heaved as she filled her lungs, as if readying for a marathon. And then she began. "You know how I was raised. My foster parents weren't very attentive, but they gave me a home. They fed me and I had clothes on my back."

They were reckless and selfish bastards. Heavy drinkers. But Dylan wouldn't say that.

She sipped water, probably needing fortification, then went on. "I was about ten when Doris and Burt went out to the local English pub one night. You might remember the one on Birch Street."

He nodded. "Darts and hard ales. I remember."

She gave him a quick smile. They had the same roots. Only, hers were laden with weeds instead of the pretty poppies little girls deserved.

"They'd put me to bed early that night and told me to stay there," she continued. "I knew they probably wouldn't come home until very late. What I didn't know was that the electricity had been turned off that day. They hadn't paid their electric bill, so when a bad storm hit that night I trembled every time there was thunder. And the erratic lightning really freaked me out. None of the lights in my room were working. I remember how black it was. And there were noises. Crazy, scary noises, shutters flapping against the house, wind howling, shrubs brushing against the outer walls sounding like devilish whispers. I ran downstairs, clicking as many light switches as I could find. Nothing worked. And then I remembered Burt kept a flashlight in a little storage closet under the stairs. S-somehow... s-somehow...as I climbed into that space, a gust of wind or something...slammed the door shut behind me. I was locked in that tiny dark space all night."

"Oh, man, Emma," Dylan said, taking her hand and giving it a squeeze. Her face was stone cold, as if reliving this memory had frozen her up inside. He could only imagine her terror that night. He had no clue what this had to do with her pregnancy, but he listened. Maybe she needed to get this off her chest. She could use him to unburden herself if that's what it took.

"It was the longest night of my life. I sobbed and sobbed most of the night, quietly, though, in case those devilish sounds materialized into something evil. My folks finally came home. It was almost dawn when they found me cowering in that closet. They told me everything was all right and that I'd be okay. Only, I wasn't okay. From then on, being in dark places has always screwed with my head."

"It's understandable that you get frightened. Those memories must be horrible for you."

Her lips tightened as she bobbed her head up and down.

He waited for more. A moment later, her sad eyes lifted to his. "Flash forward about sixteen years. It was the night of the blackout…my neighbor Eddie was having a big birthday bash on the Sunset Strip. It was one round of drinks after another. For the first time in my life, I indulged. In a big way. My friends kept my glass refilled until I was feeling no pain. My fuzzy head went on the blink, and unfortunately so did the lights. Before I knew what was happening, the entire club went black. I couldn't see a thing out the windows, either. Then I heard the rain. It wasn't a downpour, but it didn't have to be, just the steady pounding on the roof was enough. I freaked and began trembling uncontrollably. Luckily, I had Brooke on autodial, or I wouldn't have had the coordination to make the call. I couldn't reach her… She didn't answer."

Dylan leaned in, nodding his head. "Go on, Em. Then what did you do?"

Her eyes squeezed shut. This was hard on Emma but it was probably good for her to purge this memory. "When I couldn't reach your sister, I panicked and gave my phone to someone sitting on the floor next to me." She shook her head and took a deep breath. "My friend punched in your number."

"My number?" he repeated, and his forehead wrinkled as he scoured his memory for an inkling of recollection. Nothing came to mind.

"Yes… I…I thought Brooke might be with you."

His mind was a blank wall when it came to those days. "I don't remember."

Her eyes watered and she gave him half a smile, one of those unhappy smiles that tussled with his heart. "I was so scared."

"I'm sorry."

"Don't be. You came to rescue me. I just remember thinking *Dylan will come*. If he says he will come, he will come. He'll get me out of here. I couldn't wait to get out of that place."

He could've caught flies when his mouth dropped open and stayed that way. "What happened next?" And why didn't she tell him this before? She knew he was trying to piece together those lost hours before the blast.

"It's fuzzy, but I remember you finding me in the dark and carrying me out of there. You drove me home and… and…"

She gazed into his eyes then, and it hit him with dazzling clarity. He blinked rapidly several times. "You're not saying…"

She hadn't said anything yet. But a knot formed in the pit of his stomach. And he knew what she was going to say, not because he remembered it, but because she'd given him the full picture of her life leading up to that moment. And he was cast in the starring role.

"I wouldn't let you leave, Dylan." Her head down, she began shaking it. "I begged you to stay with me. I was scared out of my wits. The whole city was pitch-black and you knew I would freak out if you left me, so you agreed, and then…we, uh…"

"We made love?" He couldn't believe he was asking Emma, his little sister's friend, this question. Emma, the efficient one. The one always in control, the one who never took risks, never strayed from the straight-and-narrow path. Emma Rae Bloom. He'd bedded her?

Her eyes were filling with unshed tears. "It was my fault."

He winced. The entire script was now playing in his head. Emma had been intoxicated and scared and he'd come to her rescue and then seduced her. Crap.

He rubbed a finger over his eye. "I'm sure it wasn't."

"I wouldn't let you leave. I pleaded with you to stay with me. You kept saying something like *You've got it all wrong*, or *This is wrong*, but because of my fear and the alcohol I wouldn't listen. I just needed…you."

"I don't remember a thing, honey. I don't. So, you're sure…" Hell, what a creep he was, about to ask her if she was sure the baby was his. If it was anyone but Emma, he would ask that question. And demand proof. But Emma wouldn't lie. She wouldn't try to pull a fast one on him. Her story made sense. He wouldn't have left her to fend for herself that night. If she was in trouble, he would've gone to get her himself. But he thought he would've drawn the line at taking advantage of a frightened friend, tempting as she might have been. Damn it all.

Maybe his subconscious had known all along he'd been with Emma. Maybe that explained the reason behind his recent attraction to her. He'd always thought of her as off-limits, but after the accident, things between them seemed to change.

He kept his voice soft. "You're sure that you're pregnant?"

"I mean, I haven't seen a doctor yet, but the tests were all positive."

"How many did you take?"

She glanced away. "Seven."

"Ah, just to be sure."

"Yeah."

Dylan heaved a sigh. He realized his first words to her would have great impact, so he treaded carefully. But hell, he was stunned. And clueless about that night. He ran a hand through his hair and then mustered a smile. "Okay."

"Okay?"

"Yeah. I don't have any answers now, Emma. But you're not alone in this. I'm here. And we'll figure it out together."

He knew damn well he'd have to marry her. No child of his was going to grow up without a father and mother. He'd seen too much neglect and abuse over the years. Before Brooke came along and was adopted by his folks, they'd brought many frightened, insecure children into their family, cared for them and nurtured them until they could find a loving home. His child would have his name and all the privileges and love he could give. But now wasn't the time to propose marriage to Emma.

They were both in shock.

Dylan was trying to be charming, trying to be patient, but Emma could tell by the worry lines creasing his forehead he was at a loss. She was, too. But already, she was in love with her baby, Dylan's child, and would move heaven and earth to make things right.

She rose, steady on her feet, and Dylan bounced up from the sofa, his concerned gaze never wavering. "I need to use the restroom," she said.

"I'll walk you."

"No, I'm okay. I'm not dizzy anymore and I know where it is." Dylan's lips were pursed tight but he didn't argue as she walked away with steady measured steps and entered the bathroom.

She splashed water on her face, the cool, crisp feel of it perking her up. As her head came up from the sink, her reflection stared back at her in the mirror. The color had returned to her face. And her legs didn't feel like jelly anymore. Revealing a secret as big as this one was therapeutic, as if a light had been turned on and she could see again. She felt free, relieved and unburdened.

But that feeling lasted only a few seconds. As she exited the bathroom, Dylan was there, leaning against the wall with arms folded, his face barely masking his concern. He approached her and took her hand. "How are you feeling, Em?"

The slightest touch of his large hand on hers was enough to wake her sleeping endorphins. As they tried to spread cheer, all she could think about was pulling away from him. Pulling away from the caring way he said her name. Away from what she feared almost as much as being alone in the dark. Falling for him. Really, in the flesh, head-over-heels falling for him, leaving her broken and shattered.

She'd been unloved all of her life.

But to be unloved by Dylan would be the hardest of all.

"I'm fine. Much better actually."

"I want you to stay here tonight."

"Why?" She stared into the deep sea of his eyes. They weren't commanding exactly, but filled with expectation. Like the rest of him.

"You shouldn't be alone tonight."

"Isn't that how I got pregnant in the first place?"

It was a bad joke. Not a joke really, the truth, but Dylan didn't seem to take offense. His lips quirked a bit. "Oh, how I wish I knew."

"To be perfectly honest, I don't remember, either. My brain wasn't firing on all cylinders. I just have flashes here and there of how it was."

He nodded, staring at her as if he still couldn't believe they'd made love. As if the thought was foreign to him. He didn't say the words, but there was an apology on his expression. "Just for the record, and I do appreciate you *not* asking, but I'm sure it's your baby, Dylan. I haven't been sexually active in quite a while."

His tanned face became infused with color that wasn't there before. Dylan McKay blushing was a rare sight.

"I figured."

Her brows lifted at the quickness of his response. Had he just insulted her?

"I mean, you wouldn't lie to me, Emma," he explained. "I know you're telling the truth."

Better.

"I'm not staying here tonight, Dylan."

He'd walked her into the kitchen, where he handed her a glass of water. "You've been sick for days and you fainted just a few minutes ago. You need someone with you."

She sipped and took a moment to gather her thoughts. "You're not going to watch over me all night, Dylan."

"I didn't intend to. But there's nothing wrong with a friend checking in on a friend, is there?"

"That's what text messages are for."

He snorted, and it was sexy. How much trouble was she in?

"You're gonna cause me a sleepless night."

"Look, you can drop me off at home and then text me when you get back here. I promise to text you first thing in the morning."

"Whatever happened to phone calls?"

"Fine, I'll call you when I wake up."

"And what if you're sick again?"

"You'll come to my rescue. I have no doubt."

He rubbed his hand back and forth across the expanse of his jaw as he contemplated her words. "I wish you weren't so stubborn about this."

"I'm not stubborn, just practical. I think we need space right now…to think."

"That's my line, honey. And notice I didn't say it? Because right now, it's more important to make sure you get your health back."

"I've been taking care of myself for almost twenty-six years. I can manage, trust me."

He nodded slowly, giving her a stern fatherly look. God, she'd always hated when Dylan did that. He wasn't her guardian or big brother. "Fine, then. I'll drive you home."

Half an hour later, they pulled up to her building. Dylan insisted on coming into her apartment, his take on seeing her safely home. Her emotional well was dry and she didn't have it in her to argue the point.

"So this is where we, uh...conceived the baby?" His eyes dipped down to her belly and a searing heat cut through the denim of her dress as if she'd been physically touched. A tiny tremble rumbled through her system.

"Yes. This is it." She wouldn't say it was the scene of the crime. She couldn't label the new life growing inside as anything but wonderful. Whether or not Dylan or anyone else agreed. "In the bedroom, of course."

He shot another piercing look her way. "Right."

Dylan helped take her jacket off and then guided her to a seat on the sofa. She sat down without argument. He didn't sit, though. Instead, he walked around the room, scanning the picture frames on her bookshelf, looking at trinkets, the furniture and all the surroundings with a new and insightful eye. Then he turned to her. "Mind if I peek into your bedroom? See if it jars my memory?"

Oh, boy. This was awkward. But she understood the necessity. Things for Dylan would be so much easier if he could get those lost hours back. She nodded. "Just don't look in my lingerie drawers."

He laughed, his somber eyes finally twinkling.

He was gone only a minute before returning to her.

"Anything?" she asked.

He shook his head sadly. "No."

She understood his disappointment. All that she remembered from that night was a muscled body covering hers and the tender comfort his presence had given her. Afterward, she'd slipped into the tight cocoon of his arms and fallen into a drugged sleep. When she had woken up with the mother of all hangovers, Dylan was gone.

That next day, the power outage was old news in most parts of the city. The lights had come back on and everything had returned to normal. For most people. And the shocking death of Roy Benjamin on the set of beloved actor Dylan McKay's new film had usurped all the day's headlines.

Right now, she and Dylan were on even footing. Both were unsure of how that night had gone down. There was a chance Dylan would never get that time back. And her memory was fogged over and blurry at best. "I'm sorry."

"Don't be. It was a long shot."

His smile didn't budge the rest of his face. He turned his wrist and glanced at his watch, a gorgeous black-faced gold Movado. "It's ten thirty. What time do you go to bed?"

"Eleven."

He nodded and sat on the couch beside her.

"Let me guess. You're not leaving until I go to bed?"

"I'd like to stay."

Crapola. How many women would kill to have that offer from Dylan McKay?

"I'm just going to do some reading in bed before I turn in. You can leave now."

Dylan ran a hand down his face. "You're trying to get rid of me."

"Only because I don't need you to babysit me. I'm fine."

"Then I'll go," he said, standing up, leaving her gaze to follow the long length of his body as he straightened. "I'll text you at eleven and see how you're doing."

"My kind of guy," she teased.

His lips curved up. "You're not going to prevent me from checking on you."

She rose, too, and amazed herself at her own stability, considering she'd fainted just a few hours ago. "I'll call you in the morning. It's a promise."

"Thanks," he said, and she followed him to the door. When he turned to her, they were only a breath apart, him towering above her by six inches. The scent of raw power and lime emanated from his throat and lingered in her nostrils. His golden hair gleamed under the foyer light and his eyes, deadly and devastatingly blue, found hers. "Make an appointment with a doctor for next week. I'd like to go with you," he said.

It shouldn't have come as a surprise that he'd want to go with her, but Dylan escorting her to an obstetrician's office would be big news if word got out. And there would be repercussions. "Are you sure?"

"Absolutely," he said immediately. "I'll let you know my schedule."

He laced his hands with hers then and gave a little tug, bringing her closer. His beautiful mouth was only inches away. "I want you to move into my house, Emma. Think about it and we'll talk again tomorrow."

Without hesitation his head came forward and his lips met with hers. The kiss was brief, but amazing and glorious. A glimpse of what could be. A tease. A temptation.

And when she opened her eyes, he'd already turned away and was gone.

Yes, yes, yes would've been her answer. If only he'd asked for the right reasons.

But Dylan didn't want her. He wanted her baby.

And she wasn't about to live her life unloved.

Ever again.

Emma didn't pick up a book to read. Instead, she grabbed the phone and speed-dialed Brooke's number. She picked up on the first ring.

"Hi, Brooke. It's me, checking in."

"Emma, it's late. Are you okay?"

"Right now, I'm feeling fine. Did I wake you?"

"Gosh no. I'm dead on my feet, but wide-awake. I'm done prepping for tomorrow. Rocky and Wendy are doing their share and we're managing."

"That's great news. I've been thinking about you all day. How was the silent auction?"

"It went well. We had lots of bids and I'm guessing the charity made lots of money. I haven't tallied it up yet. That comes later tonight."

"Do it in the morning, Brooke. You sound beat."

"I am, but in a good way."

Emma's pangs of guilt resurfaced. Poor Brooke. The business side of things wasn't her forte. She had a creative streak a mile long and Pinterest could learn a few things from her when it came to party planning. But anything with numbers, and Brooke was at a complete loss.

"So, no snags for tomorrow?" Tomorrow was the celebrity golf tournament, the golf widow's luncheon and the formal Give a Dollar or a Thousand Dinner and raffle. All the celebrities golfing would attend the dinner. Their appearance made for heftier donations, but they came with a high price for their time. They were accustomed to and expected fabulous cuisine and service, so this task was even more daunting.

"Nope, not a one."

Emma breathed a sigh of relief. "Good."

"How are things with you?" Brooke questioned her in a softer tone that left no room for doubt what she was really getting at.

"You guilted Dylan into checking on me."

"Yeah, I did. I'm sorry, honey, but I'm worried about you. So, you spent time with him tonight?"

"Yes, and I…well…he knows my situation now."

"You told him!"

Her face scrunched up at her friend's enthusiasm. "Don't sound so happy. He's in as much shock as I am."

"But at least he knows the truth."

"Yeah, but nothing jarred his memory."

"That's not really the point. You can't worry about the past. At least you'll move forward toward the future."

Normally, she told Brooke everything, but tonight wasn't the night to tell her about Dylan's offer. She wasn't about to move into his mansion. And if Brooke knew, she'd probably side with her brother on this. Two McKays would be too hard to fight. "Yeah, I guess." She waited a beat. "I'm glad things went well tonight. And I know tomorrow will be amazing. You should hit the sack. That's what I'm going to do. Love you, Brooke."

"Love you, too. Sleep well."

Emma hung up the phone and undressed, slipping out of her street clothes and into her pajamas. She climbed into bed, shut off the table lamp and snuggled her face deep into her cushy pillow. Her body sank into the mattress and she sighed out loud. Nothing was better than a comfy bed after a rough day. But just as she closed her eyes, Dylan's image popped into her head.

She owed him a text.

Stretching her arm out, she fumbled for her phone on the nightstand, punched in his number and typed out her text.

I'm tucked in and feeling well. Good night.

Short and sweet. It'd been a long time since she'd had to answer to anyone. Derek Purdy, the man she now thought of as The Jerk, had cured her of that in her sophomore year of college. She hated even thinking of him anymore. He didn't deserve another second of her time.

But Dylan, on the other hand, would be in her life forever now.

He was no jerk, and from now on they would have to answer to each other.

For the baby's sake.

Five

"Rolling," the first assistant director called out as Dylan stood on his mark on the Stage One Studios back lot. The cast and crew of *Resurrection SEALs* became quiet. They were on the same dirt road where Roy had died and where Dylan had been hit with shrapnel. If being here didn't jog his memory, nothing would. Dylan tried to focus. He was a professional, and the crew had worked long hours this morning prepping this scene. The director called, "Action," and Dylan went into performance mode, delivering his lines. He stumbled once, mixing up the words, and looked to the script supervisor for his line.

Marcy offered it. "Whether or not you give me those papers, Joe, the colonel is going to hear about this."

They reshot the scene several times and Dylan went through the paces for coverage and tights on his face before his work was done. The director, Gabe Novotny, walked over and put a hand on his shoulder. "That first scene had to be hard on you. But you're through it now. How does it feel?"

"I can't lie. It's a little weird, Gabe. Mostly, it's knowing that Roy died right here, and now, here I am, doing my job, back to the status quo and moving forward without him."

"We're all feeling it, Dylan. But you managed the scene. And the next one will be a little easier, and then the next."

Dylan didn't have much choice. He was under contract, but a part of him wanted to bail on this project now, even though he'd done intense training, including daily ten-mile beach runs and weight lifting to become Josh O'Malley, Navy SEAL. "I'm hoping you're right. Still is strange to be here, though." He knew enough about survivor guilt to understand that the ache in the pit of his stomach wasn't going away anytime soon. He missed Roy, and if he'd been the one to get into the car that day as planned, instead of Roy, he'd be the one floating atop the high seas now with his ashes scattered all over the Pacific. "If we're done for now, I think I'll head back to my trailer."

"Actually, an officer from the LAPD is due in the production office any minute now. He's asked to speak to you and me, Marcy and the execs. Maury Allen was asked to be there, too, so it's something big if the police want the head of the studio there. You might remember the officer. He consulted with us early on in the film about two months ago."

"Oh, yeah. Detective Brice. He's a big Clippers fan. We talked basketball for a while."

"That's him. It's about Roy's death, Dylan." Gabe took his eyeglasses off and rubbed them clean on the tail of his shirt. "So I'm betting it's not a social call."

"All right."

Gabe glanced past the chaos of the crew taking down the rigging and spotted Marcy speaking with the girls from Hair and Makeup. "You about through, Marce?"

She slammed a folder closed, stood on her tiptoes and waved at him. "I'm coming."

Instead of golf-carting it, they walked to the offices together. When they entered the building, they were reintroduced to the detective, who was dressed in an austere gray suit. They all took a seat at a long table as if they were going to do a cold reading. But it wasn't play acting. Judging by Detective Brice's sullen expression, he didn't have good news.

"I'm here to ask a few more questions regarding the death of Roy Benjamin. After investigating the accident, it's been determined that the car in question had been tampered with before the stunt ever took place. We've already spoken with the stunt team supervisor and he's confirmed that they'd given the stunt the all clear. They went through a series of tests before Mr. Benjamin ever got in that car. There's a timeline factor that we're working with here. From the time the stunt team finished rigging the car until the actual shoot, there are thirty minutes unaccounted for."

"What are you saying exactly?" Maury asked, his brows gathered.

"Mr. Benjamin was to roll out of the car right before it blew up. But we believe someone sabotaged the rigging so that the car would blow up ahead of schedule."

"With Roy in it?" Dylan asked, barely recognizing the high pitch of his own voice.

Detective Brice nodded, his voice gruff. "That's right."

"So you think Roy was murdered?"

"That's what I'm here to investigate. Mr. McKay, do you have any recollection about that day, at all?"

He squeezed his eyes shut hating that he couldn't remember a damn thing. "No, none."

"Okay, well, if you do remember anything, give me a call." Detective Brice handed Dylan a business card that read Homicide Division. He stared at it, finding this whole thing bizarre, like something out of one of his movies. Who would want to murder Roy?

The officer proceeded to question Dylan about his relationship with Roy. How long had they been friends? How long had he worked as his stunt double? Any girlfriends? What was he like? Did he have any enemies? Dylan answered as honestly as he could, and when the detective moved on to the others, Dylan's mind wandered to some of the better times he'd had with Roy. They had a lot in common. Both liked to work out, both loved women, both enjoyed good whiskey.

By the time Maury, Gabe, Marcy and the other execs were through being questioned, they all began shaking their heads. They were as stunned as Dylan was. Then Gabe remembered one important thing. "Dylan was originally supposed to do that scene," he told the detective. "We changed the script a bit and decided the stunt was too risky for Dylan to handle."

Brice turned toward Dylan. "Is that so?"

"I don't remember, but that's what Gabe told me."

"I don't think it was changed on the call sheet for that day," Gabe offered.

"I'd like a copy of that, please," the detective said, and Gabe nodded.

Detective Brice was quiet for a while, writing things down in a notebook. "Okay. Well, until we get to the bottom of this, I'd suggest that all of you be wary of anything unusual around the studio and report any suspicious behavior. And, Mr. McKay, if that script change wasn't common knowledge, then there's a possibility that you could've been the target instead of Mr. Benjamin. Do you have any enemies?"

Dylan's head snapped up. He gazed into Detective Brice's serious eyes. "I get all kinds of fan mail. I have an assistant go through it. But she hasn't said anything about threats."

"Maybe you should ask her for details and start going through your mail for anything unusual. You might recognize something she doesn't."

"You don't really believe Dylan was the target?" Maury asked.

The detective shrugged. "It's better to take into account all the possibilities."

After the questioning, Dylan returned to finish his next scene, struggling with what he'd just learned. He couldn't believe someone was out to get him. He might have a few unhappy ex-girlfriends, but he was actually on good terms with most of them. He dug around his memory for anything else, anyone who might want to do him harm, and came up empty.

He left the studio unnerved and on the drive home made a call to his security team to beef up patrols around his house. Usually if he went out on studio appearances or interviews, he traveled with a bodyguard, so he was good there. And once he'd taken care of that business, he called Emma. She answered the call on the first ring. "Hello."

"Hi, it's me."

"Hi, Dylan."

"How're you feeling today?"

"Better. I went into the office today and did some work. It feels good to be back among the productive."

He smiled. "That's good. What if I told you I had a bad day and needed a friend? Would you have dinner with me tonight?"

Her silence at the other end of the phone made his heart race. It blew his mind how much he wanted her to agree.

"Would that be the honest truth?" she asked.

"It would."

Her relenting sigh carried to his ears. She wasn't happy

about the pressure he put on her and he was taking advantage of her good nature, but he really did need a friend tonight. He couldn't tell her about Detective Brice's visit on the set today, and even if he could, he wouldn't want to trouble her. Just seeing her tonight, knowing that she was carrying his child and something good had come out of that time he'd lost, would boost his spirits. "Then sure, I guess I could do that."

"Thanks." He released a pent-up breath. "I'll be there in half an hour to pick you up."

Emma faced Dylan across the tufted white leather booth at Roma's Restaurant in the city. Silly her, after he'd called, she'd waded through her closet and come up with the prettiest dress she could find: a soft sapphire-blue brushed cotton with lots of feminine folds and a draping halter neckline. She'd dressed for him and had been rewarded with hot, appreciative glances on the drive here.

Looking around the place, she noted that Roma's tables weren't covered with red-and-white-checked tablecloths, there were no plastic flower centerpieces and not a hint of sawdust was sprinkled on the creamy marble floors. Dylan was used to the best, and he'd come to think of these high-end places as the norm. But Emma wasn't used to eating pizza off expensive Italian dinnerware or having a violinist make the rounds from table to table, offering up a musical selection to soothe the soul.

"They make a mean eggplant parm here," Dylan said. "And the pizza is old-school, like back home."

"Eggplant sounds good," she said, folding the menu. "I'd like that."

Dylan nodded to the waiter. "Make that two, then, Tony, and two glasses of sparkling water."

After the waiter left, she picked up a wafer-like piece of

rosemary-and-garlic bread, almost hating to break up the fancy-schmancy geometric design in the basket.

"Feel free to order wine or whatever you want, Dylan. You don't have to drink water because of me."

God, tonight he looked as if he could really use a drink. He was a good actor, the best actually, but tonight he wasn't acting. His guard was down and she saw it in the pallor on his face, his sullen eyes and the twist of his otherwise beautiful mouth.

"Thanks," he said, giving her a nod. "Maybe I will order a glass of wine later."

"That bad a day?"

He glanced down at the pearly-white tablecloth. "Yeah, I guess. We had to resume shooting the scene in the location where Roy died. It was a hard day for everyone."

"For you especially, I would think."

He nodded. "It was just weird and sad."

"I'm sorry."

"Thanks. I guess there's nothing to be done about it. The show must go on," he said with a strained chuckle that barely moved his mouth.

A part of her wanted to reach out to him, to hold his hand or maybe fold him into an embrace. He looked a little lost right now. She knew the feeling and she was suddenly glad she'd accepted his dinner invitation.

"Enough about me," Dylan said. "How are you feeling?"

"I'm sitting here about ready to eat eggplant smothered in sauce and cheese and the thought of it doesn't turn my stomach, so I think I'm fine."

"No more morning sickness?"

"I didn't say that. I still get queasy, but it passes quickly and only seems to happen in the morning. Still, I'm not counting my chickens yet."

"Did you call the doctor?"

"Yes, the appointment is next Thursday at ten o'clock."

"Okay, good." He seemed pleased. He'd told her he wasn't filming on Thursday and she had been lucky enough to get an appointment with her ob-gyn that day.

"If you run into a bind or something, it won't be a problem. I can get myself there." She wanted to throw that out to him. She had other means, if he couldn't go that day. She was suddenly transported back in time to when she was a charity case, an unloved little young burden to those around her. She'd been a child then, scared of the future, but she wasn't now. Now she clung to her independence and needed it as much as she needed air to breathe. Single motherhood wasn't rare these days, lots of women did it and managed just fine. She wasn't looking to Dylan to be her savior.

"I won't run into a bind." His jaw was set as he spoke those firm words. He meant it. Dylan was a big enough star that schedules could be woven around his needs, and not the other way around. But still, she wasn't going to crumble if she did the mother thing alone.

"Brooke wants to go with me on an appointment later on," she said. "She wants to be a part of it, too."

"I'd like that. She'll be an amazing aunt."

Emma smiled. They both agreed on that. "She's been very supportive."

Dylan nodded. "What do you think of this Royce guy she's been dating? Is he the real deal?"

Ah, finally the conversation was moving away from her. She was glad for the distraction. "I haven't met him yet, but there's a bouquet of red roses on her desk at work that says he's an okay guy. She's seeing him tonight, as a matter of fact. She missed him like crazy while she was away."

Dylan made a grunting sound before he sipped the sparkling water the waiter had just delivered. "That always scares me."

"Why?"

He shrugged. "I want to see her happy. She's been disappointed before."

"Haven't we all," Emma blurted. And then squeezed her eyes shut but not before witnessing Dylan's brows lift inquisitively.

"I know."

She gave him a look that must have revealed her astonishment because his baby blues softened immediately. "Brooke told me about a guy in college you were seeing."

"When did she tell you that?" The witchy tone in her voice made her mentally cringe. She didn't mean to sound so darn defensive.

"A while back. I'm not prying into your life, Emma. I wouldn't put Brooke in that position, and if I want to know something about you, I'll ask you up front. But actually, my sister mentioned it a few years ago and I never forgot it because I thought you deserved better than a jerk who would verbally abuse you. I guess it always stuck with me. I sorta wanted to punch his lights out."

Emma pictured Dylan knocking Derek Purdy to the ground and grinned. "You've always been protective."

"There's nothing wrong with a friend looking out for a friend."

"I've always appreciated that." That was the truth. Dylan had never failed to be her champion when he was around. He had a thing for the underdog. It was quite commendable actually, but right now with her baby situation, she didn't want to be considered the underdog, or lacking in any way. "But it's old news now, Dylan. I've forgotten about him."

The meal was served and that part of the conversation ended. Emma dug in with tepid gusto, keeping in mind the capacity of her shrunken stomach and the queasiness that might rear its ugly head at any given moment, despite what she'd told Dylan. She didn't trust her gut not to act up. She was just getting used to the idea of eating a full meal and not paying the price afterward.

"It's delicious," she said. Steam rose up from the sizzling cheese and the garlicky scents made her mouth water.

"It's not too ostentatious for you?"

"The eggplant?"

His eyes twinkled with that you-know-what-I-mean look.

"The place."

"Let's see. I'm eating off handmade Intrada dinner plates while being serenaded by a sole violinist. The Waterford cut crystal and white rose centerpiece is a nice touch. Adds class to the joint. Nope, I'd say it's right on par with Vitellos back home."

He wiped his mouth with the cloth napkin. The gleam in his eyes became even brighter at her sarcasm. "How do you know all this stuff?"

"You're forgetting what I do for a living. It's my job to know about dinnerware and crystal and high-end table dressing."

"Right. I didn't put it together. You're good at your job. But you're not comfortable with all this, are you?"

"It's fine, Dylan. I have no complaints. If this is what it takes to cheer you up, then I'm all for it."

Dylan's smile faded a bit as he reached for her hand. "*You* are what's cheering me up. I enjoy being with you, Em. And I brought you here not to impress you, but because I knew you'd enjoy the food."

Her heartbeat sounded in her ears. She had no humorous comeback. "Oh."

She got a little more lost in his eyes. It was hard not to; those eyes could drown a lesser woman and she was certainly not immune. The clarity in them astounded her. Dylan knew what he was about, amnesia or not. There was no limit to his confidence, yet he wasn't arrogant or prissy. He was kinda perfect.

And that scared her more than anything.

"Maybe…uh, maybe you should have some wine now." She would if she could.

He shook his head, not breaking eye contact. "Not necessary."

"You're cured?"

He chuckled, the smile cracking his face wide-open. "For the moment, anyway." He squeezed her hand a little and a shot of adrenaline arrowed up her arm and spread like wildfire throughout her system. What was he doing to her? She'd come here to boost his spirits, not fall under his spell.

He glanced at her half-eaten plate of food. "Finish your meal, sweetheart." And he released her hand just like that, leaving a rich hum of delight in the wake of his touch. She filled up with deliriously happy hormones. "We'll talk about dessert when you're through," he added.

Dessert? She felt as though she'd already had a decadent helping of chocolate-espresso gelato with cherries on top.

The Dylan McKay Special.

And nothing was sweeter.

When they got back to her apartment, she made a feeble attempt to get inside with some semblance of grace and dignity. "Really, Dylan, you didn't have to walk me to my door," she said, her back to the front door and her hand on the knob.

His brows lifted and a lock of straight sun-streaked hair fell across his forehead. She was tempted to touch it, to ease it back into place and run her fingers through the rest.

"I never drop a lady off at the curb, Emma. I certainly wouldn't do that to you. You know that."

She did. But she couldn't invite Dylan in. She didn't

have willpower to spare right now. Yet she knew that's exactly what he wanted. "Well, now you've earned another gold star."

"I have many."

She imagined a black-and-white composition book filled with pages of gold stars. But she had to be kind in her not-too-subtle brush-off. "Thanks again for dinner. You must be tired after the day you've had. You should go home and turn in."

"I will soon enough. But you're not safely inside yet." His hand glided over hers to snare the key from her fingers. "Here, let me."

She nearly jumped from the contact and her hand opened. When he took the key, she moved away from the door and allowed him to insert it into the lock. With a twist, the door clicked open.

"Thanks again," she said breathlessly, again pressing her back to the door.

He leaned in so close she caught the slight scent of musky aftershave, a heady mixture that stirred all of her erotic senses. Oh, boy, she was in trouble.

She pressed her head against the door, backing away from him and staring at his lips that were coming way too close. "What are you doing?"

"I'm giving you a proper thank-you, sweetheart."

"The eggplant was thanks—"

And then his mouth came down on hers. Not roughly or aggressively, but not with tender persuasion, either. It was perfectly balanced, a kiss that could mean a dozen things that were not necessarily sexual. Yet as she raised her hands to push at his chest, he deepened the kiss, giving it more texture and taste, and the balance she relied on was starting to disappear. Her arms fell to her sides; there would be no shove-off-buddy move on her part. How could she think of ending something so amazing?

His hand came up beside her head, his palm flat against the door, and the darn thing moved, making her clumsily back up a step, then two. He followed her, of course, his lips still locked with hers, and the next thing she knew they were inside her dark apartment and breathing heavily. Dylan broke the kiss momentarily to guide her backward some more and then kick the door shut with his foot.

"Imagine that," he whispered. "We're inside your apartment."

"Uh-huh" was her brilliant comeback. She was too enthralled with his mouth, his tongue and the wonderful way he used them on her to think straight.

And then she felt his hand on her belly. Only someone who knew her intimately would notice the slight bulge above her waist. His fingers splayed out, encircling the whole of her stomach, and a throaty sound emanated from deep within his chest. "I've wanted to touch you here, Em. It's okay, isn't it?"

She nodded, not trusting her voice.

"I know it's not ideal, but, Emma, if there was ever a woman to carry my child, of all the women I know, all that I've been with, I'm glad it's you."

There was a compliment in there somewhere. Emma understood what he meant, but there were still issues, lots and lots of issues. She pulled away from him. "I'll turn on a light."

Before she was out of his reach, he was gripping her wrist and tugging her back to him. She landed smack against his chest and gazed up at his face, which was steeped in shadows. "Don't, Emma. You're safe with me. Don't be afraid."

She *was* afraid. Of where this was leading. "What do you want, Dylan?" she asked softly and heard the defeat in her voice. It was as if she couldn't compete, couldn't deny him, couldn't defend against him.

"Honestly, I don't know. You're good for me, Em. I like who I am when I'm with you. And I don't want to leave, not just yet."

Something almost desperate in his voice kept her rooted to the spot. Then he touched her, a light brush of his fingers feathering her face, a caress she had always dreamed about. And he kissed her again, tenderly and slowly, like a man treasuring a sacred prize. The prize, she knew, wasn't her, but the baby. She got that. She already felt the same way about the life growing inside her. She didn't blame the child for her bouts of sickness or regret the mere fact that the baby existed at all. Yet something was off. His kisses were new to her. His touch exciting and not familiar in the way she'd thought they'd be. They'd done this before, kissing and intimately touching when they conceived the baby, but she didn't remember...*him*.

"Dylan," she said softly, "we're friends."

"We could be more."

He nibbled on her lower lip. A blast of heat spiraled down to her belly and she closed her eyes, absorbing the pleasant torment while trying to contain the burning inferno that was building, building. Dylan's heat became her heat and she hardly noticed as they moved farther into her room, until Dylan was sitting on her sofa and she was being yanked down onto his lap.

His tongue danced with hers as he pressed her against the sofa cushions. His lips found her forehead, her cheeks, her chin, and then moved leisurely back to her waiting mouth. She ached for him and it was almost useless to try to fight the feeling. In her teenage imaginings, before his fame and fortune, Dylan had always been hers. She caved to those feelings now and moaned when his hand slipped under her dress and climbed her thigh, inching toward the part of her body that ached for him the most.

But Dylan bypassed that spot and moved his hand farther up to lay claim once again to her belly. He stroked her there gently and she caught a glimpse of the top of his head as he bestowed a loving kiss right above her navel over the spot where their baby resided.

She melted in that moment. Her eyes filled with tears. She bit her lower lip to keep from making a silly, revealing sound. But her heart was involved, now more than ever before. And it pained her in ways that she'd never dreamed possible.

"Dylan," she whispered.

He lifted his head and their gazes locked in the shadows. An unwavering gleam in his eyes spoke of the love he already had for his baby. He smiled. Dread pierced her stomach. She didn't have ammunition to fight Dylan when he was like this.

The next thing she knew, his hand was on her thigh again, moving up and down, rubbing away her apprehension and bringing on a new kind of tension. "You're soft, Emma. Everywhere."

Oh, God, but he wasn't. It was evident from the press of his groin to her hip. They were treading dangerous ground and she was too enthralled to put a stop to it.

He brought his mouth to hers again and again, his hand working magic over her throat, her shoulders, the steep slope of her breasts. His fingertips grazed her nipples and she jumped, sensitive and achy.

A groan rumbled from the depths of his chest and he moved more steadily over her, cupping her breast through the material of her dress, trailing hot moist kisses along her collarbones. Everything was on fire, burning, burning. The heat was combustible and then…and then…

The phone rang.

Her house line was ringing. It was used for emergencies, and only a handful of people had the number. The answering machine picked up and Brooke's voice was on the other end.

"It's me, Em. I'm looking for Dylan. Neither one of you are picking up your cell and it's sort of important. Is he there by any chance?"

Dylan immediately sat upright.

Emma gave him a nod and bounded up, adjusting her lopsided halter as she dashed to turn on a light and pick up the phone on the kitchen wall. "Hi," she said, breathless.

"Hi," Brooke said, drawing out the word. "Am I disturbing something?"

"No, no. We were just coming in from dinner. Dylan dropped me off. He's still here. Let me get him," she said. But there was no need. He was already behind her, his hands on her waist, planting a kiss on her shoulder as though they were a real couple, before he took the phone. "Hi, sis."

Emma walked out of the room to give him privacy, but her apartment had few walls and she could still see him and hear his voice. Her curiosity wouldn't allow her to turn away. "Renee?" He sighed heavily and after a few seconds said, "Okay, I'll take care of it." Then he ended the call.

Dylan squeezed his eyes shut and rubbed the back of his neck before turning to Emma. Their gazes locked and he moved toward her and grasped her hands. "I have to go. But I want you to promise you'll think about moving in with me. We could have a lot more nights like tonight. I want you with me, honey."

It was too much, too soon, and her head was still reeling from how close they'd come to making love. Inhaling a shaky breath, she shook her head. "I can't promise you that, Dylan. I'm not ready to make that kind of move."

He nodded and worry lines formed around his eyes. "Okay, but I'd like to see you again. Soon."

"Like a date?"

"Yeah," he said, his face brightening as if he was really warming to the idea. "I think we'll take one step at a time. Dating first. Can you manage that?"

She nodded. "I think so."

"Exclusively?"

Exclusive with Dylan McKay! She liked the sound of that. Not that she'd ever had a situation where she was dating two men at the same time. "Exclusively."

Seeming satisfied, he gave her a quick, chaste kiss goodbye and hurried away.

Leaving Emma to wonder about his ex Renee and what that phone call was all about.

Was *she* the exception to Dylan's rules of exclusivity?

Six

Dylan sat down at his desk as morning breezes blew in through the window, the fresh ocean air a jolt stronger than caffeine to rouse him out of his sleep haze. Each morning he'd scan his mind, hoping to get a glimpse of the time he'd lost, hoping his memory would be restored. It wasn't happening today.

He opened the drawer, pulled out his checkbook and wrote out a check for a larger sum of money than he'd normally sent Renee over this past year. The monthly checks weren't a fortune, but enough to help her get by and make sure her two children were fed, housed and clothed. She was in worse shape than a single mother. She had a lousy ex-husband who threatened to take her kids away from her on a regular basis and Renee needed to supplement her meager earnings as a waitress in order to provide for her family.

She seemed to be in a constant state of crisis.

Dylan had long ago forgiven Renee for breaking his

heart. But the fault wasn't just Renee's. He'd allowed himself to be persuaded to run away with her. He'd been crazy in love, young and impulsive, and so willing to do whatever Renee wanted to keep her happy. They'd been in a theatre production together in high school and had lofty notions of success. Later, at the age of nineteen, she'd convinced him to move to Los Angeles to pursue an acting career. He'd gone with her with eyes wide-open, understanding the risk, but when his success didn't come fast enough for her and Renee's so-called contacts in LA had dried up, her disappointment was hard to live with.

Then one day, he'd found her in the arms of another man, a director of a small theatre, an older man with a colossal ego who'd convinced her they were one step away from fame. That hadn't happened and she'd made one bad decision after another. While Dylan's career had finally launched through patience and perseverance, she'd given up on her dreams, becoming cynical and bitter, and wound up marrying someone who worked in the industry. Dylan had lost touch with her completely until last year when she'd reached out to his sister and asked if she could put her in touch with Dylan.

It was a pained conversation when they'd spoken, but Renee had touched something deep and tender in Dylan's heart as he remembered the young, vivacious girl she'd once been. She'd pleaded with him for forgiveness and he gave it willingly. She'd never once asked him for a handout, but after learning about her situation with an alcoholic, abusive ex-husband and hating the thought of her kids suffering, he'd started sending her checks.

"Knock, knock."

His head snapped up and he found Brooke dressed in a stretchy blue workout outfit standing at the threshold of his half-opened door. He gave her an immediate smile. "Hey, kiddo. Come in."

Once a week, he and Brooke exercised together in his gym on the second floor that overlooked the Pacific Ocean.

"Morning, bro. Ready for a workout?"

"Just about." He placed the check in an envelope and wrote out Renee's name on the front before sealing it. "You don't have to do this, Brooke. I can mail it."

"It's not a problem, Dylan. I know where Renee lives."

"It's half an hour out of town."

"Listen, I'm no fan of Renee's, but if she needs this pronto for her kids, then it's no big deal for me to put the check in her mailbox. This way, she'll have it earlier."

Dylan ran his hand along his chin. "Her daughter needs corrective eye surgery. She's in a panic about it."

"It's a good thing you're doing," Brooke said.

He didn't do it for accolades and no one besides his sister knew about this. Renee was part of his past, a one-time friend and lover. She needed help. Wouldn't he be a hypocrite to volunteer to help other charities and not help someone he knew personally who was in need? Why not give her a hand up?

"You have a big heart," his sister said.

"I can afford to."

"Yes, but she hurt you badly and I don't forgive as easily as you do."

"I didn't forgive her for a long time."

"But eventually you did. And she scarred you, Dylan. It was a betrayal of the worst kind."

"I'm hardly crying over it anymore."

But he'd lost his faith, and trust didn't come easily for him. He'd once believed in love, but not so much anymore. He hadn't come close to feeling anything like it since his last happy day with Renee. And then a thought rushed in and Emma's face appeared in his mind. He'd always liked Emma, and she was, after all, the mother of his child. Dating her was a means to an end. He was going to marry her and give the baby his name. At least he trusted her. As a friend.

Brooke took the check and plopped it into her wide canvas tote. "Let's go burn some calories."

An hour later, Brooke sipped water from a cold bottle, a workout towel hanging around her neck. "Inspiring as always," she said, glancing out the floor-to-ceiling windows at the low-lying clouds beginning to lift. It was going to be a blue-sky day.

Dylan set down his weights and sopped his face with his towel. "It's not half bad."

"You ready to talk to me about Emma?"

"Emma?" He sat down on a workout bench, stretched his legs out fully and downed half a bottle of water in one gulp. "What about Emma?"

She snapped her towel against his forearm. The painless rap and smirk on her lips had him grinning.

"Duh…" Brooke sat down next to him. "What's going on between you two?"

"Nosy, aren't you?"

"Concerned. I love you both."

Dylan flashed to the last night he'd been with Emma and the surprising, explosive way she'd responded to him. He'd taken liberties, but none that she hadn't wanted, and the feel of her skin, so soft and creamy smooth, the taste of her lips and plush fullness of her body against his, had him thinking of her many times since then. "I've asked her to move in with me, Brooke. She said no."

"You can't blame her for that," Brooke said. "She's struggling with all this, too. And you know her history. She's—"

"Stubborn?"

"*Independent* is a better word. And just because you're a celebrity doesn't mean every woman on the planet wants to live with you."

"I'm not asking every woman on the planet, Brooke. I'm asking the woman who's carrying my child."

"I know," she said more softly. "Give Emma some time, bro."

"I'm not pressuring her."

"Aren't you?"

"We're dating."

Brooke laughed. "Really? Like, in flowers and candy and malt shop hookups?"

His sister could be a pain in the ass sometimes. "Malt shop? I hadn't thought of that. Besides, little sis, isn't that what you're doing with Royce?"

Brooke's smile christened her flushed face. "Royce and I are much more sophisticated than that. We do art shows and book festivals and—"

"Intellectual stuff, huh?"

"Yeah, so far. We're still in the getting-to-know-each-other stage."

"Good, take it slow."

"Says the man who just asked a woman he'd never dated to move in with him."

"You're forgetting…that we—"

"Made a baby? Well, seeing as neither one of you recall much of that night, I say it's good you're starting out by dating. S…L…O…W and steady wins the race."

Dylan wasn't going to take it slow with Emma. No way. But Brooke didn't need to know that. She got defensive about Emma, and normally he loved that about his sister. She was loyal to her friends, but this one time, there was just too much at stake for Dylan to back off. He wouldn't give Emma a chance to run scared or go all independent feminist on him. He didn't want his child being raised in a disjointed home.

He had the means to provide a good life for both Emma and the baby. And the sooner she realized that, the better.

* * *

Emma tossed a kernel of popcorn into her mouth and leaned back in her maroon leather recliner seat, one of twenty in Dylan's private screening room. "I must admit, when you said you were taking me to the movies, I wondered how you would pull that off. I mean, it's not as if you can simply walk into a movie theater and not get noticed."

"Comes with the territory I'm afraid. Life has changed for me, but I'm not one of those people who complain about their fame. I knew what I was getting into when I started in this business. If I was lucky enough to succeed, then I wasn't going to cry about not having anonymity. I have a recognizable face, so I've had to alter a few things in my life."

"Like not being able to pop into a grocery store or travel unnoticed or window-shop?"

"Or take my date to a movie," Dylan added.

Emma laughed. "But you adapt very nicely."

"I'm glad you think so. So, what movie would you like to see? Chiller, thriller, Western, comedy, romance?"

"I'm at your mercy. You decide. You're the movie connoisseur."

Dylan picked an Oscar-nominated film about a boy's journey growing up and took the seat next to her. Wrapped chocolates, sour gummies and cashews were set out on a side table and a blue bottle of zillion-dollar water sat in the cupholder beside her chair.

"All set?"

She nodded. "Ready when you are."

Dylan hit a button on a remote control and the overhead lights dimmed as the screen lit up. Emma relaxed in her lounger and focused on the movie. They shared a bag of popcorn, and by the time they got to the bottom of the bag, her eyes had become a teary mess, a few escapees trickling down her cheeks from the poignancy of the film, its depiction of the heartfelt joy of family life, the struggles and cheerful moments and all the rest.

Picking up on her emotion, Dylan placed a tissue in her hand. She gave him a nod of thanks, wiped her watery eyes and focused back on the screen. It wasn't hormones that wrecked her heart this time. Whenever she witnessed a real family in action, the ups and downs and the way they all came together out of love and loyalty, she realized how very much she'd missed out on as a child. Though she was proud of the fact she hadn't let her childhood hinder her in any way. It had only made her more determined to seek a better life for herself, and now for her child.

Dylan reached over the lounger and took her hand. She glanced at their entwined fingers, his hand tanned and so very strong, hers smaller, more delicate, and she welcomed the comfort, the ease with which they could sit there together and watch a movie, holding hands.

The movie ended on a satisfying note and Dylan squeezed her hand, but didn't let her go. They remained in darkness but for the yellow floor lamps lighting a pathway around the room.

"Did you enjoy it?" he whispered.

"Very much."

"I didn't realize you're such a soft touch." His thumb rubbed over the skin of her hand in round, lazy sweeping circles.

"Only when it comes to movies."

"I find that hard to believe. You're soft…"

Her breath caught as she gazed into his heart-melting eyes.

"Everywhere."

Oh, boy.

He turned his body and leaned in, his mouth inches from hers. "I've been thinking about the other night. If we hadn't been interrupted, what would have happened?"

It wasn't really a question he expected her to answer. She thought of that night, too, so often. Wondering what if?

And then his lips were on hers, his mouth so exquisite as he patiently waited for her to respond, waited for her to give in. "Dylan."

"It's just a kiss, Em."

He made it seem so simple. "Not just a kiss," she insisted, yet she couldn't deny the temptation to kiss him back, to taste him and breathe in his delicious scent.

"This is what people do when they're dating," he whispered over her mouth.

"Is it?" Kissing Dylan wasn't anything ordinary. Not to her. It was the stuff of dreams.

"Yeah, it is," he said. "I want us to be more than friends, Em."

She wanted to ask why. Was it all about the baby, or had he somehow, after all these years, miraculously found her appealing and desirable? It was on the tip of her tongue to ask, but she chickened out. She didn't dare, because in her heart she already knew the truth.

He swept his hand around her neck and caressed the tender spot behind her ear. She closed her eyes to the pleasure and breathed deeply, soaking it in. His gentle touch and the power of his persuasion weren't anything to mess with. She could stay like this for hours, unhurried, just enjoying being the sole focus of his attention.

"I think we already are, Dylan. I'm having your baby. That puts us on a little higher level than friends."

"Maybe it's not enough," he rasped, and with a little tug, he inched her closer until their mouths were a breath apart. "Maybe we need to be more." And then he kissed her.

"What if that's not possible?"

He swept into her mouth again and deepened the kiss, his tongue working magic until her entire body grew warm and tingly. Her nipples pebbled and she gasped for sustaining breath.

"It's possible," he urged, rising from his seat and reaching for her hands. He seemed attuned to the exact moment when her body betrayed her. With both her hands in his, he gave a gentle yank and she came to her feet to face him in the soft glow of the floor lamps. "Let me show you."

Dylan was an expert at seduction; what he was doing to her now was solid proof. He took her face in his palms, looked deep into her eyes and then kissed her for long-drawn-out moments. Until her heart sped like a race car. Until her knees went weak. Until the junction of her thighs physically ached. It was too much and not enough. She was dizzy when he was through kissing her. Dizzy and wanting more.

"It's your choice, sweet Emma," he said, planting tiny kisses over her lips, his hands roaming over her body, taking liberties that she freely offered. She moaned a little when he touched her breasts and then gasped when he cupped her butt and pressed her firmly against his rigid, hard body so there was no doubt what he was about. He whispered softly into her ear, "We can take a walk on the beach to cool off, or walk into my bedroom upstairs and heat things up. You know what I want, but I'll abide by your decision, whatever it is."

She was out of breath. Her fuzzy mind told her to stall for time. As ardent as his kisses were, she couldn't wrap her head around him wanting to make love to her. It had once been her wildest dream. And yes, they'd done the deed already, but that wasn't really logged into her memory bank. Or his, either. "Is this what usually happens on your first dates?"

He laughed and took her into his arms, squeezing her tight as if she was a child asking an adorable question. "You know me. You know it's not what I do, Em."

Well, no. She'd never really quizzed him on his methods of seduction. How would she know how easily or often he took his dates to bed? He'd been in enough tabloids to wallpaper his entire mansion with the stories they'd concocted. And his sister defended him on every front. He'd even sued a few papers that had stepped over the line and had won his cases.

So, if she was to believe him now, then he was truly attracted to her. "I don't think I've ever seen your bedroom, Dylan."

He smiled then and nodded, and the next thing she knew, Dylan was lifting her in his strong arms and carrying her out of the screening room.

And up the stairs.

She roped one arm around his neck and laid her head against his broad shoulder as he marched to the double-door entry of his master suite. She felt featherlight in his arms, tucked safely into his embrace. He gave the door a nudge and pushed through, entering a massive room with an equally large bed. It faced wide windows that angled out with a magnificent view of the Pacific. Right now, only stars and a half-moon lit the night sky, but she heard the roar of the waves and smelled the brine of the sea coming through an opened terrace slider.

She wasn't sure about any of this, but lust and curiosity won over any rational sense inhabiting her brain at the moment. She'd done this before with Dylan, but now both were aware, both would remember. It was key. Monumental. Dylan would be in her life one way or another and she wanted this memory. Sane and rational or not, she simply didn't have the will to deny them both this night.

She did, after all, have secret dibs on him.

He lowered her down, her body flush against his until her feet hit the floor beside his bed. He let her go then, taking a step back to lock eyes with her and lifting his black polo shirt over his head. A rush of breath pushed from her lungs. His upper body was ripped and bronzed, his shoulders wide, the muscles in his arms bulging. He'd been working out hard for this Navy SEAL role and he had her vote. Hands down.

"We'll take this slow," he said.

Slow? She was on her first official date with him and about to get naked.

He reached for her and placed the palm of her hand flat against his concrete chest. His breath hitched and she lifted her lids to find the gleam in his eyes bright and hungry. Slowly, she moved her hand along the solid ridges that made up his six-pack and tiny coarse chest hairs tickled her fingers. He was amazing to touch, almost unreal. She'd never been with a man like Dylan before. It scared her, how absolutely perfect he was.

What was his flaw? Everyone had one, but she couldn't find it here, now.

He took her other hand, put it on him and encouraged her to explore. She did, running her hands over his shoulders, to his back and then returning to his torso. In her exploration, her fingers grazed his nipples and they grew taut from her touch. It was a turn-on, just seeing how she affected him.

He stood there, allowing her to know him, to feel his skin, absorb his heat and become familiar. She took her time, meeting his eyes once in a while, but mostly keeping a vigil on the beauty of his body.

He kissed her then, suckling her lips in a heady way that said he was ready to move forward. To take the next step.

"Should I undress the rest of the way?" he breathed over her mouth. "Or is it your turn?"

Fair is fair. She turned around and offered him her back. He didn't hesitate to unzip the long gold zipper on the little black dress she wore. The zipper hissed as it traveled all the way down to the small of her back. A shot of cooler air hit her as he pressed his hands to her shoulders and helped her shimmy out of her dress. Free of the fabric that pooled at her feet, he bestowed tiny kisses along her neck. Slowly, he turned her around and his eyes met hers once again, before drifting down her body over the slope of her ample breasts encased in her black lace bra, to her tummy that bulged slightly and the matching thong she wore. He rode his hands along her naked thighs and a tiny moan squeaked from her mouth.

"You are soft everywhere, sweetheart," he said, slipping his hand over her hip and edging up to her stomach. His palm against her growing belly, he stopped his exploration and bent on one knee to bestow a kiss there.

Her eyes slammed shut as Dylan worshipped their baby. It was a beautiful moment, so tender, so gentle, wiping away her fears. She couldn't fault him for anything. This situation was out of their control now. Maybe she'd been too hard on him, too rigid in her stance. He had a right to love their baby and want to share in the joy. She could give him that. She could try this dating thing, go in with an open mind and heart to see where it led.

He rose up then and stared directly into her eyes. "Our child will be beautiful like you, Emma. Inside and out."

Laying her hand flat against his cheek, scruff facial hair rough against her fingers, she whispered, "You're going to make a wonderful father, Dylan. I have no doubt."

Longing filled his eyes and he smiled. There was a moment that seemed to change everything; a newer intimacy and understanding passed between them in that moment.

And then Dylan reached for her again, pressing her fully against his hot, delicious body. Skin to skin, he kissed her for all she was worth. The next thing she knew, she was naked and they were on his bed and tangling in his sheets. Going slow was a thing of the past, and easily forgotten.

While one hand sifted through her long hair, his mouth created a dampened trail from her chin, along the base of her throat and farther down past her shoulders, until her breasts fairly ached for his touch. He came over her then and didn't disappoint, giving attention to one, then the other. Her back arched, the rosy nipples pointing up, hardened and sensitive, while white-hot heat scurried down past her belly, reaching her female core. A shudder ran through her, a beautiful sensual tremor as Dylan continued. She squirmed beneath him, the pleasure almost unbearable.

His mouth was masterful, his hands ingenious. When he moved, she moved and they were in sync, their bodies humming along together at a pace that suited her. She was in heaven, a bliss that she'd never encountered before. And it only got hotter when his hand slipped down past her navel, his fingertips teasing and taunting, edging closer to that one spot that would send her soaring.

She was damp and ready, and when he finally dipped into her soft folds, a tiny plea, a cry of pleasure, escaped her lips and she did, in fact, soar. The pressure, the light stroking growing firmer and more rhythmic worked her into a frenzied state. Dylan knew how to please. His kisses muffled her soft whimpers, his mouth devoured hers and his body radiated enough warmth to heat all of Moonlight Beach.

She reached a climax quickly. "Dylan, Dylan," she breathed, grasping his shoulders, clinging on, her heart pounding against her chest. He didn't let up until she shattered completely and was fully, wonderfully spent.

With glazed eyes, she watched him get up and remove his pants and briefs. Through the faint light streaming into the room she focused on the entire man, stark naked, virile and majorly turned on, and could only think, "Wow."

Before he climbed back onto the bed, he grabbed a golden packet from the nightstand, ripped it open and offered it to her as he lay down next to her. "For your protection."

There'd been someone before her. Probably Callista. And she was grateful for his concern, even though she was already pregnant with his child. She took it in her hands as he waited for her to slip it on him. The act was intimate, perhaps even more so than what had occurred just seconds ago.

She swallowed hard. When she was finished putting on the condom, Dylan wasted no time taking her back into his arms. "This all feels so new, sweet Emma."

"For me, too," she whispered, but there was no more room for small talk. Dylan was towering over her, using his thighs to move her legs apart. She was ready, watching him, his gorgeous face so determined, his body so in tune with hers, moving ever so slowly, nudging her core and finally, finally pushing forward, staking his claim.

She wound her arms around his neck and welcomed him. It was a glorious greeting, one that she'd always remember. Yet he took it slow, cautiously moving, giving of himself and making sure she was okay throughout.

He felt good inside her. As if she was home and where she belonged. As if she'd waited all of her life for this one moment. Safe. Secure. Happy.

But not loved.

She shoved those thoughts from her mind and concentrated on the amazing man making love to her. His blond hair was wild now, spiking up in sexy disarray. His chest heaving, his labored breaths fully accentuated his power and grace as he moved inside her. Muscles rippled and bunched. Skin sizzled and sensations ran rampant. Then those intent blue eyes locked on hers as he uttered her name and carried them both up, higher and higher.

Until the last thrust touched the deepest part of her.

She fell apart at the exact moment he did. In unison, they cried each other's names. He held on, allowing her to draw out the pleasure. And then he collapsed upon her, bracing his hands on each side of the bed to accept the brunt of his weight.

Looking at him now, she whispered, "Wow."

He grinned. The sexy man who'd just fulfilled her truest fantasy appeared to be quite satisfied. "Yeah, wow."

Rolling away from her, he landed on his back beside her. He took her hand and interlocked their fingers, staring out the window at the starry sky, listening to the pounding surf. She sensed him straining his mind, trying to recall that one night they'd shared before. "Anything?" she asked.

He gave her a quick noncommittal smile. "Everything."

She was taken by his sweet answer and the way he rolled over and kissed her. But he didn't remember anything from the blackout night. Nothing they did up until this point had triggered a memory.

"It doesn't matter if I remember or not. We've got this night and many more to come. We'll start out new, from here."

"I agree. It's a good plan." It was. She shouldn't dwell on the past any more than he should.

He laid his hand over her belly in a protective way. "New is good, Emma. Trust me."

She would have to trust him.

From now on.

"So everything looks good, Dr. Galindo?" Dylan asked, his face marked with concern. They were sitting in the office of Emma's ob-gyn.

"Yes, Mr. McKay, the baby is healthy and Emma's exam was right on point," the doctor said. She glanced at Emma and smiled. "All looks good. Be sure to continue to take your prenatal vitamins, and see me again in one month."

"Okay," Emma agreed. "I will."

"Do either of you have any further questions?"

"Just that," Emma began, "this isn't public knowledge, and we both expect our privacy to be respected."

Dr. Galindo gave Dylan a knowing look. "Of course. We honor every patient's privacy."

"Thank you. Where Dylan goes, news seems to follow."

The thirtysomething doctor smiled. Her eyes had repeatedly traveled to Dylan during the course of the consultation. Emma couldn't fault her. Dylan was A-list. He was hot and sought after and just about every woman from age ten to one hundred and ten ogled him. "Rest assured, your privacy will not be an issue with my office."

"I appreciate that." Dylan rose from his seat and shook the doctor's hand. "Thanks."

Emma noticed that his taut face had relaxed some as he led her out of the building and into his car. She, too, breathed a sigh of relief. "That went well."

"Yeah," he said. "The baby will be here in less than seven months. Hard to believe."

"For me, too. I'm grateful the baby is healthy. It was pretty cool hearing the heartbeat."

"It was awesome."

"I'll be big as a house soon."

"You'll look beautiful, Em," he said and started the engine.

"You're really okay with all of this, then?" she asked. He'd taken the news well and never once balked or hesitated when she'd revealed her pregnancy to him. It had been full steam ahead—they were having a baby together. Emma didn't quite understand his immediate acceptance, though she'd been grateful for it.

"I...am. I've always wanted to be a father. Just never found the right—"

He caught himself, but Emma knew what he was going to say. He'd never found the right woman to carry his child. Well, that decision had been taken out of his hands. She wasn't the right woman, but he was stuck with her. And she supposed that he was making the best of it.

He'd been attentive and had taken her on a date every night since that first one. One night they'd gone for ice cream at a local creamery, a place that Dylan's friend owned. They'd snuck in the back way and had taken a corner table, Dylan disguised in a Dodgers ball cap and sunglasses. The next night they'd gone to a concert at the Hollywood Bowl, Dylan scoring front row seats, and they'd gone in through a VIP entrance. Each time they went out, Dylan's bodyguards weren't far behind. It was kind of eerie knowing their every move was being watched, but as Dylan explained, it came with the territory.

She enjoyed her evenings with Dylan. And each night after their date, they'd wind up in bed together—sometimes in his gorgeous master suite and sometimes at her tiny apartment. They were growing closer each day, and getting to know one another on a different level. Dylan was kind and tender and as sexy as a man had a right to be. There were times when they were making love that she'd actually have to gasp for breath and remind herself this was really happening.

She had fallen in love with him. Truly and madly, and it had probably happened the night of their movie date. She'd always been halfway in love with him as a teen, but this was different. This was based on actually knowing him and spending time with him. It probably hadn't hurt that her orgasms were off the charts when they made love. Or that he was the father of her baby. Or that they shared a hometown history together.

But every morning, when she'd wake in his arms, he

would plant a bug in her ear. "Move in with me, Em. We could have all our nights and mornings like this."

It was a tempting offer, one that she debated for long moments, but ultimately always refused because, like it or not, she wasn't ready to give up her independence. To give Dylan her one last means of defense against heartbreak. He wanted to keep his baby safe and close at hand. She understood that, and it was a noble gesture, but what did that say about her relationship with him? It was what Dylan was *not saying* to her that fueled her resolve to stay out of harm's way.

"I don't understand why you don't want to, Em," he'd say. And she'd shrug her shoulders and shake her head. This was new to him, this constant rejection. He wasn't conceited or arrogant, but he'd been used to having women fall at his feet, she supposed, and he didn't understand her reluctance.

"I just can't, Dylan," would be her answer.

After the doctor's appointment, they went to lunch at a little private beach eatery and sat outside on benches facing the ocean. She had chicken salad and he had halibut in drawn butter. Afterward, Dylan dropped her off at the office. "Don't work too hard," he said, giving her a kiss.

"Never," she said, and he tossed his head back and laughed. He knew she was a workhorse, never settling until things were perfect and under control. He would tease her about that all the time. "You, either," she shot back.

"I won't. I'll be learning my lines for tomorrow's shoot. Which reminds me, the next two days will run long. We're having night shoots. I won't be home until after your bedtime. I'll miss you."

She smiled. "Me, too."

His eyes dipped to her belly. "Take care of the little bambino."

"Always," she said, placing her hand there protectively.

Touching her stomach and greeting the little one, warming to him or her and the idea of a baby, had become a habit.

She climbed out of the car, waved goodbye, and then he was off. She wouldn't see him for the next few days. Maybe that was a good thing. She watched him drive into the traffic stream before stepping into the office.

"Hey, how did the appointment go?" Brooke asked, gazing up from her desk.

"Wonderful. Everything is good."

Brooke grinned. "Great. I can't wait to find out if it's a boy or girl. I'm making up a shopping list and already have three my-auntie-is-the-best outfits picked out. Now, just gotta know if I'm buying blue or pink."

Brooke was definitely going to spoil the baby. "It'll be fun finding out."

"Yeah, but for now, I'm just happy knowing the baby's healthy."

Brooke rose from her desk and approached her. "Things are working out with Dylan, aren't they?" she asked. "I mean, you sound happy. You look happy and well. I know you've been dating, hot and heavy."

"Hot and heavy?" Emma's laughter sounded a little too high-pitched even to her ears and Brooke caught on immediately.

"Wow, so it's true. You and my brother are hooking up."

Well, yeah, she supposed they were. He'd asked her to move in with him several times, but never with any true sense of commitment. Was that what she was waiting for? Some hope, some sign that he wanted her, and not just because she was going to give birth to his child? Maybe what she wanted from Dylan was impossible for him to give. "Brooke, I have no name for what's happening between Dylan and me."

"At least something is happening." Excitement sparkled in Brooke's eyes.

"Maybe you should concentrate on your relationship with Royce," Emma countered, giving her BFF a wry smile.

"Oh, believe me, I do." Brooke giggled. "We're heading to hot and heavy, too."

"Wow, you two are moving fast."

Brooke sighed. "I know. It's crazy, but we're in tune with each other on every level."

"I'm happy for you."

"Thanks. Now, on to work issues. We've got the Henderson anniversary party on Friday night and then we've got Clinton's seventh birthday party in Beverly Hills all day Saturday. Which one do you want to confirm?"

"I'll take Clinton's party. I've made special arrangements for the petting zoo and the cartoon characters to show up and I've got the cake and food already set. I'll double-check it's a go, and you can make your confirmations for the anniversary gig."

"Okay, sounds good. It's going to be a busy weekend. Are you sure you're up for it?"

"I'm sure." Emma had been operating at 90 percent and feeling better every day. Dylan had been keeping her plenty busy at night, too, exhausting her in a good way. She'd been sleeping soundly and waking feeling sated and refreshed, but the thought of not seeing him for the next few nights suddenly cast a shadow of loneliness on her perspective.

How odd. Usually she valued her downtime and enjoyed being on her own.

"Oh, yeah," Brooke said, making a face. "I almost forgot to tell you, Maury Allen called today. Seems his event planner for Callista's big birthday bash had a family emergency and he can't continue the work. He wants us to take over. It's in two weeks."

"You told him no, didn't you?" Emma held her breath.

Brooke scrunched her face even more. "Well," she squeaked. "I couldn't do that. He used Dylan's name as a reference and made it seem like my brother recommended us to him. He's Dylan's boss and he said everything's pretty much done. All we have to do is show up and make things run smoothly."

"Brooke!"

"I know. But he took me by surprise and I didn't think I could worm out of it."

"Couldn't his planner get someone else from their company to step in?"

She shook her head. "They're all booked solid. And we're not. His secretary is overnighting the signed vendor contracts and the itinerary so we know what's planned."

Emma rolled her eyes. "That's just wonderful."

"Sorry." To Brooke's credit, she did seem genuinely apologetic. "You don't have to go. I'll get Wendy or Rocky to help out."

"Knowing Callista, it's going to be a giant production. You're going to need me."

Brooke ducked her head and looked sheepish. "I think you may be right."

Shoulders tight and arms crossed, Emma leaned against the wall and sent a disgruntled sigh out to the universe. "I guess I was destined to go to this thing."

"Destined? What do you mean?"

"Dylan asked me to go to Callista's party as his date. He said he wanted company in his misery, but I flat out refused. The woman barely gets my name right."

Brooke chuckled. "Just call her Callie, like I do. You know what they say about payback."

"I can't do that. She's our client now."

"Her father's our client."

"It's practically the same thing," Emma said. "She's got him wrapped around her diamond-ringed finger."

"True, but I wish I could be there when she…"

Brooke's expression was way too mischievous for Emma's curiosity. "What?"

"When she finds out you're carrying Dylan's child."

"Brooke! You're not going to say a thing. Promise me."

She glanced at Emma's belly bump and smiled. "I promise. But maybe I won't have to say anything. Maybe she'll find out on her own. Now, *that* would be worth the price of admission."

Emma couldn't suppress a smile. She grinned along with her friend. "You're wicked."

"Yes, and that's why you love me."

Seven

Emma dragged herself through the door on Saturday evening, her twenty-five-year-old bones aching. She was too tired to make it to her bedroom. She tossed her handbag onto the sofa, then plopped down next to it. The well-worn cushions welcomed her and she put her feet up on the coffee table. Stretching out, she closed her eyes.

Little Clinton's birthday party had done her in. It had gone fairly well for a seven-year-old's party, though there'd been a few potential disasters in the making. One of the goats in the petting zoo had escaped the pen and begun nibbling on the party decorations. The kids thought it hilarious, until the darn goat made a dash for the cupcake table and nearly downed the whole thing. Emma screamed for the zookeeper to do something, and he'd looked up oblivious to the goings-on from across the yard, giving her no choice but to navigate the stubborn animal back to the pen herself.

But that was an innocent mistake, unlike the guy dressed

in a furry purple character costume. Judging by the way he was walking, the guy must have been intoxicated. It was either that or balancing himself in the costume was too much for him. She'd kept her eyes peeled on him for the entire day and thankfully he didn't cause any trouble.

Then there was the incident at the taco bar. The kids took one bite of their tacos and their little mouths were set on fire from too much chipotle sauce added to the meat. Emma escorted those kids right over to the snow cone machine. Rainbow ice doused the flames and put smiles on their faces again. Disaster averted, but not before Emma scolded the cook. What had he been thinking?

Emma leaned forward and did slow head circles, first one way, then the other. The stretch and pull felt good, easing away a full day's worth of tension. Her cell phone rang and she had a mind not to answer it, but as she glanced at the screen name, she smiled and picked up. "Hi, Dylan."

"Hi," he said in that low, masculine tone that made her dizzy. "What are you doing?"

"Just putting my feet up. It's been a long day."

"Tired?"

"Yeah, pretty much. What are you doing?"

"Driving by your apartment."

"You are?" She bolted straight up, her heartbeat speeding.

"Yeah, I thought I'd take a chance and see if you were up to company. If you're too tired, I'll just keep on driving."

God, just the sound of his voice roused her out of exhaustion. It had been three days since she'd seen him. He'd been constantly on her mind. "I'm not too tired."

"You sure? You sound wiped out."

"I'm...not."

"I'll be right there."

A soft flow of warmth spread through her body. Her hormones were happy now. Beautifully, wonderfully happy. Just minutes later, she opened the door and he walked straight into her arms. He lifted her off the ground as he kissed her and moved her backward to the sofa, setting her down and taking a seat next to her. "I'm not staying. I just wanted to see you," he said, wrapping his arms around her shoulders.

"I'm glad. I, uh, I wanted to see you, too." It was always hard admitting how she was feeling toward Dylan. She wasn't playing hard to get. She was running scared, frightened that this big bubble of joy would pop at any moment.

"How was your day?"

"Chasing goats and kids and keeping parents happy, just a usual Saturday afternoon fun day."

Dylan smiled. "You love it."

"I do. I'm not complaining." It was what she was meant to do. She enjoyed every facet of event planning. Though it was a hassle at times and deadlines could be gruesome, the end result, a successful party, was her reward. She couldn't imagine having a nine-to-five job, although she thoroughly enjoyed keeping the books and managing the accounts, too.

Dylan grasped her hand and brought it to his knee. It was as natural as breathing for him to hold on to her this way. "I'm glad you're in business with my sister."

"Me, too. I think our talents complement each other. She's the creative one and I'm the practical one."

"You work hard. Don't take this the wrong way, but you look exhausted."

She sighed. "There's no fooling you."

"I'm quite perceptive." He smiled at her and his sea-blue eyes softened. "Turn around."

"What?"

"Turn your back to me and try to relax."

"Okay."

She angled away from him on the sofa and then his hand gently moved her hair off her shoulders. It fell in a tangle on her right side. Next, he placed both hands on her shoulder blades and began a firm but soothing massage. The tension was released immediately, and as he worked the kinks out and moved farther down her back, she closed her eyes. "Oh, that feels good," she cooed.

"That's the plan, sweetheart."

His hands on her body were a comforting, soothing presence lifting her spirits, a balm for her tired bones.

"Why don't we take this into the bedroom," he whispered, his breath tickling her ear. "Where you can stretch out and really relax."

She turned to face him.

"Just a massage, I promise. Deal?"

"Deal."

And then she was being lifted and carried toward her bedroom. Her independence had flown the coop the minute Dylan had shown up. But she loved his inner he-man and the way he took control of a situation. It was amazingly sexy.

She played with the curl of hair resting on his nape. "You don't have to make deals with me, Dylan."

"Don't tempt me. I know how tired you are and let's leave it at that."

She nodded.

A slender shaft of light from the courtyard illuminated her bedroom window. Dylan lowered her to a standing position by her bed and moved behind her. With one hand on either side of her back, he inched her blouse up and over her head, tossing it onto the nightstand. Then he helped to remove her slacks. Down to a white bra and panties, she kicked off her shoes and turned to face him.

There was a sharp rasp of breath as he looked at her. "This isn't going to be as easy as I thought," he muttered in a tortured tone. "Lie down. I'll be right back."

Emma pulled her sheets back and lowered down onto

her tummy, resting her head on her pillow. When Dylan returned, he held a bottle of raspberry vanilla essential oil. "This okay to use?"

She nodded and closed her eyes. She heard the sound of his hands slapping together as he warmed the oil and then felt the dip of the mattress as he sat beside her. "Ready?"

"Oh, yes."

He spread the oil onto her skin, his touch light and generous as he rubbed every inch of her back. The pleasing scents of raspberry and vanilla wafted to her nostrils in the most delicious way. Using his thumbs, Dylan pressed the small of her back in circular motions, his fingers resting on the slope of her behind. She tingled there and her breath caught noisily. This was quickly becoming more than a massage and almost more intimate than having sex with Dylan. He removed his fingers, using his thumbs to walk up her spine.

"Oh, so nice," she whispered.

"I'm glad you're enjoying this."

"Aren't you?"

"Too much."

She grinned and endorphins released merrily through her body.

He lifted his hands off her back and again she heard the smack of his hands as he warmed the oil. Next, he worked her legs, starting at her ankles, gliding his hands up and down, around and around, bringing new life to her tired limbs. First one calf, then the other, and then he was inching his hands up the backs of her thighs. He slowed his pace and stopped for a moment.

"Dylan?"

"I'm okay," he said, his voice quietly pained.

"This isn't supposed to make you tense."

"Too late for that, sweetheart. Just relax and enjoy."

But there was something too tempting, too genuine in

his voice for her to sit back and take this without giving something back. She shifted her position, landing on her back. One look at his gorgeous face, his gritted teeth and set jaw had her gaze moving down below his waist. She wasn't surprised to see the strain of material in his pants.

"I didn't come here for—"

"I know, and it makes it all the more sweet." She lifted her arms and reached for him. "Come here, Dylan." she said. "Let me do something for you."

"There's no need," he said, but it was too late. She grabbed him around the neck and pulled him down on top of her. He was careful where he landed and avoided plopping on her belly.

"I'm not tired anymore. In fact, I'm feeling pretty loose," she said softly. "And you deserve a massage, too."

Emma stood over the sizzling range top, flipping pancakes on a griddle, a pleasing hum running through her body. Last night's massages had turned into something pretty spectacular and now she was famished. She'd crept out of bed, leaving Dylan sleeping, to make him a nourishing breakfast. He'd sure earned it judging by the energy he'd exerted making love to her last night.

When his arms wrapped around her waist, she nearly jumped out of her skin. She hadn't heard him come up behind her. "Morning," he said, nibbling on her neck.

"I thought you were sleeping."

"I missed you."

God, he said all the right things. "Sweet."

"You're sweet to make us breakfast."

"Us?" She chuckled. "What makes you think this is for you?"

He tightened his hold on her and then reached around her body to turn the knob, shutting off the burner. "Dylan, what are you—"

He turned her around and kissed her complaint away. Then he gave her a heart-melting smile and tugged her away from the stove. He'd already put his clothes from yesterday back on. They looked amazingly unwrinkled and fresh, while she was wearing gray sweats and a pink tank sporting the Parties-To-Go logo in purple glitter, her hair in a messy ponytail.

Holding her hand, he led her to the living area. Her heart was beating fast now. What was he up to? He turned to her and the expression on his face was dead serious. "I've been thinking, Em. About us."

She gulped. Us?

"You and I, we're going to be parents soon and I guess I'm an old-fashioned guy when it comes to kids and all. I see a bright future ahead for us, the *three* of us. We'll be a family, a real honest-to-goodness family, and I think the baby deserves the very best start in life. That means having a mother and father raise the child together. I care very much for you, Emma. You know that. We're good together, if last night isn't proof enough." His smile was a little wobbly now and Emma's heart pounded even harder. He was going to press her to move in with him.

"I'm not going to ask you to move in with me anymore, Em."

"You're not?" She blinked. This was new.

He shook his head. "No. That's not the solution."

He gazed deep into her eyes. "I want you to marry me."

Emma's mouth opened and a sharp gasp escaped. "Oh."

"I'm asking you to be my wife, Emma. I've given this a lot of thought and I can only see good things in store for the three of us."

She dropped her hand from his and shuffled her feet. Inside, everything was stirring, a mad mix of emotions and thoughts flying through her head. "This is...um, unexpected."

"Really, Em? It's not so far-fetched to think that two people conceiving a child together would get married, is it?"

He made it seem so simple. He cared for her. And Lord knew, she cared even more for him. She loved him. Could they make it work, even though he didn't say the words a woman being proposed to was meant to hear? There was no claim of undying love, nothing about how he couldn't live without her and how his life would be empty without her in it. Yet Dylan had spoken honestly, giving her genuine reasons why this was a good idea.

But doubts immediately crept in. He was Dylan McKay, eligible bachelor extraordinaire, a highly sought-after movie star, a man whose life was obviously filled with temptations at every turn. Could she place her trust in him not to break her heart and soul? Could she marry a man who didn't outright love her?

"Em, you don't have to give me your answer right now. Take some time," he said, his voice laced with tenderness and understanding. "Give it some thought. I'm not going anywhere. I'll be right here."

A huge part of her wanted to say yes, but she couldn't make this decision on the spur of the moment. She was being given the moon, but was it greedy of her to want the sun and the stars, too?

"Dylan," she began softly, "I can't give you an answer right now. Everything is happening so fast."

"I know. I get it, Em. I don't want to add to your stress. Believe me, I only want what's best for you. But I wanted to get my feelings out in the open. I think it's the right move, but I won't pressure you. I'll wait until you've made your decision."

"Thank you. I appreciate that. So, um…where do we go from here?"

Dylan grinned. "You finish making me breakfast. I'm

starving and those pancakes look pretty appetizing. And tomorrow night, we'll have a dinner date at my house. Sound good?"

She nodded. So they'd resume dating, *with the option of marriage*.

So that was it. He'd proposed and now they were back to the status quo. The ball was in her court, as they say. How on earth would she be able to make this decision? Her foster parents' marriage had been a train wreck. They'd fought constantly and Emma often felt she was to blame. She'd cower under a blanket in the far corner of her bedroom and cover her ears to block out their vulgar arguments. She never wanted a child of hers to go through that kind of pain and torment. Would Emma and Dylan end up hating each other and fighting constantly, just as her folks had?

Just as important, could she possibly say no to Dylan and refuse his marriage proposal? Or even more frightening, could she allow herself to say yes to him without having his love?

"Sounds perfect," she said with a manufactured smile.

Lying to Dylan and to…herself.

Monday morning Emma walked into her office, greeted Brooke, plopped into the chair behind her desk and began working. She was in the early planning stages of a Bar Mitzvah and had many calls to make. She worked diligently, struggling to keep her mind on business.

Later that morning, she met with vendors, a florist and photographer, and then returned to the office feeling somewhat accomplished. But all day long, she'd been distracted and had a difficult time focusing. She'd made a few mistakes along the way as well, giving the wrong dates to a vendor and then having to recalculate an estimate she'd given and call back a client with the bad news that she'd made an error. That never went over well and she'd wound up giving them a 10 percent discount to make up for it.

Brooke had cast furtive glances at her all day long and no matter how much she tried to behave like her normal self, Emma figured she hadn't fooled her friend. To add to her dismay, a gorgeous bouquet of pink Stargazer lilies had been delivered in a bubble crystal vase while she was gone. They sat on one corner of her desk now and flavored the air with a wonderful floral scent.

The note read: *Just Because. Dylan*

By late afternoon, Brooke approached, taking a seat on the edge of Emma's desk. "Hey, Em?"

Emma's lips twisted. She knew the drill, but refused to look up from her computer screen. "Hey, yourself."

"So what's wrong? You've been distracted all day."

"I can make an error once in a while, Brooke."

"I make errors all the time, but not you, Little Miss Organized. You don't make mistakes."

"Well, call me perfect, then."

"Emma?" Brooke put a motherly tone in her voice. "What's up? And don't tell me nothing. Did you and Dylan have a fight or something?"

Emma finally shifted her focus and looked into Brooke's concerned eyes. "No," she said emphatically. "We didn't fight. He asked me to marry him."

Brooke's face lit up. "Really?"

Emma ran both hands down her cheeks, pulling the skin taut. "Really."

"Oh, so you're bothered by his proposal?"

"It wasn't so much a proposal, but a sort of bargain, for the baby's sake. Not that I don't want what's best for the baby. I do, but I don't know. I'm…confused."

"Did he say he wanted to marry you?"

"Yes, of course he did."

"And did he say he wanted you, him and baby to be his family?"

"Yes. That's what he wants."

"He's very fond of you, Emma. He's always liked you."

"I know that."

"So how do you feel about him? And be honest."

Emma tugged on her long braid, twisting it around and around in her hand. Her mouth twitched and she blinked a few times. This was a hard thing for her to admit even to Brooke "I've fallen in love with him," she finally said.

Brooke didn't get excited about her admission and Emma was grateful for that. Instead, she took her hand and smiled. "I see the problem." Brooke knew her so well. "You're worried he may not return the feelings."

"Ever."

"Ever," Brooke repeated softly. "Well, all I can say is that Dylan is capable of great love. He accepted me from day one when I came to the McKay house to live. Here I was this little frightened girl with no family, and there was this older boy who seemed to have it all, a nice set of parents, and friends and a decent house to live in. I was afraid he'd hate me for imposing on his family, but he did just the opposite. He made me feel welcomed, and the first time he called me his little sister, I cried big sloppy tears and he hugged me hard and said something funny that made me laugh. From then on, I was okay with Dylan and he was okay with me.

"I can't tell you what to do, Emma. You're my friend and you deserve to be loved, but I know my brother will never intentionally hurt you. He's gonna love the baby you're carrying with all his heart. And I know you will, too. You'll have that in common and that's a bond that will carry you into the future. It's up to you, to figure out if that's enough." Brooke gave her hand a last squeeze, then stood up. "Are you okay?"

Emma nodded. "I'm much better. Thanks, Brooke. It helps."

A weight had been lifted from her shoulders. Brooke's rational, though slightly biased, opinion made sense to her. She had the moon in the palm of her hands, and maybe just maybe, the sun and the stars would come later on.

Late-afternoon runs always served to clear Dylan's mind, and today's jog along the shoreline did the trick. He wasn't running the ten miles he'd been doing before the accident, but he managed five miles today without too much problem.

As he climbed the steps that led to his house, he nodded to Dan, one of his bodyguards, who'd been on the beach running behind him and watching him diligently. That was another reason he hadn't resumed the longer runs. Dan wasn't up to it. Not too many people were. Dylan had been doing endurance runs for months during his training for this SEAL movie. His bodyguard was fit but hadn't been training as intensely as Dylan had.

He went inside and stopped in the kitchen, grabbed a bottle of water from the fridge and gulped it down in three big swallows. As he moved toward the staircase, he lifted his T-shirt over his head and used it to sop up beads of sweat raining down his chest. Emma was coming for dinner soon. He'd given Maisey time off today so that they'd have time alone. Yesterday, he'd jumped into the waters with both feet, spontaneously proposing to Emma, and he hoped he'd made an impression. He had a ring ready for her, one he'd been carrying around with him for days, but putting that ring on her finger would have to wait until she accepted his proposal.

When the doorbell rang, he blinked in surprise and strode to the front door. He'd given Emma the remote control to the garage door entryway and wondered why she didn't come through the back door as usual. Peeking through the peephole, his shoulders drooped when he saw Callista standing on the threshold. He made a mental note to change the code to his front gate.

Opening the door, he greeted her. "Hi, Callista, what are you doing here?" He put as much civility in his voice as he could muster.

"I came to check on you." She glanced at his bare chest and black running shorts, smiled and whizzed by him, entering his home. "Did I ever tell you how much I love this vertical garden? It's a masterpiece," she said, eyeing the lush wall of succulents spilling down from the tall ceiling in his foyer.

Dylan grimaced before facing her. She turned back around and waited for him to shut the door.

"No, I don't think you ever have." He closed the door.

"Well, I do. I love it."

He nodded and stood his ground.

"Aren't you going to ask me in?"

She was already in, but that was beside the point. He'd have to deal with her, explain that he wasn't interested in a relationship with her any longer and hope that they could still remain friends. She should've already gotten the hint, since he hadn't called her since the day of Roy's memorial service, but Callista wasn't easily put off. "Come in, please. After you." He gestured for her to lead the way.

She walked into the living room and leaned against one of the open double doors to the veranda. "It's a beautiful time of day, Dylan. I love the sea air. I've missed coming here."

He had nothing to say to that.

"It looks like you've been running."

"Yeah, I'm getting back into it. It feels good, clears my head."

"So, you're feeling better?"

"I'm doing well."

"That's good to hear. You look amazing."

"So do you, Callista. As always."

She was a beautiful woman, her honey-blond hair cut longer on one side than the other in a sleek style, her eyes a glistening blue, her body as slim as a supermodel's. She dressed impeccably, in the latest fashion, her clothes fitting her flamboyant personality. Unfortunately what she had on the outside didn't make up for her lack of humanity on the inside. She wasn't a bad person, just self-absorbed, and he couldn't lay all the blame at her feet. She'd been spoiled and indulged all of her life by her parents and her friends, and it had taken Dylan getting to know Emma as well as he did now to make the comparison and see which woman he wanted in his life.

"Are you okay, Dylan? I mean, really okay? Daddy told me about the possible threat to your life and I'm…I'm so worried about you."

"I'm fine. And they're not absolutely sure if it was an attempt on my life. But to put your mind at ease, I've added additional security around here and I travel with bodyguards all the time now. I'm sure your father told you to keep this private. There's an investigation going on."

"Yes, of course. On any given day there are hundreds of people at the studio, Dylan. How can they possibly find out who's responsible?"

"I don't know, Callista." At least he'd be finished shooting the movie in a few weeks and wouldn't have to go into the studio anymore. "All we can do is hope the investigation gives them some leads."

"Gosh, I hope so."

Dylan softened a little. Callista seemed genuinely concerned for him. He couldn't deny that they'd had a past relationship and that they still cared for each other's welfare. "Thanks. I appreciate it. I value your friendship."

She walked over to him, placed her palm on his cheek and locked her pretty doe eyes on his. "We're more than friends, Dylan. I'd hoped you'd remembered that." She brushed her lips to his and spoke softly over his mouth. "And it would make me very happy if you'd be my date for my birthday party."

Emma shut her mind off to all of her misgivings about Dylan and looked upon his proposal more openly now. Her conversation with Brooke had helped her see things in a new perspective. She was still debating about marrying him, but at least the roadblocks in her head were slowly being taken down. She'd realized this as she was baking him a chocolate marble cake today, just like the one she'd demolished on her birthday years ago. If they could have a good laugh over it, then the cake would serve its purpose. Smiling, she entered the gates of his home, noting a foreign sports car in his driveway she didn't recognize. Oh well, so much for having a quiet evening together. He had a visitor.

Emma parked her car in one of the empty garages on his property and carefully removed the cake holder, balancing it in one hand as she went up to the house and unlocked the back door with a hidden key. When she entered, she heard voices and debated about barging in, but as she moved into the kitchen, she recognized the seductive female voice.

Callista.

Emma set the cake down on the countertop and strode quietly toward the living room. She came to an abrupt stop when she saw Callista and Dylan tangled up in one another's arms at the far end of the room. She blinked several times, not believing what she was seeing. Her first thought was how wonderful they looked together, two stunning people living in the same high-profile world, a place where Emma didn't fit. They were the beautiful people, A-listers with friends who owned islands and airplanes and villas on the French Riviera. Seeing the two of them cuddled up good and tight, whispering to each other, brought it all to light. Emma didn't belong in Dylan's universe. Jealousy jabbed at her over the unfairness of it all.

But Dylan wasn't Callista's to ensnare. She wasn't the right woman for him.

Emma had had dibs on him since forever. Was she going to give him up without a fight? Shockingly, her answer was a flat-out no. She couldn't let Dylan get away. Jealousy aside, she wasn't going to hand her baby's father over to the wrong woman. Dylan had asked her, Emma Rae Bloom, to marry him, something he hadn't done since Renee had torn his heart to shreds. And now, Emma was beginning to see a life with him and their baby. So what was her problem? Why hadn't she jumped at his proposal last night? Why was she being so darn hardheaded?

To his credit, Dylan backed away from Callista instantly, wriggling out of her clutches before she could kiss him again. He didn't see Emma standing there, so there was no pretense for her sake. He really was rejecting the woman.

"I can't be your date, Callista," she heard him say.

Emma breathed a big sigh of relief.

"Why?" She approached him again, a question in her eyes. "I don't understand."

Emma gulped air loudly, deliberately. She'd heard enough. Both heads turned in her direction. Callista's mouth twisted in annoyance and Dylan, God love him, appeared truly relieved to see her. He put his arm out, reaching for Emma's hand, much to the other woman's horror, and Emma floated over to him and took it.

He smiled at her, and before he could say anything, Emma announced, "Dylan is my fiancé, Callista. I'm going to marry him."

Callista's mouth dropped open. Clearly stunned, she darted glances from Emma to Dylan and back again. And then her gaze shot like a laser beam down to Emma's slightly bulging belly. She was sharp, Emma had to give her that. "You're pregnant."

Dylan pulled her closer in, winding his arm around her waist in a show of support. "I'm sorry, Callista, but that's not an issue here. I was going to tell you about Emma and me."

"When, at my birthday party? The one she's supposed to plan and execute?"

Dylan's eyes never wavered. He was such a good actor. As far as she knew, Dylan had no knowledge of that latest development. "Under the circumstances, that's not going to happen now. I hope we can still be friendly, Callista. We've known each other a long time."

Callista ignored Emma once again, speaking to Dylan as if she wasn't standing there, in his embrace. "You can't be serious, Dylan. You're going to marry her?"

"Of course I'm serious. When have you known me not to be?"

"But…but…"

Emma stifled a giggle. She'd never seen Callista speechless before.

And finally, "You cheated on me with *her*!"

Dylan's brows gathered; his eyes grew dark and dangerous. "Don't go there, Callista. I never cheated on a woman in my life. We were on-again, off-again, and before my accident we were definitely off. Big-time off. And you know it."

Callista made a show of grabbing her purse and stomping away. Before exiting the room, she swiveled around and glared at Emma. "It'll never last. He's just doing this for the kid. Wait and see."

The front door slammed shut behind her.

Neither of them moved.

Seconds ticked by.

God, all of Emma's fears had come full circle in Callista's venomous declaration. Those three sentences revealed Emma's innermost doubts. A tremor ran through her. Could she do this? Could she really marry Dylan?

And then Dylan faced her, the darkness of his expression evaporating into something hopeful and sweet. His eyes gleamed and the way he held on to her as if she was precious to him, as if he was truly happy, convinced her to stay the course. She'd made up her mind and couldn't bear losing Dylan. If they had a chance at a future together, she was going to take it.

"You're really going to marry me? You weren't just saying that?" he asked.

"It wasn't the perfect way to tell you, but yes. I'm going to marry you."

His brilliant smile warmed all the cold places that threatened her happiness. "Good. Okay. Good. The sooner the better."

He kissed her then, and all of her doubts flittered away on the breeze. She would give herself up to him now. She wouldn't hold back. She was all in, and she would think only positive thoughts from now on.

After a long embrace, Dylan shook his head. "I'm sorry about that scene with Callista. I didn't know she was coming over."

"She was very upset, Dylan."

"She's dramatic and only upset because she didn't get her way. In her heart, she had to know we were over. But the truth is, I never cheated on her with you or anyone. It's important that you believe me."

"I do," she said. These past few weeks with Dylan had shown her what kind of a man he truly was. The tabloids liked to paint a less-than-rosy picture of celebrities, but

Emma didn't and wouldn't believe a word of it about Dylan McKay. She'd walked in on Dylan rebuffing Callista's advances and that alone was proof enough for her. She could place her faith in Dylan.

She had to.

He was going to be her husband.

Eight

Warm Pacific gusts lifted her wedding veil off her shoulders as she stood on the steps of Adam Chase's palatial oceanside home, waiting for her cue to walk down an aisle laden with red rose petals. They, too, blew in the breeze in sweeping patterns that colored the pathway in a natural special effect.

She looked out to the small cluster of friends and family in attendance, no more than thirty strong. Their secluded little wedding ceremony was about to begin. Dylan's mother was here, and Brooke, of course, was her maid of honor. She'd helped Emma into her ivory, Cinderella-style wedding dress. Wendy and Rocky were here, her part-timers who'd actually become dear friends. Dylan's agent and manager attended as well as his closest neighbors—Adam Chase, his wife, Mia, and their adorable baby, Rose, seated next to Jessica and her country superstar husband, Zane Williams.

It had been Adam's idea to hold the wedding here, the

reclusive architect offering a place for their secretive ceremony away from any paparazzi who might've gotten wind of their engagement. To their surprise, Callista hadn't spread any ugly gossip as yet and Dylan had insisted on marrying quickly. Parties-To-Go had immediately been fired from holding Callista's big birthday event, much to Brooke's glee. Ironically, Dylan's hectic work schedule only allowed them to get married on the very same day.

The music began, the traditional "Wedding March" played by a string quartet bringing tears to Emma's eyes. Her foster parents had declined the invitation to attend, claiming illness—aka too much alcohol—so Emma began her trek down the aisle on her own, the way she'd always done things.

She didn't mind, though, because waiting for her at the end of the white aisle, dressed in a stunning black tuxedo, his blond hair spiky, his blue eyes twinkling, was the man she'd always dreamed about marrying, Dylan McKay. As she held her bouquet of delicate snowflake-white lilies and baby red roses, beautiful emotions carried her toward him, each step a commitment to making their marriage work, to having the family she never thought she'd have.

The small group of guests stood as she flowed past them toward Dylan, her eyes straight ahead. When she reached him, he took her arm and led her to the minister and the flowered, latticed canopy that would be their altar. There, they spoke their vows of commitment and devotion.

For only a minute she was saddened that no words of actual love were spoken. Wasn't it odd, a union taking place where neither of the participants spoke of undying love and devotion?

But once they were declared man and wife, Dylan cupped her face and kissed her with enough passion to wipe out any feelings of sadness. From this day forward...

she would look only to the future. She'd promised. And so had he.

"Family and friends," the minister said, "I give you Mr. and Mrs. Dylan McKay."

As they turned to face their guests, applause broke out.

"Hello, Mrs. McKay," Dylan said, kissing her again.

"Dylan, I hardly believe this is real."

"It's real." It was the last thing he said to her before they were separated and the guests bombarded each of them with congratulations.

Brooke ran over to Emma and hugged her so tight, her veil tilted to one side of her head. Brooke stomped her feet up and down several times, her joy overflowing. "I can't believe you're my sister now! I mean we always were like sisters, but now you're truly family. This is the best. The very best. Oh, here, let me fix your veil. My duty as your maid of honor."

She refastened the veil just as Royce walked up. "Congratulations, Emma."

"Thank you, Royce. It's great to finally meet you."

"Same here. And on such a special day. I feel honored to be invited."

"I'm glad you're here. Brooke looks great, doesn't she?"

Royce glanced at his date. Brooke was wearing a red halter gown, tastefully decorated with sequins along the bodice. She'd promised she wouldn't wear black, and when they'd shopped and she'd tried this one on, both knew it was perfect for her. Her gorgeous long dark hair hung in tight curls down her back and complemented the dress. "Yes, she does."

"Have you met Dylan yet?"

"No," Royce said. "But I'm looking forward to it."

"He's scared," Brooke said, grinning. "Meeting my famous big brother isn't in his wheelhouse. Isn't that right, honey?"

"Well…uh…I must admit, he's such a big star, I'm a little intimidated."

"Don't be. Dylan's a good guy," Emma said. "He's harmless."

"That's good to hear."

"I keep telling him that, too," Brooke said. "But you, Emma, are the beautiful one. You look like the happiest bride in the world, and that dress…well, you destroy in it."

Emma laughed. "Thanks, I think."

"You do look very pretty, Emma," Royce said.

"And I agree." Dylan came from out of nowhere to take her hand. "You look gorgeous today, Em. My beautiful bride." He kissed her cheek and played with a curl hanging down from her upswept hair.

Brooke wasted no time introducing Dylan to her boyfriend. The two men talked for a few minutes and Brooke seemed immensely happy that they seemed to be getting along.

Just a few minutes later, Dylan's mother walked into their circle and took Emma aside. "I've always thought of you as my second daughter, Emma, you know that. You've been part of our family since the first day Brooke brought you over to our house, but I can't even begin to tell you how happy I am that you and Dylan are married." Katherine McKay hugged her tight, just as she had when Emma was a kid. Growing up, Emma was made to feel welcome and accepted, not by her own foster parents, but by the McKay family. "I know you're going to be a wonderful wife and mother to my first grandchild," Katherine continued, her gracious smile widening. "I am very excited about the baby, in case you can't tell. If you ever need help or advice, please promise you'll ask."

"I promise, Mrs. McKay."

"I'd be honored if you called me Mom."

Tears rushed into Emma eyes. The notion was so sweet and exactly what she needed to hear. "I will, from now on."

"That's good, honey." Katherine kissed her cheek and winked. "Now, I have to congratulate my son. He's made a wise choice."

After pictures were taken and the cocktail hour was observed, dinner was served on the veranda. A stone fireplace crackled and popped, adding ambience to an already elegant day. The wedding had been small, but with attention to detail. Leave it to Brooke to make all the last-minute arrangements. She was a dynamo, and Dylan spared no expense. It was a dream wedding as far as Emma was concerned.

As a disc jockey started setting up, Adam Chase, Dylan's best man, gave a toast. "To my neighbor and good friend Dylan," he said, holding up a flute of champagne. "May you enjoy the very same kind of happiness that I have found in Mia and my daughter, Rose. I'll admit it takes a very special young woman to get Dylan to the altar. He's avoided it for too many years, so to Emma, for making an honest man out of Dylan."

Laughter rippled through the crowd and cheers went up. Everyone but Emma sipped champagne. She opted for sparkling cider and enjoyed it down to the last drop. Dylan held her hand and nodded to Zane. To her surprise, the country crooner slid a chair over to the front of the veranda near the steps, took up his guitar and sat down. "If you all don't mind, I'd like to dedicate this song to my friend Dylan and his new bride, Emma. It's called 'This Stubborn Heart of Mine.' Dylan, feel free to dance this first dance with your wife. And no, this song wasn't written with you in mind, my friend, but if the shoe fits."

Another round of laughter hummed through the guests seated at their tables.

Dylan pulled Emma out onto the dance floor. "May I have this dance, sweetheart?"

And as Zane sang a sweet, soulful ballad, Dylan took her into his arms and twirled her around and around, his moves graceful and smooth. Emma was happier than she'd ever been, but still the notion of getting married to the most eligible bachelor on the planet at a beachfront mansion and having her own personal country superstar dedicate a song to her was surreal.

"You're quiet," Dylan said halfway through the dance.

"I'm…taking it all in. I'm not used to this much…"

"Attention?"

"Everything. It's…kind of perfect."

Dylan hugged her close as the song came to an end, whispering in her ear, "Kind of perfect? Just wait until tonight."

Emma snapped her head up, gazing into his incredibly seductive, amazingly clear blue eyes.

Maybe this marriage-to-Dylan thing would work out after all.

The light of a dozen candles twinkled all around Dylan's master bedroom, but nothing was brighter than the wedding ring he'd put on her finger today. The brilliance of the oval diamond surrounded by perfect smaller diamonds had stunned her into tears. The sweet scent of roses flavored the air, and her bouquet and flowers from the ceremony decorated the room as well, reminding her, as if she could forget, that Dylan was now her husband.

He'd succeeded in making her wedding day a fantasy come true. Now she faced him still wearing her wedding gown, feeling very much like Cinderella. Handsome in his tux, he gazed upon her, his mouth lifted in a smile. "Are you ready for the rest of our life?"

"Oh, yes."

He took her hands in his. "You were a beautiful bride

today, Emma, but now it's time to take this dress off and make you my wife."

Emma's body sang from his words and the anticipation of what the night would bring. "I'm ready."

She stood still as Dylan circled around her. He lifted the tiara from her head, the veil having long ago been removed. Cool air struck her back as he unfastened one tiny button after another. Her body warmed with each flick of his finger as he skimmed her skin. Once done, he spread the satiny material off her shoulders and kissed the back of her neck. A prickling feeling erupted there and followed the path of his hands as they moved the dress down her body. His gentle touch unleashed something wild in her, even as he took his time and took care with her dress. She stepped out of it and he gathered it up and set it over a chair. She stood before him in white lace panties, and as he approached her with fire in his eyes, he undid his bow tie, shed his white shirt and unbuckled his belt.

Pangs of impatient longing stormed her body. They'd gone the old-fashioned route and hadn't slept with each other since the day she'd agreed to become his wife. Now all that pent-up hunger was ready to explode and she couldn't remember ever feeling this way before. Not even on that first night, when she'd dragged Dylan on top of her during the blackout and they'd made reckless love. She knew the difference now. She understood why it seemed so different, answering a nagging question that had plagued her foggy memory. That time, she'd been desperate, eager to have a friend banish her fears. But this time, there was no desperation, only intense passion and true desire, and for her…love.

Dylan went down on his knees, caressed her rounded belly and placed a kiss there. His hands wound around to her butt. Holding her firm, he rested his head on her stomach, and after few reverent seconds, he rose and drew her close in his arms. "Welcome home, Emma," he whispered over her mouth. He lifted her up carefully and swung her around once. "This will have to take the place of carrying you over the threshold."

He laid her down on the bed.

"Thresholds are overrated," she whispered, reaching for him.

Dylan came to her then, climbing into the bed beside her. He leaned over and kissed her again and again until her head swam, her body ached and every nerve tingled. He cupped her breasts and made love to them with his mouth. Her hips swung up, her back bowing, the straining, pink peaks of her nipples sensitized and gloriously begging for more.

She wound her arms around his neck and caressed his shoulders, her palms flat against the breadth and strength of him, solid and sure and smooth. Her fingers played in the short blond spikes of hair, the military cut grown out some, and for the first time, she could say she possessed him as much as he possessed her.

"Ah," she cooed as his tongue licked at her and her entire body strained.

She had to touch more of him, to give as much as she was receiving.

She rolled him away and came up over him, kissing his lips and flattening her palms over his chest. His skin sizzled and she absorbed the heat, gloried in the rapid heartbeats nearly exploding from his chest. She kissed every part of it and a groan escaped his lips when she wandered down and hovered around his navel. His body pulsed, his breath caught. She wouldn't deny him what he wanted. She slipped her hand under his waistband and met with raw, powerful, hot silk.

"Emma," he rasped, almost in a plea.

She wound her hand around his full length and stroked

him, settling into a rhythm. Breath hissed from his mouth, as sensation after lusty sensation drove her on. She unzipped his trousers and he quickly removed his remaining garments. He lay naked before her. He was beautiful, broad where he should be broad, muscled in a jaw-dropping way and lean everywhere else. There wasn't bulk, but rugged, hard-won sculpture. She couldn't believe Dylan was her husband. How had she gotten so lucky?

She continued to caress his upper body as she dipped her head down and took him to a place that had both of them panting and hungry. Dylan's pleasured groans inspired her lusty assault. But then he grabbed her shoulders and backed her away. "Enough, sweetheart," he said. Yet his expression said anything but. His restraint was endearing and tender, even as both of them were nearly destroyed.

He rolled her under him and began the same kind of lusty assault, using his hand first and then his mouth. Pleas and moans slipped from her lips, over and over, until she reached the very edge of pleasure. Her release came fast and hard. It shattered her, split her in half and half again. It was powerful, explosive, the pinnacle of pleasure. When she came back to earth, Dylan's eyes were on her, watching her in awe. She couldn't pretend she wasn't immensely satisfied, nor would she want to. Dylan was an expert lover and she was attuned to him and his body.

She reached up to touch his face. He placed a kiss in the palm of her hand. She slipped her index finger into his mouth, and his hazy eyes widened, new energy erupting from him. No words had to be said. He growled and rose up over her. Within seconds, they were joined. She'd already gotten used to the feel of him inside her, the surge of power even as he took things slow, making sure she was comfortable. He couldn't possibly know how right this felt to her, how her body wrapped around his with possession and adoration. She had let go of her fears when she was in bed with him and gave of herself freely.

Dylan appreciated that—she witnessed it in his expression. She'd never tire of watching him make love to her, to see the complexities on his face, the hunger, the passion and raw desire. She watched him and he watched her and they moved in unison, his thrusts coming stronger now, filling her to the max, giving her another round of hot pleasure.

Dylan's guttural groan echoed in her ears. He reached as high as he could go. She, too, was there with him, arching up and taking that final earth-shattering climb. And then they exploded, sharing the precarious cliff and taking the fall together.

She gloried in the aftermath of his lovemaking and lay beside him, with no words, just feelings of total acceptance and tenderness and protection. If Dylan couldn't give her his love, at least she had that.

Dylan grasped her hand, lacing their fingers together. "My wife."

It was like a song to her ears. "My husband."

"After I finish this movie, I'd like to take you on a real honeymoon, Em. I have a place in Hawaii, or we can go to Europe. If the doctor says it's okay. If not, we can go somewhere locally. We'll find a hideout, maybe up north. A friend of mine has a cabin by a lake."

"Any of the above sounds wonderful."

"Really?"

"Really. I'm low maintenance, Dylan."

He turned onto his side to face her. Leaning on an elbow, he twirled a thick strand of her hair around his finger. "I love that about you, Em. You're easy."

"Hey!"

He laughed and the sound was beautiful and husky and

filled with joy. "I meant you're easy on the eyes, easy to get along with, easy...and fun."

"You think I'm fun?"

His eyes narrowed and his brows lifted in a villainous arch. "So fun," he said. He removed his hand from her hair and used his index finger to circle and tease the pink areola of her breast. Both nipples grew hard and pebbled. Gosh, she *was* so easy.

He bent and kissed both breasts and then sighed. "I should really let you get some sleep. You must be tired."

"Not all that much." Being in bed with him gave her energy and excited her as nothing else ever had. She ran her fingers through his mop of spiky, military-cut hair, grateful to have the freedom to do so—to touch him whenever she wanted. "Did you have something in mind?"

"You don't want to know what's on my mind." His mouth twitched, his smile wicked. But then he gathered her up in his arms and covered them both with the sheets. "Sleep, Emma. I'm not going to wear you out tonight."

"Darn."

He chuckled.

She rested her head on his chest and closed her eyes.

She'd have a lifetime of nights like this with Dylan.

She couldn't imagine anything better.

Cameras flashed like crazy as a dozen photographers on the red carpet of the premiere of Dylan's romantic comedy, *A New Light*, caught sight of him with Emma as they exited the limousine. Just one look at her and they started tossing out questions.

"Who's your date, Dylan?"

"You've been holding out on us!"

"Are you going to be a father? Is she your baby mama?"

Dylan hugged Emma closer, his arm tight around her waist. She looked gorgeous in an organza gown he'd had tailored just for her. Her belly bump couldn't be hidden any longer, but the Empire style of the dress and the floral colors showcased her skin tone and her pregnancy in a beautiful way. "Sorry, honey. This is my life."

"It's okay, Dylan," she said. "You warned me about this."

Selfishly, he'd wanted Emma by his side tonight. Hiding the news of his marriage and the upcoming birth of his baby was proving harder each day. He'd talked to his publicist and they'd both decided that tonight during the movie premiere would be the best time to introduce Emma as his new wife to the world. At least the media would get the scoop from him, and not have to speculate or make up lies to fill their pages.

So right there on the red carpet, with a crowd gathering and the media in his face, Dylan proudly announced, "I'd like to introduce my new bride, Emma McKay. We were married last week in a small ceremony on the beach. Emma and I have known each other since my days in Ohio. I'm happy to say we'll be parents by early next spring. She's an amazing woman and we're both thrilled to have a baby on the way."

"Is it a boy or a girl?" someone shouted.

"We don't know that yet."

"When did you get married?"

"Last Saturday."

"What is Emma's maiden name?"

"Bloom," Emma answered, and Dylan slid her an appreciative glance. She wasn't going to let him take all the heat. She'd have to learn to deal with the media and it might as well start now.

The reporters angled their microphones her way now. "How do you feel marrying the world's most eligible bachelor, Mrs. McKay?"

"I've never really thought of him that way. He's just

Dylan to me. His sister and I have been best friends since grade school."

"Are you going to—"

"Please," Dylan said, putting up a hand. "My publicist will issue a statement in the morning that will answer all of your questions. The movie is about to begin and my wife and I would like to enjoy the premiere together. Thank you."

With bodyguards in front and behind him, Dylan moved through the crowd keeping Emma right by his side. It wouldn't be long now. He'd make headlines and their secret marriage would be a thing of the past. He felt the loss in the pit of his stomach. He loved the anonymity, the intimacy of having Emma all to himself these past few days. Now the news would be out and their lives would change, once again. Lack of privacy was a penalty of fame and he accepted it graciously for himself, but there was Emma to consider now. And their baby.

"You handled yourself pretty damn well, Em," he whispered in her ear.

"I winged it."

"I like a woman who can think on her feet."

He took her hand and entered the iconic movie theatre. It was one of the last few truly historic theatres in Los Angeles, with its plush red velvet seats, sculpted walls and miles and miles of curtains. "Well, what do you think?"

Her pretty green eyes took all of it in. He wanted so badly for Emma to experience the same sort of awe that he did. Moviemaking was in his blood. He was producing more and planned to continue to direct other projects in the future.

"I've never seen anything like this, Dylan. I can picture this theatre back in the day. All those classic movies flashing on that big screen. The actors, directors and producers who've taken their seats here. It's all so…grand."

He smiled. She got it. Emma *was* an amazing woman. He hadn't lied to the press today. He was falling for her and it didn't scare him, or make him nervous. Brooke had said Renee had scarred him for life, but maybe it had taken a woman like Emma to make him realize he was completely healed.

He kissed her cheek then, and she glanced up at him. "What was that for?"

"Can't a man kiss his wife just because?"

She smiled and his heart warmed. He took her hand again. "C'mon, Mrs. McKay, there are bigwigs who would love to meet you. I guess we should get this over with before we take our seats."

"I'm down with that," she said. And he cracked up.

So far, marriage to Emma had been anything but dull.

Nine

"Honey, I'm home," Dylan called out as he entered his house on Monday afternoon. He'd always wanted to say that, but now that he had, his wife was nowhere to be found. He was home fairly early from the set, though. He took a look at his phone and saw that she'd texted him.

I'll be home a little late. Behind on work today. See you at 6ish.

Dylan was disappointed. Each day, he looked forward to coming home to Emma. He'd find her doing pregnancy exercises or poring over a book of baby names or helping Maisey make a healthy dinner for the two of them. Each day also brought him closer to fatherhood, something he discovered he could hardly wait for now. He and Emma had plans to design the nursery. It would be just another few weeks before they found out the sex of their baby.

"Emma's not here, Dylan," Maisey said, greeting him

in the hallway off the kitchen. "I've got dinner ready. It's in the oven, keeping warm. If you don't need me, I'll be heading home."

"Thanks, Maisey. Sure, go on home. I might as well take a run. Emma's going to be a little late."

"Have a good evening, then," Maisey said.

He waved goodbye and dashed up the stairs to change his clothes.

A few minutes later he was on the beach, the shoreline nearly empty as he began to jog. He started out at a good warm-up pace and did at least half a mile before he kicked it into higher gear. It was cloudy and cool, making the run more enjoyable. What had started out as a chore—a fitness program for his role as a Navy SEAL—had become a ritual lately, one he enjoyed. His runs helped him think, helped him work out his upcoming movie scenes and gave him a way to reflect on his life. He'd asked his bodyguards to keep their distance. They had trouble keeping up anyway and he loved the idea of solitude on the beach.

Once he got going, his mind clicked a mile a minute and he made mental tallies of his thoughts as they rushed by, one after the other. And as he ran, he thought back on the night of the blackout. If only he could remember his last day with Roy…

And then images popped into his mind. He was sitting in his house, drinking with his buddy Roy. He was laughing and they were talking about the upcoming stunt and then his phone rang. It was Emma. She was freaking out and slurring her words. She was drunk. She'd said there was a blackout in the city. Dylan's lights were still on. The power outage hadn't reached the beach. He still had full power. Emma was looking for Brooke to come pick her up. Dylan immediately told her to stay put, and he'd come get her.

Dylan slowed his pace, thinking back, happy to have

the memory return. To see Roy in his mind, who looked so much like him they could've been brothers. To remember their laughter and then…then he remembered Roy getting pissed at him. "Dylan, you're in no shape to drive. You've worked your way halfway through that bottle of Scotch. Give me your keys. I'll go get Emma."

The scene played out in his head. He'd been stubborn with Roy, but when he'd tried to rise to go get Emma, the room began to spin and he'd sat back down.

Holy crap.

He came to an abrupt halt on the beach, his feet digging into the sand. His limbs wouldn't hold him; they were like rubber now. He dropped to his knees, his face in his hands. He saw himself handing Roy the keys to his car.

Dylan's face crumpled. Tears burned behind his eyes.

Images that he'd prayed would return now haunted him. He'd let Roy pick up Emma that night, because his friend had been right—Dylan was in no shape to get Emma. Roy picked Emma up that night. Roy…made love to Emma. It was Roy all along.

And the next day on the set, right before Roy got into that car, they'd argued. About Emma. Roy told him what happened and said he'd let things get carried away with her that night. Dylan had gotten hot under the collar, accusing him of taking advantage of Emma. And minutes later, the car exploded, with Roy inside. A fire cloud went up and Dylan was hit with shrapnel.

Dylan dug his fingers into the sand to keep from collapsing entirely. His head was down as he rehashed his thoughts, trying to contradict what he knew in his heart to be true. A woman walked over to him, the only other jogger on the beach beside his bodyguard. "Are you okay?"

Dylan nodded. "I'm…okay," he told the woman. "J-just need a little break."

He warned Dan off. The woman wasn't a threat, but he

might never be okay again. His whole future had been destroyed. The baby Emma carried wasn't his. He was married, but his wife had lied to him. Was it all a ruse? Had she deceived him on purpose? How could she not know what man she was screwing?

The woman walked off slowly and Dylan waited until she was out of sight before he tried to rise. His legs barely held his weight. His entire body was numb from neck to toes. His head, unfortunately, was clear for the first time in weeks, and the clarity was enough to squeeze his gut into tight knots and suck the life out of him.

He walked along the beach, feeling broken, each step leading to his house slower, less deliberate. He was more broken than when Renee had dumped him.

More broken than at any other time in his life.

Emma tossed her purse down on the living room sofa and went in search of Dylan. His car was in the garage; he must be home. She couldn't wait to see him. They'd talked about planning the nursery and she'd brought home paint samples of blues and pinks, greens and lavenders. The sex of the baby would determine the color themes, and they'd find that out pretty soon. At least they could narrow down their options, if Dylan wasn't too tired tonight to help her make some selections.

Unless he had other things on his mind, like taking her to bed early. Lately, they'd been doing a lot of going to bed early and *not* sleeping.

She smiled as she walked the downstairs hallway, popping her head inside rooms in search of him. A delicious aroma led her to the kitchen. She opened the oven door and peered at the meal Maisey had left for them. The garlicky scent of chicken cacciatore wafted in the air.

She closed the oven door when she heard Dylan enter from the beach. He was dressed in a tight nylon tank and black running shorts. Her heart skipped a beat, he was so gorgeous.

"Hi," she said. "How was your run?"

Dylan didn't answer right away. He headed to the bar in the living room. She followed behind him, noting the lack of pep in his step. His shoulders slumped and he was extremely quiet. "Dylan, are you all right?"

Silence again. She waited as he poured himself a drink of some sort of expensive whiskey and gulped it down in one shot. "Did you have a bad day?"

He looked at her then, his face ashen, his cloudy blue eyes dim and lifeless. There was something so bleak in the way he looked at her. "You could say that. I got my memory back."

"Oh? Isn't that a good thing, Dylan? It's what you've been hoping for."

"Sit down, Emma," he said, his voice ice-cold. He pointed to the sofa and she sat. He poured another shot of alcohol and took a seat opposite her, as if…as if he needed to keep his distance. Her heart pounded now as a sense of dread threatened to overwhelm her. Something was very wrong.

"I remember it all, Emma. The night of the blackout, the call you made to me."

She nodded and blinked her eyes several times. Dylan's teeth were gnashing. He had a grip on his temper, but just barely. "I didn't come for you that night," he said, looking down at his whiskey glass. "It wasn't me. It was Roy."

"What do you mean it was Roy? You came for me. I called you looking for Brooke and you…you—"

He was shaking his head adamantly. "I was drinking with Roy that night. Roy didn't think I was sober enough to drive. He took my keys out of my hand and picked you up."

"No, he didn't." Emma's voice registered a higher pitch.

"Yes, he did."

"But…but…that would mean—" Emma bounced up from the sofa. This wasn't right. This wasn't the truth. Dylan had it wrong. It was all wrong. "Dylan, that can't be true. It can't be."

Dylan rose, too, his blue eyes hard and dark as midnight. "It is true. Are you denying it? Are you going to tell me you don't remember sleeping with Roy?"

"That's exactly what I'm saying. I didn't sleep with Roy. I wouldn't do that."

Dylan stood firm, poured whiskey down his gullet and swallowed. "But that's exactly what you did. You slept with Roy, and after he died, you told me the baby was mine."

"I…uh, oh no! I didn't. I mean, if I did, I didn't know it was him. I wouldn't do that, Dylan. I didn't lo—"

"Which is it, Emma?" Dylan asked, in a voice she didn't recognize. He sounded harsh and bitter. "You knew you were screwing Roy, or you didn't?"

Tears welled in her eyes, the truth slapping her hard in the face, but it was Dylan's mean-spirited words that hurt the most. How could she come to terms with what Dylan was implying? She thought she was making love to Dylan that night. Even in her drunken state, even as scared as she was, she would've never knowingly slept with Roy.

Yet he looked enough like Dylan to fool his fans. And he'd come for her in Dylan's car. Because of the blackout and her blurry head, it could have been Roy after all. But she never once thought he wasn't Dylan coming to her rescue.

But Dylan didn't believe that. And he probably never would.

Her memory sharpened to that night and all the things the man she thought was Dylan had said to dissuade her. *You've got this wrong. It's a mistake.* Those pleas made sense now, because she wasn't imploring Dylan to stay with her, it had been Roy all along. Roy who had held her tight and comforted her, Roy who had finally given in when she pressed him to make love to her. No wonder there were differences in Dylan's lovemaking since that first night. She couldn't put her finger on it before and blamed it on her drunken state. But now she knew why it had felt different making love to blackout Dylan versus the real deal.

The truth pounded her head. The truth hammered her heart. The truth made her stomach ache.

"I'm carrying Roy's baby," she said, her voice flat, monotone, as if saying it out loud would make it sink in. She trembled visibly, her arms going limp, her legs weakening. She wanted so badly to sit back down and pretend this wasn't happening. But she couldn't. She mustered her strength, though she bled inside for the life she might have had with Dylan. The bright future she'd only just come to believe in had been snuffed out forever.

She should've known her happiness wouldn't last. When had she really been happy? Only lately, working with Brooke and starting their business. "I can hardly believe this."

When she lifted her eyes, wondering if there was a way around this, a way to make this right, a way to preserve the goodness that had come from marrying Dylan, she met his hard, glowering stare. He blamed her for all this. He didn't believe her. He thought she'd betrayed him.

Like Renee.

Nothing was further from the truth, but it didn't matter. She saw it in the firm set of his jaw. Ice flowed in his veins now. He was convinced she had deceived him.

She faced facts. She wouldn't be Dylan's wife much longer. She'd file for an annulment and wouldn't take a dime of the prenup Dylan's lawyer insisted she sign. She didn't want his money. She had only hoped one day to earn his love.

"I'll pack my things and be gone in the morning, Dylan. Have your attorney contact me. I don't want anything from you. I'm sorry about this. More than you could ever know."

"Emma?"

"Don't worry about me, Dylan," she said, biting her lip, holding back tears. This news crushed her, but she didn't want his pity. She'd never wanted anyone's pity. "I'll land on my feet, as usual. We both know you only married me because of the baby and now that we know the b-baby isn't y-yours…" She couldn't finish her thought. She'd been robbed of the joy of carrying Dylan's child. She'd love her baby, but now her child would never know its father and never have the love of both parents.

Dylan was quiet for a long time, staring at her. His anger seemed to have disappeared, replaced by something in his eyes looking very much like pain. This wasn't easy for him, either, but she had no sympathy for him right now. She was in shock, devastated beyond anything she could ever imagine.

"I'll make sure the baby wants for nothing," he said.

She shook her head stubbornly. "Please, Dylan…don't. I really don't need anything from you. I'll manage on my own. Goodbye." She turned away and kept her head high as she made for the door.

"Emma, wait!"

She stopped, her tears flooding her face. She didn't pivot around. "W-what?"

"I'm…sorry for the way things turned out."

"I know. I am, too."

Then she dashed out of the room.

Dylan sat in his dressing trailer, on the studio lot, feeling uncomfortable in his customized honey wagon, staring at his lines for this evening's scenes and repeating the words over and over in his mind. Nothing stuck. It was as if he was reading hieroglyphics. He hadn't been able to concentrate since Emma had packed her bags and left home two days ago. Brooke had told him that Emma had returned to her apartment. She still had time left on her lease. And his ears still burned from his sister's brutal tongue-lashing that had followed. Brooke had defended Emma and basically called him a jerk for letting her leave that way.

He'd been hard on her. But how on earth could a woman make love to a man and not know who he was? The idea seemed ludicrous to him and yet Brooke had believed her without question and insisted that a man worthy of Emma should have, too. Which told him maybe they weren't meant to be together. Maybe the marriage had been a mistake all along.

Keep telling yourself that, pal.

He'd tried to convince himself he'd done the right thing in letting her go. He didn't love Emma. She was a friend, a bed partner and his wife for a little while longer, but he couldn't deny the reason he'd married her. The only reason he'd married her. He thought she'd been carrying his child and he'd wanted to provide for both of them.

Now the loss seemed monumental. He'd fallen in love with the baby he presumed was his and the notion of fatherhood. He'd begun to see his life differently. Having a family had always been a dream, something he'd wanted sometime in the future.

Now that future was obscure. He was more confused than ever.

He missed Emma. And not just in his bed, though that was pretty spectacular. He missed coming home to her at night, seeing her pretty green eyes and smiles when he walked through the door. He missed the infectious joy on her face when they'd talked about the baby and fixing up the nursery.

All of that was lost to him now.

Someone pounded on the trailer door. He rose from his black leather lounger and peered out the window. It was Jeff, one of his bodyguards. Opening the door, he took a look at the guy's face and the hand he held over his stomach. "Hey, Jeff. What's up? You're not looking too good."

Which was an understatement. His skin had turned a lovely shade of avocado. "Must've been something I ate. I'm sorry, Mr. McKay. I've put in for my replacement. He'll be here in an hour."

"Don't worry about it, Jeff. Go home. Do you think you can drive?"

He nodded and the slight movement turned him grass green. "I'll wait for Dan to get here."

"No, you won't. You can barely stand up. You go home and take care of yourself. There's plenty of security around here. I'll be fine and the replacement will be here soon. You said so yourself."

"I shouldn't."

"Go. That's an order."

Jeff finally nodded. Gripping his stomach, he walked off and then made a mad dash for the studio bathroom. Poor guy.

Dylan grabbed his script and took a seat again. He had to learn his lines or they'd all be here until after midnight. Sharpening his focus, he blocked out everything plaguing his mind and concentrated on the scene, reciting the words over and over and finally getting a grasp of them. He closed his eyes, as he always did, to get a mental picture of how the scene would play out—where his marks were and what movements he would make throughout.

The caustic scent of smoke wafted to his nostrils and he was instantly reminded of the day Roy died. The memory of the blast and the smoke that followed had now fully returned. It was so strong that every time he came upon a group of people smoking on their coffee breaks, he'd relive that moment.

He shook it off, determined to run through his lines one more time before rehearsal was called. But his throat began to burn and he coughed and coughed. That's when he noticed a cloud of gray haze coming toward him from the back end of the trailer. Seconds later he saw flames darting up from his bedroom. Right before his eyes, the fire jumped to the bed and wardrobe racks. Within moments, his entire bedroom was engulfed in flames. He ran for the trailer door and turned the knob. The door moved half an inch, but something was blocking it from opening from the outside. He pushed against it with his full weight. It wouldn't budge. Peering out the window, he looked around and shouted for help.

Flames lit the entire back end of the trailer, the heat sweltering, the smoke choking his lungs. Dylan darted quick glances around the trailer, looking for something sharp to break the small kitchen window. He grabbed his wardrobe chair and shoved the legs against the window above the sink with all his might. Once, twice and finally the window shattered. He broke out as much glass as possible with the chair and then dived headfirst, tucking and rolling his body the way Roy had taught him.

"Ow!" He met with gravel, landing hard, and instantly sucked fresh air into his lungs. The flames were blazing now and he struggled to his feet. He had to get away before the whole thing blew.

Members of the movie crew had now seen the fire and came running over. Two of them grabbed his arms and dragged him away from the trailer. In the distance, he heard sirens blasting.

"Are you okay?" one of the crew members asked.

"Dylan, talk to me." He recognized the assistant director's voice. "Say something."

"I'm…okay."

"Mr. McKay," another voice said, "we're getting you to safety. Hold on."

Once they were fifty feet from the trailers, a blanket was tossed onto the ground and he was laid down. Blood oozed out from scrapes on his body and his clothes were torn from the leap out the window. The stench of smoke and ash permeated the area. Within seconds, the studio medic arrived and assessed him. An oxygen mask was put over his mouth and soon a fresh swell of air flowed into his throat and down his lungs.

"Take slow, normal breaths," the medic said. "You got out in time. Looks like you're going to be fine."

Dylan tried to sit up but he was gently laid back down. "Not yet. You're not burned, but you do have abrasions on your arms and legs. You banged up your face pretty good, too. An ambulance is on the way."

He groaned. "Someone tried to kill me," he said.

"We figured. Those honey wagons don't just light themselves on fire. And we noticed how your door was blocked with a solid beam of wood from the Props Department. The police are on their way."

"I can't believe you didn't call me last night," Brooke was saying softly near his hospital bed. Concern over him was the only thing keeping her from unleashing her wrath.

Accompanied by a police escort, he'd been taken here for observation and to clean up his wounds last night after the fire, and decided not to call his sister until dawn. She didn't need to worry about him and lose sleep over this, but he had to call her before the story hit the morning news.

"There's a freaking police guard outside your room, Dylan. I had to practically strip down to my panties to get in here to see you."

"I bet that was fun," he said, winking the eye that wasn't bruised.

"Ha-ha. Well, at least you haven't lost your sense of humor. But this is serious, brother," Brooke said, her eyes misting up. "You're all bandaged and look like a train wreck. God, I don't want to lose you."

Brooke had a blunt way of putting things, but he knew what was in her heart. He took her hand and squeezed. "I don't want to be lost. They'll find whoever did this, Brooke. It has to be someone with access to the studio lot."

Brooke frowned. "That narrows it down to about a thousand or so."

"I'll be fine, Brooke. I'm going home with a police escort this afternoon."

Dylan flopped back against his pillow. A part of him was disappointed that Emma hadn't shown up here. Had Brooke told her? He couldn't ask, because then his well-meaning sister would give him another lecture. Emma would find out soon enough, if she looked at a newspaper, logged onto the internet or turned on a television set.

He'd already spoken to his manager, his agent and his publicist. They were taking care of business for him. He was set to be released from the hospital later today. Not that he wasn't grateful to the staff, but if one more person told him how lucky he'd been last night, he would scream. Someone was out to kill him. A crazed fan? Some lunatic who wanted fifteen minutes of fame? Or was it someone he knew? A tremor passed through him at the thought. Who hated him enough to want him dead?

He'd been questioned extensively by the police last night and he'd told the detectives everything that had happened that day. They'd been thorough in their questioning, and unfortunately, Dylan was still at a loss as to who might want to murder him.

"I called Emma and told her what happened to you,"

Brooke said, her chin tilted at a defiant angle. "She's your wife, Dylan, and has a right to know. At least she won't hear about it first on the morning news. She's pretty messed up right now."

"I didn't mean to cause her pain, Brooke." Yet that's exactly what he'd done. She was pregnant and his wife, and even though the baby wasn't his, he should've treated her better than he had. The fact that he wanted to see her, wanted her to come just so he could look into her pretty face and be comforted, made him question everything. "Please tell her that I'm all right and that she can talk to me anytime, but honestly, Brooke, until they figure out who's doing this it's best that you and Emma stay away from me."

Brooke opened her mouth to protest just as the nurse walked in. God, he'd never been so happy to have a medical procedure in his life. "Time to get your vitals and check on your bandages, Mr. McKay," the woman said. "If you don't mind stepping out of the room, please?" she asked of Brooke.

"Of course. I'll see you a little later, Dylan," she said, blowing him a kiss. "Be safe."

By five in the afternoon, Dylan was home. Both of his bodyguards were on the premises, keeping an eye out for anything unusual. His first order of business was to go through the past few months of fan mail. He'd had Rochelle skim the letters back when suspicions had first been raised about the cause of Roy's accident, but now that he was certain someone was out to get him he sat behind his office desk and read through each one. His cell phone rang and he sighed when he saw the caller's name pop up on the screen.

"Hello, Renee."

"Dylan, thank God you're all right. I heard about the fire at the studio." Renee sounded breathless.

"I'm fine. I got out safely."

"Oh, Dylan, I hope I'm wrong about this, but I think I know who's out to get you."

Dylan bolted upright in his seat. "Go on."

"My ex-husband is a maniac. I mean, Craig's gone off the deep end lately. He's been trying to get custody of my kids for months now. A few weeks ago, he stormed into the house, screaming at me. He found out about the money you've been sending to help us. Money he thinks is keeping him from getting his hands on the kids. Dylan, I don't know for sure he's behind it. As you might know, he... he...has a background in film and stunt work. He might be working at the studio. And I know he hates you."

"Why does he hate me? Aside from the money?"

"I guess he's always been jealous of you. He knows about our history, Dylan. And, well, he got it in his head that I'm still in love with you. That I compared him to you and he always came up short. I don't know... I guess I did. I've always regretted the way things ended between us. But I never thought he'd go to such extremes. Like I said, I'm not sure...but my gut is telling me it's him."

"Okay, Renee. Sit tight. I'll call the police. They'll want to question you. And, Renee, thanks."

"Of course, Dylan. I couldn't stand it if anything happened to you. Be careful."

"I will."

After hanging up with Renee, he called Detective Brice and relayed the information about Craig Lincoln. He gave him Renee's address and phone number and Brice thought it was a good lead. If her ex was involved, he wouldn't be hard to track down if he worked on the studio lot. Even if he'd used an alias, crews would recognize his face.

Dylan's heart raced. He hoped Renee was right and that Lincoln would be caught. A man like that could be dangerous to her and her kids, too, if he would resort to murder.

Dylan ran a hand down his face.

He needed a drink. As he headed toward the bar, one of his bodyguards entered the house and approached him. "Here you go, Mr. McKay." Dan handed him today's mail.

Dylan wasn't allowed outside to pick up his own mail. He was trapped in his house, a prisoner to the whims of a killer. The studio had shut down all production until the investigation concluded.

"Thanks." He poured himself a whiskey as Dan headed back outside.

He took his mail over to the kitchen table and sat down. Thumbing through ads and bills, he came across an unmarked letter. There was no postal stamp or address on the envelope. It simply read "McKay."

His gut constricted. His breathing stopped for an instant. There was something about this that didn't pass the smell test. He should turn the letter over to Detective Brice, but that could take hours.

It could be nothing or…

His hands shaking, he peeled the envelope open carefully and unfolded the short note.

"You took my family, now I'll take yours."

Dylan froze, staring at the threatening words. Momentary fear held him hostage. His mind raced in a dozen directions and came to a grinding halt. Emma.

His wife.

She could be in danger.

And Brooke, too.

His sister.

He had to get to them. "Dan! Jeff! Get in here, now!"

Ten

Emma sat at her desk at Parties-To-Go working on the numbers for an upcoming wedding. It was after five in the evening, but she'd rather be here than in her lonely apartment. She went through the motions robotically with none of her usual enthusiasm. Debbie Downer had nothing on her. She'd sent Wendy and Rocky home early. She needed to dive into her work with no distractions. She'd been on the receiving end of their sympathetic glances and worried expressions all afternoon. No one knew about her breakup with Dylan yet, aside from Brooke, but her employees were astute and of course had heard about the murder attempt on her husband's life. She was worried sick about Dylan, and missed him so much. She'd spent a good part of the night at the hospital waiting on word of Dylan. Once she knew he was doing well and they expected a full recovery, she'd breathed a sigh of relief and left the waiting room. She didn't want to bring him any bad memories by showing up. He didn't need a confrontation and he'd made himself clear about how he felt about her and their situation.

Resting a hand on her tummy, she closed her eyes and then…the baby kicked! It was more like a flutter, a butterfly taking flight, than an actual kick, but oh, her heart pinged with joy. This was amazing and so absolutely miraculous. A miracle that should be shared and treasured, and her mind went back to Dylan and how happy he'd been thinking he was going to be a father.

She couldn't dwell on what wasn't to be anymore. She was on her own, and her focus had to stay finely tuned to the child she carried.

From now on, she wouldn't be totally alone.

The back door jingled. She stopped to listen. Someone was trying to get inside. Her heart raced and she rose from her desk. She did a mental tally: the part-timers had been sent home, Brooke was on a special date with Royce. She heard more jingling and a couple of loud bangs as if someone was pressing their body against the door, struggling to get in. She glanced around, picked up a kid's baseball bat left over from a party and strode to the door just as it burst open.

"Brooke! You scared me to death."

"Sorry," her friend said. "The dang lock keeps sticking. We've got to get that fixed."

"I wasn't expecting anyone. Aren't you supposed to be with Royce tonight?"

Brooke shut the door and glimpsed the baseball bat in Emma's hand. That's when Emma noticed the hollow look on her friend's face. "What is it?" Bile rose in her throat. "Is it Dylan? Is he okay? Did something else happen to him?"

"Dylan's fine, honey. I've talked to him three times earlier today. He's been released from the hospital and had a police escort home. There's no damage to his lungs and his bruises are superficial. He told me he wanted to rest. Translation—stop bugging him. And I got the hint."

"Oh, thank God. But he's all alone there now. Are the police watching him?"

"He's got two bodyguards round-the-clock and you know about the added security he has around his house. He told me not to worry."

"How can you not? Someone tried to kill him."

"I know. Freaks me out." Brooke took the bat out of her hand. "Must've freaked you out, too."

"Yeah, well…this whole thing is so scary."

Brooke took a shaky breath. Her eyes were rimmed with red. She moved into the office and sat down. Emma did the same. "So why are you here? Shouldn't you be with Royce tonight?" she asked carefully.

"Royce and I are over."

Emma's brows lifted. She didn't expect this. "What do you mean, you're over?"

"I walked out on him, Em."

"Why?"

Brooke sighed. "When Royce said he had something special he wanted to give me, I thought, oh my goodness. A key to his place maybe, or a piece of jewelry, maybe even a ring. I let my imagination run wild. I mean, come on, he knows what I've been through this month with Dylan. And he actually used that. He told me he knew I was worried about my brother and that he'd probably have time on his hands, now that the studio shut down production, so—"

"He didn't!"

"Oh, yes, he did. He gave me three scripts for Dylan to look at. Scripts that were his pride and joy. He said he'd been working on them for two years and he knew Dylan would love them and want to produce and star in the movies once he read them."

"Oh, Brooke, I'm so sorry. You must've been…"

"Pissed and hurt and most of all shocked. That's the part that gets me. I was shocked and I shouldn't have been. I really thought he was the one guy I could count on, who didn't want to get close to me because of my brother. He's in finance, a Wall Street type. I didn't think there was a creative bone in his body. And I loved that about him. I mean…I really thought… Oh, I shouldn't feel sorry for myself. Not in front of you."

"Are you saying I have bigger problems than you?" Emma leaned in to give Brooke a goofy smile. "Is that what you're telling me?"

"No. Yes. You know what I mean."

"I do know. So, we're both hurting right now."

Brooke nodded. "But I'm not going to let that idiot ruin my life. I'm not going to fall to pieces."

"Promise?"

"I…uh…well, maybe a little crumble." Her voice shook.

Emma took Brooke's hand and they sat there for a few minutes, holding on to each other and trying not to cry.

"You know what?" Brooke said. "We should get out of here. They're showing a special screening of *The Notebook* at the Curtis Cinema down the street. If we're going to cry, it might as well be over our favorite chick flick. Let's go and then have a late dinner. Just like old times."

"I like the sound of that. No more moping."

"Pinkie swear?"

They locked their pinkie fingers, just as they did when they were kids. "Pinkie swear."

"We'll shut down our cell phones and have a night free of worries."

"Shouldn't you check in on Dylan?" Emma asked.

"I will, as soon as the movie ends. Deal?"

"It's a deal," Emma said, her spirits lifting for the first time in two days.

* * *

"Damn this traffic." Dylan sat shotgun as Dan navigated the streets leading to Emma's apartment, cutting in and out of the lineup of cars on Pacific Coast Highway whenever he could. "It would have to be the busiest time of day."

After Dylan had called Detective Brice about the threatening letter, he was ordered to stay put at home. That had lasted only half an hour. His nerves had been bouncing out of his skin and there was only so much pacing he could do. How could he sit around and wait when Emma's and Brooke's lives could be in danger? Neither of them were answering their phones and their part-time employees confirmed they didn't have an event tonight. He'd left countless messages at their homes and at the office, which had gone straight to voice mail. His texts hadn't been answered, either.

He'd moved fast then, ordering Dan to drive, while Jeff followed behind, both in black SUVs. The first stop was Emma's place. She should've been home from work by now. Dusk had settled in, a gray cloud cover shutting out the lingering light.

His unanswered voice mails put fear in his heart. Emma was in danger, he was sure of it. That creep Lincoln couldn't get at him after two failed attempts and now he was going after his unsuspecting pregnant wife.

Emma.

As soon as he'd read that damning note, his first thoughts were of her and the child she carried. *She* was his family now, along with the baby. That child was his best friend's baby, an innocent in all this, and someone who deserved to be loved. Dylan was ashamed of himself for turning away from Roy's baby. He hadn't been thinking clearly. He'd felt the same sense of deceit and betrayal from Emma as he had from Renee. It had all been too much; his hopes and dreams had been paralyzed and he'd lashed out at the injustice, but none of it was Emma's doing. He believed that now. Deep down he'd always known Emma wouldn't resort to that kind of devastating deceit.

Good God, had his heart been so hardened that he couldn't recognize true love when it slammed him in the face? Had it taken a threat to her life to make him realize what she meant to him?

He was in love with her.

And the very thought of Emma and the baby being hurt was too hard to imagine.

"Hurry, Dan. I can't let anything happen to her."

Once they finally reached Emma's apartment building, Dan parked on the street and Dylan threw open the car door.

"Wait!" Dan ordered. "You can't go running in there. It might be a trap."

Jeff raced over, blocking him from getting out of the car. "Then what are we going to do?"

"The smart thing is to wait for the cops to arrive," Jeff said.

Dylan shook his head. "Think of another option."

His cell phone rang and he immediately picked up. "Dylan, it's me."

"Brooke, thank God. I've been trying to reach you. Are you okay?"

"I'm fine."

He got out of the car now, listening to the sweet sound of his sister's voice. "Where are you and is Emma with you?"

"Yes, I'm with Emma. But first tell me, are you okay? I panicked when I saw a dozen missed calls from you. Your texts said Emma and I were in danger?"

"Yeah, you might be. The creep who tried to kill me sent a note saying he was going after my family. You're sure Emma's fine?"

"Uh, well, she will be. We were at the movies and she started feeling weak. When I looked at her face, she had gone completely white. I didn't let her argue with me. I drove her straight to the emergency room. We're at Saint Joseph's."

Dylan stopped breathing. God, if she lost the baby, he'd never forgive himself. He loved the both of them with all of his heart. "What's wrong with her, Brooke? It isn't the baby, is it?"

"The baby's fine. Emma's been under a lot of stress lately. She hasn't been eating and, well, she's been upset and crying lately. She's dehydrated. Could've been really dangerous, but we caught it in time. They're pumping her full of fluids now and the doctor said she's going to be okay."

Dylan ran his hand down his face. "Okay." He heard the relief in his own voice. "I'll be there in a few minutes. And I'm calling Detective Brice to put a guard on her door. Don't leave the hospital under any circumstances."

"That won't be necessary." At the gruff-sounding voice, Dylan turned and found Detective Brice approaching, a frown on his face that would scare the devil. "You don't listen very well, do you, McKay? You almost blew our cover coming here."

"Brooke," Dylan said into the phone. "I'll call you back in a sec. Just stay with Emma." He hung up the phone, surprised to see Brice. "What do you mean?"

"We had the apartment under surveillance since this morning. Your sister's place, too, just as a precaution. Sure enough, we found Lincoln tonight, lurking in the bushes in the courtyard. He's in our custody now and he's not going to be able to harm anyone ever again."

The courtyard gates opened and Dylan faced the man who'd murdered Roy. Blood ran hot in his veins. Here was the man who'd tried to kill him twice, who was lying in wait to harm his pregnant wife. Lincoln was in handcuffs, two officers flanking him and three others following behind. All Dylan wanted to do was meet him on equal turf and beat the stuffing out of him. He took a step toward him and Brice got in his way, his hand firm on Dylan's chest. "McKay, don't be an idiot."

Lincoln's eyes bugged out of his skull when he saw Dylan. "You sonofabitch! You home wrecker! You don't deserve to live!" Lincoln was out of his mind, wrestling with the officers restraining him. "You think you can take my kids, my wife. Ruin my life! You hotshot, you'll live to regret this!"

Two of the other officers grabbed Lincoln, restraining his arms and maneuvering him into the squad car that had pulled up behind Jeff's SUV.

Dylan shook his head. "He killed Roy."

"He'll pay for that," Brice said. "And all the other crimes he's committed."

Dylan nodded. "Yeah."

"He's deranged, but something set him off. You said over the phone his ex-wife called you."

"Yeah, she was the one who figured it out after she saw the headlines today about the attempt on my life. I don't know too many details about her life, just that we were close once and that more recently she was near poverty, trying to raise her kids and keep her ex away from them. I've been sending her money to keep food on the table for her children. That was my crime. That's why he hates me."

"He's going away for a long time." Brice patted Dylan on the back. "It's over now, McKay. You can go on being a superhero, *on film*," he said, giving him a teasing smirk.

"There's only one person I want to think of me that way."

And unfortunately, it was the one person he'd hurt the most.

"Are we through here?" he asked.

"I'm going to need your statement," Brice said.

"Can I give it to you later tonight? I just found out my wife's in the hospital and I want to see her as soon as I can."

"Sorry to hear that." Brice puffed out a breath. "Okay. Sure. Go check on your wife. You both had some close calls lately. I hope she's going to be okay."

Dylan hoped so, too. "Thanks." Dylan shook the detective's hand. "I appreciate what you've done for my family. Your team did excellent work."

"It's all in a day's work. Sometimes things go sideways, but this one turned out in the best way possible. No one got hurt today. I'm proud of these guys."

Dylan left the detective to speak with his bodyguards. He dismissed them for the night, thanking them for their help, explaining that he wanted to see Emma on his own. He needed time alone to think things through on the drive over and he didn't want to show up at the hospital with an entourage. He'd had plenty of experience sneaking in and out of places—fame did that to a man, made him hunt for ways to go undetected. He borrowed Jeff's ball cap and his oversize gray sweat jacket as a disguise.

Dylan called Brooke back on the way to the hospital and told her the entire story. His little sister nearly broke down on the phone and he couldn't blame her. What had transpired was like something out of a bad B movie. But they were all safe, he assured her, and he told her to hang tight. He would be there shortly.

As the SUV's tires hit gravel on the way to the hospital, one thought continually nagged at him. How in hell was he going to make this up to Emma? He had no doubt he was responsible for her unhealthy state. She hadn't been eating well and she'd been terribly upset lately. All because he'd misjudged her and had the foolish notion that he couldn't love completely again.

At the hospital, he found Brooke sitting in a waiting room. She took one look at him, bolted up and flew into his arms, tears streaming down her face. "Dylan, my God... to think what could have happened to you. To Emma. I'm a freaking basket case."

"I know. I know." He brought her into his embrace and held on tight. Her face was pressed to his chest, her quiet sobs soaking his terrible disguise. "We're all going to be fine now, Brooke. The police have the guy in custody. He's not going to hurt anyone anymore."

"He murdered Roy."

"Yeah, he did." Dylan would have to live with that guilt the rest of his life. "How's Emma? I need to see her, Brooke. I need to tell her... I just have to see her."

Brooke pulled out of his arms, sniffled and gave him a somber look. How quickly she'd transformed into a mother hen. "Dylan, she's sleeping now. They gave her a sedative and she'll stay here for the night. She needs to rest and she especially needs no further drama in her life. Doctor's orders."

"I got that covered, sis."

"Are you sure? Because you can't mess with her, Dylan. She's not as strong as she looks. She's had a rough life. And she—"

"Brooke, I know what my *wife* needs."

Brooke's lips lifted in a smile and the defiance in her stern eyes faded. "And you're going to make sure she gets everything she deserves?"

"Yes. I've been a fool and I plan on rectifying that now. But I'm going to need your help. Are you willing to help me win my wife back?"

"Is it going to cost me her friendship?"

"No, it may even earn you a spot as godmother to the baby."

"Well, shoot. I've already got that in the bag."

"But you'll help me anyway because you love me?"

"Yeah, big brother. I'll help you. Because I love you *and* Emma."

Emma sat at her office desk and laid a hand on her belly, thanking God that her baby was thriving and growing as it should. The scare she'd had the night she went to the movies with Brooke couldn't happen again. She couldn't let her emotions get the best of her like that anymore. She was eating well now, drinking gallons of water a day, or so it seemed, and taking daily walks. All in all, she felt strong. Facing the future didn't frighten her as much as it once had. Emma adapted well and she was learning how the new life growing inside her only encouraged her own private strength.

"Look what just arrived for you," Brooke said, walking over with a vase full of fresh, snowy-white gardenias. "I love the way they smell."

"Your brother has a good memory." Emma admired the flowers Brooke set down on her desk. "Either that, or he's a good guesser. It's my favorite flower. You didn't tell him, did you?"

Brooke shook her head. "No. He must've remembered how you'd always ask Mom if you could pick a gardenia off the bush to put it in your hair. You'd wear it until the leaves turned yellow."

A fond memory. Emma smiled. "That's when the scent is sweetest."

Every day since her hospital stay, Dylan had done something thoughtful for her. The day she was released from the hospital, he'd sent her a basket of oils and lotions to pamper herself along with a gift certificate good for a dozen pregnancy massages with a message that simply read "I'm sorry."

Yesterday, he'd sent her an array of fresh fruit done up in the shape of a stork. It was really quite ingenious, with wings made of pineapple slices and cherries as eyes. Again, there was a note, which read "Forgive me."

And today, the flowers. She lifted the note card from its holder, her hand shaking. She wasn't over Dylan, not by a long shot.

He'd wanted to see her. To apologize in person, but she wasn't up to that yet. She needed time and strength and to make sure the baby was thriving again. She feared seeing Dylan would break her heart all over again. Luckily, because Brooke warned him off visiting her, he hadn't pressed her about it.

Brooke had already walked back to her desk. It wasn't like her *not* to nose around and ask what was going on. But then, Brooke's heart had been broken, too. She didn't believe in love anymore. Together, they were the walking wounded.

"I miss you," the note read.

Tears pooled in her eyes. The gifts were getting a bit much. Why was he torturing her like this? Didn't he know that she needed a clean break from him? That he owned her heart and soul and she was fighting like mad to take them back.

The capture of his stalker had made headlines and Dylan hadn't been back to work yet, according to Brooke. The investigation had shut down production at the studio for a few days. His adoring fans had been outraged at the murder attempt and the police thought it best for him to keep a low profile. Dylan had his hands full with news helicopters circling his home, reporters at his front gate and paparazzi trying to get glimpses of him. He'd hunkered down at his mansion on Moonlight Beach and had his publicist offer a statement, thanking the police for their diligence, thanking his fans for their support and asking for the press to abide by his privacy during this difficult time.

Emma, too, had been the source of news, especially since she'd been a target as well, and as Dylan's newly estranged bride, well…her life had become very public, very quickly. Emma refused to comment to the press and Dylan assigned Jeff to escort her to and from work each day to basically stand guard over her. It was weird having her own personal bodyguard, but she appreciated the gesture. No one had gotten near her, thanks to Jeff. Today, an equally juicy scandalous news story had broken and she hoped that she and Dylan were off the hook, at least for the time being.

This afternoon, she was working on a retirement party for a man who'd started his own business in foldable cartons back in the early 1950s. The exuberant senior citizen was finally retiring at the ripe young age of ninety-four, giving up the helm to his grandson. The party would be full of guests of all ages and she and Brooke worked tirelessly to throw an event that would encompass every one of the three generations attending.

Brooke turned away from her computer screen for a second. "Are you still on board for our meeting with the manager of Zane's on the Beach tonight?"

"Yep, I'll be there."

"Okay, he'll make time for us at around eight and we can go over the details for the party. I'll meet you there, though. I have to run a few errands after work."

"Sure. Jeff and I will meet you." Emma lifted her lips in a smile.

Brooke rolled her eyes. "It's for your own sanity, you know. Dylan's used to having a swarm of reporters dogging him, but you're not."

"The reporters have backed off. Dylan's probably getting the brunt of it."

"He can handle it. The press loves him. Especially now. Since his murder attempt they're treading carefully and trying to give him the space he needs."

"For his sake, I hope so," Emma replied. She'd lived in his world for a short time. There was never a time when people weren't gawking at him, sneaking peeks or flat out trying to approach him.

"Me, too," Brooke said. "Love that guy. I'll be forever grateful he wasn't hurt by that creep. I only wish…"

"What do you wish?"

"Nothing," she said, dipping her head sheepishly. "I've got to go." Brooke tossed her handbag over her shoulder and then bent to give Emma a kiss on the cheek. "See you later, Em."

Emma closed up shop at precisely five o'clock, exited by the back door and found Jeff waiting for her by her car. He stood erect in his nondescript black suit, waiting. When he spotted her, she put her head down, stifling a frown. "I'm going home to have dinner. And then I've got an appointment."

"Okay. I'll follow you home. What time are you going out again?"

"Seven thirty. And I want you to eat something before you come back. Promise?"

He nodded and a silly smile erupted on his face. She was mother henning him to death, but in some weird way she thought he actually liked her fretting over him. If she was a better liar, she'd tell him she was calling it a night and going to bed early, but with her luck, she'd get caught in the lie and then feel bad about it for weeks. So, the truth had to be served.

Once she got home and Jeff was on his way, she created a healthy chicken salad with vegetable greens, cranberries and diced apples. She took her food over to the sofa, plopped her feet in front of the television screen and turned on the news until a report came on about Dylan's would-be killer. She hit the off button instantly, shaking her head. She knew all she wanted to know about Craig Lincoln, Renee's homicidal ex-husband, thank you very much. Her stomach lurched, but she fought the sensation and ate her salad like a good mother-to-be.

After dinner, she walked into her bedroom, took off her clothes and stepped into the shower. Until the warm spray hit her tired bones, she didn't realize how very weary she was. For the past few weeks, she felt as if her emotions were on a wacky elevator ride going up and down, never really knowing where she was going or when it would finally stop. She lathered up with raspberry vanilla shower gel and lost herself in thought, allowing the soothing waters to take effect.

After her shower, she threw her arms through the sleeves of a black-and-white dress that belted loosely above her waist. There was no hiding her pregnancy any longer; her baby was sprouting and making its presence known. A cropped white sweater and low cherry heels completed her semiprofessional look. Next, she applied light makeup, eyeliner, meadow-green shadow and a little rosy lip gloss. The last thing she cared about right now was how she looked, but this was an important meeting.

She stepped out of her apartment at precisely seven thirty and there was Jeff, waiting for her. How long had he been standing guard outside her apartment? Gosh, she didn't really want to know.

"Hi again," she said.

Jeff stood at attention, his gaze dipping to her dress, and a glimmer of approval entered his eyes. Something warmed inside of her that she thought had been frozen out. She told him where she was headed.

"I know the place" was all he said.

She arrived at the restaurant a little before eight. She

didn't see Brooke's car in the parking lot so she waited until eight sharp and there was still no sign of Brooke.

She got out of her car, and Jeff did the same. It was dark now, except for the full moon and the parking lot lights. The roar of the ocean reminded her of Dylan and the time she'd spent living as his wife and she sighed. Fleeting sadness dashed through her but she had no time for self-pity. She had a client to meet.

Jeff did a thorough scan of the grounds as he approached her. "I'm meeting my partner here," she said, "but since it's already eight, I'd better go inside to start the meeting."

"I'll walk you inside."

"Is that necessary?"

He smiled. "It'll make me feel better."

She smiled at his comment. He'd taken a page from her mother-hen book. "Okay."

When they reached the front door, he opened it for her. "After you."

"Thank you." She stepped inside the restaurant and her heart seized up at the sight before her eyes. Hundreds of lit votive candles illuminated the empty space. "Oh, no. We must've gotten the date wrong. Looks like someone is setting up for a party," she said to Jeff.

When he didn't answer, she turned around. Jeff was gone. Vanished into thin air.

Her heart pumped harder now and she was ready to scurry away, when a figure walked out of the darkness into the candlelight—a man wearing a dark tuxedo with lush blond hair and incredible melt-your-soul blue eyes.

"Hello, Emma. You look beautiful."

Her hand was up at her throat. She didn't know how it got there. "Dylan?"

He smiled, eyes twinkling, and walked over to her. She nibbled on her lip, trying to make sense of all this, and when he took her hand and held on to it, as if for dear life, she was beginning to see, beginning to hope that she knew what all this meant.

"I've been a fool," he said.

Oh, God, yes. Not the fool part, but that, too. He was here for her. "Why do you say that?"

"Come," he said, pivoting around and guiding her with their hands still clasped to a table set for two overlooking Moonlight Beach. Roses and gardenias at the center of the table released an amazing sweet aroma. A chilled bottle of sparkling water sat in a champagne bucket, along with two flutes. The crystal glassware and fine bone china reflected the candlelight, added sparkle and a heavenly aura to the room. Right now, that's exactly how she felt: out of this world.

"As you might've guessed, there is no appointment for you to keep tonight. Just dinner with me."

She blinked and blinked and blinked. "You arranged all this?"

He nodded, but his smile seemed shaky and unsure, not the usual confident Dylan smile. "I know the owner."

Zane Williams. Of course. He'd attended their fateful wedding. "And I wanted to do something for you that was as special as you are, Emma."

"I'm not that special," she whispered.

"To me, you are. To me, you're everything I've ever wanted and it's taken me nearly losing you to that maniac to figure it out. When I thought you were in danger, I panicked and my thick head finally cleared. I was willing to do anything to keep you safe."

"Jeff told me you were ready to risk your life for me."

"Jeff, huh? Well, it's true. The thought of you getting hurt made me realize that my life, all of my success, everything I have now, would mean nothing if you weren't right there beside me. You and the baby. God, I've been so selfish, Emma. I only thought of what I'd lost when I found out you were carrying Roy's baby. But I never stopped to realize what I'd be gaining. Until I almost lost you."

"I was never in any real danger."

"Not that night, no. But if Renee hadn't called to warn me, things might've turned out differently. He threatened your life. He probably wouldn't have stopped until... I can't think about it."

"Well, I'm thankful to Renee for putting the pieces together."

Dylan nodded. "I owe her for that. And the best way to repay her isn't by sending her money. A friend of mine has a job waiting for her, as a personal secretary. She's going back to work and she's happy about it. The job pays well and she'll be able to hold her head up high again and support her family."

"Dylan, that's wonderful. You're giving her a second chance."

He nodded. "I hope so."

"You're a good man, Dylan."

"Good enough for you to give me a second chance?"

"Maybe," she said softly. "After the attempt on your life, I came to the hospital and made Brooke promise not to tell you. I wanted to see you so badly, but I didn't want my being there to upset you, so I stayed outside your room until I found out you were going to be okay."

"I wanted to see you. I'd hoped you would come."

"I didn't think it would be wise."

"Emma. I'm sorry for how I've behaved. I'm sorry about everything. I should've stopped you from walking out on me. I let you leave my house pregnant and alone to face an unknown future. I hope you can forgive me for being obtuse and selfish."

"I think I already have, Dylan. I couldn't hold a grudge when your life was in danger. And I've made mistakes, too. I shouldn't have lost my head and gotten so drunk that night that I didn't realize what was happening. I told you the baby was yours. It was only natural for you to be disappointed to find out the truth. I'm sorry you were hurt. Truly."

"Apology accepted. Now it's time for us to put those mistakes in the past and look to the future." Dylan went down on one knee then, and her out-of-this-world experience got *real*, really quickly. "Emma, I want to do this right this time. I love you with all of my heart. I love the child you're carrying, my best friend's baby, and it's my hope that we raise the baby together and—"

"Wait!" She put up her hand and the hope on Dylan's face waned. It wasn't that she hadn't heard him the first time or that she wanted him to stop, but she'd waited a long time for those words. They were worth repeating. "Can you say that again?"

"The I-love-you-with-my-whole-heart part?"

"That's the one."

"I do, Emma, I love you," he declared. "I didn't think I'd ever let myself love again. After Renee, it was just easier to have casual relationships with women. No risk, no injury. I guess it was a way of protecting myself from ever feeling that kind of pain again. I'm not making excuses, but for me, falling in love wasn't an option, mentally and emotionally. I wanted no part of it. Everything changed, though, when you became part of my life. Suddenly, everything I've ever wanted was right in front of me. It took a blackout and a baby to make me see it. It was a strange journey to be on, but I can't imagine my life without you and the baby in it. You're my family, and I see a wonderful future ahead for us. So, sweetheart, will you please come back home…to me? Be my wife, mother of our child. I propose for us to stay married and love each other until the end of time. Could you do that?"

Tears of joy streamed down her face. Dylan's proposal

was everything she'd ever wanted. She loved him beyond belief. How could she look at that man, see the truth in his humble blue eyes and not love him? "I can. I will. I love you, Dylan. And I want a life with you. That's all I've ever wanted."

On bended knee, he caressed her growing belly and placed a sweet kiss there. The outpouring of his love was evident in the reverent way he spoke about the baby, spoke of his love for her. She believed in his love now, believed in their future.

Then he rose to his full height, his gaze clouded with tears. "I love you, Emma. And our child. The best I can do is promise to share my life with you and try to make every day happy for our family. Is that enough?"

"More than enough," she whispered.

She was drawn into the circle of his arms and he bent his head to claim her mouth in a deep, lingering kiss. By the time he was through, her mind was spinning and only one fulfilling, delicious thought entered her head.

She'd finally claimed *dibs* on Dylan McKay. And quite fantastically, he'd also claimed dibs on her.

And that would be no darn secret anymore.

* * * * *

MILLS & BOON®

Helen Bianchin v Regency Collection!

6_MB520